D1500372

HANS FROST

HANS
FROST

BY

HUGH WALPOLE

1929

DOUBLEDAY, DORAN AND

COMPANY, INC.

GARDEN CITY, N. Y.

No Portrait of, or Allusion to, any living person is intended in the pages of this novel.

For ADA and JOHN GALSWORTHY
a small emphasis on the happiness
of twenty years' friendship

"All the windows were broken. . . . The sun streamed in and the statues, the rare editions, and the cabinets of precious stones blinked and twinkled before the splendid blaze."
— THE DUCHESS OF PARADIS

CONTENTS

Part I
SEVENTIETH BIRTHDAY

Part II
JOURNEYS OF COLUMBUS

Part III

TO ST. SERVIAN!

Part I

SEVENTIETH BIRTHDAY

CHAPTER I

Nathalie Swan

No ONE perhaps in the United Kingdom was quite so frightened as was Nathalie Swan on the third day of November, 1924, sitting in a third-class carriage about quarter to five of a cold, windy, darkening afternoon. Her train was drawing her into Paddington Station, and how she wished that she were dead!

She sat in a corner on the hard, dusty seat, her hands clenched, her heart beating with hot, thick, hammering throbs. She wished that she were dead. She was an orphan. No one in the world needed her. The Proudies whom she was abandoning had been very, very good to her, but certainly did not need her. The famous Mrs. Frost to whom she was going would almost surely not be good to her—and as to needing her . . .

Open upon her lap was a number of that shiny geographically illustrated paper the *London News*, and among other portraits was one of Hans Frost, and under it was written:

Mr. Hans Frost, whose Seventieth Birthday occurs on November 3. His friends and admirers are marking the occasion with a suitable presentation.

Kind Samuel Proudie had not known that the photograph was there, when at Polchester Station he had bought illustrated papers and flung them onto her lap. She herself had, of course, not known it, and it had been with a kind of shock that she had recognized the well-known features, the square rugged face with the deep, penetrating eyes, the round head with its short, thick, black hair, the face austere like a priest's, the shoulders broad, the body rather squat, the short sturdy legs, standing there in the beautiful book-lined library—no man of seventy here surely. Not even a man of letters. Rather priest plus prize-fighter plus (in some implied kindly geniality) Father Christmas without the beard.

And then at the last something enigmatic. . . . Or did one imagine that because one knew how great he was?

Nathalie was nineteen years and no fool. She had had this face in front of her, framed in a neat black frame for the last six years, had carried it with her everywhere, had had it always in her bedroom wherever she might be. For was he not her uncle, her famous, marvellous uncle whom she had never seen but had made her hero, her conception of God, indeed, ever since she could remember?

How tiny, but how defiant, she had been on that first morning at the Polchester High School, when, hemmed in by tormentors, she had boasted: "You can do what you like, but I've got a grander uncle than you have!"

The name, Hans Frost, had meant nothing to them until they had enquired of fathers and mothers at home, but then, after those enquiries, she had received her coveted glory.

"Mother says he's the most wonderful writer. What's he like? Does he take you to theatres when you're in London?"

And then must come the sad confession that she had never seen him, that he had perhaps never heard of her, that he was her uncle only because he had married her aunt.

And yet some glory lingered. The time had come at last when she read his books. Always surreptitiously. They were forbidden. Mrs. Proudie thought them shocking. All except the fairy stories, and they might also be shocking, did one understand what they meant. . . .

Nathalie read some of the fairy stories first: *The Crystal Bell*, *The Duchess of Paradis*, *The Palace of Ice*. She did not at the time bother about inner meanings. She took the pictures for what they were. The Prince in *The Crystal Bell* crossing the Lake of Fire, the Duchess of Paradis opening the casket of jade, the Dwarfs in *Green Parrots* tying the tails of the monkeys together while they slept. Then (she was seventeen now) she came to the novels. She saved up her money and bought *The Praddons*, *The Silver Tree*, *Joy Has Three Faces*, and *The Chinese Miracle*.

Of these she liked *The Praddons* best. She could follow that easily with its crowds of people, its London scene, and its definite story of Isabel Praddon and her unhappy marriage. She noticed that the later in his life the books appeared the more difficult they became.

She always cut pieces from the paper when they concerned him. The greatest time was when, in his fifty-ninth year, he was dangerously ill. The whole of London, the whole of England, even the whole of Europe and America, waited breathlessly.

She read how groups of people lingered outside his door,

how the King and Queen sent enquiries, she remembered
the newspaper headlines on the morning after the crisis of
his illness was successfully passed.

He had never, perhaps, been quite so famous again. The
war had immediately followed. Uncle Hans' mother—dead
many years—had been a German. He had lived in retire-
ment during the war, had said very little. After *The Chinese
Miracle*, which came out in the autumn of 1914, he had
published nothing in the war years save his volume of
essays, *The War and the Artist*.

At school during those years she had been torn between
her loyalties. She was patriotic, of course, but Uncle Hans
was as much her god as ever. It wasn't her fault or his that
his mother had been a German. But she had not mentioned
him when she need not. She had not been a coward, but
perhaps—a little of a diplomatist. . . .

She worshipped Uncle Hans, but she did not worship Aunt
Ruth. For one thing she had never seen Uncle Hans and had
seen Aunt Ruth. Aunt Ruth had, in 1919, spent two whole
nights under the Proudie roof. She had been visiting friends
in Cornwall, and, passing through Glebeshire, stopped for
two nights in Polchester to "see her little niece." She had
been all kindness and condescension, lovely to look at and
lovely to smell. Very sweet to the Proudies, who were no
relation and had looked after little Nathalie all these years,
simply because Mrs. Proudie and Nathalie's mother "had
been girl friends together."

Nathalie had been only fourteen at the time. She had
been given holiday from the high school, and Aunt Ruth had

taken her for a drive—and that drive had been for Nathalie the most terrifying of all her life's experiences.

Aunt Ruth had been determined to be kind, and was probably satisfied that she had been. As they sat on the broad back seat of the handsome motor-car Aunt Ruth had asked many questions in her melodious, but very deciding, voice. Was Nathalie happy at school? What was her favourite subject in lessons? Did she like games? And, at the last, was she a good little girl, because she would have to earn her living when she grew up?

There were certain things in Aunt Ruth that reminded Nathalie very oddly of her mother, who had been Aunt Ruth's sister. Oddly, because the same things that were adorable in Nathalie's mother were in some strange way terrifying in Aunt Ruth—a note in her voice, a smile, a gesture with her hand. These things brought back her mother to Nathalie so desperately, because in a way they seemed to attempt to betray her, as though now that she was gone and had no one to defend her they were attacking her, that Nathalie to her own surprise and chagrin burst into tears.

Here would have been an occasion for aunt and niece to come together, and had they done so the lives of many people might have been changed, but it happened that the motor-car was just reëntering Polchester, and Mrs. Frost had a keen sense of public absurdity and a wise consciousness of the necessity for self-control. And Nathalie hated herself for crying and hated her aunt for seeing her cry. So Mrs. Frost left Polchester thinking her niece "a silly little girl," and Nathalie thought her aunt "simply terrifying."

How astonishing then, all these years afterwards, to discover that Aunt Ruth wanted her to live with her "for a time" in London. There could be no question about Nathalie's acceptance. The Proudies were keeping her only out of kindness; she was nearly grown up and must soon be "looking after herself"—and her aunt's house in London would be a splendid place to jump off from!

And then there would be the famous, wonderful Uncle Hans, who must surely sometimes be visible when you were living under the same roof with him! If only she were not so terribly frightened of Aunt Ruth! But perhaps now she wouldn't be! It was, however, as Mrs. Proudie had so often told her, her worst fault to be frightened. She had never, possibly, recovered from that awful morning when, only eight years of age, she had been with her father and mother in a pony-cart in the lanes above Rafiel and the pony had run away, turning over the pony-cart, throwing them all out, killing her father at once. Her mother had died six months later.

She had never, possibly, recovered from that, but nevertheless she had a brave spirit. When she was frightened of something she strung herself up, summoning all her forces like the Princess about to meet the dragon. She had her aids on these occasions, superstitions for the most part, like counting fifty and allowing nothing to stop her, saying the Lord's Prayer, praying to her father, and thinking of Uncle Hans.

And now, how odd, it was as though she were praying to

Uncle Hans to defend her against Aunt Ruth! Odd and shocking too. How she wished that she was not trembling, how she detested and despised her own cowardice. Nineteen years of age and near to tears, because she was going to stay with her aunt.

She could not think of London through whose grimy and sordid side streets she was now entering. She did not see the rows of windows with flower-pots and undergarments and occasional human heads painted onto the swaying background of checkered brick. She did not look down onto the strips of long snaky street let into the sombre walls. She saw nothing. Only she longed for Mrs. Proudie with her large heaving bosom, her capacity for gasping amazement at quite ordinary things, her conviction that food and drink would solve every problem; for Canon Proudie, Precentor of the Cathedral in public and the husband of Mrs. Proudie in private, that meek mild man with the beautiful voice and passion for cricket; and for Edgar Proudie, eldest Proudie child, soon to take Holy Orders, vowed to celibacy and the Higher Anglicanism; the very thought of them made the tears hot behind her eyes. The train drew into Paddington Station blurred and wobbly with smoke and noise and clatter, trying vainly to cover an inexhaustible loneliness.

CHAPTER II

The House

She had been told that there would be someone to meet her, and at once after leaving her carriage she saw a plump, rosy-cheeked, young chauffeur coming towards her.

"Miss Swan?" he asked, touching his cap.

"Yes," she said shyly. She was comforted a little, because he looked as though he were from the country. Smart, though, but strong and sturdy. She knew that he would not smile at her luggage for being shabby or turn up his nose at her timid air.

The luggage was found. The car, very large, dark blue, waited scornfully quite close to the platform, sniffing at the taxis that were quivering with anxiety lest they should miss their fares. The station glittered with glass, screamed with naughty impatience, choked in its own smoke, and was gone. Nathalie slipped into London.

She found that her terror did not diminish. Argue with it, talk to it like a mother, scold it—nothing did it any good. It just sat there in its dark corner, refusing to be exorcised. It did not make things better to observe that London was indifferent, that the lights flashing now about the streets displayed the world with its head up, and that what the world was wise enough to disregard Nathalie might dis-

regard also. The world had not seen Aunt Ruth as Nathalie
had seen her, there was only one Aunt Ruth for one
Nathalie, and to change her into a common denominator
helped not at all.

Antagonisms are made up of personal furniture, and there
is no pincushion in one's wardrobe that has not its share in
one's hatred of Cæsar.

They rolled into silence. The roar of London was checked
as though a hand had been laid on its bawling mouth.
Water gleamed beneath lamplight. As the door opened, trees
rustled into the car: autumn leaves lay underfoot.

Nathalie stood, alone and defenceless, on the steps of
what seemed in the shadowed starlight a huge house. Yes,
water was over the way and dark spaces. A shrill scream
broke the shadows.

"Oh, what's that?" she cried.

"That's the Zoo, Miss," said the chauffeur, waiting beside her for the opening door.

The bell of some clock struck five as the heavy door
opened. A large, stout, and flat-faced man received her. She
disliked him at once, because he was so ugly. His face looked
as though it had been trodden on in childhood. Afterwards
she was to wonder whether he had ever known that savage
and innocent state. His name was Bigges. Later on she
would know him for the laziest man in England.

She waited, standing, as it seemed to her, in the middle
of endless lighted space, while Bigges brought in her meagre
luggage and very officially closed the door. The nice rosy-
faced young man was shut out.

She didn't know that Bigges was saying to himself: "Yes, you would be arriving just at the busiest time when everyone's got their 'ands full. You're going to be a nuisance, you are."

Before they moved on, however, she was comforted by seeing a large, splendid portrait of Uncle Hans hanging over the big stone fireplace. Head and shoulders. Such a picture, so strong and so kindly and so humorous! It was as though, after all, he had been there to greet her and wish her well. . . .

"Mrs. Frost would like to see you at once, Miss."

She followed.

The house in Polchester had been one of the small ones under the shadow of the Cathedral—bright small crooked rooms overcrowded with ancient treasure, garden in front and garden behind, all colour and comfort, but tiny beside the clang and echo of the Cathedral bells.

How vast and grand and empty, then, this House, the passages endless, the rooms stiff and splendid, one's feet silent on the thick carpets, no voices anywhere! Oh! had she no pride, no self-defence? There was nothing of which she need be ashamed. She was as good as another.

But, arriving at last in the drawing-room, so huge to her country eye, so rich in brown and gold, so stiff in its icy distance between sofas and chairs, Nathalie lost the last remnant of her pluck. She looked, as she went to meet Mrs. Frost and her two lady friends, like a beautiful, rather shabby, and sulky child.

Mrs. Frost, clad in golden armour, introduced her to the two ladies—one sheathed in silver like a mermaid, Lady

Thingumety, and the other in black silk like a bathing dress, Mrs. Whatyoumayplease.

Mrs. Frost was very kind. She kissed Nathalie twice. She seemed to be glad indeed to see her. Nathalie, gazing at her glorious bobbed amber-coloured hair, wondered how her aunt, who must be fifty at least, could be bobbed and have a figure so straight and not seem in any way absurd. Mrs. Proudie, who was not a day more than forty, if bobbed rather than bunned . . . !

Through her wonderment came Aunt Ruth's explanation: "And so, darling, if you won't mind just for a night . . . I really should have wired and asked you to come on Wednesday, but I couldn't bear to put you off. . . . You see it's rather an occasion. It's going on at this very moment upstairs, and then there's the dinner-party. Besides I expect you're as tired as anything after your journey and would rather have something on a tray in your own room. And then you can go to bed as early as ever you like. Ask Elsie for anything you want. We'll have *such* a talk in the morning. Your kind friends quite well? That's good. I'm *so* glad. . . . So goodnight and happy dreams."

Nathalie found herself moving out just as she had moved in, as though under the command of some inexorable law. She didn't *want* to stay, but at the same time . . .

A thin starched woman was waiting for her in the passage.

"I'm Elsie, Miss. If there's anything . . ."

CHAPTER III

Presentation

At this precise moment the Presentation was going on.

In the beautiful library Hans Frost was sitting and Mr. Frederick Osmaston, standing spiritually like a stork on one leg (he was tall and thin, untidy in odd places like a shaggy umbrella), was reading from his document:

"We, your friends and admirers, feel that it is impossible to allow your Seventieth Birthday to pass without a sign from us of our affection and esteem.

"You have now for nearly forty years shown us all how Art may be nobly served. In an Age that offers continual evidence of the temptations to cheapness and hurry, you have with unswerving honesty and undoubting faith pursued the only honourable path. You have made it evident that the grand Art of Fiction is inexhaustible in her resources, is for ever opening new ways of adventure for those who follow in her train, and your wit, your gaiety of humour have proved again and again the generosity and wisdom of your known genius.

"But best of all, your knowledge of the human heart, your tolerance and generosity of spirit, have created for us a

14

world of companions, enriching our lives with fresh and enduring characters. So long as the English tongue may last, the earth will claim for its noblest inhabitants the Duchess of Paradis and Hunter Clive, Isabel Praddon, Clarissa French, the King of Wizards, Mont St. Leger, and the Queen of the Crystal Sea, Berenice. Whether in the green woods and glassy lakes of your world of magic or in the everyday streets of your earth-bound cities, the human note is never absent and the tender love for your fellow-men makes life happier for every one of us.

"May destiny allow you many more years in which you may add masterpieces to the English language, and splendid hours to the lives of your friends."

"That's pretty awful," thought Hans Frost, and then immediately afterwards: "Very jolly of them to take all the trouble." Then a little later: "They like doing it though. Gunter's been in the Seventh Heaven. . . . 'Follow in her train'—that's bad. . . . Whole thing too flowery. . . . Nice of them to do it though. . . . Why does Osmaston always half shave himself? Better not do it at all."

There was a pause. It was time for him to reply. He rose to his feet.

"I must say I think it's delightful of everybody. I don't feel like seventy, you know. But you make me realize that I've been an unconscionable time at the whole thing. It's all very well for you to say that you'd like me to go on for years and years, but we've got to make way for the young

people, you know. . . ." (He looked across at the rather
supercilious, thin young man in pince-nez, Maurice Follett,
who represented in the deputation the Young Generation.)
"And yet it's hard to stop. I can't promise you that I will,
and, as there are no reporters present, I may as well confess
to you that I'd *hate* to stop. We're like that—eh, Gunter?—
becomes a habit." (He looked down at Martha, the notori-
ous dachshund, who, her head on her paws, was regarding
young Follett's thick and ugly shoes with arrogant suspicion.) "All the same I'm immensely touched by your taking
this trouble. I've done what I can, but you know as well
as I do that the thing's a snare and a delusion. I can only say
at seventy what I wouldn't have said at thirty, that it's
damned difficult to write a decent sentence and that the
best things come after all by accident. . . . But you don't
want me to preach to you. I can only thank you and all the
friends whom you represent and to whom I hope to reply,
for your goodness, kindness, generosity."

He sat down. Martha looked up at him sharply as though
to say, "Not so bad. Might have been better," and settled
down to the ironical study of Follett's shoes again. But now
the real moment had arrived. Sir Giles Gunter, K.C.B.,
rose rather ponderously from his chair and approached with
grave solemnity towards a paper parcel lying on the table
close at hand. Osmaston also gravely approached.

Gunter, pushing up his gold-rimmed spectacles, spoke
with an odd bark that resembled nothing so much as an
elderly seal at feeding-time:

"We took much counsel together and decided at length,

my dear old friend, that the enclosed would—ahem—yes—
would be more gratifying to your artistic feelings than
anything else we could find for you."

Gunter was moved, his emotion was choking him. He put
his large hand on the shoulder of Hans Frost, who had risen
and was approaching the parcel with the eagerness of a child.
He had, all his life, adored presents. He got that, perhaps,
from his German mother. Anything with paper round it.

His heart warmed to Giles Gunter, whom he had known
for thirty years and with whom he had quarrelled a thousand
times. Gunter's feminine nature adored quarrels, because of
the reconciliations that followed them. And to-day Gunter
really loved Hans Frost, a little because he loved him, a
little because he was a great man, and a good deal because
he, Giles Gunter, was officiating at an important ceremony.

The other two members of the deputation stood modestly
in the background, Peter Westcott because he *was* modest,
and Follett because he was too arrogant and aloof to push
himself vulgarly forward.

Osmaston produced a pair of large scissors. The string
was cut. Gunter, his round, red face illuminated with a kind
of sacred priestly fervour, lifted the object out of the paper
and with a bow and a triumphant smile as though he, and
he alone, had just at great personal sacrifice given birth to
this lovely thing, presented it to Frost.

And it *was* a lovely thing! It was a very small oil painting
and the artist was Manet.

The picture had for its subject two ladies and a gentleman
outside a print shop in Paris. One lady wore a blue crinoline

and the other a white; there was a little fuzzy white dog; the glass windows shone in the afternoon light, and beyond the pearl-grey wall of the old house there was a sky of broken blue and swollen white cloud. It was a very lovely little Manet. . . .

"Oh!" cried Hans Frost, and Martha gave a sharp short bark, because she perceived that something exceptional was happening.

"We thought you would like it," said Sir Giles, fingering the old gold frame with proud, possessive fingers. "We were fortunate that it turned up in the market when it did. The very thing, I said when I saw it, the very thing for my old friend."

Meanwhile Hans Frost was unconscious of Sir Giles and of everyone present. He saw only the picture. He had always adored Manet, a painter closer to his soul than any other. He entered into the heart of a Manet at once, as though it had been painted for himself alone. He could be critical about everything else in the world (and was so), but not about Manet. When he was depressed or troubled by his liver he went and looked at Manet. . . . And now he would have a Manet all of his own, his very own—that deep and tender beauty, that blue crinoline, that fuzzy little dog, that white cloud against the gentle blue; these were his for ever.

His eyes shone with happiness as he turned round to his friends. He held out his hands to Gunter and Osmaston. He smiled beyond them to the friendly Westcott and the superior Follett. "What am I to say? What *can* I say? That you should have thought of me at all—and then thought of this!

I'm seventy to-day, as you remind me, and perhaps I shouldn't be thinking any longer of possessions, but how can I help it when you thrust under my nose such a lovely thing? I'm an acquisitive creature, I fear. I have always been. I love beautiful things, and I have a fancy that they return the affection that one gives them! But this! I can't say any more. . . . I'm overcome. . . . I truly am. I'm touched to the very heart."

And he was. He had in his eyes the look of the child that knows, to the exclusion of everything and everyone else, that the immediate moment is supremely good. Generosity, ardour, unselfish delight, all the fine emotions were there, and there was nothing to cloud them.

Follett himself was touched. He rubbed his large shoes the one against the other.

"It's the least we can do—all of us—for what you have done for us." And yet only the night before, to a chosen gathering, in his high falsetto voice, he had proclaimed:

"Frost! . . . The Dark Ages. . . . Fairy stories, I ask you."

But Hans was not yet conscious of any of them. On his short, sturdy legs he went about the room, holding the picture at arm's length, propping it now against the Epstein bust on the mantelpiece, now against the blue Chinese clock, now against the marble lion—one of two book-rests—now against the drawing of his wife's head by Sargent.

Then, laying it down, he turned again to them, laughing:

"But after all, my friends, from whom is this lovely thing? Am I not to have their names?"

Osmaston, who by his right as secretary of the Authors' Society was the official head of the deputation, unrolled a large and handsome parchment.

"Here they are, Mr. Frost."

And there they were, some three hundred and sixty of them, all neatly laid out in alphabetical order—ANKER, ALFRED L.; APPLEWARD, RICHARD; ARON, ARTHUR . . . Yes, many of the finest names, not only of Great Britain, but of Europe and America as well.

He took the two sheets and smiled upon them. He would look at them carefully in a while. He put his hand on Sir Giles' massive shoulder.

"This *has* been an occasion. . . . I shall only realize it slowly. I'm a little overcome, to tell you the truth. Yes, just a little. I'm seventy, you know. You've said it yourselves. Giles, my wife's waiting downstairs to give you all tea. Lady Gunter's with her, I believe. Will you go down? I'll join you shortly."

He beamed upon them all. They passed him down into the hall, where Bigges was waiting.

He stopped Westcott for a moment. "Mr. Westcott . . . I was greatly pleased to see you here. I'd like to tell you, if I may, how immensely I enjoyed an article of yours—somewhere. I read it at the Club the other evening—an article on Henry Galleon."

"Yes," said Westcott, smiling. "It was in the *Westminster Monthly.*"

"You knew him evidently?"

"Only very slightly, I'm afraid. I was at school with a

son of his, and when I was a young man in London I had an evening with him—an evening I shall never forget."

"No, he was a very remarkable man—a great man. He was a close friend of mine, one of my closest. There's not a day that I don't miss him. I'm glad you knew him. You got him wonderfully well in that article."

"Thank you, sir," said Westcott.

"And I enjoyed that last book of yours, *Wandering House*. I've watched you for a long time. A good book."

"Thank you," said Westcott again.

"Will you come and see me some time? Come in bachelor fashion and smoke a pipe."

"I'll be proud."

"All right, then. I'll get hold of you."

Westcott closed the door behind him. The library was left to Hans and Martha.

CHAPTER IV

À la Recherche du Temps Perdu

IT WAS a beautiful room. The long, high windows, veiled now with deep blue curtains, looked out across the strip of water and the green levels of the Park. The ceiling was dark blue; the length of the room on the side opposite the windows was lined with unbroken rows of bookshelves, pale ivory in colour. The fireplace was between the windows.

There was no room for pictures. One etching—Rembrandt's "Three Crosses"—hung over the fireplace. Beneath it was an Epstein head of a woman. There was one long writing table and two small ones, two armchairs of deep blue, a deep-backed chair that had once belonged to Dickens at the writing table. On the table itself perfect neatness, a writing pad, an old shabby ink bottle shaped like an owl (this had belonged to Henry Galleon), a round crystal bowl edged with gold that held now dark amber chrysanthemums, on his right hand a photograph of his wife, on his left a photograph of Galleon, a small bronze (a copy of the Donatello David), a silver paper knife, a stick of red sealing wax, a heavy blue paper weight.

His library was evidently a working one. In the centre there was a square of bookshelf protected with glass; here were such rare editions and association copies as he had:

first editions of the *Essays of Elia* in their green backs and
pink paper labels, the copy of *Vanity Fair* that Thackeray
gave to Dickens, some notebooks in manuscript kept by
George Borrow while in Spain, a first edition of *Ballantrae*
with "To my friend Hans Frost from R. L. Stevenson"
inscribed on the front page.   Charlotte Brontë's Italian
Grammar, some Kelmscott volumes, a number of Galleon's
novels, with very affectionate greetings in that fine, rich
rolling hand, and three volumes of Proust's great and unend-
ing chronicle sent with the homages of the author. . . .

These were the principal treasures. For the rest, the
working library divided meticulously into its proper sections.
This labour from the devoted hands of Miss Caparis, the
entirely excellent secretary.

Frost, holding the Manet in his hands, went over to the
shelves. This for That! Tit for Tat! The Manet and the Roll
of Friends in return for his own, how many volumes? He
stood before his own collected "Burshott" Edition. Here
they were then.

Aware that some crisis—the nature of which he could
only as yet dimly perceive, but its approach was heralded by
a quiver in the spiritual air about him—was imminent,
he stood, held, it seemed, by some dominating trance, and
read their names.

It was as though he were saying to the Manet: "Here!
See at what you are valued. . . . Make yourself aware of the
home to which you have come."

He, who for many a day now had not glanced at their
covers, read over their names. They had been published in

Chronological Order. (Ah yes! the Grand Edition! How, five
years ago, he had detested the bore of it with its neat little
prefaces, its photogravure frontispieces of places asso-
ciated with the books . . . And then, after all, no one had
bought the damned thing. A White Elephant if ever White
Elephant blew its own trumpet.)

And they were:

1889	The Crystal Bell
1891	The Praddons
1892	The Blissful Place
1893	On the Road (*Poems*)
1895	The Duchess of Paradis
1896	Queen Rosalind
1898	The Miltonic Spirit (*Essays*)
1899	The Palace of Ice
1900	Laura Merries
1903	Green Parrots
1904	Friendly Places (*Travel*)
1905	Goliath
1906	The Philistines
1907	In Israel
1909	The Silver Tree
1910	Troilus (*Poems*)
1912	Walter Savage Landor: Critical Study
1913	Joy Has Three Faces
1914	The Chinese Miracle
1916	The War and the Artist (*Essays*)
1919	Eumenides (*Poems*)
1922	The Scornful Sun
1924	King Richard the Fourth

He looked at them with dispassionate eyes. Such a number and, for the most part, having so little to do with him!

How many of them retained any life for him still? *The Praddons*, with a certain youthful freshness, *The Duchess of Paradis* for its poetry, the Trilogy for some of the people in it, *Joy Has Three Faces* for its irony, *King Richard* because it was the last . . . but for the most part how thin, how touchingly shadowy, how, as they looked at him, they seemed to beseech him not to forget them, because if he did not remember them who in Heaven's name would?

No, what they did stand for was—not their artistic beauties, poor withered things—but certain stages in his immortal life.

He went back to his chair, settled down in it; Martha, sighing luxuriously, rested her head on his shoe. What was the matter with him? The Manet lay on his lap, the whites and blues and pearly greys looking up at him already with familiarity. What was the matter? He was disturbed. He looked restlessly about him.

Something was going to happen.

The deputation had unsettled him, not because it had emphasized that he was seventy but—but what? Was it the deputation or was it the Manet? Was it, perchance, the Manet that in its perfect and rich beauty pointed so ironic a contrast with his own deformed children? He moved restlessly, Martha's head slipped from his shoe, and she murmured resentfully.

He was unhappy. He wouldn't go down to tea and listen to their silly chatter. He must stay there and face the thing that was troubling him.

The Crystal Bell. His first published work, 1889.

Thirty-five years of age.

Not an infant even then. Fifteen years of good experience behind him. A clerk at the Foreign Office where, as it had seemed, he had been settled for life—settled with a pearl pin in his tie, a cup of tea, and a dispatch case. He wrote by accident. He had no fervour, no inspiration, no heated blood, and certainly, at that time, no genius.

He saw one sunsetty evening Nelson climb down from his column and ride away on the back of one of the lions. So he wrote about it. For his own satisfaction. Those were days at the end of the 'eighties when the New Realism and Romantic Fantasy were walking arm-in-arm together. Not that he had ever believed in those tea-caddy definitions. He detested them. But people liked the way he wrote and so he went on writing. That was the way of it. Once you began you couldn't stop and, after the beginning, what happened to you was neither your fault nor your merit.

What happened to him was that he caught the eye of Stevenson and Henley, wrote for the *National Observer*, and had the time of his life. He would never have such days again of course—not *those* days of flaming, arrogant, abusive, triumphant, self-confident youth. Although he wasn't in reality young. Forty was less young in the 'nineties than it is to-day perhaps.

With *The Praddons* his bell rang and with *The Duchess of Paradis* he was lifted onto a little throne. Quite a small little throne, but raised so that you could look down upon other people. He didn't look down on other people—that had never been his habit—but for a while he was considered unique; no one else had ever written quite *his* thing; no one else could manage the Romantic Fantasy one minute and the Realistic the next. . . .

Oh well, it was all jargon, the kind of jargon that he detested. All he knew about it was that he had very pleasant rooms in St. James's Square and a cottage near Lewes, and that he wrote down what came to him.

Then with his Trilogy he was made—for ever and for ever and a day. *Goliath* in 1905, *The Philistines* in 1906, *In Israel* in 1907.

He knew that these books were good. He knew it then and he knew it now. They were his especial thing; the very sweet kernel of his very own nut. Every gift that he had was in them, his fantasy and his realism, his poetry and all his philosophy. Moreover, in them he created crowds of people, real live breathing people, a whole world of his own, embracing town and country, the Dome of St. Paul's, and the smallest squirrel skipping up a tree in the darkest little wood. The three books together were a long affair, and there wasn't a page too many.

By then he was more than fifty years of age, and he married Ruth, who was only twenty-five. Too great a difference, but he was madly in love with her—yes, as he had never been in all his life before.

He had always liked women, and twice he had been in love. But some fastidiousness had always been in the way, not of passion, but of complete surrender.

But to Ruth Curnow he surrendered—yes utterly—surrendered to her, mother and all.

She had been married before—very happily married—
to Francis Curnow, who was vastly rich, adored, oh, adored
her, got pneumonia, died, and left her every penny.

And he, Hans Frost, adored her too—adored so that he
did what he had sworn to the jealous gods he would never
do, married a woman with more money than he had himself.

With a great deal more money because, although he was
on his little throne, and had a body of work behind him,
including his famous Trilogy, he did not make very much
money. In America they liked him as a reputation rather
than a buying proposition—and in England, of course,
nobody buys books.

The question was—why did Ruth marry him? This was
a question that he had never very honestly faced. He loved
her so desperately that he knew that it was wiser not to ask
questions.

She did not love him desperately. She had no desperation
in her, but she accepted him very readily, without a moment's hesitation. She was probably tired of being a widow.

She was extremely beautiful; she was like a fire at night,
a sunrise at morning, a golden flower, a goddess in amber.

She had a great deal of the goddess about her, very tall,
carrying herself superbly, her head high, looking down upon
mankind. But she was very gracious, and she was not stupid
and, if people behaved to her rightly, she liked them very
much.

She was exceedingly good to Hans. There was nothing
she wouldn't do for him, and she made it easy for him to

accept her blessings, because it gave her so huge a pleasure to bestow them.

Oh! she was large, fine, and generous! She was indeed!

If only she had not had her hideous old mother with her— but, then, nothing in this Jack-in-the-box world is perfect.

Mrs. Marriott was even then a dried-up old lady. She was, when Hans Frost first saw her, fifty-five years of age (she was only five years older than Hans) and fifty-five is no terrible age, but she wore lace caps and black silk dresses, carried in her hand a handkerchief with a thin black border, and read frequently in a large purple book of devotion.

Her one object in life, as she told everybody, was her daughter Ruth, the most marvellous woman in the world.

She was one of those old women who are for ever slapping the face of the present with the dead hand of the past. She was propriety itself, and was so frequently shocked at the persistent coarseness of Nature that how she had ever suffered the processes necessary for the production of children was an eternal wonder to her son-in-law.

It must be confessed that he disliked her from the first, but she went with Ruth and so must be accepted.

Must be accepted, yes, but with the years an increasing nightmare. That was really what she was, the old lady, a nightmare!

There had been a time just before he was ill in 1913, when he had felt that he simply could not endure her any longer. His illness, in fact, had been a climax to many things.

In 1910, the year of his most difficult and obscure volume of poems, *Troilus*, he had suddenly, obeying an impulse that he did not understand, and that did not seem to be his, published at intervals in the columns of the august *Daily World* a number of poems about the man in the street. They had been rather colloquial, slangy, poems, and some of the higher critics had denied that they were poems at all, but they had immense force and energy and were as simple as Tennyson's "Mr. Wilkinson."

Some of them, "Miss Battle," "The Man with the Coal," "Crossing Sweeper," had swept the country. Everyone learnt them by heart, lines from them crept into the language and, sure sign of universal acceptance, his name figured in contemporary musical comedy.

He delighted a wide public, because he provided something very rare now in England and always acceptable—literature that was acknowledged to be fine superior literature, and that yet could be understood by everybody. It was expected that now he would write a great English picaresque novel with all the energy, simplicity, and creative genius of a Dickens, and the subtlety and beautiful prose of a Henry Galleon. But, of course, he did not.

In 1913 came his illness, and this, following so swiftly on his new popularity, made him a Figure.

Figures can be made in all sorts of ways in England— by imprisonment, by eccentricity of dress or food, by the refusal of honours, by bad manners, by the accident of foreign birth—and the surest way of all, have you the patience, is to wait until you are eighty, grow a white beard, and live in the country fifty miles from anywhere so that people must make a Pilgrimage.

Hans had no wish, of course, to become a Figure—it was the last thing that he wanted, but it was thrust upon him, first by the sudden unexpected twist of his genius and, secondly, by his nearly dying in public.

He was too ill at the time to think of it and after his recovery too lazy, but had he considered the steps of his becoming a Figure he might have found them odd. The time was to come when he would consider them.

Meanwhile there followed the war and, for the time, he vanished. His mother had been German, and German ancestry was not for some while popular; but here again Fate worked for him a queer twist in the pattern.

In his volume of Essays, *The War and the Artist,* published in 1916, some of the finest, noblest, and sincerest utterances about the war in any language appeared. It was generally recognized that this was so. They were accepted by Patriot and Pacifist alike, because in them the true nobility of Hans' character, its depth, width, freedom from petty egotism, tenderness, and unpriggish passion for humanity were openly displayed.

Then when at length the end of the war arrived, his volume of poems *Eumenides* was so commanding in style and lyrical splendour that he emerged at last as a Great Man— someone who would thenceforth be written about as though he were already dead.

For himself, his principal sensation was that during these years he had been incorrigibly lazy. It had not been a mental laziness nor, regarding the war, which he felt with the deepest poignancy, an emotional one. He had felt the war, he had felt and enjoyed his intellectual passion, but in his human personal relations he had been as lazy as a cat.

Men and women had been to him as trees walking. Even Ruth's horrible mother had been merely a kind of toad or baby alligator confined to the back garden. He had been even able to watch quite passively her habits as, at the Zoo, one observes a tortoise absorbing a lettuce.

So, from 1914 until now, this day, his seventieth birthday, he had lain in the arms of Ruth—lain there because he was too sleepy to move.

It had been a long while since he had lain there from instincts of physical passion. After his illness he had been aware that that was over for him, once and for all.

A great peace had descended upon him. The anxieties, triumphs, and sudden ghastly disappointments of physical love were to be his no longer. He felt no shame and no regret. Work and friendship and love of his fellow-men remained, nay, could move the more nobly forward now unimpeded by the thickets and tangled undergrowth of that dusky wood.

Nor did Ruth offer objection. He could have realized now, had he investigated it, that physical passion had never been for her an impulse towards him. He did not examine it, but dismissed it, in company with a multitude of husbands, by deciding that she was sexually "cold," making his individual experience of her a general rule.

He knew that his sexual withdrawal from her gave her no ground of complaint, because the old woman, her mother, did not blame him for it.

He would have heard—oh yes, he would have heard—had he in this committed sin.

Meanwhile Ruth made him ever more comfortable. He was lapped round with luxury. The house grew ever more luxurious, more tranquil, more soft-footed. Bigges the butler, Miss Caparis his secretary, were ideal. They understood his needs before he uttered them. They were like his physical properties—his hands, his feet, his eyes. They were always there and they were never in the way.

Moreover, had he considered it, he would have seen that nothing but flattery and adoration came across his path. He did not consider it, because he did not want flattery and adoration. That is not to say that he did not care for an adroit compliment. Clever praise makes all men happy— a reassurance against the eternal fear of the hidden enemy— but he was at heart too simple, and by nature too generous, and intellectually too wise, to require incense.

He grew also intellectually lazy during these years. He ceased to have curiosity about his fellow human beings. Before this his interest in them had been a peculiar mixture of irony and tenderness, and in this same mixture he was himself involved save that in his view of himself his irony exceeded his tenderness.

Watching those around him he saw—and of course had long before this seen—that the only difference between one man and another was as to whether he were a poet or no. This difference had nothing to do with the actual creation of poetry nor with the delighted perception of it. Investigating his immediate household, for instance, it was plain that

Bigges his butler was no poet and that Crouch his chauffeur
was one. He was willing to admit that the decisions that he
made were influenced by his personal liking and dislike. A
poet to one is no poet to another, and it might be that to
Mrs. Bigges, Bigges was Keats and Shelley pressed into one.
But he knew what he meant. He had only to consider
Crouch's straight and steady gaze and the sullen droop at
the corner of Bigges' mouth to be aware that one was march-
ing to glory and the other not.

He was immensely attracted to simple and good-hearted
people, but he liked no one's company for very long.
He became dissatisfied with himself rather than with them.
It was incredible that human beings could be so stupid,
so uninquisitive, so muddle-minded, but it was incredible,
too, that they could offer so bold a front to undeserved
misfortunes, could snatch time from their own problems
to consider others. An ironic tenderness was the only emotion possible.

He made during these later years no close friends, and
took but little trouble with old friendships. He had long ago
perceived that among writers contemporary friendships
were almost impossible to sustain. You could be paternal to
a younger writer, would he only consent to be filial. You
could, when young, yourself be filial. But the rivalries,
jealousies, egotisms of the literary world (no fiercer, of
course, than in any other artistic world) were disappointing, disturbing, sterile.

He had loved Henry Galleon with a deep and reverent
love, but that on the whole had been the last of his reverence

for his kind. Reverence was not the emotion that they aroused.

And so, for this reason as well as all the others, he snuggled into the lazy comforts that Ruth provided for him. He allowed her to make what she would of him so long as she did not worry him.

To himself he was no sort of a Figure at all. With the good that there had been in his work he seemed to have but little to do. The mistakes, clumsinesses, stupidities, they were his, but even there he could not worry himself very deeply, he had been born like all other human beings a fool, and a fool he would remain.

He was dimly conscious, as one may be in a dream, that Ruth was very happy in making a Legend of him. Well, if it amused her, why not? He did not object. He even liked some of the consequences of it. No one can be flattered for ever and ever and not, at last, react to the flattery. Not grossly and not to the grossest. But still the thing is there and it will be missed when it is there no longer. . . .

English people are not clever in their flattery of artists because, thank God, they do not care very greatly for art. The only countries where art really flourishes are those in which the artists are left alone and work, in little isolated numbers, not against hostile surroundings but indifferent ones.

Hans knew that he had won his popularity by the elements that were least important in his work, but because the other elements were there also, he was someone who had a longer history. . . .

So he listened to the flattery at times, despised it and liked it. It did not change him, make him complacent or irritated by hostile criticism, but it bound him still more closely to Ruth, because she saw that he got just the kind of flattery that he could swallow.

He thought meanwhile increasingly in literary terms. Methods began greatly to interest him. He read the newest writers with a great deal of appreciation and sympathy. They could do things that he would never be able to do— and at the same time there were things that he had done for which they were too external and brittle and self-satisfied.

He wrote three articles on "The New Novel" for one of the monthlies, and the house echoed: "Wonderful to take such an interest in the young generation"; "Marvellous modesty . . ."; "This is real genius. . . ."

He knew that it was neither marvellous nor modesty nor genius, but only a literary vanity. He caught echoes beyond the house of "Old Frost trying to catch up with the young people," "Why doesn't he lie quiet in his grave?"

He wasn't hurt by these distant voices—not at all—but he snuggled closer to Ruth.

When he went abroad he was a Figure. He wore a distinct sort of uniform, a black hat that was too short for a top-hat but too square for a bowler, with a large, curly brim. A buff waistcoat with gilt buttons, a broad dark blue coat, grey spats. A heavy black cane with a gold knob.

He was always immaculate. He hated untidiness of any kind. Spotless linen seemed to him next to the Grace of God.

He was a well-recognized figure in the centre of London.

As he climbed slowly the broad steps of the "Acropolis" Club the chauffeurs of the cars ranked in the square, the policemen on duty, the drivers of crawling taxis, all knew him. And often a casual passer-by wondered who that distinguished, swell old gentleman might be.

Yes, he was a Figure.

CHAPTER V

Ma Marriott

MARTHA stood up, looked in her master's face, and yawned. Frost started. For how long had he been sitting there? He shivered. He was still permeated with this sense that some crisis had come to him, as yet veiled but in a moment to be revealed.

Ruth would be hurt at his not going down to her tea-party. But he would not go down. He did not want to see any of them or indulge in the silly, smirking kind of talk that would be provided with the tea and bread and butter.

Silly? Smirking? Were these the words to use about Ruth's tea-parties, those gentle, well-bred ceremonies instituted especially for himself? But tea-parties . . . things that no man should attend. And yet how many during these last years he had attended!

In his own house, of course. Coming into the dignified, cheery, curtained room a little late, a few chosen spirits already there, some silly woman murmuring as she rises, "Ah, here is the Master!" Standing there, his cup in his hand, listening to the gentle almost whispering conversation, breaking in upon it with an occasional remark, stupid enough, but saluted by everyone as though it were an Olympian judgment. . . . Ruth in the background, beautiful, dignified, serenely pleased. Why now did the contemplation of this make him shiver?

He rose, stretching his arms, and yawned. Martha yawned too. She looked at him cynically, wagged her tail a trifle, and examined the carpet.

He addressed her:

"Shall we go downstairs? What do you think? Are you also ashamed of society? You are always a little ashamed of me. Now I come to think of it you have been ashamed for some time. Why? What have I done that's disgraceful? Or is it simply that you're bored with me and all my works? Well, I'm bored with them myself. They are beneath contempt perhaps. And you and I are beneath contempt too. The Manet is worth a hundred of us. What do you say, Martha? Shall we do away with ourselves and come out in a new incarnation? You as a Peke, perhaps, or a bulldog, I as a great newspaper magnate or a pimp in a small French watering place. What does it matter as long as we have bellies in good working order and can have our eyebrows lifted?"

He swung round, and there was Henry Galleon surveying him from his gold frame, the wise broad brow, the kind benignant eyes, the slightly ironic mouth. "Yes, you were a Master. . . . Not the kind of sham I am. But didn't you think yourself a sham? Hadn't you moments of ironic horror at yourself? No, you were a tranquil man. You liked your joke, but you were secure because you saw so far. But I . . . I . . . I'm myopic. I can't see my own hand."

He stood feeling a distress and an agitation that he had

not known, he fancied, for years. The room seemed to him overpoweringly hot. He was stifled. He must get out. But where?

He thought then of his mother-in-law. So uncomfortable was he that he wanted to add to his discomfort. He would rub salt into the wound. Despising himself as he did, he would inflict upon himself the most intolerable company he could find—and that was most certainly his mother-in-law's. He would spend ten minutes in her company, just to prove to himself how low humanity could sink!

He went into the passage, Martha following him.

How still the house was! Not a sound anywhere. The long, dusky passage seemed to invite him to mysteries. At the end of it, like an old witch brooding over her toad-and-snake cauldron, was his mother-in-law. Perhaps it was she who had thrown this spell over him. She would love to do him any kind of harm. He would go and investigate.

She had for some time now decided that she was an invalid and could move only with difficulty. He was convinced that there was nothing whatever the matter with her, save that she ate too much and did not take any exercise.

She was, it was true, an old woman, but had, he was sure, a sort of demonic good health, and the only way that she would ever disappear would be on a broomstick swinging through the night to Satanic revels.

How he hated her—and he was in the mood just now to spend time with someone he hated.

He went down the passage and knocked on the door.

A soft echo came from within the room.

"Come in."

She had arranged her room according to her fancy, and her fancy was for everything dark and dingy. The window curtains were of some heavy dull brown material. The chairs and sofa were of a thick grey padded stuff, as though hippos had spawned their young. On the walls hung photogravures of "Queen Victoria Receiving the News of Her Accession," "The Charge of the Guards at Waterloo," and a large representation of "Mr. Gladstone Addressing the House of Commons."

She was taking her tea. She sat in a vast armchair over which her black silk dress billowed in multitudinous folds. Her face was yellow and peaked and lined, but her eyes were alive and bright. Her grey hair, spare and thin, was pulled back tightly over her scalp and parted in a sharp white line down the middle.

She wore black mittens and, when he came in, was peering into the teapot, as though she expected to find a hoard of gold there.

She greeted him very briskly and with a kind of coy amiability. She pretended always that she was devoted to him and that they were the best of friends.

She hated Martha and was offended when he brought her with him. So he always brought her.

"Well, Hans! Not having tea with Ruth?"

Her eyes were the only part of her that she could not control, and she gave him a bright, hostile glance before she again investigated the teapot.

He stood looking at her. "No. It's my seventieth birthday,

and I think that so important an occasion should be spent
in monastic seclusion."

She never knew whether he were laughing at her or no,
which was one reason why she disliked him. "Leaving poor
Ruth to entertain all those gentlemen alone? Naughty,
naughty!"

She waggled a finger at him and then poked a teaspoon
into the teapot.

"Oh, they'd had enough of me. They've been making me
speeches."

"Speeches?" she echoed, her voice muffled by the teapot.

"Yes. Telling me I'm a wonder. Which of course I'm not,
as you very well know, but they must have their little bit
of fun."

She poured herself out some more tea, drank it thirstily,
shrugged her old shoulders.

"Ruth thinks you're a wonder," she said at last. "And
what have you come to pay me a visit for?"

He smiled.

"I like a word with you once and again."

"What can you see in a stupid old woman like me?"

"I see all sorts of things."

"Not nice things, I'll be bound. Oh, I know what you
think of me. You needn't pretend."

"And what do you think of me?" he asked her, laughing.

"I don't think of you—except in relation to Ruth. When
an ordinary old woman like me has got an extraordinary
daughter, a wonderful, marvellous daughter, who is always so
good and kind to her, the most unselfish creature in the

world, why, then, the old mother wants only her happiness. So long as you make Ruth happy I'm content."

"And don't I?" he asked her.

"It isn't you that makes Ruth happy. It's her character. She's so noble and fine that she's bound to be happy."

There was something genuine here. He hadn't reached his seventy years without knowing that there was fineness in the worst of human beings, and this old woman, nasty though she was, was not the worst by any means.

At that moment there came to him something that Coleridge had said about Sterne: "There always is in a genuine humour an acknowledgment of the hollowness and farce of the world and its disproportion to the godlike in us," or something of the kind.

Well, there was a scrap of the godlike in old Mrs. Marriott, only a scrap, but still something.

"But still I don't make her unhappy."

"Nobody could make her that. She's got too complete a command of herself. She's proud of you. That makes her happy."

He looked at Martha.

"She's proud of the position she's made for me. But do you think she's proud of what I've done?"

There was a new note here. The old lady pricked up her ears. This sounded strangely like a criticism of her dear daughter.

Her voice rang sharp as she answered. "Well I never. . . . What a thing to say! Of course she's proud of what you've done."

"I wasn't sure," he answered, smiling. "I'm not very sure of anything this evening. My seventieth birthday has upset me. Didn't you feel that a little on *your* seventieth birthday?"

She eyed him sharply. Again she didn't know whether he were laughing at her or no. Her eye, in its suspicious whirl, caught the dog. She was sure that Martha was laughing at her.

"I can't think what you want to bring that dog around with you everywhere for. Dogs are messy things, in my opinion. . . . No, I don't think my seventieth birthday upset me. One birthday's like another."

"That's just where you're wrong. One birthday isn't like another. Every birthday's one nearer the end."

She eyed him with hatred. He knew how deeply she resented to be reminded of her dissolution. It was an insult to her egotism. "You must trust in God more," she said.

He leant forward, resting on the back of a chair and staring at Victoria in her nightdress.

"He, too, has changed with my birthdays," he answered. "Seventy is a lot for Him to take an interest in."

She recovered her pretended amiability. "You're a very clever man, Hans, far too clever for me. I've never been clever. I'm an old woman, as you say, and should be preparing for my end. It will come soon doubtless, and no loss to anybody."

She fished in his eyes for a contradiction (she had a very determined vanity), but she caught nothing. He wasn't for the moment thinking of her.

"I don't feel old," he said. "That's the devil of it. I feel as though I were just beginning life, which is absurd. I want to be taken out of myself. I'm as sick of myself as any young man of twenty can be. Books . . . silly, futile things, unless you're not a writer of them. And then anything can do the trick. The *Family Herald* just as well as *Adonais*, if you're in the proper receptive mood.

"Well, well, I'll have a bath and dress at my leisure. There's nothing pleasanter."

He could see that she was uneasy. There was something unusual about him to-night, and this something unusual might threaten her daughter. She sniffed peril to Ruth, as the native sniffs the tiger. There was something in this old man's eye that boded ill. And, in any case, what was he doing up here instead of entertaining Ruth's guests downstairs? Why hadn't he gone down?

She hated him. He made her restless. Always thinking of himself. But she smiled at him, her dry, wintry, withered smile.

"Ruth's waiting for you all this time downstairs. You should go down and help her."

"They've gone, or at least I hope so. I'll send Martha down to see." Martha, at the sound of her name, looked up hopefully. She detested this room. She knew that no one loved her here.

"Martha! Really, the way you go on about that dog! One would think that she was a human being."

"A human being! She's far finer. Devoted and wise. She's elegant and humorous and knows what she wants. She doesn't change with every wind. My seventieth birthday is neither good nor bad news to her. I'm a fixed object to her.

Were my face all boils she'd love me just as much. Of how many humans can that be said?"

Mrs. Marriott shook her black silk.

"You never say what you mean. I think it's a pity myself."

He shook his head at her laughing.

"Perhaps I do—more than you think, Good-night. Sleep well."

He went.

CHAPTER VI

Unknown Guest

OUTSIDE in the passage again he looked at his watch—half-past six. He must have stayed there thinking in the library a long time. Slept perhaps? That's what old men were for ever doing, sleeping when they didn't know it. Maybe, just as Alice bounded across the brook or Cæsar crossed the Rubicon, so he, on receiving the Manet . . . Anyway he felt devilish queer. Death perhaps. The beginning of an illness, the instant change from a fine, taut body to a trembling, helpless, aching mass of flesh and bones, disintegrated, fading.

He peered down the passage as though he expected to see his own ghost at the end of it. Then, with a little smiling sneer at his own folly, he pinched his arm. Solid firm flesh. He stroked his chin. *He* was all right. He saw suddenly breaking into the tissue-paper of the passage all the world's old men taking exercises, clad only in their vests, on the floors of their bedrooms, rising slowly on their hams and sinking again. Faces purple, arms mottled, stomachs protruding. At the sight of that disgusting vision he turned tail and sought refuge in the things of the spirit, the Holy Grail, and the last agonizing leap up the dark mountain side until the summit is grasped! That was better. He had shaken

47

the old lady off his shoulders. Let her weave her spells under the shadow of "Gladstone Addressing the House of Commons." He defied her.

Eight o'clock dinner. Nearly an hour and a half to bathe and change. Something within him snuggled together at the anticipation of the pleasure. Water, hot as hot, bath salts, softly scented soap, the slow, tranquil, half-sleepy comfort of the relaxing body, thoughts like indifferent, glittering, tail-flicking goldfish slipping along his brain, silence everywhere, the soft glow of the electric light on the white tiles. There, now that you are seventy, is your principal sensuous pleasure. A warm bath and silence. A warm bath and silence. Better than all the glories of the arts and the tender intimacies of any woman's embrace—now that you are seventy.

He padded along, Martha sniffing as though she scented the possibilities of a rat, a little ahead of him. His bedroom was on the next floor. Ruth had hers on this one, down the passage beyond the library. He had chosen his because it was almost an attic, the roof sloping a little, and a wonderful view over the Park. The servants' rooms were only just beyond his, and one of the guest rooms, the guest room for the quite unimportant guest.

His only discomfort was that he felt sometimes as though he were spying on the servants, on Bigges, and Mrs. Carlyon the cook, and the maids. Or that they might think he were. Servants were so odd. You meant them to be just like yourself, they doing their job and you doing yours. No servant and master any more, but only human beings performing services each in his or her own way.

But they wouldn't have it so. They talked among themselves and watered the private gardens of their own private souls, growing their own spiritual cabbages and turnips. Very indignant if you asked them for one of their own special lettuces. Nor would they exchange. Bigges, for instance. What did he know about Bigges? Nothing, except that he was an efficient servant and very unpleasant. He would love to rid himself of Bigges. He would love to say:"Now, Bigges, you go this very minute." And Bigges would say: "Why?" And he would say: "Because you are so efficient. Because you never make a mistake. Because I hate the neatness of your hair and the breadth of your chest and the way you swing your hams when you walk. Reason enough. Now go."

But Bigges wouldn't go because Ruth liked him and thought him an excellent servant, and were Hans to say: "Bigges must go, because of the way that he swings his hams," Ruth would think him mad, and also indecent.

He walked slowly upstairs to his room. Yes, something was certainly wrong with him. He had never actively wanted to get rid of Bigges before.

Entering his room he was at once dissatisfied with it. It was too luxurious and comfortable. On the pale cream-coloured walls were four beautiful pictures: a painting of a French street, by Utrillo; a faintly coloured drawing of two long-legged nude women, by Augustus John; a flower piece of peonies, by Bracque; and a blue hill behind dark fields, by Duncan Grant. The carpet was dark wine-purple and very soft. Everything was soft, the bed, the electric light, the deep armchair, the dark blue curtains at the window. The only hard thing was the electric horse in the corner, on whose back he took his morning exercises, and even that had a soft seat. Hanging over the foot of the bed was a thick-padded orange dressing gown and below it two deep brown wool-lined bedroom slippers. Everything was soft.

He took off his coat and waistcoat, his collar and tie. He looked at himself in the glass—funny old man with his bare neck and the grey hairs on his chest curling between the ends of his open shirt. Funny old man nearly dead in this soft electric-lighted room. Nearly dead and nothing to show save a few ill-written, childlike books. No warmth anywhere, no real friend, no real wife, no real butler even.

No real life anywhere—only the silly reflection in this looking-glass and the padded dressing gown waiting to fold itself about his naked body.

He had left his door half open. He turned to close it before he stripped. He heard a sound. He stood by the door listening. Yes, there could be no mistake. Someone, near at hand, was sobbing.

The sudden reality of the sound breaking on the empty unreality both of his room and himself startled him profoundly. Who was it? One of the maids perhaps. But no, not at this hour.

He thought then of the guest room. The guest room! Could there be anyone there?

He remembered then that he had heard something—Ruth had told him—something about a niece. The daughter of her sister, an orphan. He had been told weeks ago; he had scarcely noticed. Could this be she? But no. Modern girls didn't cry. Tears were no weapon in *their* armoury.

But the sobbing went on, broken, half checked, desperately unhappy. He could not endure it. He went hastily back into the room, slipped on the dressing gown, went down the passage.

Yes, it was from the guest room; the door had not been completely closed. He pushed it softly open and looked in.

Lying on her face on the bed, her head in her arms, was a girl. She lay there almost without movement.

He could not spy upon her. At once he said:

"Hullo! Anything the matter?"

She sprang up and kneeling on the bed turned to him a face childish, stained with tears, and flushed with surprise.

She sprang off the bed and, standing like a young animal at bay, said fiercely:

"What is it? . . . I thought the door was closed."

"Well, it wasn't. . . ." Then he added, smiling: "I beg your pardon for coming in."

She had hated to be caught. She looked at him with hostility. Then she blew her nose on a very small and, as he could see, very damp handkerchief.

"You're Uncle Hans?"

"Yes," he said.

"I'm Nathalie Swan, and I was crying because I was homesick. I never did anything so silly before in my life and I never will again."

"Oh, there's no harm in crying," Hans said. "I often wish that I could. It's a great relief. One always feels better after it. Men aren't supposed to—I'm sure I don't know why. But I like women to. It shows they're human."

She gave her nose a final blow.

"I haven't been away from home before. I went to the high school in Polchester. This house is so big and silent. But it was dreadfully silly of me. . . . How do you do?"

She came towards him, her hand outstretched. They shook hands.

"I suppose it isn't very proper," he said, "to come into a lady's room in a dressing gown, but it's my seventieth birthday and after seventy one may do anything."

"Yes, I know it is," she answered. "I read about it in the paper."

"Well then, because I'm seventy, and because I'm your uncle, and because you're my guest, I may go further. Tell me what I can do to make you happy and comfortable."

"You've done everything," she answered timidly, "by our meeting. I saw your picture in the hall when I arrived, but I felt somehow as though that was as far as I was going to get."

"When did you arrive?"

"Late this afternoon."

He was going to say something about his wife. He checked himself.

"But how foolish to think that you weren't going to get further than that very indifferent picture. We're under the same roof. We'll be meeting every day."

Her eyes shone with pleasure. "Oh, shall we?"

"But of course—why shouldn't we?"

"You're a great man. And you won't have time——"

He shook his head impatiently. "What nonsense! In the first place there aren't any great men. In the second I've all the time in the world. I've nothing to do."

"Writing books must take a great deal of time."

"I don't expect I shall ever write another. There are far too many in the world already. If you can stop my writing them I shall be deeply grateful."

"Other people won't. They'd murder me."

She was sitting on the bed. She looked tired and dishevelled.

"Dinner's at eight," he said.

"I'm not coming down to-night," she answered. "There's a grand dinner-party because of your birthday. And I'm going to have what I like better than anything in the world —dinner in bed."

He was about to speak. Again he checked himself.

"Perhaps that's best to-night. You must be tired. But it isn't a grand dinner-party, only a stupid one, when no one will say what they mean."

"It would be awful if they did, wouldn't it," she answered him. "I don't mean at your dinner-party especially, but always. Mrs. Proudie has a brother who comes to stay sometimes and he always says exactly what he means. The results are frightful."

"Mrs. Proudie?"

"The Proudies are the people I've been living with. They have been so wonderfully kind to me—always. I think that is why I was crying. They spoilt me. I couldn't help thinking of them. I love them terribly."

"We'll try and be kind, too," he said. "It will do us all good here."

She was brightening. He saw how young she was by the way that the colour was stealing back into her face and all her form returning, her curly bobbed hair resuming its order although she had not touched it, the traces of the tears vanishing from her cheeks although, after the first surprise, she had not wiped them, faint rose like soft re- flected light shadowing the face under the dark eyes and the dark hair.

She was adorably young. She might be his beloved grand- child.

"You might be my grandchild," he said, not knowing why he said it.

"I could easily, couldn't I?" she answered, smiling with all her body.

He saw that she was adoring him, gazing at him as though in five minutes from now he would be wrenched from her sight never to be seen again.

"My father and mother were killed in a carriage accident when I was very young," she went on, very serious again, not seeing him now, only her father and mother. "So that I've never had any real relations. The times I missed having them most was always in the summer when we went to Buquay. Everyone was part of a family. So was I of course. The Proudies were the same to me as to their own children— only, of course, I knew the difference."

He saw her as a very little girl, her dress pinned up round her waist, in striped little bathing drawers, with a bucket and spade. Very serious. In the bucket, floating in sandy sea water, were an amorphous jellyfish and a pale yellow starfish.

She was looking for shells. Very seriously. And in his nostrils was the tang of the fresh biting salt, and glittering fragments of sand stuck to his hands, and there was sand inside his canvas shoes. Boom, boom went the waves. There was some surf to-day, a bright sunshining breeze, and gulls were clustered over some glorious fragment there where the wet sand shone in reflected light. Behind them the lodgings stood, and in front of each window, heavy and wet, hung towels and bathing costumes. She was looking for shells. She found several beauties and brought them to him to look at. One was indeed lovely, faintly rose and fading to cream at the edges of the rim. He looked from the shell to her round chubby serious face; on her cheeks were glistening fragments of sand, and coiled round her spade like the spoils of a hunter's chase a clinging fragment of red-gold seaweed.

"Yes. That's a beauty . . ." he said. "Don't you lose it."

"Don't I lose what?" she asked, looking across at him from the bed where she was again sitting.

"I was thinking of you as a little girl on the sea shore looking for shells. I was with you. You showed me a beauty."

"I wish you had been," she answered. "I'd have brought you all my spoils."

"A jellyfish, a starfish, a piece of golden seaweed . . ." he thought, looking back to his own childhood, so long, so very long ago.

"The seaside I knew when I was young wasn't so romantic. A place called Seascale in Cumberland. It's a fashionable watering-place now, I believe. Then it was nothing but a row or two of houses and a long wet beach. It was my first sea, though, and it was marvellous in my eyes. We stayed in a village called Gosforth three miles inland. I was about eighteen and I used to bicycle over—one of those bicycles, you know, with a seat as high as the stars and a huge wheel in front and a little one behind. I went over every Thursday, because just above the beach at Seascale was a little stationer's shop with bottles of sweets, balls of string, buckets, and spades. And they sold a weekly called, I think, the *Weekly Telegraph*, or some such name. It was printed on rough yellow-looking paper, and it had rough smudgy pictures and —the most marvellous serial stories in the world. Stories like Miss Braddon's and Mrs. Henry Wood's—and a page of correspondence at the end. I was in touch with all the world through that paper. And I would buy rock cakes and toffee and my *Weekly Telegraph*, then go and bathe, and then sit on the sand eating my toffee and reading my serial . . . Now isn't that odd? I've never told anyone before about those times. And now they're all around me. I can hear the long wave curling over, dragging back the sand, and the sea-gulls calling, and I can feel the rough paper under my hand. . . ."

"And have you never gone back?" she asked.

"No, never. I'd be afraid to go."

She caught her breath in a little gasp. "Now if we never have another talk it will be worth while having come to London just for this one."

He discovered that he was excited. "You've made me a present—a jellyfish, a starfish, a rosy shell, and a piece of seaweed. Now what shall I give you?"

"Nothing—except that we'll talk sometimes."

He shook his head. "My dear, you'll soon get very tired of me. I'm an old, old man. Martha's the only one who can stand my company for long."

"Martha? Who's Martha?"

"My dog. She knows me precisely and has no illusions."

"Who else is there in the house?"

"My secretary, Miss Caparis, the cook, Mrs. Carlyon, the maids, Bigges, whom you know—and your grandmother."

"Oh, what's she like? I've never seen her."

"You won't see her often. She's an invalid."

"I *am* sorry. Does she suffer terribly?"

"Not so much as you might imagine. No. You won't see her very often. She stays in her room."

Then the girl's voice sank into a whisper.

'What shall I do if Aunt Ruth doesn't like me?"

"Of course she'll like you."

"No, but if she doesn't."

"Well—what then?"

"You see I can't go back to the Proudies. At least I'm determined not to. They've been so good to me for so long. Of course they'd *have* me back, but it wouldn't be right.

They're not well off, and although they say that it doesn't make any difference, my being there, of course it does. I eat such a lot."

"There's plenty of food in *this* house."

"Yes, but I must find a job. I'm sure that I could learn typing and shorthand in no time I must look around."

She said this in a very grown-up fashion.

"You mustn't look around yet anyway. You'll be a splendid companion for my wife."

"Do you think so? I know so little. I'll seem to her terribly stupid."

"Oh, you'll soon pick up the London jargon. You'll find out who are the writers and painters, and then in two months when they all change you'll change too, almost without knowing it. It's in the air. My wife has a bookcase downstairs with the newest writers, French and English—only the very latest. Study that for half an hour and you'll be all right. Now I must go or I shall be late for the birthday party."

They looked at one another. He wanted to go across to her and kiss her. He did not. He said, "See you later," and vanished.

He lay in his bath thinking about her. He was still excited —as though he had been given some wonderful, unexpected present—but because in his life he had always found that things were less good than they ought to be, so now he refused to consider this affair.

He would expect nothing. He would demand nothing. He

knew nothing about her. She was very young. She thought him wonderful. He detested anyone who thought him wonderful.

He considered his round pink belly, his ugly toes, his bumpy knees. Anyone who thought him wonderful was a fool.

He lay luxuriously despising himself and with himself all the universe. Ridiculous, preposterous, noisy, aimless, imbecile universe. And after despising it, he loved it and felt deeply tender towards it. Touching, aspiring, courageous, enterprising, adventurous universe. He looked at his body and gave it a pat on the back, because here he was at seventy and hardly an ache. He considered then its ugliness, its absurd protuberances, its rag-tag and bobtail odds and ends. He pinched his thigh and, holding his nose, dropped his head under the water. There was a great roaring in his ears. He rose again. He kicked his legs like a baby in the water. He sat up and soaped his face. He felt clean, wrapped about with beautiful odours. He was content.

Standing on the bath-mat rubbing himself, he thought again about this child. What had his wife invited her here for? The answer came at once, as though whispered in his ear by a dark enemy. To increase her own glory.

For an instant his heart seemed to stop beating. What was he about? What had happened to him? He had never been disloyal to his wife before. This was disloyalty, nay worse, treason. How ridiculous! How could the coming of this child increase Ruth's glory?

She wants to show off, you know—to have someone to

show off to. She always wants that. No, no, she does not!
He flung down the towel and rushed naked into the bedroom.
He saw himself in the long glass, a ridiculous naked old
man, betraying and traducing his dear wife, who had done
everything for him.

Then, very quietly, slipping on his vest, he said out loud:
"It's true. I know it's true."

He felt again a great tenderness for Ruth. He wanted
to put his arm around her and protect her against a hostile,
critical world. Then he saw her as she would be to-night in
her beautiful clothes, her head high, afraid of nothing and
nobody. How absurd that he, clad only in his shirt, his hair
on end, should want to protect this glorious creature. She
needed no protection. That was the trouble. She had never
needed any.

But this child needed protection. Poor little thing, flung
helpless into this hard London world, with no friends, no
parents, and her ridiculous confidence in himself. He would
have to change that, show her that he was of no use as a
protector, that he was too old, too selfish, too lazy. Much too
selfish!

At the mere suggestion that he must change his habits,
his comforts, his indulgences, his heart shivered. He at seventy! What was the value of being seventy if you were not
safe at last, safe from emotions, duties, new influences? Of
course he was safe. He drove his studs fiercely into his shirt.
He slipped on his silk socks, his trousers.

He went to the glass to brush his hair.

He loved to brush his hair. It was wonderful that at

seventy he should still have such stiff, strong hair, and so much of it.

But she was charming. What a child she had been as he had first seen her stretched on her bed crying! How adorably she had trusted him, confidence shining from her eyes; how quickly, when she had seen that it was he, she had been happy, as though all that she wanted was that he should be there.

And he was sure that she would not invade his privacy nor trespass on his daily life. She would have great tact and discretion. A word from him would always be enough. And how pleasant to have someone to whom he could show things, his books, the Manet, his favourite things in London, like the Aquarium at the Zoo, the odds and ends in the London Museum, the pictures at Dulwich, the Caledonian Market, and the rooms at Hampton Court. She would be excited and interested, but not too much so. She had, he fancied, a little irony, and she would be grateful without being sentimental. . . .

There was a knock on the door. Bigges was there.

"The guests have arrived, sir." Damn the guests!

"All right." He frowned at Bigges. He would love one day to pull Bigges' hair and see what he would do.

"Bigges, suppose I don't come down to dinner?"

"Are you unwell, sir?"

"Not in the least. But it's my seventieth birthday. I ought to be able to do what I like to-day."

"Yes, sir. Of course, sir."

"I would like to have dinner in bed, and read a bad novel."

"Yes, sir."

"Don't you ever feel that way yourself?"

Bigges coughed, but didn't answer.

"No, I see that you don't. You keep me in my place."

Bigges coughed again.

"All right, I'll be down in a minute." Silly fool. If you threw Bigges out from the top floor, when he bumped on the pavement he would rise immaculate, unhurt, every hair in its place.

He sighed. He must take the greatest care or he would be rude to someone to-night. He must take the greatest care or his seventieth birthday would be marked by a scandal. In the passage Martha awaited him. They went down in solemn state together.

CHAPTER VII

Dinner

THERE they all were waiting for him. The drawing-room
gleamed and shone about them. Ruth was magnificent in a
dress of old gold, and the guests were all talking with the
amiability that comes from having reached the right house
at the right time, and the prospect of a good dinner.

How well he knew them, how terribly well! Stout and
cynical Carl Reynolds, eager and active Mary Malpas,
shining and polished Horace Clay, and—Jane Rose.

Carl Reynolds was his contemporary, two years older
than he. Casual, careless, cynically contemptuous, omnis-
cient, the best and greatest critic in England, who had read
more than anyone else, remembered more than anyone else,
written more living, twisted, and ungrammatical prose than
anyone else, the greatest authority in the world on Early
Nineteenth-Century English Literature, so that he knew
just what De Quincey had for tea on August 5, 1808, what
books Southey was reviewing in November, 1810, and
exactly how far Coleridge went in his love-making with dear
Dorothy Wordsworth. He was married to an old woman who
was so impossible that no one ever asked her out anywhere,
dropped food on his clothes, had hair in his ears, and a very
red nose. Ruth, Hans knew, detested him, but asked him,
because he was important.

Hans loved him.

Against him, was Horace Clay, whom Ruth loved and Hans detested. Well, to say that Ruth loved him was perhaps too strong, but he stood for everything that seemed to her good. He was fifty, and slim, with a beautiful profile, small eyes like marbles, and an eyeglass on a thick black cord. In the season he dined at other people's houses, and out of the season he stayed with whom he might. He had, before the Revolution, had something to do with the Russian Embassy. He had now something to do with the City, whither, however, he never turned his steps.

He cackled like a hen when he laughed, smiled with all his teeth when he saw a friend, and left other gentlemen to pay taxis and supper bills. He gossiped among his familiars like three women alone at bedtime, and was very popular in his own world.

Then there was Mary Malpas. She was a tall bony woman with blonde hair. She was a widow, and not very rich, but entertained artistic celebrities.

She gave amusing parties in her little house in Charles Street. Everyone went to these, laughed at her afterwards, and then said how much they liked her, because they wanted to go to more parties.

In absolute fact she was an exceedingly kind woman, loyal to her friends, intelligent and amusing. Her great problem was how to have room in her very small house for the new artistic celebrities, and still to retain the old ones. They *would* increase so fast.

Hans did not dislike her, but she *would* call him the Master.

Jane Rose was quite another pair of shoes. Ruth didn't like her, but had asked her because the new generation in London thought her important.

She looked like the wife of a Pre-Raphaelite painter, her dark hair brushed back in waves from her forehead, her grey dress cut in simple fashion, her thin pale face quiet and remote. She was, Hans thought, the best living novelist in England. She wrote the most beautiful prose in the most beautiful way. Her three novels, *The Haycock, Garlands Passage,* and *The Cattle Boat,* were lovely, wonderful things. Oh! if he could write like that, if he could observe and remember like that, if he could translate onto the page pity and irony and tenderness and humour like that! . . . But he could not. Here was a gulf between her generation and his fixed! Never, never, try as he might, could he win her lovely revelation of human nature, unwitting that it should be revealed.

Her London street and park and summer sun, her sea and sand and distant hill, her triumphant evocation of the drama of little things, her seemingly casual assembling of tiny significances that were the waving flags and beating drums of life's procession!

She had in her last novel spoken of the beam from a lighthouse "stroking the floor of a lodging-house bedroom"—so her art illumined, gently and tenderly, the world that he knew. The debt that he owed her could never be paid.

Ruth didn't like her, because she looked odd and always

in conversation (with Ruth at least) answered the last sentence but one. There was something terrifying in her gentle remoteness.

Ruth could not understand her novels, all about nothing, with a chair here and a duster there, and someone talking about cheese one moment and life and death the next.

However, people like Mary Malpas who "knew" thought her "dreadfully clever," so Ruth asked her. And Jane Rose came, because she liked and respected Hans.

There they all were and, as he came in, he knew that although he had been cross and rebellious coming downstairs his official "charm" was, at sight of them, poking up its head. He couldn't but be "charming." He was expected to be. He was expected to smile that jolly, humorous, semi-sarcastic smile. He was expected to employ that easy, friendly voice, he was expected to be his public self. Hans Frost, the great (if slightly embalmed) writer, who had a lovely house and a lovely wife and a lovely position, whose books were already classics, although no one any more very much read them.

He heard himself saying: "I'm so sorry I'm late. I do hope that you haven't been waiting. How are you, Carl? Good evening, Mrs. Malpas. How do you do, Miss Rose? Well, Clay, how are you?"

Everyone was very well.

They all went in to dinner.

Hans had on his right Mary Malpas, and on his left Jane Rose.

He was not hungry: he was excited and could not think

why. Something had happened to him upstairs. What? He would not open the door and look, lest what he saw should be disappointing. So he remained sensationally in a mist, holding in one hand a jellyfish and in the other a piece of golden seaweed—and in the meanwhile, from a long way off, Mary Malpas was saying:

"But truly, *cher maître*, I think she would amuse you. If one day you'd honour my poor roof. . . . She's so young that her impertinences aren't offensive. *Si jeunesse savait*." (Mary Malpas's French accent was a poor one.) "Why not try her? Really her poetry is remarkable. Everyone is agreed. . . ."

He looked at his soup, which was a clear translucent brown, and in it floated tiny lozenges of vegetable. It was one of those soups in perfect taste but without vitality— well bred and *fin de siècle*. He sighed. Martha, whose head was resting on his shoe under the table, sighed also.

"I'd like her, would I?" he asked, wondering whether it were true, as he'd read somewhere, that in Teheran the famous Persian gardens contained only trees and running water. No flowers at all. Very disappointing if that were so, after all the fuss the Persian poets had been making. . . .

"Tell me about her," he said.

"There isn't very much to tell. She's taken everyone by surprise. No one *dreamt* that she had *Fly-by-Nights* in her. In fact some people say . . ."

Carl Reynolds was in trouble. He had spilt some soup onto his waistcoat, and he wouldn't have cared—oh, not in the least—had Horace Clay not been sitting opposite to

him. Horace Clay made him feel as though he had been discovered in Piccadilly Circus with no clothes on—not that
he would have minded that in the least had Piccadilly Circus not minded, but as soon as the Circus minded (which of
course it did) he was unhappy.

He was a violent, abusive, ironical old man, but absurdly
enough he could not bear that other people should be unhappy or that he himself should be laughed at. Now his hostess was unhappy, and Horace Clay was laughing at him.

He had spilt his soup—and a good deal of it—because
he had become deeply interested in explaining to Ruth
about an article only this very day completed on the Ettrick
Shepherd and the virtues of his story *The Brownie of
Bodsbeck*. When he talked of James Hogg he saw at once
the Edinburgh of that day, the fine folk riding down Princes
Street, and Burke and Hare skulking in their holes, and Scott
coming out of the Court House and . . . So he spilt his soup.

He wiped it with his napkin. Ruth ever so faintly flushed.
Carl saw his ancient mother—two years deceased—and his
two ugly sisters, whom he loved, and his plain brown-faced
wife (who was never asked anywhere and preferred not to be
asked, but Carl felt always a traitor because he left her at
home), all of them insulted, all of them contemned through
the eyeglass of Horace Clay.

He stammered, trying to return once more to the
"wynds" and windy places of Edinburgh, but he could not.
He had been cast out from them, because he had spilt his
soup.

Hans, glancing over the brilliant shimmer of the round

table, over the blue bowl on whose surface floated the heads of pale yellow roses, saw it all.

And at once when he saw it he felt everything within him rise to champion Carl. Carl was his friend and Horace Clay his enemy. Carl he understood and sympathized with and loved, as though they had leapt together from the same womb and had never from that moment been separated. He loved neatness and cleanliness, but he felt as though he himself had spilt Carl's soup and Carl, in a spirit of wonderful generosity, had taken the crime upon himself.

And he hated Horace Clay: he hated his eyeglass and his hen's cackle and his beautiful profile. Clay should have been a procuress in Dieppe or Ostend. Clay . . . But he must rush to champion Carl. So he raised his glass and cried:

"Your health, Carl. It's splendid to have you here again."

But, alas, this was most unwise, because it was Carl's only failing that he was inclined to drink too much when under the roof of a friend who knew what good wine was like, and Carl knew that and would do his utmost, on a fine occasion, to drink only lemonade or beastly barley-water.

It was tacitly understood that he must not be encouraged; but now Hans had encouraged him, and Carl turned and said to Bigges: "I think, after all, I will have a little sherry"; and after that there would be champagne and after that port . . and the end of the evening would be perhaps disgraceful.

Hans knew at once that he should not have done this, and he knew that Ruth was angry with him, and so he, in return, was angry with Ruth.

"We must all drink your health soon, *cher maître*," said

Mary Malpas. "Ruth tells us that they have given you a Manet. To be given a Manet, what bliss! We are pining to see it . . . and, indeed, it is no more than you deserve."

So the Manet was to be insulted too. He resolved instantly that they should not see the Manet—none of them, not even Jane Rose.

Not to-night at least. She should come by herself to tea and he would show it to her then.

He turned to her.

"On my seventh birthday," he said, "I was given a Noah's Ark with a red roof. I've never liked any present so much since."

"I was lost on my seventh birthday. The nurse went off with a soldier and I followed the man with the balloons. I was lost for a whole afternoon. I sat in the police-station for an hour. I've loved policemen ever since. They were so very kind to me and gave me a piece of seed cake. But don't you think," she added, "that possessions are a pity? Don't you feel sorry for your Manet, that it isn't free dancing about on its own—a little like the tigers at the Zoo?"

"It shall be free," he said. "It shall do whatever it likes. I won't complain if it flies out of the window."

"No, you wouldn't," she said, smiling at him. "You know what freedom means."

But did he? Or, if he knew, had he got it?

No, he had not got it. He had had it possibly once, but now it had been stolen from him—stolen from him by Bigges, who was pouring out champagne, stolen by the beautiful saddle of mutton, the currant jelly, the crackling brown potatoes—stolen from him by the cheque-book in his dressing-room table, the roses in the flower bowl, and the electric wires that ran behind the boarding—in any case they should not see his Manet.

But Horace Clay who thought he knew about pictures (he took his ground mainly on the Russians, saying that no one could judge Tchekov unless they'd seen Stanislavsky and Knipper in *The Three Sisters*, which, of course, no one had. He had also drunk tea with Kuprin and vodka with the author of *Sanine*) took the Manet under his wing.

"Of course we must see the Manet. Of course we must see the Manet." He was just like a hen scratching in a dust-heap.

"I'm afraid you won't see the Manet." Hans, as though he were observing himself from the outside, was surprised at the tremor of excitement in his voice. "Nobody's going to see it to-night."

His voice was almost harsh. Certainly peremptory, rude, on the edge of violence. He knew that they were all surprised, as though he had taken up one of the plates in both hands and flung it to the ground. He knew also that Ruth was offended, deeply offended. He knew it still more surely when she laughed—her gay social laugh that was like a little gilt nail that you drove in somewhere with a sharp little tap to prevent a catastrophe.

"Why, Hans, what *do* you mean? Of course we're going to see the Manet. Why, *I* haven't seen it yet!"

He tried to laugh it off.

"I'm afraid not. It doesn't want to be seen to-night. It's

shy after so much public exposure. I felt quite sorry for it
this afternoon."

"Oh, but when *I* ask you——"

"No, darling. Anything else to the half of my kingdom——" (Everyone was aware that husband and wife were
in conflict.)

"Now come, Hans, I never heard anything so absurd.
He *will* have these ridiculous ideas, you know." (This to
Horace Clay.) "I insist on seeing it."

"So you shall, my dear, to-morrow."

"No, to-night. We must *all* see it."

"Greatly distressed. . . . Manet invisible."

"But really, Hans, this is too bad——"

Just that note too much in her voice—note of personal
vexation, true irritation, rising anger. Horace Clay recognized it and—was it because he wanted to save her or to
accentuate the trouble?—he raised his glass. "Never mind
the Manet," he cried in his shrill and slightly effeminate,
shop-walking, gently foreign, accentuated voice (as though
he were an assistant in a very smart shop selling only the
best Russian fabrics). "We must drink to our host. The
Master and his glorious works! May there be seventy more
birthdays and seventy more masterpieces!"

"The Master!" called Mary Malpas shrilly. Jane Rose
looked at him, smiling quietly and drinking in silence.

But Carl Reynolds rose to his feet. "My friend! My
friend!" he shouted huskily, his voice thick with champagne and great feeling.

Everyone saw that he had drunk too much. He sat down

again and began peeling in a crazy way an apple while he
related to them all how at one of George Eliot's famous after-
noons George Henry Lewes had stood on his head to show
them something he had observed in the country, and had
looked exactly like a little performing dog, while George
Eliot, seated in her chair, had been like a performing horse
snorting through her nostrils and talking about Kant to
Herbert Spencer. He might have his details wrong, he said.
It was a considerable long time ago, but that was exactly
what Lewes had done—stood on his head and waved his
little legs in the air.

Everyone was greatly distressed. No one knew what Carl
Reynolds' next gesture would be. Ruth rose in dignity and,
followed by Mary Malpas and Jane Rose, moved off towards the drawing-room.

But Hans didn't care. It might be true that Carl had
drunk too much, but Carl was his friend. He got up and
moved to the chair next to Carl and put his hand on Carl's
shoulder. He knew that he should have said something
pleasant to Horace Clay, who was sitting now all by himself
in a débris of fruit skins, wine glasses, and crumbled bread,
but he could not. He was damned if he would. . . .

"It *is* jolly to have you here again," he said to Carl.

That was enough for Carl, who, with another glass of
port, would be in a vinous heaven, but had reached, without
the extra glass, only the outer portals. His eyes were filled
with tears, and he waved his hand in the air.

"You understand me, Hans," he said. "We understand
one another. There's hardly anyone but ourselves left.

Everyone dead, and a damnable new generation that doesn't know good writing when it sees it. A cold-blooded, whoring, ignorant generation. Why, there's that fool Mortlake despising the classics just because he never went to a university. University all wrong because *he* never went there. Latin and Greek all wrong because no one ever smacked his behind when he didn't do his Greek verses. Greek verses ... Greek verses. . . . My God! . . ." He choked over a piece of apple, and a tear, moved by his choking, stole down his cheek. "All this nonsense . . ."

Horace Clay, smiling only too courteously, leant across the table. "Well now—Greek verses—do you really think they've ever done any good to anybody?"

Carl's chest heaved. "Good! Good!" Then, like Parsifal, he asked violently, "What is good? . . . Good to whom? Good to what? Good to your stomach? Good to your pocket? No. But good to your soul. But perhaps you don't care about your soul. Souls are old-fashioned. I'm old. And you'll be old one day and wonder what the world's coming to. Each to his taste. . . ."

He was angry, his voice shook, not only because he had drunk too much, but because he saw the Athenian streets screaming with motor-cars and Mount Olympus trodden by the gilt shoes of cinema ladies—also he hated Horace Clay. He didn't know who he was, he didn't care. He was to him like a dirty street boy cocking a snook at Sappho.

It was Horace Clay's art to allow nothing to ruffle him. He saw before him only a drunken old man who had spilt soup down his waistcoat, so he said, still smiling:

"I'm sure you're right. I never had any education. I think
our modern world's absurd, of course, but as we belong to it
we may as well make the best of it."

"I don't belong to it! I don't belong to it!" Carl shouted.
"I'm better dead and buried, of course, but it isn't a question of you or me. Greek art and Greek literature are greater
than either of us, and if we don't take what they offer, what
do they care? The sun will shine whether we sneeze at it or
no. Yes, it will, thank God. We don't matter a damn."

He was becoming rhetorical and on the verge of great
personal rudeness, so Hans pressed his shoulder and said:
"Let's join the others."

But as they walked into the drawing-room he was greatly,
greatly excited. What did it matter whether Carl were drunk
or no? With his clumsy fist he was pushing this door ever
wider and wider. What door? The door that he had discovered only this afternoon, whose knob he had turned, and
now a thin line of light was showing, and soon . . .

He had himself perhaps drunk a little too much champagne. But it didn't matter. He would drink more if only,
by so doing, he could open the door more widely.

And then—would you believe it?—in the drawing-room
Mary Malpas began once again about the Manet. She came
to him with that air she had (she practised it only with the
acknowledged great) of being on intimate and unique relations. She looked him in the eyes and said:

"Dear Master, won't you allow us just a teeny, teeny
peep at the Manet? I know what you feel. We won't tell a
soul that we've seen it. . . ."

Know what he felt? Indeed she did not. He answered:

"Dear Mrs. Malpas, take it as an absurd whim of mine. I hate to refuse you anything, but there it is. I'd rather it were left to itself."

Then Ruth's voice broke in. "Don't be ridiculous, Hans. Go and get it. I never knew you so absurd."

He bowed.

"I am absurd. It's my seventieth birthday, the one day in one's lifetime when one's allowed to be absurd. The Manet is gone, vanished. It isn't there any longer, so how can I go and get it? To-morrow morning it may return. Who knows? As Miss Rose says, we've got to leave it its freedom. We can't capture it just because it's passed through the hands of some literary gentlemen. I'm sorry. When it returns I'll let you know."

He was laughing, and Ruth was laughing too. How beautiful she looked in her dress of old gold, and the lovely carriage of her head, how beautiful and how remote! She looked at him as though she loved him. Why was he so sure to-night that she did not?

"Have it your own way. It's your picture." And she turned, still smiling, to barricade herself off with Horace Clay, who sat down on the sofa beside her as though they had a special code of their own, something that was nearly Russian, but because Ruth had never seen Stanislavsky in *The Three Sisters* couldn't be quite.

Poor Carl had reached the stage when he was ashamed of himself and wanted to go home. He had been rude, had he not? But to whom? To that man with the eyeglass who didn't

like Greek verses? Shame upon him for an untidy, worthless,
old man. He was very near tears indeed, and Jane Rose,
seeing this, because, having both heart and brain in equal
splendour, she was able to understand the simplest distresses,
took him under her wing. How tenderly and with what loving care she did it, Hans thought, making the old man sit
down beside her, praising his book on De Quincey and his
Critical Essays, 1770–1830, asking him exactly about God-
win and the novels of Bage. . . . Yes, out of goodness of
heart all the splendours of life must come!

He himself stayed with Martha and Mary Malpas. Mary
wasn't so bad, would have been very good indeed had she
not been bitten by this curious social bug. But he could
attend to her only slightly. He was listening—listening—for
what? Was somebody sobbing somewhere? or was it laughter
—very faint? Was somebody having dinner in bed and reading a bad novel, the book propped up against the coffee pot?

Martha seemed to know. She was listening, her head on
her paws, her beady eyes fixed upon the door.

They were going. They were saying good-night. They
were all happy now, all wishing to be twice as friendly now
that they wouldn't have to be friendly any longer.

"You will come, won't you? I'm in almost every afternoon
at five. . . ."

Jane Rose had asked Carl to come and see her. He was
radiant. Bigges handed him his large woollen muffler. He
was grasping Hans' hand.

And now they were all gone. Hans turned back from the
door to see what it was that Ruth would have to say.

CHAPTER VIII

Intimate Truths

HE WENT straight back into the drawing-room. Ruth was waiting for him. But he would not have it out here.

He stood in the doorway.

"I'm going up. I'll come in and see you for a moment."

The words were of vast importance and they both knew it. For many years—ever since his illness indeed—he had not been near her room.

She said "All right" and then, as she passed him, rested for a moment her hand on his shoulder. She said, smiling, "You *were* funny to-night." She kissed his cheek lightly. Then added reflectively, "It's the last time Carl Reynolds dines here."

From the second step of the stairs she called back to him: "You won't be long? I'm tired."

"No. I won't be long."

He waited in the drawing-room. Out of the silence Bigges appeared. "All right, Bigges. I'll turn the lights out."

He was tired and sat down, alone with Martha.

He called after Bigges: "You can take Martha."

Bigges appeared again as though Hans had been some magician summoning figures from the vasty deep. He bent down to pick Martha up and his huge back stretched and

78

stretched. Martha, superior and scornful under his arm, yawned. She was thoroughly aware of all that was occurring.

Yes, he was tired, but tired with this anxiously pressing excitement. It wasn't good for anyone of his age to be excited. He seemed to be suddenly contemporary with himself as a very young man in Weimar looking at the relics in Goethe's house, where he had a rendezvous with a young flaxen-haired German woman. At that time he was virgin of sexual experience, and he knew that in another hour he would no longer be so. He had looked, he remembered, at Goethe's bed and had thought that it would be astonishingly fine to obtain the use of it, just for one evening, for the young flaxen-haired woman.

"I was a literary prig of the first order. That at least I am no longer. Or am I not? Perhaps I mislead myself. She had teeth like a rabbit, the young woman in Weimar. But fair-haired women were always my danger. That, at any rate, is over. Thank God! . . . or thank my years. But love—real love . . . Is there no one in the world any longer whom I love?"

He got up and walked in great agitation about the room. Was he already a corpse then, or at best a body without soul? This soul that Carl talked about. And a sentence from Henry Galleon rang in his brain: "The only desire left to him was that he should have watercress for tea."

The little gold clock on the mantelpiece rang the half hour, and he decided that it was time to visit Ruth.

What would he say to her? He didn't know. "Watercress for tea. . . ." But it would be something momentous.

He found her sitting in front of her mirror, brushing her short red-gold hair. The room was beautiful. Ivory and silver, and the floor, after the fashion of a year or two ago, was in lozenges of black and white.

She attacked him at once, without losing a moment, gazing into her mirror, putting down the brush, pinching her cheeks.

"Hans darling. *How* odd you were to-night! What *was* the matter with you?"

He sat down on the sofa at the foot of the bed and looked into the fire, one deep cavern of amber glow.

"*Was* I odd?"

"You know you were. It was the most tiresome dinner-party we've ever had, and I'd arranged it so carefully."

He looked at her lovely body, her white arms raised above her silver peignoir.

"And all I really want," he thought, "is watercress for tea."

"That horrid old Reynolds man. What *did* you ask him to have wine for? You know he isn't to be trusted."

"No. You're right. He isn't to be trusted."

There was something so odd in his voice that she abandoned pinching her cheeks and turned round to look at him.

There was something so odd in his face that she said: "Poor Hans. I forgive you. You're terribly tired. Trot off to bed."

"And I forgive you," he said solemnly.

"You forgive *me* ? Whatever have you to forgive me for?"

He shook his head. "Oh, I don't know. We have all to
forgive each other all sorts of things."

Then she knew that he wasn't well and, really alarmed,
came over and sat beside him on the sofa. "Certainly on to-
night's score you're my debtor. You hated the whole affair
and showed it. Was that being a good host?"

She spoke to him with tenderness, and gently, as though
he had been her little boy who had gone to the circus when
he had promised—oh! most solemnly promised—never to go
unless Mother took him.

This quite suddenly infuriated him.

He jumped up. "I'm *not* nineteen! I'm *not* nineteen! Oh
yes, you think that I am. You can't deny it. You know you
do. You'd arranged a nice dinner-party for me, so, of course,
I ought to like it. I'm an old man now and must do what
I'm told, and be fed through a spoon. Well, I'm not old.
I'm younger to-night than I've been for years, and I won't
be called *cher maître* by Mary Malpas, and what does it
matter if Carl does spill his soup on his waistcoat? Carl's
worth all of us put together, and then a lot more. . . ."

He paused for breath. He hadn't shown anger with anyone or anything for ten years. It was delightful, invigorating.
He hoped that he would be able to go on being angry. He
wasn't at all sure.

Ruth laughed.

"Dear Hans—so that was what annoyed you? Mary Malpas is a fool, of course, but one has to ask her. And why
shouldn't she call you *cher maître ?* It's a little affected, but

men like Anatole France and Rodin didn't mind, so why should you? And to-day especially, when you've been honoured by the whole of literary England. And then again— don't you think that it was a little absurd of you to make that fuss about that picture? Now, that *was* affectation if you like—and quite unlike you . . . you're generally so simple about those things."

His anger was gone, alas, alas! He couldn't simulate it. He must be gentle while waiting for its possible happy return.

"Yes. I don't defend myself. If Horace Clay didn't wear that eyeglass, things would be different. You're very patient with me, Ruth—and I wish you wouldn't be. Lose your temper. Let's have a scene. We haven't had one for years."

She smiled. He was his old self again, which meant perhaps that she had got him just where she wanted him to be.

"Dear Hans—what one forgets is that a day like this must be exhausting for you. After all, it's been one of the days of your life——"

"One of the days of my life!" he interrupted her. "And what do you think the days of my life have been if this has been one of them? I haven't had a real day, what you can call a day, for years. . . . Listen . . ." He sat down beside her. "That's what I want to talk about. I want to go away for a bit. I want to go right away from everybody and everything. The South Seas or—no, they've become artistic—well, Greenland or Manchester or Buenos Ayres. I want to shake everything off. Yes, to shake everything off. My ridiculous clothes and my reputation. I'll start again. I'll write under another name, John Jones or Horace Clay. Anything will do. And I'll catch fish in a cloudy stream and sit in the gallery of a provincial music-hall. Would you mind? For a little while? I would send you post cards signed Jones, 'Hoping all's well as it leaves me at present.'"

He felt her agitation. The room of ivory and silver was suddenly filled with real emotion, waves of it running up and down the walls and across the floor.

"Hans, you're mad. At your age. To go away. Of course it isn't possible for a moment." He realized then, in a flash of dazzling intuition, that this was *the* dread, *the* peril that had for years haunted her life. Not because she loved him, not because she wanted him with her, but because her whole married life had been given in its body and soul to this one purpose—to make herself a glorious position through her grand elevation of himself. *He* was her position, he was her achievement, her splendour, her throne. Let him go, even for a week, and evil tongues—because, of course, like all of us, she had her enemies—would say that he had left her, that he was tired of her, that she was nothing to him and— worse than any of these things—that he had made, and could continue to make, his position himself, that she was nothing but Hans Frost's wife whom now no longer anyone wanted.

Yes, this was it, or if this wasn't exactly it, if there were many other elements yet to be discovered, this was the shape of the animal, the colour and form of the lurking tiger.

He looked at her curiously, as though he were seeing her for the very first time in his life.

"Wouldn't you like," he said gently, "to be rid of me

for a very little while? I must sometimes be a nuisance. I know that I am. You've had such a lot of me for so long."

She had recovered from the first shock. She was prepared —and with amazing quickness—to fight her battle.

"The thing's absurd. Go away by yourself? Why, you know you couldn't. You would be wanting a thousand things. Of course you don't realize how dependent you are. With many men it would be easy enough, but with you—I flatter myself that I've managed all these years so that you don't know how dependent you are. I wouldn't like you to know. You'd be sending for me after the first hour."

"Isn't that rather humiliating for me? Just because you've made me so comfortable all these years that I can't get on by myself. Everyone is independent now. After all, seventy is nothing nowadays. A holiday apart from one another might be good for both of us——"

Her hands were raised for a moment and then fell again onto her lap.

"And *this* is all I get! All I get for everything, for our years together, our friendship. . . . You want to go away, you're tired of everything that I've done for you. . . ."

She broke off, and really it seemed that there was despair in her voice. But there was not. He knew well that there was not.

And, oddly, he caught in the timbre of this last sentence the echo of countless others.

In a further flash of revelation he saw her building up with endless little social strokes the public story of his helplessness.

"I'd love to come to-morrow night, but I mustn't. Hans doesn't like me to go without him, and nothing would induce him to come, I'm afraid."

"Of course I'd be with you if I could but I can't leave Hans. He isn't *quite* the thing. Oh no, nothing serious, but he'll have to stay in, and I must stay in with him."

Or again:

"Ah well, when one has a famous husband, you see, one has one's duties. Hans *pretends* he doesn't mind, but in fact . . ."

And then the dark shadow of Ma Marriott behind:

"If there's a devoted wife in this world my daughter——"

Summed up in that one final sentence: "I'm sorry, I don't like to leave Hans."

The illumination, now flooding for him the past years, showed him also how easily he had succumbed to all this, preferring again and again out of the most idle laziness to stay in of an evening, to have a cozy dinner, a long read in the library, with Ruth and her mother scarcely figuring in the scene at all.

His genius! His genius! Damn his genius!

"You can't defend the position," he said, "that it's going to ruin our lives if I go away for a week by myself."

"Of course not," she answered him easily. "Go when you like *if* you're determined. I only say you'll be back in an hour. But why this sudden passion to be rid of *me*? Is it all because I confessed to an irritation that old Carl Reynolds would drink too much at my dinner table?"

She had made it personal. As soon as she uttered the word "ME" she vanished from his sight. Here, a moment ago, had been someone whom he was supposed to love and did not. Now, at her dominating personal challenge, he saw nothing there at all except a trap. That alarm that each sex is for ever feeling before the possessive tactics of the other— so that marriage is often enough nothing but guerilla warfare among mountains impassable and filled with echoes— seized him. He felt as though, in another moment, she would put out her hand and grasp his arm. If she did that they would both, in an instant of time, become fighting, snarling animals. He would slap her face, perhaps, although his courtesy to ladies had always been proverbial.

Awful things would occur because she wanted to hold him when he wanted to go.

However she only said: "What about our going to Blackmoor for a week?"

That was her next move then!

Blackmoor with its laurels, its bound sets of the classics, and three grandfather clocks. . . . Blackmoor. . . .

"But don't you see," he said to her very gently, "that Blackmoor can't settle it? I want to go away by myself somewhere. It isn't that I don't want you. I don't want anybody. I tell you what it is. I'm emptied of life. I'm nothing. I've lost myself, my emotions, my desires, my heart. . . . Why, damn it!" he sprang up from the sofa. "You're living with a corpse; it isn't decent. Everyone would be shocked if they knew. Horace Clay would never dine with you again. Old Carl to-night saw what the matter was.

That's why he drank so much. The discovery shocked him. And so it should."

She had, he saw, in the last few minutes come to some secret and, for herself, most satisfactory solution. She was, once more, perfectly serene.

She smiled up at him.

"You're tired. You can say you're not, but you are. And so, as a matter of fact, am I. We'll talk it over to-morrow."

She got up, put her hand on his shoulder, bent forward, and lightly kissed his cheek.

"Good-night, Hans dear, and sleep well."

He looked at her and then drew back. "You're a mysterious woman," he said. "Now why didn't you tell me that you had a niece staying under our roof?"

The question was unexpected. She coloured very slightly as she answered:

"A niece? Oh—Nathalie? Little Nathalie Swan. I never thought to tell you. I didn't think you'd be in the least interested. Poor little Nathalie. She's always had such a miserable time. She's an orphan, you know, and has been stuck away in the depths of Glebeshire. I saw her down there and thought her an attractive, pleasant child. I thought it would be agreeable to bring a little fun into her life, so I asked her up here."

"Always thinking of others," he said.

"Not at all. Thinking of myself too."

"How long will she be here?" he asked.

"Oh, I don't know. A week or two perhaps."

"And then?"

"I suppose she'll go back to Polchester again."

"I see."

"But I promise you, Hans, that she shall be kept entirely out of your way. You shan't be bothered with her."

"Thanks." He moved to the door. "Good-night then."

"Good-night, dear Hans."

CHAPTER IX

Friends Met

ALONE once more in his room he realized that sleep would
not for a long while come to him. To that he was now well
accustomed, for, as the years advanced, they had taken
from him one hour after another. He did not complain of
that: he even liked to lie knowing that beyond the windows
the day was breaking, hearing the twitter of the sparrows,
the faint early rustle of the trees, seeing in his mind all the
Park stir under the faint grey shadows of the first light.

But to-night it was something different; his restlessness
was other than physical. He stood listening, as though expecting to be confronted by some ferocious event, as though
the house were to be broken in upon, or he suddenly to be
summoned by frightened servants to some awful discovery.

He went to the door and listened. Everything was still.
No one was sobbing now.

Then, impelled by a force that he could not deny, he stole
a little way down the passage and listened again.

Someone was snoring—Bigges it might be—and behind
the snoring was the skirmish and rattle of a motor-car in the
road outside.

His hand was on the handle of the door and, as though
he were somnambulistic, he had turned it and slipped inside
the dark cool room.

An instant later a voice came, quiet and gentle and not at all alarmed. "Who is it?"

He switched on the light. She was sitting up in bed, and at once when she saw him she smiled.

"Hush! Hush!" he whispered. "I thought you'd be sleeping . . . only came to make sure that everything was all right."

"I heard your step in the passage," she whispered. "I knew that it was you."

"Well, that's enough," he answered sternly. "You know that you should be asleep."

"I couldn't sleep. At least I was asleep for a little—but now I'm terribly awake."

He closed the door behind him so that he should not rouse anybody.

"Disgraceful . . . stealing into a lady's bedroom at this hour." He was smiling because she looked so charming. Had he had a grandchild she would have been just like this.

"Oh, stay, now that you're here," she said eagerly. "A little while. I promise you that I can't sleep. Are you terribly tired yourself?"

"No, I'm not. Old men are never tired. But I'm not going to stay. You'll be worn out if I do, and to-morrow you've got to see all the sights. You'll have to be at your freshest."

"Here—come here." She patted the bed. "Come and tell me about the dinner-party."

He came across slowly, then, after a moment's hesitation, sat down on the edge of the bed.

"You've no right to tempt me like this. I'm doing wrong to stay. What would Bigges say if he found us?"

"Oh, Bigges is fast asleep. I've been listening to his snoring."

They both listened, and the snore came, steadily, monotonously, through the wall paper.

"Well—only five minutes then." She settled down luxuriously into the bedclothes.

"Was it a good dinner-party?"

"No, a very bad one."

"Why?"

"Nearly all dinner-parties are bad, unless you can speak your mind without fear or favour. It's only when you're young and expect to meet a miracle round every corner that dinner-parties are amusing. But I forgot. Young people nowadays don't believe in miracles."

"No, I suppose they don't. They rely on themselves, which is much better. You can't be let down then." She touched the back of his hand for a moment with hers—then very quickly took hers away again. "Do you believe in miracles?" she asked.

"I didn't—until to-night. But now—it seems to me anything might happen."

"Why to-night?"

She let her hand lie now very lightly on his thigh.

"I don't know. What does one know about anything? Things come and go as they please. One's helpless."

"I don't agree at all," she answered indignantly. "I'm

sure one can make of life what one wants to. I'm going to have just the life I want."

"Are you? Perhaps you are. Perhaps you're one of the lucky ones."

"And fancy your talking like that," she went on. "You who've had everything—who've got to the very top, written books that will last for ever——"

"Last for ever? Why, already most of them are dead. Nobody opens them any more. Only one or two still stir a little. And if they do live—one or two—for say fifty, even a hundred years? A hundred years! A moment of time! And myself unaware . . ." He put his hand down on hers.

"No, my dear, that's not the prize. I'm damned if I know what the prize is. But don't you listen to me. I have my good times or I used to fancy that I had——"

"You've made things," she broke in eagerly, "beautiful things that have helped people to see how many beautiful things there are."

"Yes, I've tried." He broke off. He took her hand firmly in his. "So we're going to be friends? You're going to take me out for walks and show me the world? You won't do it for long. You'll find ever so many more entertaining people. And don't you pretend, mind, when at last you find it boring, that you don't. Say quite frankly: 'Uncle Hans, I'm bored to death with you. Go back to your library and let me alone.' And I'll go. Without a grudge. Perhaps I'll be rather relieved, because it's a strain, you know, coming out of your grave when you've been buried for so long and blinking your eyes and buying a new ear-trumpet. . . ."

"Buried?" she said.

"Oh, well, I suppose it's how you look at it." And he saw, staring into the bright glittering room, the way that *he* looked at it—putting aches in the legs and a passion for Steak Minute and the Manet and the ironic disappointment of fixing pretty sentences together, all, humble-jumble, on the table of his mind: "There you are. That's what life has brought you. How do you like it?"

And Nathalie, staring at him with all her eyes, saw none of these things. She saw a splendidly distinguished old man, exceedingly smart in his evening clothes, broad of chest, with his white shirt gleaming, his face so alive, the kindly wrinkles creeping out of the corners of his eyes, his cheeks with their healthy colour like a child's, his strong wiry black hair, the bright intensity of the eyes themselves—surely not seventy, this old man!

His grasp of her hand was firm and strong, his thighs thick and sturdy, his back upright and challenging—surely not seventy, this old man!

And above all, something in him that she had not seen in anyone before. A light, a fire, an eager, devouring spirit! Was it his genius? She had heard that so many geniuses looked nothing at all, that you would not think of them as anyone especial did you see them and not know who they were.

But of course she had never seen a genius before. Above all what he expressed was energy. Perhaps that *was* genius? Genius was vitality strongly directed towards one special aim. But no—it was something stranger than that. A drop of magic transforming the ordinary clay.

But the thing that she principally felt, as she realized the beat of the pulse of her hand within his, was that she must have him for her own. She had got him—she knew that she had, as she saw his eyes shining into hers—and she must never lose him again—no, never, never, never!

"Buried——?" she said again.

"A lot you know about it," he said, smiling at her.

"I know enough about it," she answered defiantly, "to tell you that if you think you're buried, I'm going to dig you up. Anyway," and she drew a little closer to him, "we're friends now, aren't we—and for ever?"

"Friends—and for ever? What a little you know—but of course you don't know. How could you at your age? Friends —and for ever? I said it once—just like that. And now, looking back, how many friends do you think I've ever really had?"

"As many as you've wanted."

"One—exactly one. Friendship is the hardest thing, keeping it up, standing the shocks, making allowances, keeping your temper, remembering to put stamps on envelopes, not snorting at meals, dividing fairly the eggs and bacon, seeing the good points in objectionable intruders, forgetting geographical distances, getting up when the alarm clock strikes, surrendering your independence and keeping it at the same time, being critical without personal satisfaction, praising without jealousy. . . ." He broke off. He saw Henry Galleon, Galleon lying back in his chair asleep, Galleon with that odd, sudden twist of arrogance and supremacy, Galleon putting on his grey tie with the red spots, Galleon laughing, his head

back, his body bent, Galleon suddenly tender, his hand
pressing one's shoulder, Galleon lost in dark distant worlds
whither no one might follow him.

His eyes misted. Unconsciously his hand withdrew from
hers, he was gone from her miles and miles away. She could
not touch him. She was frightened and lonely, just as she
had been that afternoon when she had first come to the
house. She had been presumptuous. She had been going too
fast. She hadn't realized what the difference in their generations must mean.

At last she said shyly:

"I didn't mean, of course, that I could be a friend like
any of your real friends. But perhaps no one can be that to
you now. I only meant that if you'll let me be with you
sometimes, I'll be glad and proud. Of course I know how
much you must be by yourself sometimes."

She broke off.

He was back. He was right with her there. He took her
hand again.

"My dear child, that's beautiful of you. I didn't mean
that *we* couldn't be friends. Of course we are, now and always. I was thinking of something else, friendship with
someone of your own age when you're young and vigorous,
and think you can do anything with the world if you try,
and that you'll stand side by side always and never need
another. That's over for me—has been for years, and I'm
lucky to have had even one friendship of that kind——"

He shook off the sentiment: "You'll have to tell me so
much about yourself. I know nothing yet. What you like

and don't like. What you want to do, where you want to go. I want to know everything."

"I want," she answered, "to make a fine career for myself as women do nowadays. Not to be dependent on anyone for anything. Not to owe anybody a penny. I want to work and work and have a fine time. And now that you've come, I know that I can."

That touched him terribly: it was really terrible the pain that shot through him as he felt her confidence and courage and innocence. Depending on him! Poor child, poor child! And loving him with such complete trust, without a doubt, a hesitation.

He knew that in that moment something fresh, strong, and wonderful had come to him. His life was going to be disturbed, his peace threatened, all his composure gone.

He would love this child and go into new worlds that had been, he had thought, closed to him for ever. He saw, in a flash of revelation, that the old life was not going to give up without a struggle. Ruth would be there. There would be battle and conflict, not only with the outside world, but with himself.

But now he realized only that this new delight had come to him. He put his arm round her, felt her draw as close to him as she could, her hair brushed his cheek.

Holding her tightly, he bent down and kissed her.

"My darling. . . . I'll look after you with all the strength that I have left. I'll love you as well as I know how."

END OF PART I

Part II

JOURNEYS OF COLUMBUS

CHAPTER I

Nathalie's Visit to Grandmamma

NATHALIE was several days in the house before she saw her grandmother. It didn't matter; she could manage without seeing her; she didn't suppose that she would be so terribly attractive. And, in any case, there wasn't, in Nathalie's excited feelings, room for anyone *more* to be especially attractive, so entirely adorable and lovely were Aunt Ruth and Uncle Hans.

Very different, of course. Nathalie, looking out of her bedroom window at a taxi-man arguing with a thin stick of a woman about her fare, considered how *amazingly* different they were.

Auntie Ruth was all sweetness and light—the thin stick of a woman was feeling in her pocket for more money; the taxi-man, from the height of Nathalie's observation, looked like a gigantic squashed marrow; he had on closer observation red moustaches and a fiery nose—while Uncle Hans was—well, what was Uncle Hans? Certainly *not* altogether sweetness and light.

He sometimes lost his temper. He was sometimes young and gay like a young pony—and here a very lively, brown, shaggy young pony went dashing across Nathalie's bedroom, kicking his heels over the pink sofa with the brown flowers,

coming to a stop before the bed; leaping it and whirling, a
happy ghost, through the closed door. . . .

And sometimes he was exceedingly aged. One morning
Nathalie had peeped into the library, and there in his vast
armchair Uncle Hans was sitting in a black alpaca jacket,
bright crimson leather shoes, and on his head a black skull
cap. Moreover, on the end of his nose was a pair of thick
tortoise-shell-rimmed spectacles. In his hand he held an
immense silver paper knife, and he was reading out of a big
book spread open on a reading desk at his side.

Seen thus in his skull cap with his brown lined face and
his intense absorption he looked nine hundred and ninety-
nine at least. So absorbed was he that Nathalie hadn't dared
to make a sound, but after observing him for an instant had
hurried, frightened, away. Yes, frightened, because although
he hadn't moved or stirred she was nevertheless convinced
that he had seen her, and she had been to him less than a
gnat or a wandering tickling fly.

The thin stick-like woman was standing now looking about
her, as though she were lost entirely. She gazed at the water
and the trees of the Park passionately. She was like someone who had just woken up.

There was a third Uncle Hans quite distinct from the
other two. This was the Public one.

Nathalie had met him first on her second morning in
London when he had taken her on an expedition to the
Tate Gallery. Coming down the broad steps, her mind a
small, very confused cupboard where Blake sat upon Turner,
and Watts hung a vast naked angel on a gold nail in the

wall, they were confronted with two gentlemen and a lady. These two gentlemen and lady became at once a Public Meeting, and Uncle Hans, on a vast platform, accompanied by nothing but a glass of water and a small deal table, was receiving orations.

Nathalie did not listen to the remarks made by the Public Meeting. Her sharp (and for her age penetrating) glance was concentrated on Uncle Hans.

He stood, isolated on the broad steps, the River Thames bowing in front of him and all the pictures in the Tate clapping their hands behind him, looking very sweet in his square black hat (that was only half a top-hat and not quite a bowler), in his waistcoat with the gilt buttons, and his beautiful spats, and he was one of England's well-known Celebrities. It was not that he was consciously celebrated or that he appeared to be especially pleased with the oration of the Public Meeting (the female part of which was smart, gushing, and tender) but that in his smile, his reserved gravity, the set of his thick stocky body and the kindly intonation of his gracious words, he found and held his transformation.

Nathalie was both excited and distressed. She realized that she had perhaps forgotten in the delightful intimacy of the last two days how truly celebrated a man he was. She had taken it all too easily and too readily for granted. She saw in the devoted glances and reverent attention of the Public Meeting that this was, for the P. M., a very great and never-to-be-forgotten occasion.

The P. M. would speak of it with bated breath in the

sanctity of its several homes—"*Who* do you think we met just as we were going into the Tate? . . ." and it wasn't the P. M.'s fault that, at that exact moment, two gulls, rising angry from their wasted investigations in the river mud, should shriek derisively and contemptuously "Who?"

The P. M. moved on, and Uncle Hans was at once his own darling and private self. But there it was. That was what, on certain occasions, he undoubtedly became.

And when he was cross! Here Bigges figured. Bigges most certainly was just now exasperating to Uncle Hans. On this occasion he had not, Nathalie must reluctantly confess (because of course she hated Bigges), done anything very terrible. He had only, as Uncle Hans, dressed and ready for going out, had reached the bottom of the staircase, said: "The car is at the door, sir," and Uncle Hans had replied: "Well, it can wait, can't it?" But he had looked at Bigges as though he would love above all things to crash him on the head with his gold-headed cane. There was something very especially irritating in the top of Bigges' head. It was sleek and shiny and—yes, stagnant. It was in a mysterious fashion immensely pleased with itself as though it said: "I use a hair oil that is *facile princeps*, I am treated only with the best brush and comb, and my parting is superb."

Nevertheless, there was no reason here for ill-temper, and Uncle Hans had, for a moment, looked like a very wicked, malevolent, and murderous old man.

He had continued, too, to mutter as they passed into the car: "Idiot! Crass imbecile, self-satisfied idiot! . . ." There were other expressions that Nathalie did not catch.

So that Uncle Hans was not altogether that lovable, endearing human being that he had appeared to be on the first never-to-be-forgotten night when he had sat on her bed, put his arms around her, kissed her, and called her his darling.

But how could he be? Uncle Hans was a great man, and everyone knew that great men were peculiar, must be shown every kind of indulgence and be yielded full room for the play of their genius.

Aunt Ruth, then, was much simpler. Aunt Ruth was a darling.

At this moment the thin-as-a-stick woman drew herself together, as though she had come at last to some very important resolve and, astonishing mystery, hailed another taxi that happened to be passing. She spoke to the taxi-man with deep impressiveness. He nodded as though he were proud to be trusted with her secret and would, on his life, tell no one.

The thin-as-a-stick woman vanished, leaving some trees, an expanse of grass, two dogs, and a noise of chattering birds.

Aunt Ruth was so beautiful. Her appearance was a perpetual joy and glory to Nathalie, who passionately loved beauty. Her slim, graceful body, her exquisite clothes, the carriage of her superb head, her red-gold hair, the colours she wore, her mingling of daintiness and strength, her queenly aspect, indifferent and yet participating, above and beyond you and yet sharing also in your little affairs. Oh! she was a queen indeed!

Moreover, she had been exceedingly kind to Nathalie, and

Nathalie at this stage in her growth was like a puppy who could believe no wrong of any kindly person.

After that first evening she took Nathalie right into her arms. There was the dressmaker's where Nathalie was given some exquisite frocks, there was a morning's shopping in Bond Street (how Bond Street shone in retrospect with its silver—George III sugar castors and teapots—its picture shops, its dog shop, and its window filled with the richest, most glorious of motor-cars, all with their heads to the street as though, once the magic word was passed, out and away they would go!).

There had been the evening, too, when Aunt Ruth had taken her to the theatre (Uncle Hans staying at home to read in his library). How wonderful that had been! A musical comedy all smiles and music, with a hero whose hair was crimped like the waves of the sea, and a funny man who slid *up*stairs with all the ease in the world.

But best of all had been Aunt Ruth's confidences—confidences sitting together in front of the fire in the drawing-room, Nathalie's hand in Aunt Ruth's and Aunt Ruth confessing that she needed someone to love her, that Uncle Hans was a darling, but that he was, of course, a genius and couldn't be expected to have the time for the domestic affections that more ordinary people would have.

Nathalie's heart rushed out and threw itself at the tips of Aunt Ruth's gold shoes. Anything, anything she could do; and she saw herself rushing from the burning building into the cold night air, learning from the excited cries of the multitude that Aunt Ruth was yet within, darting back again (although the multitude did everything it could to prevent her), and then ... Or better still, perhaps, Aunt Ruth walking in the very path of a mad bull (mad bulls had always been to Nathalie the very Last Word in Terror), and Nathalie darting forward, catching the bull by the horns ... and the fire spurted in little tongues of amber flame and the sand-wiches faded on the lovely dark blue plate, and the gold clock on the mantelpiece chimed the flying quarters.

Nathalie lay awake thinking what she might do for Aunt Ruth. Aunt Ruth had everything, including the most superb pearl necklace that you ever saw in your life. There wasn't much you could give her except your love. That she should have, pressed down and running over, for ever and ever.

Behind Uncle Hans and Aunt Ruth there was Grand-mamma.

Nathalie had never seen either of her grandmothers. One had died years and years ago, and erected herself for ever in Nathalie as a bright green bottle standing up in the sun. That was because when Nathalie had heard of her death she had been a small girl nursing a nigger doll and gazing at a bright green bottle that stood on the window ledge.

"Your grannie's dead, darling," and it had meant nothing at all except that, because of the sad gravity in Mother's voice, a cloud came down and tried to hide the glittering light that leapt in sparks of fire at the very centre of the bottle. But the cloud could not. It was not powerful enough. And the heart of Pongo Jane, the black doll, leapt with joy when she saw that it was not able.

This other grandmother had been alive all the time and

had done nothing about Nathalie. She had not sent her presents at Christmas or at birthdays, nor even written a letter.

She was, in Mrs. Proudie's opinion, "a wicked shame."

But Nathalie had, even at this early time, a strong conviction that "people should be allowed to do what they wanted to do," and if Grandmamma didn't wish to be bothered with her granddaughter, then that was her right.

Nevertheless, the picture of this grandmother was unattractive. She was an invalid, and Uncle Hans didn't like her. Nathalie knew that he didn't like her, although he had never said so.

Honestly Nathalie was frightened at this coming interview, frightened because the old lady seemed to threaten something. To threaten what? Nathalie didn't know. Some change. A change for the worse.

She saw from her watch that it was four o'clock, so she washed her face and hands, stood for a moment hesitating, then went downstairs. She hoped that it would soon be over.

Aunt Ruth was waiting for her in the little silver room beyond the drawing room. She was dressed in dove-grey, and the lovely rope of pearls was round her neck. If not the real pearls then imitation ones, so fine that you couldn't tell the difference. (Why, then, ever have real ones?)

Aunt Ruth was a little vexed. Nathalie noticed this at once. She was sitting at a lovely little desk writing a letter. She said: "Wait a moment, dear. I must finish this," quite sharply, and Nathalie at once sat down on a chair of gilt and dark red brocade and felt shabby. She felt as she used to do years ago when, because she was very hungry, she came down to breakfast in a hurry, not having brushed her teeth. She hoped, as she took the top off her boiled egg, that no one would discover the fact. Now, in exactly the same way, she hoped that Aunt Ruth wasn't really cross.

She was not, it seemed. She had, as she rose from her chair, a shining protecting smile.

"That's right, darling. We're going up to see Grand-mamma, aren't we? Grandmamma will love to see you." Then she looked vexed again. "It's too tiresome," she said. "Ruggins ought to have known better than that." Ruggins (whoever he might be) instantly swung down from the ceiling and stood like a great bear with protruding teeth all over the little sitting room.

"Ready, dear?" said Aunt Ruth. "Shall we go up?"

They went up, Nathalie's heart beating in spite of her modern determination to be frightened at nothing; but it seemed that Ruggins (whoever he might be) accompanied them up the staircase, lolloping behind them and breathing stertorously. "You've never met your grandmother, have you? Of course she's been an invalid for a long time, scarcely going out at all. She's been so brave, never complaining, taking cheerfully everything that comes." (Nathalie saw her grandmother as a dear old lady in a white cap and mit-tens, smiling bravely although racked with pain.) "She has often spoken of you." (How did Nathalie know that this was untrue?) "It will be delightful for her if you can go in and see her sometimes. She has a pretty dull life, I am afraid."

All this time Nathalie knew that her aunt was not thinking about her at all, but was preoccupied with something else, Ruggins in all probability.

They were at the door. Aunt Ruth knocked, and then, in a very sweet voice indeed, asked: "May we come in?"

They went in. What an ugly room and what a grim old woman sitting reading a book! The room was shadowy, so that at first it was hard to see anything very clearly. Then the pictures came out one by one, "Queen Victoria Receiving the News of Her Accession" and "Mr. Gladstone Addressing the House of Commons."

Then a strange, dreary, little smell stole out, a smell of medicine, straw, sweet biscuits, and window curtains. Then at last a voice, very old, very dry, and a little peevish:

"So this is my granddaughter. Come here and let me have a look at you."

Nathalie approached. She was aware of an old yellow face, two thin white hands blue-veined, and billowing cascades of rather faded black silk that spread over the chair. "So you've come to see your grandmother at last? Thank you, Ruth, dear. Just a little farther. Thank you, my dear.

"You're a pretty girl, I must say. And are you happy to be in London?"

"Yes," said Nathalie.

"You ought to be, I'm sure. It's very kind of your aunt."

"Nathalie," said Aunt Ruth cheerfully, "is going to be a great companion to me. It will be delightful for all of us having her."

But Nathalie's thought was: "Shall I be like that one day, so old and ugly and helpless? Is that what old age is? Must

one . . .?" But no, one need not. This old woman was more
ancient by only a few years than Uncle Hans, and how lively
and fresh and healthy he was. And why wasn't she filled
with pity and tenderness? Why didn't she want to do something for this poor helpless old woman? She did not. She
wanted only to slip away as soon as decency permitted.

"Now then sit down, my dear, and tell me everything.
Yes, that chair will do nicely."

Nathalie saw that the meeting was to be staged like something dark in a melodrama. Aunt Ruth had withdrawn to
the dusky end of the room where, near the bed, she stayed
with her dove-grey dress and her red-gold hair, a coloured
shadow.

"So it's all this time that you've taken before coming to
London to see your grandmother. Times change. It's long
since I've had even a photograph of you. And I must say
that you're prettier than I had expected. Now tell me
everything."

How could Nathalie tell her everything? This awful old
woman. . . . How *could* she be Nathalie's mother's mother—
Nathalie's mother who stayed always a lovely ghost seen
in candlelight, laughing, and through the window the sky
powdered with stars? Or Aunt Ruth's mother, Aunt Ruth
with her lovely body, her coloured freshness, her strength?
Was *this* again to what all youth and loveliness must
come?

Everything? Tell her everything? The Polchester streets
on a summer evening when the sunlight shone through the
little gardens in the Precincts; about the Proudie dogs,

Boomer and Sand; the teas in the Proudie schoolroom with
saffron cake, strawberry jam, and muffins; the market place
on market day when the dark cavernous arches were filled
with life, piles of tomatoes, and bottles of sweets, and cabbages as large as your head, and farmers, and sheep, and
calves so funny that they brought tears to your eyes; about
making cowslip balls in the lanes above Orange Street, and
early in the morning hunting for mushrooms in the fields beyond Bodger's Street; about reading *The Chaplet of Pearls* in
front of the fire on Sunday evenings and a chocolate all round
between the chapters; about the expeditions in jingles to
Rafiel and St. Mary's Moor, and picnics on the beach with
sand getting into the jam sandwiches and the waves licking
up the trenched castles; about that first ball in the Assembly
Rooms and the new dress, and the little gold chain Mrs.
Proudie gave her; about the time when the massed choirs
sang "The Messiah" in the Cathedral, and the tennis on
summer evenings in the Dean's garden; about the present-
giving on Christmas evening and waking up in the middle
of the night to hear the waits singing "Good King Wences-
las" under your windows when the moon was shining and
the air glittered with frost——

Tell this old woman? . . .

So Nathalie said: "It's been very nice in Polchester,
thank you, Grandmamma. The Proudies have been awfully
good. . . ."

She was aware that her grandmother wasn't listening to
her and was thinking of something else. It was soon plain of
what she was thinking.

"Ruth, darling," the voice was querulously sharp, "why are you sitting where I can't see you? I'm sure you want to hear about everything too."

"Yes, Mother dear."

So that was it. At once Nathalie's heart was filled with tenderness and compunction. This old woman was very human after all. She loved Aunt Ruth, she *adored* her. It was evident enough now in the way that she moved in her chair, her trembling hands trying to arrange something, her body jerking forward. She leaned to the side and dragged a chair. She seemed to be suddenly filled with energy, and Nathalie saw that she was neither old nor feeble but pulsating with life and vigour.

"That's all right, Mother. I'll sit here. I thought you'd like to talk a little alone with Nathalie."

"Oh, you must come too. You must come too. Your aunt's so unselfish, she'd do herself out of anything. Copy your aunt and you won't go wrong. . . . Well, that's all very interesting what you've been telling me. And now what are you going to do with yourself in London—see all the sights, eh? Are you sure you're comfortable, Ruth? Are you quite all right, dear?"

"Quite, Mother, thank you."

The old woman was uneasy. Her thin, glassy-white hands beat the arms of the chair.

"What's Hans doing?" she rapped out like a challenge.

"Working in the library, I expect," Aunt Ruth answered.

"Always thinking of himself. Never was such a selfish man."

"Oh no, Mother dear. He has important work to do, and many people to see."

"People! people!" the old woman broke in. "Just to feed his vanity. He doesn't think of you half as much as he ought to, and well you know it. You spoil him, and that's the truth."

The old woman gave her head a vigorous shake. Nathalie was forgotten. Her grandmother had no interest in her, no interest at all. This visit had been a form, and now that it had been made there need never be another. But Nathalie was excited now by a deeper drama than her own. There was something going on here that was as yet hidden from her. But she could catch glimpses, flashes of it. Grandmother loved Aunt Ruth and hated Uncle Hans. That was part of it. And Aunt Ruth didn't mind that Uncle Hans should be criticized. That was another part of it. And Uncle Hans? How much had he to do with this? What part did he play?

The room was growing ever stuffier and closer, and the smell of stale biscuit and straw was ever bolder. Ruggins, the stertorous bear? Was he not here hiding in the dark, waiting for his moment to spring? Was there not some sort of incantation here, spell-whispering? Why had Nathalie so sleepy a headache, why was Queen Victoria in her nightdress moving out of the picture, her finger to her lip? "Hush, there, hush. Hush, there, hush," and from a great distance came Aunt Ruth's voice:

"And then, Mother, I told him that three pounds was just thirty shillings too much. Why, Whiteley's would——"

And the brown curtains moved, fattening as though a

breeze blew them, and the hands of Grandmamma, glassy white, swelled above the arms of the chair, and Nathalie's head nodded.

The door quietly opened, and Uncle Hans (oh, dear beloved Uncle Hans!) was standing there.

"May I come in?" he asked, poking his head into the half-light. You could see that he was smiling.

"Is that you, Hans?" said his mother-in-law. "I was just asking where you were."

He came in amongst them. He was wearing his alpaca jacket and his crimson slippers, but he didn't look old at all. He was bubbling with vitality; also he was wicked—wicked and foreign, as though he belonged to some other country. Again Nathalie felt his remoteness.

He looked at her, he looked at his wife, he took them all in. His legs were planted wide, his head a little on one side, his hands behind his broad, sturdy back.

Aunt Ruth got up from her chair. She spoke to Nathalie.

"I expect your grandmother's tired." She bent forward and kissed her mother.

"Now that's too bad," said Uncle Hans, "to get up and go just when I come in. It's a little marked, I fancy."

Aunt Ruth laughed.

"Nonsense, Hans. We've been here a long time." (They had not, and Nathalie was aware that Uncle Hans knew just how long.)

"Nathalie dear, I have a nice invitation for you tomorrow night—and you too, Hans. Mother darling, are you all right?—nothing I can get you?—the Heskeths'—a musi-

cal evening. Prokolonotay is going to play the fiddle. They
are especially anxious that you should come, Hans."

Nathalie had risen. She had distinctly seen Victoria, her
finger still to her lip, retire into her picture, pat her nightdress, and listen once more with girlish dignity to Lord
Conyngham's interesting announcement.

She also saw Uncle Hans make a little bow.

"Dear Ruth," he said, "that's charming of the Heskeths,
and I am delighted to realize that so many people will have
the pleasure of hearing M. Prokoli-something-or-other. I,
alas, shall not be one of them."

"Oh, but, Hans, you must." Ruth's voice was sharp.
"I've promised for you."

The old lady's dress rustled. It might have been the stir
of some dangerous animal hiding in the thicket.

Hans smiled. Then drew Nathalie towards him, putting
his hand through her arm.

"Nathalie and I are already promised."

"Nathalie?"

"Alas, yes."

Ruth was angry. Even Ruggins was frightened.

"But Hans, how absurd! You've promised for me without a word to me?"

"Well—but you had promised for me."

"That's different. You like me to make social engage-
ments for you."

"Do I? Perhaps I do. But not this time."

Ruth laughed.

Grandmamma from her chair remarked: "I'm sure that's

very nice for you, Hans. To go with Ruth to an evening party."

"Nothing I like better," Hans assented cheerfully. "But this time I've given my word."

"Well, you can just ungive it again," said Ruth cheerfully, moving towards the door. (How did Nathalie know that Ruth disliked that Hans should have his hand through her arm?) "We are going to the Heskeths'."

"We are not," said Hans, also cheerfully.

"Nathalie and I are, in any case. There are some people there that I especially wish her to meet. Anyway who are these people into whose company you wish to drag me?"

"I don't wish to drag you." He hesitated a moment, then went on: "To tell the truth, I wasn't intending to drag you. You weren't in fact asked."

There was a silence into whose thunderous depths the curtains, the pictures, the old lady's white hands dipped and quivered.

"Not asked?"

"No. People you don't know."

"Who are they, then?"

"He's a writer—Westcott. He was here last night smoking a pipe with me. He invited me then. I asked if I might bring Nathalie with me. He was delighted. You'd be bored. No one there who would interest you."

The old lady was indignant. "Ruth bored? Why, she's never bored. Everyone interests her." Ruth laughed, and if ever an irritated temper used a laugh for its manifestation . . .

"You see what Hans thinks of me, Mother. But really, Hans, it's ridiculous to drag Nathalie off to a crowd of second-rate people, not one of whom means anything to her."

She pulled herself together. She patted Hans on the shoulder. "Have your old party, and much good may it do you. Now really we've tired Mother to death. I'll come in for a moment before you go to bed, Mother."

She bent down and kissed her.

Mrs. Marriott settled herself back in her chair. "Never mind, dear," she said. "I'm sure the Heskeths will love to see you, even though you're alone. Anyone would."

Hans, at the door, looked back.

"Good-night. Sleep well."

Then, with his hand through Nathalie's arm, he went out.

CHAPTER II

Westcott Evening

A MIRROR rimmed with gold hung on the wall opposite the door; the side walls were covered with books, save where the fireplace framed a gold-pressed cavernous glow of light and colour.

Into and out of the mirror everything had entered and faded—now it was still, because the dancing was over and they were quiet, scattered in little gentle groups about the room. The mirror caught the door, the shining floor, and a broken pattern of colour, the silver tissue of a fragment of dress, shoe buckles, arms and legs, the body of a young man leaning up against a chair, the corner of the bookcase with the covers of the books shining in the firelight.

It was Millie, Peter Westcott's wife, who had insisted on the mirror. They had had one, she said, in her family when she was a girl in the old London house, a mirror that had reflected all the room and especially the green carpet. Then one day her brother Henry had thrown a book at the mirror and broken it. Then someone said that you couldn't break a mirror by hitting it with a book, however hard you tried, and someone had wanted to try—poor Willie Payne with the crooked nose; he had been killed a year later in a motor accident.

So they had had new glass in the mirror, and Peter had

grown very fond of it because it had held in its embrace, one time or another, all the happiness that he had ever known, his married life, the antics, questionings, and beautiful submissions of his two children, friends and parties and, better than anything save Millie and the children, long hours with books and books and books. . . .

He was waiting now for Hans Frost, and he was happy to know that that figure, too, would be soon the mirror's property. The white door that the mirror held would open and there would be drawn on the mirror's surface that sturdy person, that humorous genius whom Westcott admired as he had admired no one since Henry Galleon.

Looking round the room—he was supposed to be talking to Millie's friend, Frances Laike, but she went on and on and there was no necessity to listen—he wondered how the others there would strike the old man. He had not yet recovered from the shock that he had received when the old man had consented to come, because it was well known that Frost went out nowhere save on official occasions and then always with Mrs. Frost exceedingly in attendance. But like a flash, Frost had agreed. "Of course I'll come. One evening soon. What about Friday?" and afterwards, with a sort of chuckle as though he were pursuing some secret plan that he had in his head: "And I'll bring my niece too. She's pretty. She'll enjoy it."

Not a word about Mrs. Frost.

Westcott would have liked to get together a truly splendid assemblage—all the people whom he thought wise and noble and beautiful. There weren't—he must confess—very many.

But how could you at so short a notice? "Of course," Frances Laike was saying, "that's his character. It all comes from some deep conceit. He pretends to be as modest as anything, but he just doesn't listen to you. All the time you're talking he's thinking how fine he is."

So there was someone else who doesn't listen to Frances? Of course there were thousands—almost everyone. She was one of those thin, eager, flushed, excited people, who would never be listened to, because they had so much to say that wasn't interesting.

A vague wash of melancholy that would often sweep in, like a long level rush of water unexpectedly and as though with a sudden secret purpose invading the shore, attacked him.

Here he was in middle life with a wife (a splendid wife), two children (two splendid children), ten published works (not, alas, so splendid), a reputation (middle class), high and dry on a wet and slippery rock with a drab seashore, a beautiful yellow sky, and three sea-gulls-and nothing very much ahead of him.

What had he done with that exciting surprise packet Life? Where had he mislaid it? "And I said to him," Frances was going on, "that it's all very well to think one book of poems and a play produced on one wet Sunday evening are fine things to have done, but there are such a lot of people who have had the same experience. Dozens. It's like the Heath on a Bank Holiday."

But you couldn't expect that life should go on for ever with its surprises. His early years had been surprising enough—and he saw in the mirror the dark fierce anger of his father, the high broad shoulders of Stephen his friend, round fat Zanti, Clare's fair hair, the agony of loneliness, the pain of betrayal, and the way that once, on his uppers in London, a man down at the Docks had treated him to a ham-and-eggs supper, the finest meal of his life. . . . Well, but didn't he love Millie? Indeed he did. And Bobby and Norah, the children? Indeed, indeed he did. And his work? Wasn't he for ever hoping that this time it was going to be a masterpiece? Indeed he was. And didn't he love all the daily things—the London trees and the tulips in the Park and Grock and an exhibition of French pictures and boxing at the Ring, and suddenly finding that your cold was gone when you thought you'd got it for another week at least? Indeed, indeed he did. And wasn't his stomach all right and his eyesight fine, and didn't he sleep as long in the morning as the children would let him, and weren't his hours with Millie more jolly even than they had been in the first married year?

Yes, yes. Well then——

"Peter," said Frances indignantly, "I don't believe you've heard a single word I've been saying. . . ."

He reassured her and looked around at the others. There were not very many. He had thought that Frost would not care for a crowd.

Millie, and Katherine, Millie's sister, and Philip, Katherine's husband, and Henry, Millie's brother, and Lady Poole, Katherine's friend, and on his side Rops and Beckett, two of his friends, and Nancy Beckett, Beckett's daughter.

And then the Russians.

He hadn't really intended that they should be there—Andrey Shapkin and his sister Sofya, and his nephew Vladimir and their friend Mihail Klimov—a queer group bringing into the mirror another world, a world of vodka and executions without trial, and the plays of Tchekhov, and Tolstoi wandering off to die by himself, and the Labour Party's desire for a new world without any idea of how to make one, and poetry that no one, try as they might, could take any of the strange glory away from.

He was, after all, glad of the Russians. Frost would be interested. They would be something to show to Frost.

It was Klimov who was really his, Westcott's, friend.

Klimov had been young Henry Trenchard's friend first. (It was the habit to go on speaking of him as young Henry, although he was no longer young, in reality being forty if he was a day.) Henry had found Klimov at one of those strange, very unwashed Communist parties to which he went, had loved him at sight, and supported him in his flat for weeks. Klimov had not been supported because he was penniless or hungry or for any such reason, but only because, being a traditional Russian, he was absent-minded. He had quite a proper home of his own, and the Shapkins were only too ready to look after him if he hadn't, but he stayed in Henry Trenchard's flat and was fed by him simply as he stayed anywhere that Fate placed him. Henry, loving him very much, would have kept him there for ever, but Millie and Philip, who were the stern and practical ones of the Trenchard-Westcott family (Katherine and Peter being the soft and romantic ones), told him not to be a fool, so Klimov was sent back to the Shapkins.

Millie had said that he was exactly like Alice's White Knight, not physically, because he was round and fat and as bald as an ostrich egg, but in every other way. He was traditional Russian, Philip declared, and Philip, because he had lived in Russia when he was young (you would never think it nowadays), must know. Peter was not so sure. In any case, he was very lovable, although not at all tidy and (at any moment) capable of stripping himself naked to emphasize some idea. He had all the Russian's passion for ideas. The Shapkins said that he had been once on a day a practical serious man of business, but his sufferings in Russia in '18 and '19, when his wife and child had died of starvation, had affected his character.

The Shapkins themselves were very practical indeed. Andrey was a tall thin man with a black beard, and Sofya was tall and stout with pince-nez. Andrey had quite a good position in some shipping firm.

The nephew Vladimir was the handsomest young man in the world. Peter Westcott did not like beautiful young men, beauty only too seldom going with brains, but he was compelled to admit that Vladimir was clever, amiable, and amusing. He was slim, dark, with splendid eyes and features, so aristocratic that he must be the son of a prince. Millie had a romantic legend about him.

He refused, however, to consider himself romantic. He was twenty-three years of age, writing plays and making love whenever the opportunity offered. He loved life, worked all day in an office in the City, thought himself a prodigious cynic, the English too naïve and agreeable for words, and life, because he loved it, something to drop at any instant.

Behind all this was a profound unchanging pessimism. At the final count he believed in nothing and nobody.

There the Russians were, then, and it was odd how, even in this very friendly evening, they remained apart although showing great friendliness and a readiness to talk to anybody.

At this moment Andrey Shapkin was engaged in a very violent argument with Millie and Henry, while Katherine, Janet Poole, and Beckett listened, smiling and amused.

A moment later Hans Frost was in the room.

It was incredible to Peter that he should be actually there.

Peter had little reverence left for other writers. Writers were nothing—*as* writers. They might be good married men, or adulterous swine, or kind ladies with ink in their hair, or little boys with inquisitive noses, or young men with reminiscences, or old men fond of their food, or girls with liaisons, or old maids with psycho-analysis—anything you pleased, just as coal-heavers, actor-managers, politicians, or farmers were. The fact that they were writers meant just nothing at all.

But it did mean something with Hans Frost.

Hans Frost was a swell, not because he had written some good books (although he had), nor because he had known great men in his time (although that made him interesting), nor because he was now a Figure. He was a swell because he stood by himself, gave himself away to nobody, compromised in nothing and, for so many years, had Kept It Up.

This Keeping It Up was, Peter knew by now, in any of the Arts, the hardest possible thing. Easy enough at the beginning to do a thing or two. Easy enough to be acclaimed as a Future, harder to be acknowledged a Present, the Devil and all to be admitted a Stayer.

And Hans Frost had stayed. He had written poor books in his time, of course, but he stood out now in the great country of Modern Letters in a little city of his own. He had made his world; it resembled no other. It had its own laws and customs, its own history, its peculiar geography, towns and villages, mountains, plains and rivers, its own uncharted seas.

He was a creator. Like him or no, that was not to be denied. His faults, lacks, limitations, of themselves gave shape and colour to his world.

He was Hans Frost, independent, free. There had never been a Hans Frost before; there would never be one again.

So Peter was proud to have him in his house and to offer him his bread and salt. But he would not flatter nor fuss him. He realized that he had come here to-night because he knew that he was safe. A refuge. A refuge from what? Westcott did not know, but he would see that he was secure.

"Certainly," Hans was thinking, "this is very unusual for me"—unusual just as it would have been to have muffins for tea. He would *like* muffins, but he simply for years hadn't had them because, once long ago, he had been told that they were indigestible.

Just as Daisy Ashwin, that friend of Ruth's, had heard,

so she informed everybody, that there was a little place in Greenland, a village of some five hundred souls, where you could be "made over" by a local doctor so that you were thirty years younger. But you just didn't go to Greenland. It was outside the daily "run."

And then he had always felt about literary parties that they shouldn't occur—just as he felt that Roman Catholic priests would be much better not writing would-be funny articles in the newspapers, or that famous actresses should refrain from publishing works about Plato. There was nothing against any of these things; he had simply considered himself on the other side of the wall.

He had jumped the wall. He had broken through the Looking-glass. What would he find? He was conscious at once that he was going to enjoy himself. He liked the room, the mirror with the gold rim, the piled-high books, the coziness, the friendliness, and his own physical well-being, so that to-night he wasn't tired, no part of him anywhere was aching, not that tooth one from the last on the lower left jaw, nor that odd sharp needle pain that came sometimes in the calf of his left leg, nor the general weariness that for the last two years had chosen to send him suddenly to sleep in the most unlikely places.

And then he had with him Nathalie. He was terribly proud of her. This was the first time that, publicly, he had been in charge of her. Not only pride. Something deeper, more heated, more vulnerable. Let them not be nice to her and he would show them!

But everyone was finding it very easy to be nice.

Hans was introduced, quickly, with no ceremony. He was one of them immediately. It seemed to him that he had seen them all before, that pretty, slender, gay one (Millie West-cott), and that rather stout, motherly one (Katherine Mark), and the loose-limbed, excitable, untidy one (Henry Trench-ard), and the severe, handsome, cocksure one (Philip Mark), and the large fat one like an elephant (Beckett)—and then the Russians.

He was greatly pleased to meet the Russians. He had met, in his time, one or two distinguished Russians. He had even years ago had tea in Paris with Turgenev, a kindly, ironic tea, with the pale Paris sunshine, the dark ironwork in front of the dove-grey buildings opposite their window, the great jar of pink carnations, and Turgenev sucking his tea through his slice of lemon, suggesting in his soft melancholy French that Dostoevsky was a demon.

But these were post-Revolutionary Russians, and all his tenderness—most easily stirred now when he was warm and comfortable and happy—went out to them. *What* a good-looking young man! His eyes—his marvellous eyes, the finest Hans had ever seen (save Galleon's)—were at once on Nathalie. He hadn't wasted a moment. He was talking to her in his excitable foreign way. Well, they were the handsomest creatures in the room. It was splendid to see them together.

"Sir," said (in the softest of voices) the fat round Russian with the very bald head, "I am honoured extremely to be speaking to you and you must forgive me if my ideas are tangled, untidy, in a nasty mess. I am suffering to-night from a toothache, and I have always noticed that a toothache is the most unintellectual pain in one's body, just as, in all probability, a stomach-ache is the most intellectual. Have you ever noticed, sir, how bright and clear one's brain becomes between the spasms of indigestion? But perhaps that is my own especial personal experience."

"I'm sorry you have a toothache," said Hans.

"I'm sorry also," said M. Klimov, "and I am a great coward about the dentist. I fancy that I am a coward about everything, but I don't know myself with any certainty. I am continually surprising myself. But what I really wanted to say, one among very many things, is that I would like you to tell me why the English (whom I immensely admire) have never, with all their excellent arrangements, learnt how to cook vegetables?"

"I know," said Hans, "that that is one of the most constant criticisms levelled against us."

"And with justice. I am myself a vegetarian—partly, I admit, from principle, although I consider that for a human being to bind himself to any kind of principles is a weakening limitation of experience, and partly from preference. I dislike meat, although that fact cannot be of the slightest interest to you. But the fact is that, search England as I may, I cannot in any restaurant, or English home, discover vegetables that are fit to be eaten. The English vegetable is of itself a fine thing; one sees it growing magnificently in English gardens, but by the time it reaches the table it has passed through some process that has drained from it all its life, energy, and personality. Even the potato——" He broke off, nervously rubbing the buttons of his waistcoat with his fingers. Then he looked in Hans' face with a gentle, appealing smile.

"I hope that you are not angry at my criticizing this feature of English life. I assure you that England is the only part of the world that I would care to live in, now that I am unable to return to my country."

"There are," said Hans, smiling, "a number of restaurants in London where you can find foreign cooking and, I should imagine, excellently cooked vegetables. Soho, for instance."

"Yes, yes," said M. Klimov eagerly. "I have been to them. But when I am in England I like to be in the English atmosphere. And I am a great deal, thanks to your wonderful English hospitality, in English homes. I live myself under the care of the kindest of landladies, a warm-hearted, generous-natured woman if ever there was one, but her cabbage is a horror and her potatoes little better." He broke off again, looking about him as though he had just awoken from a dream. "I must tell you," he went on, "what a pleasure it is to me to meet you. I read a great many English books, and though some of them, I must confess, seem to me sentimental, and written for the entertainment of children, I find something very noble and honest in the best of English literature." He stopped. Put his fingers into his mouth like a distressed child. "My tooth is disagreeing with every word that I say. It is a Bolshevik tooth," he ended, smiling.

And at once everyone else seemed to break in. They had not heard a word of what he, Klimov, was saying. They were intent on their own affairs—and the main question to be immediately settled was whether this wasn't the best possible time to be alive in. Of course it wasn't. Of course it was. What about the Eighteenth Century, which Millie knew was adorable? It was as though she had been living then and perhaps she had. Mr. Pope, Horace Walpole, and the Miss Berrys, Ranelagh, and Fanny Burney. The coach staggering along the highroad under the full moon. . . . But Katherine who was more romantic at heart than Millie, but also more practical, thought of the smallpox and ill-treatment of children, Press Gangs, and Public Executions.

"The Renaissance for me!" cried Henry, and then a moment later wondered why he had said the Renaissance, because truly he didn't care a bit about it, knew nothing either, his Renaissance mind a sort of paste of *Romola, The Ring and the Book*, and M. Merezhkovsky. But he was excited because Frost was here, Frost whom when he was with the younger heretics he affected to despise, whom secretly he both loved and envied. Oh! to be such another and, because he was a dreadful egoist (with nice unselfish moments), he saw himself an accepted classic, old and revered and given Seventieth offerings. To be immortal! That was all that he wanted. Only to know beyond question that one small work (bound preferably in dark blue with a white paper label) would go down the ages, and that the homeliest meal that he, Henry Trenchard, had ever eaten, would be of thrilling interest to ladies and gentlemen a thousand years hence.

Fancy, if we should know exactly what Shakespeare ate and drank on the evening, say, of September 3, 1610!

"The Elizabethan for me!" he cried loudly, and then blushed and was ashamed, because Hans Frost was talking.

Frost was saying that it all depended on what you wanted, that in all probability more people were moderately happy now than ever before in the world's history, that there was less difference in comfort between one and another, that more was known about the human body than ever before, more diseases curable, more operations successful, more . . .

He caught himself talking on and didn't care. What did it matter if it was all nonsense that he was saying? He felt to-night a quite extraordinary absence of caution and decorum. Once as a young man staying with a friend near Derwentwater, suddenly, in the woods that bordered the lake, he had felt that he must have a swim or die. He had flung off his clothes and dived in. It had been a morning of unparalleled splendour. With strong firm strokes he had cleft the blue water, speeding out towards the purple hills and the faint line of sun-drenched yellow shore.

Afterwards his friend had said what about it if anyone had seen him naked. Everyone wore a costume. And they had returned to a cottage sunk in flowers, and there had been eggs and honey for breakfast.

So now he didn't care. No one else cared either. In half an hour they were all talking as though God never intended that they should part from one another again. And perhaps He did not. He was pleased, sitting on his large fluffy cloud, pleased with all of them, as they drank their coffee and ate their plum cake. Hans, who had not for many a moon eaten plum cake, had to-night three pieces.

And Nathalie? He looked around him and found her. She was sitting on a table near the mirror swinging her legs, and beside her, eating her with his beautiful eyes, was the lovely young Russian.

She was happy. She was radiant. She was in the Ninth Heaven.

Hans' heart as he saw her was carried away as a pigeon carries a fragment of golden corn. What was this joy that he felt for her, this deep tenderness of love, this divine protective care?

He who knew so well what life must be, its ironies and bitter partings, its pains (but thank heaven to-night the sharp needle pain in his left calf was leaving him entirely alone), its disastrous ebbing of satiated passion, its bills and empty purses, its dusty cupboards and wind-blown floors, did he dare to sing Triumph once again at the absurd pathos of a happy, contented child?

He should run to her, should warn her, should snatch her swiftly from the lovely young man, should pack her in a box and carry her home and never let her loose again.

But, he thought, sucking his finger (because the cake had been sticky. It was, thank heaven, one of those cakes that are damp inside), there had been the lady in Munich who, wanting to know when she could get a ticket for Offenbach's *Schöne Helene,* had taken him for a drive (he was twenty-four at the time) and had given him a week of utter bliss and her photograph; didn't he remember how, as she spoke to him in the hall of the hotel, at that very first instant happiness had swept down upon him straight from under the stout blonde concierge's hat (or so at least it had seemed), and sitting beside her in the carriage, blushing, he had told her of his life and ambitions, his hand timidly touching the shining silk of her tight blue dress?

Yes, so it had been with him, and so it must be now with Nathalie. And he would care for her and watch over her and see that she came to no harm.

His life, as he stretched out his hand for yet another piece of cake, seemed to be opening at last, like a flower—a glorious flower with petals of gold and a fragrance of delicious tenderness.

CHAPTER III

Soul of Ruth

RUTH, in Zanti's shop, was wondering whether she ought to afford the little box of gold and crystal. On every side of her were beautiful things, a painted Spanish crucifix in red and orange, an old necklace of amethysts set in silver, a piece of gold brocade, an ivory clock with the moon and stars and a bejewelled jester striding the world in pearls and diamonds, a pair of turquoise blue earrings, boxes of every sort, gold and silver and agate, and ivory and mother-of-pearl—but this was the one—of gold and crystal—that had caught her fancy.

"Lady Poole recommended me to come here," she said, smiling graciously at Zanti, who, fat and shining, stood awaiting her orders.

Zanti bowed.

"Lady Poole is my very good friend," he said. "Once, the first time, she come in here by chance and want to buy my rose-coloured bowl she see in the window."

"And did she?" asked Ruth, who had not heard a word that he had said.

"She did not buy it," Zanti said, smiling. "She take it away with her though."

Ruth was not in the least interested in this fat smiling

133

man, who was so foreign that surely he would smell of garlic
had he not so smart a shop in so smart a part of the town.
The whole of her mind—extremely prehensile, active, fierce
and militant—was fastened, octopus-like, around this little
box that she wanted to possess, that indeed she must possess
—but must also give as little for as was humanly possible.
She did not need the box in the least, but she was going to
fight for it with every energy that was hers.

"What is the price of this box?" she asked.

Zanti told her.

"Oh, but how monstrous!" She turned and faced him,
flinging onto him the full glory of her splendour and beauty.
He seemed curiously unaffected, and as soon as she saw that,
she began to criticize him to herself, how fat he was, and only
a foreigner would wear black clothes, and how podgy his
hands were.

"Now," she said in her most military manner, "what will
you let me have that for?"

Zanti named the price once more.

"Now you know that that's absurd. Lady Poole told me
that you were most moderate in your charges." (Lady Poole
had done nothing of the kind.) "I can't call that moderate.
Now what do you say?"

"You see, madame," said Zanti, "I don't care in the least
whether I sell anything—or not. I prefer indeed not to sell.
These things are friends of mine. It distresses me to lose
them."

"What do you have a shop for?" asked Ruth haughtily.
She had never heard such nonsense in her life!

"Ah! One must do somezing. And one makes friends of
one's customers. Lady Poole, for example. I am very proud
of being Lady Poole's friend."

Ruth held her box in her hand. She must have it. "Well,
what about——?" She named half his original sum.

He bowed. "I am extremely regretful. I cannot change the
price. It is a fair price, but if it was unfair I must not change
it."

Ruth tossed her head.

"I shall tell my friends that your prices are ridiculous,"
she retorted, and swung out of the shop. She had lost her
temper. A moment later, in the sunshining street, she re-
gretted that. She hated to lose her temper. Stupid, and got
you nowhere. She paused, half tempted to return to the shop,
smile at the man, and pay what he asked.

No, she was damned if she would. She found her car in
St. James's Square, told the chauffeur to take her home, sat
back and discovered that she was extremely irritated. Why
had she abandoned the conflict so suddenly? She had wanted
the box—heaven knew why, there were plenty of others
just like it—and had been determined to have it. And now
here she was in her car alone with her exasperated temper.
That man was hateful, fat, greasy foreigner. And then
with that by now practised and customary spiritual mas-
sage she set to work on herself and, in five minutes' time,
just as the china plates and cups of South Audley Street
were swinging into view, she was sweet and amiable and
kindly again.

There was one thing that Ruth, with all her social practice, had never yet learned to do—to be kindly and pleasant to people who seemed to her at the moment unimportant. This failing—of which she was supremely unaware—came from two things—just that she had no idea of how unpleasant she was on certain occasions, never dreamt how deeply these same unimportant people resented her (had she realized it she would at once have altered her behaviour) and, secondly, there was her egotism which limited, surprisingly, her vision —simply because when she was after a thing she was after it like a contestant in a race, her loins girded, her every muscle strung, her eyes fixed relentlessly on the goal. Nine times out of every ten she secured her prize, but at a considerable (although to her quite unrealized) cost. She thought that she was an extremely charming and important woman. She had every reason for thinking so. She was beautiful. People (the finest, noblest, and most interesting people) came to her house with the utmost readiness. She was gay and clever, and amusing (not quite so clever as she fancied, and to some people not at all amusing). But, above all, she knew what she wanted.

Once and again someone was rude to her, or some loving friend told her that someone had been rude about her. She was then quite honestly amazed. She could not conceive what anyone could have against her. All that she wanted was for others to be happy. She arranged her parties so that people who wanted to meet one another should meet—(she had some cousins, two old maids, who longed to meet some of the splendid guests, but they were never invited). She

wished well to all the world—so long as it did not stand in
her way.

And especially it was her gospel that she was a genius at
seeing through people. No one whom she could not sum up
and place. No fault or silly weakness in her friends that she
could not recognize, and then most nobly she overlooked
those faults and weaknesses and was more charming than
ever. (She had no conception of the irritation that she caused
by exercising this noble forgiveness.)

And beneath all this was a touching and sympathetic
childishness. Her trouble was perhaps that she had changed
so little from the small girl with auburn hair, screaming at a
party, "I want that toy." She had been grasping then, she
was grasping now; she had been vain then, she was vain
now; but she had also been anxious to be noble-spirited
then, she was anxious to be noble-spirited now.

Finally, although she had not the least idea of this, she
was one of the loneliest women in London.

By the time that the car was halfway up Baker Street she
had transformed the incident of the little box into a pretty,
quite noble affair. Because, after all (just look at those ridiculous women crossing the street without looking anywhere
at all! How dare they, and a good thing for them if they had
an accident just to teach them!), it would have been absurd
to have shown anger to a man like that, a common foreigner
without even good manners. And, as she had again and again
noticed, something prompted one to take exactly the right
line on those occasions, although at the time one might be

quite unaware that one was taking it—as, for instance, at Venice last year, when the little worm of a Fascist official at the railway station had been so abominably vulgar about Ruth who had wanted to bring all her bags into her compartment with her—and Ruth saw the Venice railway station stretching from the Bakerloo Tube as far as Canuto's, a vast overhanging wing of foreign impudence, and her own figure (she could remember even the hat that she was wearing that day, dark blue with a soft grey feather curling about it), beautifully courageous, beautifully successful. And the hat made her think of Hans, because he had been with her when she bought it, and thinking of Hans (they were almost home now, turning in through Clarence Gate, and behold all the water was ruffled by the evening breeze) she was, she must confess, a little disturbed at the way that he was going on.

She would be home in a moment and have no time to think, because Adele Manson was coming to tea. It was as though Hans had hurled himself straight through the window of the car, presented a pistol at her head, crying: "Now what are you going to do about it?" What? ... Indeed what? ... But was anything the matter? Only that a few evenings ago he had gone with Nathalie to a Bohemian party. So unlike him. And here the car stopped, and the chauffeur was off his seat and standing at the door. No, it had rather been his manner. Something determined and secret. And that odd talk that he had had with her after the dinner-party.

She got out and stood for a moment looking at the large

yellow cloud, like a cow that was going mooning about the sky as though it desperately wanted milking. Was there something in him of which she was not sure? Had there always been something? Yes, there had. She knew it only too well, as the cow split up into four sofa cushions and a pink ear-trumpet—something that he put on like a disguise, an invisible mantle—he passing beside her like a ghost that is felt but not seen.

She shivered, drawing her furs a little closer about her. Some anticipation—unexpected, without precedent, like a stranger addressing her in an unknown language—touched her shoulder. She could not bear to be alone. She hastened, as though fearful of the open sky, the gleaming water, the bare and unfriendly trees, into the house.

CHAPTER IV

The Zoo

HANS, feeling, as he always did in the Zoo, a mixture of conscience-stricken shame and a pleasurable schoolboy excitement, was aware (he and Nathalie stopping in front of the little coloured birds) that the thing (if he ever did it, which was most unlikely) must be called "The One-eyed Commander." That was its one and only conceivable title. Two little birds with crimson bodies and bright blue wings sat very close together on a slender swaying bough. Were they unhappy and desolate, or loving and private, or simply cold? He asked Nathalie.

Nathalie, who was so happy that it was impossible for her to believe at this moment in the unhappiness of anyone or anything, was sure that they were enjoying every moment of the sun, the stir of life, the perfect companionship. And did Uncle Hans know from what part of the world they had come? She would like if she knew where it was to go there—and she had a vision of a glittering blue-acred country where monkeys threw cocoa-nuts into the air, and the roars of the lions could be heard quivering the silences in the thickness of the jungle. Uncle Hans, putting his arm through hers and drawing her gently forward, knew, he informed her sadly, little about birds. It had been always in his novels his trouble that he had to go so carefully when birds were in the air, naming only the ones of whose family he was certain, leaving the others to sing their songs in a beautiful golden mist.

"And the danger is," he continued, "that you can have too much golden mist. It's so damned easy. There's no reason why you should ever stop."

He saw the One-eyed Commander come charging down the path, scattering the family from Putney, making the little girl with the bag of biscuits for the monkeys burst into tears.

Ah, the Commander was fine in his vest of silver, his coat of green velvet, and the silver buckles on his shoes. But that was at the moment all that Hans had discovered. He was excited because he was out in the sunny air with Nathalie, and because it was the first time, for many a day, that inspiration had visited him. He wasn't dead then? His old vessel was to be boarded once again by those daring devils. With their oaths and cutlasses, driving him, at the edge of the plank itself, to plunge into the great sea of imagination.

"Now, what about the monkeys?" he said to Nathalie. The monkeys were, as always, too terribly human to be comforting. Five of them huddled together on the wooden bar resembled so exactly a family of infants left out in the snow on a lonely Christmas Eve that their sentimentality was revolting to a modern realist.

Hans was not that, but he could not endure the pathos of their beseeching gaze as he moved on hastily to an ancient member of the Athenæum Club, busily engaged in searching for the soul of a piece of red calico. Here there was an an-

cient boredom that spoke of centuries of lonely club meals,
Times leaders, and flights from other members' aimless lo-
quacities. "No," thought Hans, staring into the sad, timeless eyes of this Ancient, "the One-eyed Commander is
wearing no silver buckles nor coat of green velvet—he is
driving up in a broken-down cab on a wet and windy night
to the mansion with the garbage heap just to the right of the
front door. His family are waiting for him. He has sworn
that he will never return to them, but circumstances have
been too much for him. . . ."

"It's terribly stuffy in here," said Nathalie. "Let's go
out and find the lions."

She, too, had been depressed by the monkeys' faces. Her
happiness had for the moment been twitched from her as
though it had been a lightly worn mantle. On what basis
had she, during these last three days, been building all her
glory? On the rocking, trembling foundation of one meeting
and a letter. It was true that the letter had said wonderful
things. It was near her heart now, and her hand went up to
it feeling the crackle of the paper beneath her dress, while
the Ancient, realizing that life is but vanity, flung to the
floor the piece of red calico, swung to the top bar of his cage
and screamed his discontent with this perpetually cheating
world. What had not that piece of calico promised him,
while in reality. . . .No, Nathalie thought, as she followed
Uncle Hans into the sunshine again, she had but little to go
upon. With a Russian, too, you never could tell. Everyone
knew how uncertain they were. Look at the present state of
their country. On the other hand, he had said—she knew

the words by heart— "Such moments of wonder and delight come but seldom. Why should we permit to pass us a happiness such as perhaps we shall never encounter again?"

The English that he used was a little strange, but would he say such things if he did not mean them? And she thought of his splendid beauty, the frank honesty of his eyes, the pressure of his hand as they said good-bye, and so, trembling at this picture, found that a little boy, running away from his family to see at closer view the splendour of the elephant, who took passengers, had nearly tumbled, and caught her dress to save himself.

He fell almost but not quite, and then, straightening himself, was off like a shot from a gun, pursued by urgent cries of " 'Enery, 'Enery!"

She was happy again. She was in a splendid reassuring world, where the camel and the elephant moved, children swaying delirious on their backs, where the cries of strange birds rent the sky and the boughs of the trees waved in the blue warm air—so warm for the time of the year that everyone was a little abnormal and unusually demonstrative, because this couldn't last for more than an hour or two and was like a Royal Procession or a visit of the French President.

Hans also was reassured again now that he was in the sunshine. The name of the Commander's family was Hellicent, an absurd name, but that was what they were called. He didn't know as yet how many of them there were, but he could see Francesca the wife, an ugly beetle-browed mountain of a woman, jealous and unfaithful. Yes, she had had many lovers, and it was perhaps to avenge himself that the

Commander was returning. Up through the soppy, leaf-sodden avenue his old cab stumbled, while he, sitting sternly and with fierce concentration inside it, meditated the form that his arrival should take. While Francesca all unwitting . . .

"I think this is the way to the lions," said Nathalie. "Round to the right."

With a rush of eager affection he returned to her. How pretty she looked this afternoon in her grey dress and dark furs and little hat with the rosy feather. Never had girls, in any time in the world's history, looked so pretty as they did now. Prettiness and health together!

And she was his. She had come into his life never again to leave it. He would see to that.

Even when she married he would be allowed still to care for her and look after her. That was an old man's privilege. But then there crept in the sadness that is at the heart of all love. What in a little while would she want with an ancient monster like himself and growing with every second of time more ancient—because, after seventy, every day makes a difference. He saw himself being shovelled into a grave by careless and indifferent grave diggers whose eyes were already active to see who was next.

Ah well, he would make the most of his time, and he whispered suddenly, putting his face close to hers:

"Do you love me, Nathalie, do you love me? Say you do, even though you don't."

And she answered, laughing up at him, "I do. Of course I do. I've never loved anyone so much."

It was true. This raging madness that during the last three days she had suffered, was not love. It was rather a choking, a strangling, a fire at the throat, a chill at the heart, anticipation, starting up at every sound, lying at night awake, staring, staring, waiting—for what?

This madness, then, was new. She had heard of it, read of it, been superbly remote from it, then like an aëroplane from the sky it had swooped down, caught her up, swung her far into the burning brilliant air.

No, this was not love—this was something deafening, blinding, and without a name.

But did you talk about love—and here they were in the Lion House, and it was ten minutes to three so that very shortly now the lions would be fed—then she had never loved anyone before as she now loved Uncle Hans.

She had loved in faint memory her parents, she had loved in comfortable fireside fashion the Proudies, but something she had kept to herself away from all of them. They hadn't known that, they had thought her so wonderfully spontaneous and open-hearted. So in a fashion she had been, but now, staring into the dreaming sombre gaze of the lion who was marked like a tiger, it seemed to her that here suddenly in front of these splendid imprisoned beauties she had come of age, matured, grown up, and that that night when Uncle Hans had come into her room had been the magic moment of that transformation.

And now seen through the thick rich smoky haze of her new experience, how long ago already that night seemed! Here, although she had opened her heart to him, was something already of which she had not told him. How much did he know or guess? He was so very sharp and clever; standing there now, one knee up on the outer bars, leaning his wise old chin on the knob of his walking-stick, he looked a terrific swell.

Because it was feeding time the place was crowding with people, families with eager excited children, some grand ones who kept apart and tried to conceal their interest, some shabby old men who were there to pass the time away—how magnificently from them all he stood out, with his clothes so quiet and so distinguished, his splendid head, his kind wise eyes, his mouth a little arrogant, secret, determined, humorous, his thick strong body—who would ever dream that he was seventy years of age? Yes, if he were not anybody at all everyone would notice him. "Who is that fine-looking man over there? He must be somebody!"

"It is just two minutes to three," said Hans. "They are always very punctual."

"Let's move on to the next one," said Nathalie. "I like the real lions better, don't you, Uncle Hans? This one looks as though someone had been playing jokes with him and he's unhappy about it."

So they moved on to the next one, a very fine fellow with a huge dusty mane and an expression of affectionate, almost sentimental, amiability. He would do beautifully for a poster advertising the purposes and spirit of the League of Love and Kindness, a new society whose pamphlets Hans had received a few days ago. But why was it you could not go into his cage, fasten him, smiling amiably, with a daisy chain, and lead him down the Charing Cross Road? And why could you not, after that, arrange in his place the stout lady with the little beady eyes who was at this very moment staring at him with a gaze of haughty patronage? It was a platitude that many animals were superior to many human beings, but, platitude or not, it made one uncomfortable on every occasion that it was brought home.

Hans turned for comfort to Nathalie, his darling and his pride. He drew her close to him. He whispered to her, putting his cheek very close to hers:

"Are you enjoying yourself? Do you like to come out with your uncle? Isn't it good that we're friends? Do you mind how sentimental I am, or are you one of those hard, cynical, modern young women?"

"I am not," Nathalie whispered back. "I love to go out with you anywhere, and I'm terribly proud of you—not because you've written great books, but because you are such a darling."

"And would you defend me," he went on, "no matter how all these people in here attacked me? Will you stick to me through thick and thin?"

"I'll stick to you through thick and thin," she answered.

"And will you in the same way stick to me through everything?"

"In the same way I'll stick to you—through everything."

"No matter whatever I did?"

"No matter whatever you did."

He caught her hand and held it tightly. Why must fear and apprehension run at the heart of love? Why did he seem suddenly to see in the large amber dreaming eyes of the lion the threat that he was going to lose her, that this wonderful thing that had come to him so unexpectedly in his old age was fugitive, vanishing? Oh! he must keep it! He must keep it! She was true and loyal if anyone ever was. She said only what she meant. She was, oh, surely she was to be trusted in this vain and faithless world!

"Here comes the man!" said Nathalie.

Yes, here was the man shovelling in another moment under the bars the lumps of bloody meat, then while the children cried, "Look! Look!" and everyone else said, "Ah!" the noble animals proceeded to show what they would do had they got these same children under their noble jaws. Crunch! Crunch! Tear! Tear! . . . No daisy chains any longer and no sentimental gaze wasted upon the emotion-loving public.

Hans was suddenly tired. He wasn't, in these days, altogether accustomed to these continuous expeditions. This last week had been exhausting.

He wanted, with an immediate pressing need, the library with the deep blue ceiling, the ivory-coloured bookcases (Gibbon in calf and gold, Macaulay in dark green, and the Elizabethan dramatists in crimson morocco), the hush, the peace, the fire gently stirring—yes, and the Manet. The adorable Manet and its soft colour, its lovely gentle light. This crunching, this tearing——

"Shall we go?" he said. "We'll be back in time to have a nice laze before tea."

Nathalie at once agreed. She had had enough. Her eyes

had flown forward to the moment when she would be alone in her bedroom, would take the letter from her dress and read it again and again, while the curtains blew ever so slightly before the open window and the croaks and mutterings of the birds came up from the dusky Park.

So they moved away, away to the main entrance where the car would be waiting.

And as Hans, loving to feel Nathalie close beside him, trotted away, once again the One-eyed Commander leapt upon him.

He had pulled the bell-chain now. The echo of the clanging rang all through the house. Behind him he could hear the horse pawing the soaking ground and the stealthy stir of the rain through the black wall of laurels. Ah! someone was coming with a light! The key was creaking in the lock. The door was swinging. . . .

"There's the car!" cried Nathalie.

CHAPTER V

Nathalie in Russia

APPROACHING the Park she took her hand out of her uncle's, as though she were about to test his fidelity and patience and wanted to see how he would feel about it.

"I hope you'll approve," she said a little timidly. (Why was it that with people even like Uncle Hans, whom she loved and could utterly trust, cowardice *would* keep creeping back?) "I'm going to spend to-morrow evening with Millie Westcott." What she meant to imply was—whether you like it or not I'm going to do it, just as any modern girl would; but she wasn't, it seemed, quite modern enough, because her voice trembled into a little quaver of anxiety.

"Millie Westcott?"

"Yes, you know—the wife of Peter Westcott."

Of course he knew, and at once a sharp pain ran up the calf of his left leg (where all his emotions in these days seemed to be seated). Of course he knew, and it wasn't Millie Westcott whom she was going to see but the young Russian. She hadn't lied to him. She wouldn't do that, but nevertheless Millie Westcott was a blind.

He had a furious, heart-heating impulse to turn to her and say: "Look here! Tell me everything. You love this boy, don't you? It has fallen on you like a thunderbolt. You can think, morning and night, of nothing else. Let me share it with you. I'm old, I know, but I'm wise. My love for you has come on me, too, like a thunderbolt. It's different from your love, but perhaps because it's different it's more real and more lasting. I want to protect and help you. It's the only thing now that I care for. I'm your father, your guardian, your friend, everything that an old man can be. Trust me. Trust me."

All that he did say was:

"Why, of course, dear, if you want to go. Have a nice evening. They're pleasant people. I like Peter Westcott especially."

"I think"—she paused an instant—"that Mrs. Westcott is taking me to the house of those Russians who were there the other evening."

"Yes," he said.

"The Westcotts like them very much. I think Mr. Westcott's a very trustworthy man—about people, I mean. Don't you?"

"Oh, very," he said, patting her hand.

"Do you think Aunt Ruth will mind?" she asked.

"No. Why should she?" he answered rather sharply. "You're free. All young people are nowadays, I suppose. Only—" he took her hand tightly in his own. "We neither of us have the slightest hold over you, of course. We wouldn't wish to have. The only hold I have is that I'm your friend for you to come to if you want any advice or help. Anything —it doesn't matter what it is. I'm there behind you."

"Oh, I know." She bent forward and lightly kissed his

cheek. "That makes me so awfully happy. I've never been so happy before."

But it wasn't he that was making her happy, he reflected, as they went into the house together.

He had a strange, crazy impulse as he slowly climbed the stairs to his room to curse the Westcotts and all their damned Russians. What did this child know about life? . . . and she suddenly, just as he reached the door of the library, was beside him with the bucket and the spade, the glitter of sand on her cheeks, breathless with some news, the sea-weed trailing from the spade.

"You don't know a thing about life," he said to her, as he pushed open the library door.

"Oh, come and look at the starfish I've found," she gasped out, her eyes shining with the glory of it.

"A pretty sort of starfish," he muttered, as he went angrily over to his favourite chair.

The One-eyed Commander was so far away that he was quite certainly never going to exist again, but the Manet was there, and Martha, who looked up at him with her comical eyes, patted his leg with her paw, then posted herself between his thighs, raised her paws onto his waist-coat, and looked up at him with an amused, ironical glance.

She knew at once when he was unhappy. She never surrendered sentimentally to that unhappiness; she had too ironical a spirit for that. Moreover, she knew that he despised his own discontents and disliked extremely any sympathy, scorning the sympathizer.

She paused, however, in the middle of her own secret purposes and pursuits, surrendered her egotisms for long enough to assure him that she laughed at his moods, but was his friend all the same.

With slow, strong fingers, he stroked her sleek, shiny back. Her eyes never left his face, but very gently she wagged her tail, partly because she liked to be stroked by him and partly because she knew that her pleasure pleased him.

"I was tempted, Martha, to believe for a moment that I was to be active again, kick my heels in the air, have some fun, but a young Russian gentleman has thrown me out of the window. . . . Well, no harm done. I don't suppose I could have stood the pace——"

He took out his large tortoiseshell spectacles, settled himself in his chair, Martha arranged herself at his feet, and with a sigh half of comfort, half of humorous distress, he opened the book on the reading desk—the *Socrate Chrétien*, of M. Jean Guez de Balzac. . . .

Millie Westcott, standing in the middle of the mirror, waiting, a little impatiently, for Nathalie, had still certain fragments of her children clinging about her. She had only five minutes before closed the nursery door behind her, but closing the door did not hold captive everything within the room—Norah's slight ghost of a cough, for instance, really no more than her little polite cough of ordinary society, but mightn't it perhaps be more? Had it been wise perhaps to-day . . . that wind . . . Kensington Gardens . . . ? Oh, well, keep her in bed to-morrow if necessary—this time of the year. Also Bobby's terrible way of saying "Shan't." Hadn't they for ages been trying to rid him of this very thing, and there he was again saying it to Miss Cleaver, who, after all, was very patient with them, although she did, quite rightly, insist upon discipline.

Perhaps if Miss Cleaver's mother had only insisted when she was a child that she should wear one of those bands across her front teeth, she wouldn't have such dreadfully prominent ones now. It was the only thing against Miss Cleaver, but of course Bobby, who showed an astonishing feeling for beauty at his age (he was only three and a bit), would listen to Miss Cleaver more obediently were she a little better looking. And Miss Cleaver was, we must all admit (and here Millie looked round at a deep, dense circle of accusing and criticizing friends and relatives), the only one left now to whom he said "Shan't," and he hadn't said it to her now for several months. It was only to-night that there was that unfortunate scene about Julius Cæsar. It was, of course, foolish of Miss Cleaver to insist that Julius Cæsar was a great man if Bobby, on that particular evening, was so determined that he was not. And Bobby, after all, was determined only because he had seen a picture of Cæsar somewhere, and had thought him hideous, which wasn't, however, as Miss Cleaver had pointed out, a reason for his not being important. A great many ugly people were important—to which Bobby had said that they couldn't be, and when Miss Cleaver had said that she could give him instances, Bobby had said something very rude indeed, and then had been told to apologize. It was at that point that he had said "Shan't," had been sent to bed supperless, and then long afterwards,

when he should have been fast asleep, had burst suddenly
into floods of tears. That was what made him so odd and
surprising. It was only his father who seemed really to understand him.

Millie, placed there in her pale blue dress in the very
middle of the mirror, sighed. The trouble with her was that
she didn't feel like a mother at all. She didn't feel married
even. She didn't, as an honest fact, ever feel a day older. It
was a pity. Everyone else was getting older, but she wasn't.
Peter, Katherine, they were getting older. You had only to
look at them. She saw instantly Peter's habit of scratching
his left ear reflectively; that was an odd thing to do, there
he was right in front of her, his legs spread apart, his affectionate but rather serious gaze upon her. Yes, he *was* serious
and she wasn't. She couldn't be; something was always
happening, like one afternoon the mud at the corner of Mr.
Symons' nose, or the ridiculous puppy, Arnold Barnabas,
that Henry was dragging about with him just now. One silly,
ridiculous thing, and there she was forgetting everything,
ready to go and play leap-frog down the Strand. . . .

That was the very quality that Peter had loved most in
her when he married her. It was undoubtedly the quality
that he loved least now. Was that always so with marriage,
was it also so with life—which she saw as Henry's puppy,
all legs, ears, and a gaping, snapping mouth—couldn't one
ever get life into just the right shape like a box neatly made
for Pope's poetry? No, obviously not, because everyone was
always complaining.

But why, then, must she act as she did so constantly on

impulse—was that Bobby crying? She went to the end of the room and listened. Take to-night, for instance. There had been no reason to ask this girl, who was pretty, but in all probability nothing else at all. Only the Russian boy had suggested it, and Millie had said yes at once, as though it were the thing in all the world that she wanted to do; and it wasn't—or at least it wouldn't be until she was there in the very middle of it, and then she always enjoyed herself.

But now that it was settled, she would see that she enjoyed herself. You never knew who would be there or what would happen before you came home again. And she began to flush with excitement and to smile to herself and to dance a few steps down the room, and to think what darlings Norah and Bobby were, and how perfect Peter was (only he mustn't get too serious), and what a pet Katherine was, and what a lovely thing life altogether must be when you had babies and just money sufficient, and a husband like a rock, and a woman who really didn't cook so badly (especially the things she knew how to do, like shoulders of mutton and fig puddings—she was a *plain* cook from Glebeshire), and real celebrities, like Hans Frost, coming to supper. Sham celebrities. Real celebrities. There were so many of the former. They were always coming and borrowing money, she was certain, from Peter, who was terribly generous.

But *real* celebrities. People who were *so* real that they didn't care whether they were or no.

And beginning to dance again, she saw Hans Frost with his kindness and beautiful appearance and benevolence, and she loved him and loved everybody (except that it was a terrible pity that Miss Cleaver hadn't had something done to her teeth when she was young), and danced breathlessly, happily, straight into Nathalie's knock on the door.

Then, as sometimes happens when one sees someone for the second time, not having been very much struck with them on the first, Millie fell straight into love with Nathalie, standing as she did, rather timidly, in her rose-coloured dress at the door. It wasn't because she was so awfully pretty —although that, of course, had something to do with it—nor that she looked eager and anxious to be friendly, but really because she looked such a baby that Millie's maternal heart —and Millie was more maternal than anything else—was caught and held.

She went straight up to her and kissed her, then held her hand up warningly.

"Hush, did you hear Bobby? . . . I thought I heard something." Nathalie, too, listened seriously. There was nothing.

"No. It's all right. I'm so glad you've come. And now we must be off right away. It's eight already."

"Am I late? I'm so sorry."

"No. They're only off Russell Square. It's no distance. We'll have a taxi. We've got a car—only a Morris—but Peter's got it to-night. He's gone to a first-night. He sometimes does notices for the *Once a Week*. He's pretty good at it, I think. But of course I'm prejudiced."

Nathalie was happy at once. All the fears were gone. She had felt, as she always did before approaching a strange house, as though she were going to the dentist's. Now it was as though she had known Millie for years. She liked Millie—

yes, tremendously. Five minutes earlier she had thought her rather stuck-up and distant.

She had passed, in fact, as she was always doing, from a state of dismay to a state of ecstasy.

But beneath both the dismay and the ecstasy there was this furious current running. In another instant she would see him, in another instant her hand would touch his, she would hear his voice. "Because," said Millie, out of a thunderous distance, "they are the most unpunctual people in the world, so it doesn't matter."

"All Russians are, I suppose," said Nathalie with an air of profound wisdom.

"Have you ever met any before?"

"Never," said Nathalie. (What an absurd falsehood, when she had known Vladimir for ever and ever—when he was a star and she a cabbage perhaps.)

They were in the taxi, and London belonged to them. They sat up proudly and ordered Piccadilly Circus to take care of its manners, Shaftesbury Avenue to mind what it was doing, and the Prince's Theatre to watch its steps.

Millie talked incessantly, but Nathalie heard from a vast distance. Suppose, when he saw her to-night, he didn't like her any more. Russians were that way. Everyone said so. But no. No one could look at her as he had done and not mean it for ever and always. "So then Bobby said 'Shan't!' Well, of course, he oughtn't to have done it, and he had to be punished, but *I* know just what he was thinking, poor lamb. If Miss Cleaver weren't so ugly, if she hadn't

got such *dreadful* teeth it never would have happened, but
the trouble is that if you get a girl who's really pretty she
never knows her job and can't manage the children a
bit——"

(But *what* was the next step? Would he ask her to
marry him? It was terribly soon. But she had made up her
mind. She didn't care how little money he had. She would
work like anything. And he went down to the City every
day. They must pay him something for that.)

"Norah's quite different from Bobby. I do hope I'm not
boring you by talking about my children. Children *aren't*
exciting, and I do try not to bore people about them. Philip
says I never talk about anything else, but Philip's always
finding fault with something. I wonder if you noticed him
the other night. He's awfully good-looking and devoted to
Katherine. But then who wouldn't be? She's such a darling,
anyone would be ready to die for her. All the same I sometimes think Mother was right years ago when she tried to
prevent their marrying. Katherine's happy in a kind of
a way, but he's so full of his career and making a name for
himself. I don't think it matters making a name for yourself
if you've got just enough money. The chief thing is being
happy. That's what I tell Peter——"

(Being happy? Was Nathalie happy? Was this happiness?
No. There was dread in it, and fear.... Supposing he should
look at her coldly, hardly speak to her....)

Ah, here we are! Here before this dark house in a dark,
silent street with no eyes to any of the windows.

The taxi was paid and went lurching away. There were a number of little bells with names above them. The door mysteriously opened. They climbed black stairs, stumbling as they went.

"I do hope," said Millie, "they haven't forgotten all about it. It would be just like them if they did." Then, quite casually, she added, "It may be just the two Shapkins. They said no one was coming. I do hope you won't be bored."

Nathalie's heart jumped and died. Only the two Shapkins! The whole evening without him, when she had counted on this as she counted on God. And if he weren't there, it would be because he didn't want to see her. It would be deliberate. The kindest way to show her that he hadn't meant a word that he had said, that it had been only a moment's fun——

"This must be the door, I think," said Millie. "Yes, there's the name."

She pushed another little bell. They could hear it echoing. There was a pause. Someone was coming. The door opened, and there was the tall, stout, bepince-nezed Madame Shapkin standing to welcome them.

A moment later Nathalie knew that it was all right. He was there, haloed with light, and an untidy tablecloth, plates of ham, loaves of bread, and piles of newspapers for his foreground. Not only was he there, but he had seen her instantly, had stepped forward, smiling. . . . He was glad that she had come.

At once she was reserved. She wouldn't show him that she was glad, not immediately at any rate. She looked around the room and at everyone but him.

What a room! What a mess! What a noise! There seemed to be hundreds of people there, the room was thick with smoke.

A large table covered most of the space. She thought at once of Alice's Tea-party. Plates and knives and forks and cups were everywhere, thrown about carelessly, as though they had tumbled from the ceiling. Dishes with ham and fish, and jam and butter, and at one end piles of newspapers which two men, talking excitedly, were turning over. Someone was playing the piano. One man, short and stout, was standing on his head before a group who, for some strange reason, were clapping their hands to a measured beat.

This was madness. She shrank back behind Millie, who seemed to be finding exactly what she had expected. They were led through all the people, who paid no attention to them at all, into another room where there was a vast bed, a large dressing table, a cracked looking-glass, collars, hats, a large bandbox in the middle of the floor, and numbers of lost and desolate shoes.

"Throw your things onto the bed, there's a darling," said Madame Shapkin in her deep bass voice—then turned and shouted: "Darushka! Darushka!" and then when a tall slim girl with a long nose and laughing mouth appeared, after a torrent of Russian, ended abruptly and very absent-mindedly:—"There's a darling."

"I thought there wasn't to be anyone here but yourselves," said Millie, tidying her hair in the cracked glass.

"So did I," said Madame Shapkin amiably. "But it's Kostia's name-day, so he came along with some friends.

Thank God, he brought some food with him. And Gaier Gemzonitch has come. He was one of the finest comic actors in Petrograd. Such a jolly fellow!"

Beaming upon them both and pushing back her pince-nez, which were for ever slipping down her nose, she shouted again: "Darushka! Darushka!" and when the tall laughing girl once more appeared, poured out another torrent of Russian.

"I hope you don't mind the noise," she said, smiling at Nathalie. "English people are so quiet, I find. Come along now. You must be starved. There's still something left to eat."

They came back into the room and sat down at the table. Mr. Shapkin came and greeted them, but very absent-mindedly. It was plain that he had not the least idea who they were.

Nathalie was glad to be left alone for a little; she could not but admire Millie, who was able, in a moment, to take the pulse of the room, to smile first at one then at another, to laugh at the man who had been standing on his head, but now was pulling faces under a paper cap, and to eat the strange mixture of cold ham and fish that was piled on her plate, and to listen at the same time to the grave, melancholy discourse of Mr. Shapkin, who was apparently talking about stamps on letters and the difficulties of English coinage.

She herself was very glad to be left out of things for a little. She had never been to a party like this before, and she wanted to feel her way; moreover, in her heart there was the unceasing consciousness that Vladimir was standing near to her, that soon he would come and speak to her, and that then her cup would be filled with happiness. Nevertheless, he was more remote from her than he had been on the other evening. He belonged to this strange, foreign, noisy world. He was part of the little company gathered round the piano, singing now to a very soft accompaniment a melody that repeated again and again, and sounded to her ignorant ears like—

> *"Boshe, boshe, meely moi*
> *Kreek—ibushna*
> *Boshe, boshe, meely moi*
> *Ibushna—la."*

Very beautiful it was, and beautiful, too, to see how their faces were absorbed and lost, their eyes soft, their bodies strung to a devout attention.

> *"Boshe, boshe, meely moi*
> *Kreek—ibushna*
> *Boshe, boshe, meely moi*
> *Ibushna—la."*

What did it mean? What every other song in the world meant. What her own heart meant, as, trying to pretend that she enjoyed the ham and the fish and the tea in a glass at her side, her eyes filled with tears; and Vladimir seemed to steal closer to her with every moment.

Someone had sat down beside her, and a very gentle voice said in her ear:

"Mihail Alexandrovitch Klimov."

She turned and saw the stout round man with a head as bald as an egg, who had been at the Westcotts' the other evening and had talked to Uncle Hans.

"How do you do?" she said, smiling.

He looked at her with large, melancholy eyes that reminded her of a cow, a dog, and one of the vergers in Polchester Cathedral. She found it difficult to hear what he said, because his voice was so soft.

"I do hope that the splendid Mr. Frost is well," he said, "and took no harm from the other evening."

"He's very well, thank you," she answered. Vladimir was standing quite near to her now, talking to Madame Shapkin, and his eyes were always on her.

"That is a very great man," said Mr. Klimov, nodding his head excitedly. "I would follow him round the world if he invited me to do so. There are very few great men anywhere in the world to-day. It is also very difficult to be a great man and not to be aware that you are one."

"Yes. I suppose that it is," said Nathalie.

"I find," continued Mr. Klimov, "that the marks of a great man are that he is like a child and a very wise, experienced man both at the same time, that he is kindly of heart, but allows no one to possess him. All these things are apparent in Mr. Frost." Mr. Klimov sighed. "It must be a fine thing to have your thoughts in order as Mr. Frost must have them. All my life I have desired to bring my thoughts into some kind of order, but the essential thing escapes me. I admire that in the English; although their thoughts are

very seldom of the first importance, yet they have them all arranged very neatly. It must be exceedingly comforting. I had unfortunately a toothache on the night when I met Mr. Frost and, therefore, I was able to think even less clearly than usual." He gave another deep sigh. Then suddenly his face broke into a radiant smile.

"However, I shall never forget the good fortune of speaking to Mr. Frost. He was exceedingly kind to me."

"He is the very kindest man in all the world," said Nathalie.

"I'm sure that he is," said Mr. Klimov. "He was even interested in my desire to find well-cooked vegetables in England. Something that must have been to him of the very smallest importance. May I ask whether he is a relation of yours?"

"He's my uncle," said Nathalie very proudly. They had left the piano now, but more had gathered round them, and they were all singing in harmony, softly, those words that sounded to Nathalie's ignorant ears like—

> *"Boshe, boshe, meely moi*
> *Kreek—ibushna*
> *Boshe, boshe, meely moi*
> *Ibushna—la."*

Mr. Klimov was caught in. He, too, began to sing. They were all singing.

Then under cover of the singing, Vladimir came close to her. She felt his nearness. She dared not look. She dared not move.

At last he spoke to her, bending towards her, his cheek close to hers.

"What a noise! Shan't we go to the other room?"

She got up. She moved trance-like, noticing that the comic actor from Petrograd had unbuttoned his waistcoat; that the tall girl with the black eyes had stopped singing and was looking into the green curtains that protected the windows, as though she were asking them a question; that the two men who were reading the newspapers were now arguing fiercely. She noticed all these things, but they were in her dream.

Vladimir led her into a little room and closed the door upon it. The thing that at once she noticed was a picture— a picture in very vivid colours of a green tree, a pool deeply blue, two brown cows, a lady and a gentleman in eighteenth-century clothes talking under the tree, and in the background against a sky of faintest blue a snow-white house, and over the snow-white house a snow-white cloud. All very still. Not a leaf stirring. The heat of a summer's day.

"Oh, what a beautiful picture!" she cried.

"Yes," he answered, looking at her and not at the picture. "It is by one of our most celebrated painters, Konstantin Somov. Mr. Shapkin brought it out of Petrograd."

But he spoke as in a dream. He drew close to her, never moving his eyes from her face, then gently, softly drew her to him, laid with a protecting gesture her head on his breast, bent down over her, murmuring, "I love you. . . . I love you. . . . Little darling, how I love you! *Ya Lublyoo Tibeer.* . . . *Ya Lublyoo Tibeer. . . . Lublyoo. . . . Lublyoo. . . .*"

CHAPTER VI

Blackmoor

HANS surrendered to Blackmoor with surprising swiftness. Before he knew where at all he was he was selecting the books for Bigges to shove into the top of the bag (and it was a kind of desecration for Bigges even to touch them), two volumes of Chapman's *Homer*, a volume of Galleon's Letters, and *Crotchet Castle* and *Melincourt*.

And while he stood watching disgustedly Bigges' broad beam, he was thinking: "Why the devil . . . to surrender to that old woman's whims! . . . And Ruth will be more possessive than ever."

But that was perhaps why he had done it—to return to the old situation once more. His little plunge into life was over. It had failed. The most that it had done for him was to drag the One-eyed Commander up out of the marshes, but indeed he had sunk back into them again as completely as ever. The other thing that it had done was to show him to himself as a ridiculous old fool, letting his heart go once more, as for years he had not done, throwing it at the feet of a child who was far too young to know what to do with it, who had at the first chance thrown *hers* into the lap of a worthless young Russian. And then at the very thought that Nathalie might suffer, might be hurt, his heart began

167

to beat rapidly, his eyes to burn. What was he doing, flying off to Blackmoor (although only for a week) and leaving her to the tender mercies of her ignorant passion? But let him stay, and what good could he do? She would tell him nothing. He had not the impertinence to ask her for her confidences, nor would his vanity risk a rebuff. That was the way, too, with these modern youngsters. They must find out life for themselves. They insisted on that. It was their own risk, and they were proud to take it.

Therefore when Ruth had suggested Blackmoor for a week he had instantly (and very much to her surprise) agreed. That this was part of her campaign he knew—to drag him back into the old position, to be sure once more of her dominion. . . . Oh, well, let her! It was easier that way after all. Too old a dog for new tricks. Too old a dog. . . .

He would be spared, at least, the sight of Bigges for a week.

"Take care of those books now," he snapped, pushing his spectacles up his nose and frowning. He hated to see Bigges handle books. They seemed to cry out under the damp pressure of those soft hands. Bigges, bent forward over the bag, his thick fat arms swelling in their shirt sleeves, sniffed.

He would adore to kick Bigges' vast behind. He had to turn away, so strong was the temptation.

When he had told Nathalie that they were going, fear had flashed into her eyes.

He wished that he did not remember that. If he thought of it too long it would force him to change his purpose.

All that she had said was:

"Oh, must you?"

"Yes, my dear, I must. Duty."

"I shall miss you terribly."

"Nonsense—you young people never miss anybody."

She had turned away. She had been, he could swear, on the edge of telling him everything. He wanted to go and put his arms around her and kiss the back of her neck, where the hair had been bobbed. But he was shy, damnably shy. He didn't know after all these years how to set about it. And perhaps she would laugh at him—or hate him, thinking of her handsome young Russian.

After all it was only for a week, and these modern children were marvellously wise in their love affairs. . . . But still . . . But still . . .

And she had suddenly turned, flung her arms about him, passionately kissed him, and run from the room.

Oh yes, it was better that he should go. The trouble was that the One-eyed Commander showed no signs whatever of coming with him.

Since the day at the Zoo he had not put in an appearance. There he was still waiting in the rain among the laurels, the bell echoing its peal through the dark house. . . . Well, damn it, if he chose to stay there he should. On the other hand, to go to Blackmoor without any work—those heavy stuffy rooms crammed with hideous furniture, the overgrown, weedy garden, the Wiltshire woods dripping in the rain, Ruth's snobbish visits to Wintersmoon and Farinford and the other big houses, the old dark witch glowering in her stuffy bedchamber, the ancient library crowded with ser-

mons, political pamphlets, and the works of minor eighteenth-century poets——

He was peevish these days. Nothing was right. His peace
here was disturbed. His creative fire had for an instant flick-
ered and died again. His heart had been stirred, but to
what purpose? And he was old. Oh, damnably, damnably
old!

He said farewell to Nathalie in the presence of Ruth and
Mrs. Marriott, who, muffled in black coats and cloaks, resembled an early Victorian crow.

"You won't be lonely—it's only for a week?" he asked.

"Lonely!" Ruth broke in laughing. "Why, everyone in
the house is going to look after her. And you have your own
friends, haven't you, darling?"

Ruth kissed her. "Strange," Hans reflected, "how Ruth
never forgives or forgets anything. That's one for the Westcott evening!"

Nathalie was looking lovely, but strange, with bright
shining eyes and pale cheeks. While she was kissing Hans she
pressed a piece of paper into his hand. He slipped it into
his coat pocket. Kissing him, she clung to him for a moment.

His eyes were misty as he climbed into the car.

Later on, when they had left London, and fields and lanes
enclosed them, noticing that Ma Marriott slept (and in sleep
she was most horrible) and that Ruth was engaged in some
deep spiritual calculations, he took out the paper and read
it.

It was a little letter, and the effect of it upon him was to
cause him, for a moment, to determine to insist upon turning

the car round and to drive back to London again, but the fear of a scene, some dominance that these two women had over him, dread of scandal in which Nathalie herself would be involved, held him down without action.

The letter was:

DARLING UNCLE HANS:

Don't let anyone else read this. Of course you won't. Why must you go away just now? I hate your going away—any time. But especially just now. I wanted to ask you not to, but I hadn't the courage. I'm writing this up in my room when I ought to be dressing for dinner, so I mustn't be long. I'm afraid you're very disappointed with me, and of course you must be. I must seem so stupid to you, and I'm not what you thought me that first night when you came into my room. But you're so clever that when you've got over your disappointment and don't expect anything from me any more perhaps you'll like me again. I've wanted to speak to you so badly all these days, but I haven't had the courage. You've got so many things to think about that you can't waste time on me, but I don't know who to ask advice from.

I've never been in love before, but now I am terribly. It's the Russian who was at the Westcotts' that night. The young one. He says he loves me too, and I think just now he does, but he's Russian, and they are different from us, aren't they? Only I feel I can't live without him. When he isn't there I'm so unhappy, the sort of feeling I've never had before. I'm so sorry about this, I didn't mean it to happen. It just came. You're so wise that you'll tell me when you come back what I ought to do. *Don't tell Aunt Ruth;* she'd think me so silly.

Your loving, *loving* niece,
NATHALIE.

When he had finished this he read it again and then again. A storm had come up and the trees seemed to roll in the rain; the sky was grey with slashes of pale light. The rain tingled against the panes of the car. It was so dark that he couldn't see the faces of his companions.

He sat back wondering what he should do. He knew now that his fancy that he could go back to his old life was illusive. He could never go back. His love for Nathalie—protective, paternal, maternal, *passionately* protective—filled his heart. She was his, and she must come to no harm. She was his and asked him to help her. Every phrase in her letter reproached him. What had he done to help her? Nothing. He had known the danger that she was in and had not moved a finger. He was afraid of trouble, of making a fool of himself, of losing his comfort and security.

She had waited for him to come to her, and he had not come, but she had no word of reproach for him.

He would go back to London by train to-morrow morning. He would get out now, when they passed through Salisbury, and catch an evening train back.

But was that wise? What would Ruth and the old witch think? Better to wait until to-morrow.... But when he went back what could he do? See the young man and ask him his intentions in approved Victorian fashion?

"Young man, your intentions?"

"Oh, go to hell, you silly old man." Did any young people care these days about anything old people said to them? Of course not. But Nathalie cared. She would listen to his advice. But would she obey it? when he advised her never to see the young man again. . . .

But perhaps the young man meant, as the old phrase went, "honourably by her." But was that the kind of world into which Nathalie, so simple, so ignorant, could happily go? That messy, Russian, inchoate world. And the young man—was he of the sort to be faithful to her for a single moment? As good-looking as that, would women leave him for an instant alone? Of course they would not.

Completely miserable, holding Nathalie's letter in his hand, listening to the rain making the darkness vocal, as it seemed to him for hours, he came to no decision. And so they slipped on to Blackmoor.

"Well, here we are," said Ma Marriott, waking from a deep sleep. "What a miserable journey!"

Blackmoor was dry and barren. Neither rain nor storm, frost nor snow could impress its naked ill-temper. Until the day of judgment it would stand, impervious, discontented, and arrogant.

That night, after an ill-cooked dinner and a restless pacing up and down the dark cumbrous library, in his room, before he undressed, he wrote her a letter:

DARLING NATHALIE:

I read your letter at once and wanted to turn and come back immediately. But I don't know whether that is what you would wish, and in any case it's better to wait until to-morrow, because your Aunt Ruth might think it odd and ask questions.

My darling, I'm so bitterly ashamed of myself for not speaking to you sooner. I knew what was happening—don't be afraid. Only I know, Aunt Ruth hasn't the slightest idea, but I was shy of interfering. I've lived so much by myself these last years that I'm more timid than I used to be. It was just wretched cowardice. But don't imagine for a moment that I have ever been disappointed in you. I have loved you more every day, but I have thought that perhaps you wouldn't want an old man like me interfering in your affairs. That was my mistake as I see now. But never doubt me. I will be at your side, as I promised you, for anything or everything.

I don't know what to say at the moment except that I would be happy if you would let things be as they are until I come back. But the worst of love is that it won't stand still. I know that well enough.

Only, you see, the young man is something of a mystery to us both at present, isn't he? I see from your letter that you think so too. Although he is young, he knows probably more about love than you do, and, although he may wish all that is good for you quite sincerely, what *he* thinks good for you may not be quite the things that you and I would wish.

I put all this very clumsily, I know; you must forgive my inexperience. But I trust you. I know you are wise and believe that however strong our desires may be, there are things that are unworthy of us. I'm not preaching when I say that. It is sound practical advice, and although I've made countless mistakes in my own life and done numberless silly things, I've never really had any doubt of there being always a fine thing to do if one's got enough courage.

Then for a woman these things are more dangerous than for a man, even in these days.

You are very young, with a splendid life in front of you, and you don't want to start it with a bad mistake.

If I seem to have been preaching it's only because I love you so much. Preaching is not really my rôle, you know, and if you saw what a mess I've made in many ways of my own life you'd wonder how I had the impertinence to offer advice to anyone else.

Send me a wire at once if you want me. In any case I shall return in a day or two, and then we will see this through together. I shall be thinking about you all the time.　　　　Your most loving uncle,

　　　　　　　　　　　　　　　　　　　HANS.

How insufficient and unsatisfactory, and yet, as he folded the paper and pushed it, almost savagely, into the envelope, it was as though his very heart went with it into the confined space. What an insufficient letter, and how dark the room! Dark and creeping with draughts, the rain crawling about the windows, two large sham Indian vases in bright yellow

and black that had been the fashion about 1850, bulging
their corpulent sides at him, a wheezy clock, a flapping
blind, a dark, dark house.

Nathalie, Nathalie, Nathalie. . . . He was drawn back. He
was at her side. She was more to him than all the books,
than all the comfort the world had ever contained.

He got up from the chair, stretched himself like an old
dog, and started to undress. He shivered. Ugh! how cold it
was. Why had he not asked to have a fire in his bedroom?
Why always in this house did he feel as though he were a
child, in possible disgrace at any moment, afraid to ask for
a fire?

There slipped into his mind lines of which he had not
thought for many a year. But his memory was wonderful.
Almost as good as Macaulay's, he used to say, boastfully, to
Galleon, when Galleon cried out in his vibrant fashion:

"I can't remember a damned thing . . . hang it, why can't
I?" and Galleon was there in the room, astride that shabby
rug with the faded flowers, his head up, his eyes smiling,
his mouth indignant; and Hans, turning and mockingly defiant as though he saw him there, murmured to that adored
ghost the words (murmured, perhaps, to himself by old Ambrose Phillips, deserting his warm but inattentive heaven to
persuade even one listening mortal on this rainy, frowning
earth):

> "The vast Leviathan wants room to play,
> And spout his Waters in the Face of Day;
> The starving Wolves along the main sea prowl
> And to the Moon in Icy Valleys howl;

> O'er many a shining League the level Main
> Here spreads itself into a glassy Plain—
> There solid Billows of enormous Size,
> Alpes of green Ice, in wild Disorder rise.

"Alpes of green Ice, in wild Disorder rise," he repeated. "Damn good. . . . Damn good."

And old Galleon cried back to him:

"And later on—don't you remember?

> "Soon as the silent Shades of Night withdrew,
> The ruddy Morn disclosed at once to view
> The Face of Nature in a rich Disguise,
> And brighten'd ev'ry Object to my Eyes,
> For every Shrub, and every Blade of grass,
> And ev'ry pointed Thorn, seemed wrought in glass.
> In Pearls and Rubies rich the Hawthorns show,
> While thro' the Ice the Crimson Berries glow.
> The thick-sprung Reeds, which wat'ry marshes yield,
> Seem polished Lances in a hostile Field."

"And you say you can't remember anything, you old liar!" Hans cries.

"Ah, but," the ruddy ghost returns, "I can *now!* I've a pull over you now, Hans, my friend!"

And the fluttering shadow of poor Ambrose, thin veil against dripping pane, chuckles, because he is once more remembered, and far out across all the storm-swept sky calls triumphantly:

"They have me yet! They have me yet!"

While Hans, stepping forward that he may touch once again that old friendly arm, repeats:

> "In Pearls and Rubies rich the Hawthorns show,
> While thro' the Ice the Crimson Berries glow. . . ."

The door opened and there came in someone far indeed from ghostly—Ruth.

He turned, surprised and defeated. The ghosts were fled.

She sat down in the large, hideous armchair near the fireplace, smiled up at him, took him at once in charge, dressed him in a sailor suit, and told him he should have jam for tea if he were good. She did not, however, he could see it lurking in her eyes, forget altogether the possibility of a suddenly returning maturity.

"Well, Hans, isn't it jolly now that we're here?"

He blinked at her, pulling up his trousers with a sort of defensive movement. He had been about to throw them off before she came in. Now they were on for ever.

"Jolly?" That seemed the very last word to use.

"Yes. I don't know if you feel about this old place as I do. Oh, I know it's old-fashioned and untidy, but the moment I get back to it I'm at peace. I feel as though I'd got you again, that we belong to one another once more, just as we used to do, and—oh, you don't know how happy that makes me!"

"Got me again . . . belong to one another!" He seemed to be able to do nothing but repeat her words parrot-like. "But of course—when haven't you got me?"

She jumped up with a movement, in its intensity and impetuosity, sharply unlike her. She went to him, came close to him, so that her breast pressed against the hard glossy front of his shirt, laid her cheek against his, murmured:

"Yes . . . I was so happy when you said you'd come down here. I've been feeling these last weeks that I was losing you . . . that you didn't want me any more . . . and . . . I couldn't bear it."

She turned, ever so slightly, her warm arm was against his collarless neck, she pressed her lips on his. He put his arm around her to hold her and stood there—rigid.

She was all about him. The scent that belonged so especially to her, the warm softness of her arm, his hand pressed into the deep, yielding, gentle strength of her side. Oh, he was old! damnably, damnably old! He felt only infinite weariness, a longing to yawn, a shiver of age and awkwardness, shyness and ennui that trembled through his soul.

And she knew at once that that was what he felt. She stayed for a moment, then withdrew.

"Aren't you glad we've come? Isn't it time after all these ages in London that we were alone together again?"

You could always touch his heart, even though you touched many other things at the same moment.

He felt what he so rarely felt about her, pathos, loneliness, something unassisted and unsupported.

He smiled at her with that odd smile that she had known so long, but never understood, a smile, roguish, affectionate, and a little malicious.

"I'm glad if this place makes you happy, my dear. Of course I'm glad. I love you to be happy, you know that I do. As to the place——"

"Oh, I know it's old-fashioned and filled with ugly things. But Mother likes them. They remind her of the days when she was happy. Surely you can put up with them for a little while?"

"My dear, have I said anything against——?"

"No, only, of course, I know what you feel. One can tell, if it's only the way you've stuck up your precious Manet there on the dressing table. Besides, I think them awful myself as far as that goes. What I value is our having some time together to ourselves. Will you be able to stand a fortnight of it, do you think? Do say you will. It will make me so happy. I haven't, as a matter of fact, been awfully well lately, although I've said nothing about it. I need some quiet here—"and she ended, dropping her voice ever so slightly, "a fortnight with you."

A fortnight? A fortnight here in this horrible house with that horrible old woman pervading every corner of it? A fortnight alone with Ruth? . . . And Nathalie? Nathalie alone. . . .

He steadied himself. He realized how vast a distance had he and Ruth already travelled that she should be compelled to put forward this elaborate pleading and persuasion. Three months ago she would have made her statement, her cheerful, determined resolve: "I think we'll be here a fortnight or so, Hans; it's jolly to be by ourselves for a little"— and he would at once have submitted, out of laziness, indifference, hatred of argument.

He smiled at her, scratching his head and yawning a little—"Ugh, I'm sleepy. . . . A fortnight? That's as it may be. Possibly I shall have to run up to town for a night or so and then come back. You won't mind that?"

"Now, Hans, that's precisely what I don't want you to do. What's the good of our being down here at all, if you're breaking into it all the time? Besides, whatever have you got to run up to town for? Is it Nathalie you're thinking of?"

"No, why should it be? Modern girls don't want looking after. But there are some people I have to see. One or two picture-shows. I'm not ready to give up the ghost entirely, you know, darling."

The moment that he had said it he knew what a mistake he had made. He cursed himself for a silly blind old fool. He turned, moving towards her. But the mischief was done.

"Well," she said dimly, "that's not exactly compliment-ary to me. I'm not dead either, you know—not by a very long way. Good-night. Think over it. See if you can't oblige me."

She kissed him very lightly on the cheek and went.

The following day was one of the most miserable and con-fusing of his life. New emotions—or rather emotions that in the dark ages of the past he had known, but since had lost all track of—returned and swept in upon him in baffling, be-wildering succession. All morning he shut himself away in the dark, dim library, staring at the funereal rows of faded calf— Withering on *British Plants* (there's a name for a botanist!), Lister's *Life of Clarendon*, Hampton's *Polybius*—seeing them, not seeing them, feeling the rheumatic twitch in his leg, thinking of food and drink, religion, astronomy, and the thin long legs of beautiful women—not thinking of any of these things—and always, always this increasing knowl-edge that he was in the hands of some power that soon, un-less he pulled himself together, would swing him off his feet, hurl him into the air and bring him down, a thousand

miles away in mid-ocean somewhere, with a devastating
ruinous splash.

But pull himself together? There was nothing to pull.
"Is there?" he enquired of Polybius. And Polybius, with an
air of infinite boredom, answered, "Nothing."

He wanted Nathalie. "Yes," he assured Bingley's *Animal
Biography*, "I want Nathalie."

"Well, go after her then," said Bingley.

"But I'm an old man of seventy. Tired and bored."

"Then don't go after her," said Bingley.

No hope there. Moreover, it wasn't Nathalie that he
wanted. It was rather to be assured of her happiness and her
safety. Yes, her safety. What was happiness to her? Even
now, perhaps, she had taken some rash step. . . . At one
moment, looking fixedly into the blind, stony eyes of a very
bad bust of Cicero, he decided that he would tell Ruth
everything. Everything? What was everything?

Simply that he was fond of his niece and that *she* was
fond of a Russian young man, who wasn't to be trusted. And
at once Cicero, a very wise man, showed him coldly (not at
all out of friendship, but simply because he flattered himself
on his ability to give good advice), showed him how foolish
that would be. Tell Ruth about Nathalie? Nathalie would be
dismissed immediately and for ever. Deliver Nathalie's secret
to Ruth's tender keeping? The ruthlessness of the hungry
tiger is not to be compared with the ruthlessness of a woman
whose vanity is unexpectedly wounded and whose sense of
possession is so threatened.

No, no, no—a thousand times no.

In the afternoon he took Ruth for a walk. In the evening there took place one of the really amazing interviews of his life.

The walk was quiet and amiable and sham. Neither alluded to anything of importance. They walked through a pale misted country with pale shadow moving behind pale shadow. They climbed crooked and shadowy lanes to an open and shadowy down. Sheep could be heard and not seen; silver clouds promised the coming of the sun, but no sun came. There was no air, but a waiting suspended hush.

Ruth was gay and amusing and very friendly, so Hans was gay and friendly too. But he had never in all their married life felt so far away from her as to-day. He was miserable and alone. The life of the last ten years—easy, slothful, dying—was gone, and no other life had as yet taken its place. Beneath her talk he saw that she was deeply disturbed and determinedly resolved.

The sense of an impending talk excited her—it depressed him like a bad dream. He had not for ten years had a quarrel or dispute with anyone.

Now he knew that he was in for a series of contests. He was. He encountered the first of them that evening.

Mrs. Marriott did not, as in London, confine herself to her own room. She made the whole of Blackmoor hers. She was indeed as restless here as she was motionless in Regent's Park. She could be felt rather than seen wandering from room to room, her long black dress trailing after her with a murmurous, ominous whisper.

Her favourite room was the drawing-room, a long dingy room papered in dark faded red and littered with little tables and chairs as though it were a restaurant. On these tables there were innumerable photographs. Long thin pinched windows looked out with a kind of dusty despair upon unkept lawns and woods in whose enclosures the sun was never seen to shine.

She would move from chair to chair in this room, helping herself with a thick ebony cane. Once and again she would sit down at a piano much neglected and out of tune, strike some screaming notes, listen with twisted head to their discordances and then move again from chair to chair.

This was her place, her fortress. It had belonged to her father and her father's father. No one could change a thing in it without her wish. Here she was dingy and melodramatic queen.

Hans coming in after his walk with Ruth, and finding her there, was thoroughly conscious of her melodrama. She was sitting, a large photograph album on her lap, a dirty yellow sky against which the trees were humped in shadow behind her.

A lamp covered with a hideous crimson shade threw light over her, leaving the rest of the long room in obscurity.

As soon as he saw her he would have withdrawn. He was in no mood for a conversation with the old woman, but she called to him to stop.

"I hope you will give me three minutes, Hans," she said.

He realized at once that she was in a raging temper. He

had not seen one of her tempers for at least five years, but he instantly now, at the tone of her voice, recalled them (visualizing them, as he stood there, in a kind of whirling rainstorm, feathers flying and pieces of calico and sticks and stones, chickens running shrieking for shelter, and all the trees bent wildly by the wind).

He knew well that she hated to lose her temper, that the loss of it troubled her vanity and diminished her power. He had thought that with her fading physical strength her rage, also, was ebbing.

He was to learn in the following ten minutes that he was wrong.

"Certainly," he said, threading his way through the little tables and coming over to her. But he did not, as he generally did, smile and indulge her. His voice was stern. He had neither time nor patience for her tantrums.

"So," she began looking up at him, her fingers tightening about the knob of her stick, "you have told Ruth that staying with her here is like being buried alive. A pretty thing for Ruth to feel after she has given up her life to you, and has come down here only because she thought you were tired and needed a change."

(A pretty thing! A pretty thing! something repeated inside him—who wants this pretty thing?)

He answered her quietly: "I said nothing of the kind to Ruth. She asked me whether I would mind being here for a fortnight, and I said that that was for her to decide, that I might have to be in London for a few days, but that could easily be managed."

Mrs. Marriott, shaking with anger, plunged into the cataract.

"Look here, Hans Frost . . . I'll tell you . . . I'll let you know . . . I've been longing to for years." Here she broke for a moment into a breathless, convulsed coughing. There was an awful moment when, the coughing subdued, but her breath not yet returned, she looked at him with a cold, apprehensive stare, as though some other person inside her seized its opportunity and looked out of the window, someone quite different, a stranger; someone from the cellar who knew not Hans, was concerned with no private quarrels, but was busy day and night digging for its own private treasure. The creature vanished. Mrs. Marriott was once more in full control. "For years I've been longing to tell you what I think of you—you with your conceited arrogance, you thinking yourself so grand, because of your little books and the rest of it. Books! Why, everyone can write books these days. Schoolgirls write them, little boys at college, and books as good as yours, I'm sure. And who's made your reputation for you? You think it's your books that have done it, but I tell you, you wouldn't be anywhere at all if it weren't for Ruth. You think you've been so fine all these years, but I tell you, you haven't done a thing. If you hadn't married Ruth, you'd be nobody. You think people like your books, but I can tell you there are thousands of people can't read a word of them. I can't myself, for the matter of that, and I'm no fool. Tiresome, silly stuff. But Ruth's worked like a slave just because she's loved you. She's done everything, arranged everything, asked the right people. And you,

you've just sat back and been so pleased with yourself and thought what a grand man you are, and now when you're old and ought to know better, you tell Ruth that being with her is like being buried, and you think you'll run back to town and be a gay young man again, and take your pretty young niece about. Oh, yes! I know all about it! There isn't much goes on that I don't see. . . . But there's plenty goes on you don't see, yes, with all your cleverness. You think you're a grand one, but I know how they laugh at you behind your back, with all your conceit and the rest of it. Ruth, the finest wife a man ever had, worth a hundred of you; and you treat her, you treat her——"

Her coughing once more had its triumph. She was suddenly an old broken woman, a bag of shaking bones. He had to go to her and arrange her in her chair, pick up her stick for her; she choked, gasped, sat up straight again, stammered out—"And now you know," then leaned her head back, glaring at him.

"Yes, I know." He answered her very seriously. He knew that the time for chaff had gone by. There was justice in what she had said. She was defending her young, and through all the vibration of her anger, there was the truth of his coming disloyalty to Ruth. This old woman had scented it in the air, and by her prophetic cry she convinced him that the crisis had arrived.

"You are right," he said quietly. "I am, I've no doubt, a ridiculous old man. So are we all, all ridiculous old men. That is neither my fault nor yours. But what is my fault, perhaps, is that I want a holiday. We both want one, away from one another. You say that she has done everything for me. I know that she has. That's why I want to get away for a little."

The yellow had faded from the sky. The room was thickening with dusk. He could scarcely see her face. Her voice came out of the shadow.

"Why should you have a holiday if Ruth wants you to stay? She's spent the best years of her life in giving you what you want. Why shouldn't you give her what she wants for a change?"

"She's had me," he answered wearily, hating the place, the scene, the close, stuffy air, the vindictive old woman, with a physical nausea, "for years. Now it's time we were apart for a little."

Mrs. Marriott rose from her chair. She came towards him. He thought for an odd, fantastic moment that she was going to strike him with her stick. He stood his ground, his head up, his legs wide planted. But she only said, as she passed him to the door: "I know what you want. . . . You want to flirt with your beautiful young niece. . . . I have my daughter's happiness to fight for. . . .

"Look out!"

The last two words which she flung out of the dusky end of the room had the true melodramatic ring, but they seemed oddly to be spoken by some other voice, from the far side of the door, a warning to him that he must regard.

"Look out!" Ah, he would look out all right, that is if he could keep awake. The little battle had tired him extraordinarily. He almost tumbled into the stuffy, sticky, velvet-covered armchair, leaning his head back, and at the touch feeling as though jammy, dusky fingers reached out and caught him. What a loathsome old woman! What a vile house! He had always hated it—hated it as when once, as a little boy, playing hide-and-seek in an old house, he had shut himself into a cupboard, been forgotten, closed the doors and then been unable to open them again.

Oh! the agony of that, the close smell of pitch pine and moth balls, the strangling, suffocating terror of the doors that would not open!

He was pushing with his hands, his knees, his feet! Oh, suppose it were never to open again! Suppose that that vile old woman had closed it on the other side, was waiting there maliciously smiling to hear his strangling cries! He must get out! . . . He must get out!

He jumped from his chair, stood there blinking. Someone had come in. Someone had placed a lamp on the table and was speaking to him. He blinked again. It was Ruth.

"Hans, Mother has just been here, bothering you. I know she has. What has she been saying?"

He was still too stupidly confused. He could only stand there blinking at her.

"Hans, I must know what happened. What did Mother say to you?"

He, as though to steady himself and bring himself safely back out of that other world into this one, put his hand on her shoulder.

"Why, my dear? Why, nothing." He could feel that she was trembling.

"It's hateful. You won't tell me anything, and Mother won't either. And yet I'm the one chiefly concerned. I will know. You and Mother have had a row—a bad one. She's shaking all over and muttering to herself. What's it all been about? I insist on your telling me."

He was now thoroughly awake again, although Ruth in the soft, shaded lamplight gave him the impression of something immaterial and, unfortunately, unimportant. And yet she *was* important—for herself, for him, for all of them. And yet he could not take her seriously. She was evanescent, like water poured from a bottle, the kind of glistening shower that you get when you are using your watering-can on a sunny day. And as he felt her evanescence his own firmness of purpose grew.

"I was simply telling your mother, my dear, that I thought the time had come for us to be apart a little—for us both to take a holiday."

"So it's come to that, has it?" she murmured.

"My dear, it's come to nothing except what it always comes to, once and again, with all married people. We haven't separated for years. It isn't good for either of us."

She began to give little hysterical, breathless sobs. "It isn't good enough for you, you mean. . . . Oh, I know! . . . It isn't as though I haven't seen—and Mother's seen too. I know when the change began. . . . I know what you want. . . . I know, I know. . . . But you shan't have it, do you hear? You shan't have it! You shan't have it!"

She was crying and beating the floor with her foot. He was suddenly very exasperated. Tired and sick of the whole thing. He wanted to beat her, to crumple her up and throw her out of the window, and with her the whole race of women—ridiculous, play-acting, unscrupulous, unreal! . . .

"Well, you can take it or leave it," he shouted back at her. "I loathe this house and everything in it. I won't stay in it another twenty-four hours. I'll go up to town to-morrow morning."

He pushed past her, feeling like a naughty but suddenly liberated schoolboy, who, bent over the schoolmaster's knee, has broken free and run for his life.

He even, as he trotted up the dark stairs to his room, repeated to himself, "To-morrow morning! Yes! To-morrow morning! I'm damned if I stay here another day!"

CHAPTER VII

Return

HANS jumped out of the car, let himself in with his key, and stood in the hall looking about him as though he were seeing it for the first time. The house was silent and bathed in sunshine. The chauffeur came quietly past him and then vanished up the stairs. Not a sound. Not a creature.

How long was it since he had been alone in the house like this? Oh, but years and years! Not a sound. Not a creature. The sunshine lay in pools and splashes of colour on the gleaming boards and the dark rugs. The deep mezzotints of the eighteenth-century ladies and gentlemen lay back on the pale, creamy walls with a gesture of proud resignation. He had not noticed them for years. Not a sound in the house. He did not move; the luxury of this was so great. And they would not return for several days. The car would go back to-night. To-day at least he would have the glorious free afternoon, the magnificent liberated evening. He sighed deeply. Yes, this was wonderful.

There was a sound on the stairs. Looking up he saw that Martha was coming down. She had started her descent in her usual, casual, indifferent fashion, slowly, with grand superiority. She saw him. She stopped. Then, most miraculous of dogs, seeing that he had his finger on his lip, she checked her shrill bark of welcome, but forgetting everything now, save her eagerness to welcome him, hurriedly pattered across the hall, and was leaping up at him, pushing at his trousers with her short legs, shoving her cold, long nose into the cup of his hand, biting in an extravagance of joy and pleasure his fingers, licking the thick gold signet ring that was for her one of his especial properties, and especially her own affair.

He sat down, there and then, on the little chair under the portrait of Madame de Sévigné (whose letters were surely less brilliant than people supposed them), took Martha into his lap, and stroked the sleek warm head with a luxury of pleasure. She gave a little humming sigh of pleasure, laid her head on his arm, and fell instantly asleep. He sat on basking in the sun. The clocks about the house struck the hour; his eye wandered from rug to rug, from picture to picture. He nodded his head as though to say: "Yes, I've never seen any of you before. I apologize. I won't forget you again."

At last he rose. The library was demanding him. He got up slowly, stood Martha (who had doubtless been dreaming glories of putting other dogs in their places) on her legs, and savouring every moment of his independence, mounted the stairs.

The sunlight, the silence went with him. Why should not life be always like this? Even as he turned the last stair it seemed to him that the One-eyed Commander came out to meet him. Yes, that was how he would be inside the house now, standing, listening, his great head erect, and then calling in a voice that rang like a gong against the walls of the passages, a name. . . . What name? . . .

He pushed open the library door. This room also was bathed in sunshine, but someone was here. Bigges was here. Bigges, in his shirt sleeves, and an apron round his stout waist, a feather duster in his hand, was moving about. Even as Hans looked in, Bigges had picked up the pencil drawing by Grantby Stein (considered by most to be the best drawing of Hans), and looking at it held at a distance in his red fist. distinctly and clearly uttered: "Pah!"

"Well, Bigges," said Hans.

Bigges wheeled round. First he carefully replaced the drawing on the table, then he wiped his mouth with the back of his hand, then gasping a little like a strangling fish, he stood there, a slow, purple shadow creeping into his cheeks and nose.

"So it's 'Pah', is it, Bigges?" Hans said, coming forward and smiling. "I've long suspected that it was. Please forgive me for overhearing your confidences. I didn't know that anyone was here."

Bigges gulped, rubbed his mouth once again with the back of his hand, then started slowly towards the door.

"Tell me," said Hans, "why it is 'Pah.' As man to man." Bigges straightened himself.

"I beg your pardon, sir . . . I was ignorant of your return."

"Of course you were. You've committed no crime. Quite the contrary. We can speak honestly to one another. Tell me what you've got against me."

"It's what you've got against *me*, sir. These last weeks I've been irritating you something terrible. Everything I've done is wrong. You've been despising me at every turn. It isn't human not to mind, sir. I do my best. Certainly I do. I try my 'ardest, yet you can't bear the sight of me.'

"Why do you think it is, Bigges?" Hans asked.

"I can't say, sir. I've thought and thought. Of course you're not like other gentlemen, sir. You can't be expected to be, but it's hard to be mocked at, morning, noon, and night. I feel it, I can tell you, sir."

"Then why don't you give notice? You're so good a butler that you could get an excellent place in half an hour."

"So I could, sir, but until you took against me, sir, this was the best place I've ever been in. And I've been hoping it would pass, your being irritated by me, so to speak."

"Have I changed, then, in the last month or two?"

"Yes, sir, you have. Everyone's noticed it."

Hans spoke gravely. "You must forgive me, Bigges. I didn't know that I was behaving so badly. Your mistress appreciates you highly, you're a perfect servant. I'm a cross, malicious, selfish old man. When you're seventy, you'll either be an angel or a pig. For your own sake I hope you'll be an angel—for the sake of those who live with you I don't know—the angels are sometimes harder to live with. And remember—everyone is hard to live with. Everyone. The only hope is to be a bearded hermit, and even that state they say has its drawbacks. . . . I apologize, Bigges. That you do irritate me there's no denying. That it isn't your own fault is also true. If you find me too impossible, just tell me, and I dare say I can go away somewhere. . . . Is Miss Nathalie in?"

"Yes, sir. In her room, sir."

"Would you let her know that I'm here and would like to see her?"

Bigges withdrew, carefully, as though eggshells strewed the carpet. Hans sat down in the big armchair simply to revel in the feel of it. On the reading stand at his side was the old Balzac book, closed but waiting, he was sure, with one old eye upon him until he should turn to open it. Martha had lain down at his feet, her head on his shoe, as was the eternal custom. The afternoon sun stroked the book-shelves tenderly . . . blessing Lord Macaulay, condoling with Mr. Carlyle on his indigestion, and showing a dignified sympathy with Mr. Pope's eight volumes of Letters. The Manet was not yet unpacked, but soon it would be there. Comfort and sincerity everywhere. But he well knew what it was for which he waited. He was leaning forward listen-ing, the smile of anticipation on his lips. The door burst open. She ran to him. She flung herself into his arms. His lips were on her cheeks, his hands caressed her hair. He felt her heart beat against his. He knew now how deeply he loved her, and that he must never, never lose her again.

"You're back! . . . but . . . it's marvellous—wonderful. . . I never dreamt . . . Why are you back? What made you? Oh, I'm so glad! All night I've been awake, missing you so. After your letter this morning I couldn't be without you. . . . I was thinking I might go by train and meet you somewhere. This is wonderful—like a dream. When Bigges came in I couldn't believe it. I said 'Bigges, it isn't true.' Why, for half a minute I quite liked him—and you've come back all alone. When's Aunt Ruth coming? This evening by the train? Why didn't she come with you?"

She waited, however, for no explanation, but, dragging a cushion from another chair, sat on it between his knees, leaning her head back against his waistcoat, his hands resting on her shoulders. Martha, dispossessed, waddled to the centre of the room, where she stretched herself sighing, her eyes reproachfully on her master.

He sat there knowing that one of the great moments had come. Was this too illusion? And there swept in upon him other moments, coming to him in an instant of time, presenting themselves with "We are not illusion. We are more real than ever before."

His first hearing of "Don Giovanni" in the little red and gold theatre in Munich, bathing at Gassirtz, reading *The Rape of the Lock* on a summer evening in the hay-scented fields in Watendlath; the evening when Galleon and he had known that they loved one another, saying nothing personal, walking back through Leicester Square and Piccadilly under the stars, and piling up enthusiasm for Goethe and Jean Paul. A late night in a hotel on the lake at Vevey, finishing *Goliath*, knowing it was good in his heart, a great mixture of sadness and triumph, the first time that he kissed Ruth walking home on a shining, snowy, star-lit evening in the Tyrol; his first married night, lying awake at her side, listening to the striking of the clocks, the murmur and suction of the sea, staring into the grey room, she sleeping, his head between her breasts—and vague, timeless

memories, the full moon above a rushing tide skimming
onto a silver beach; great moments of reading, of pictures,
of music—*Karamazov;* a volume of Marlowe; *Quixote* for the
first time in Spanish; Beddoes' *Jest Book;* the first "Meis-
tersinger"; César Franck somewhere; a room in the Luxem-
bourg, a little room with only a Cézanne, a Manet, a Renoir.
. . . And now another moment eternally captured. Whatever
might come, sickness, betrayal, loneliness, at the last death
(and all these were duly approaching him now swiftly),
nothing could rob him of this moment, of the anxiousness of
this love that had, it seemed, no baseness, no meanness, no
rapacity, but a purity and a generosity that were the best
gift of his old age. It was as though he could now cry out
to all the sensual, vulgar betrayals of his spirit by his
body. . . . "I have had to pass your way to come to this.
I regret nothing."

"I gave Bigges the surprise of his young life. He was
murmuring 'Pah' to that drawing of me, as I stood in the
doorway. It was mean to overhear him. I have been unjust
to Bigges. I dislike him a little less now that I know his
dislike of myself."

"And we're all alone in the house?"

"Quite alone."

"For how long?"

"I don't know. Two or three days perhaps."

"Won't Aunt Ruth be angry?"

"No, my dear, why should she be?" That was a lie. Ruth
was furious. Would continue to be furious, and would dis-

cover some means of effectively showing her fury. It was of no use to pretend that this was not a crisis. It was a crisis —one of the most serious of his life. He was amazed at the feeling of vigour that this knowledge gave him. His muscles seemed to swell beneath his sleeves. He could run five hundred miles (those young men running at dusk up Portland Place with white shorts, motor-cars hooting on every side of them).

"And now tell me about your young man," he said.

"I haven't seen him. Not since I went with Millie Westcott to the Russian party. I swore that I wouldn't, until you came back. He's been writing every day," she added.

"Has he asked you to marry him?"

"Yes. He wants us to marry at once. He says that he doesn't think marriage important, but that if I care about it he cares too! Marriage is important, Uncle Hans, isn't it? Still, in spite of being modern."

"Yes." Hans drew her closer to him as though to guard her. "Yes, it's important, my dear. Has he got any money?"

"Not very much. He's making three hundred a year and he's got debts and he helps other Russians. But I can work. There are lots of things I could do."

"Are there? What, for instance?"

"I could be a secretary or go on the stage or be a companion to an old lady."

"I see. But you and he wouldn't be much together that way."

"Oh, it would be only for a time. Besides, married people are better when they aren't together all the while."

"Perhaps they are and perhaps they aren't. It depends. And can you trust him not to fall in love with other women, and would you mind if he did?"

He felt a little tremor run through her body.

She was silent, then answered slowly: "When I am with him I can trust him, but when I am away——"

He laid his hand on hers.

"Why is that, do you think? Is it because you don't know him enough yet, or is it because there is something in his character—something that will always be there?"

She turned her body round, that she might look into his face.

"How do I know? How can I tell? I'm in love with him— and he's Russian. And he doesn't think physical fidelity very important—perhaps it isn't."

She sighed.

"Oh, doesn't he? Anyway, a lot you know about physical fidelity. That's the trouble with you modern children. You use these phrases like counters to play a game with. The game's all right *as* a game, but when suddenly it isn't a game any longer the counters can spring into life on their own. I've a kind of idea that physical infidelity doesn't matter, but the point is that it's mixed up with so many other things that do matter. Blowing your nose would be important if every time you did it you were liable to knock someone else's life to pieces. . . . Do you think," he went on rather shyly, "that I might go and see your young man and have a talk with him? I promise I wouldn't preach as I've just been doing to you. It isn't really my habit. I'd like to have a talk with him. I got no idea of him the other evening."

"Yes, of course. . . . It would be sweet of you." She leaned up, put her arms round his neck, kissed him, then settling down she went on more gravely: "But I want to say one thing. I do hope you won't be hurt. It's difficult. Uncle Hans, I don't want you to go on bothering about Vladimir and me. Of course, it's wonderful to have your help, and I didn't know how I was ever going to wait until you came back, but all the same I'm so afraid you're going to make yourself unhappy over this, or that it will bring you some trouble. I know that I'm young and inexperienced and haven't been anywhere yet, but I *do* understand how it all is. I'm not going to be so foolish. . . . Besides it wouldn't be good for Vladimir if I were. And whatever happens to us, it will make it all twice as bad if anything happens to you."

"Happens to *me!*" he broke in, laughing. "Why, what *can* happen to me?"

"Oh, a lot of things," she answered gravely. "You were all settled in and comfortable before I came along—with your books and your work and your friends and Aunt Ruth. Nothing could touch you, could it? And now already I've broken it all up. I didn't mean to, but I loved you from the first moment I saw you. I couldn't help myself. But I never knew that you'd care so much, and why should you? You'll only make yourself unhappy, and then I shall be twice as unhappy as I would be otherwise."

He looked out beyond her, to the long high room over which the dusk was now creeping. To the long rows of books, seeming now in his close contact with her so dead and far away. . . . Life and letters—letters and life. How could he ever have doubted as to which was the more important?

"Happiness?" he answered slowly. "This happiness and safety you want me to have? My dear, I've never been very happy except at moments. . . . Who is? Wouldn't it be all wrong if one were? But I was dying, and a touch of your hand on my forehead saved me. Is that very sentimental? Well, let it be. I don't care a damn. I was sinking into a nice cozy coma; I hadn't actively cared for anybody for years. Oh! I don't mean your aunt. Marriage is something different. For one lucky man in a hundred it's exciting to the very end, and if there are children it's alive anyway. But if there aren't any children—well, it's better than being single, that's the best you can say. Your aunt's been too good to me all these years—and the world's been too good to me too. If I'd been poor all my life, read nothing, only a few fine things, kept away from the literary life, broken my head and my heart—ah, then, I'd have written a book! Just one—the book of my dreams. One book that all my life I've been going to write—yes, so I fancy. But maybe not—you can live like Flaubert or you can live like Borrow. You can die like Keats or survive to be a pompous old ass like Tennyson. One has precious little to do with it. But I know that I've missed all my life the one thing I wanted to do, and if you hadn't come I'd have perished like a pig in a stye."

He drew himself up in his chair. "Not that I pity myself. I'm an ass like the rest, but I've had my good moments and shall have more yet. Life's marvellous, more and more marvellous the older you get. It's luck enough for any man to have tasted a bit of it. Even when I'm with your grandmother I'm aware of that. I hate your grandmother, my dear. God forgive me. She's a bad old woman and ought to have been cremated years ago. Yes, don't you reproach yourself. You are giving me the best thing I've had since I fell in love with your aunt. You are indeed."

She sprang up, rested a hand on his shoulder, stood there facing the dark rich room trembling under the light of the flickering fire. "There, that's all right. We'll go along together whatever happens. But what you've said has encouraged me to take all the risks. If you feel like that, isn't it right that I should? I'll never love anyone so much as Vladimir again. Never, never. And isn't it better I should have all that to look back on when I'm old? Even if I do love someone later on I won't be as young then as I am now. It won't be the first time. It won't be as exciting. . . ."

"Yes," he broke in, "but remember you can do something now that will spoil your whole life. I mean that. There are things I've done that I'd give everything now never to have done—the experience I won wasn't worth the things I did. Love your young man, but keep it fine. Don't let it be mean and furtive and shabby. There is something in us that can be damaged, almost irreparably. I know that now. It's taken me all my life to have it. . . ."

He broke off. Although the door was closed he had caught a sound. He turned—frowning.

"I thought . . . It can't be . . ." The door opened, and Ruth came in.

She stayed in the doorway and nodded to him. She was furred to the chin, and her eyes shone; her cheeks glowed under the little silver fur hat, over the silver fur collar.

"Now, aren't you surprised? You were quite right. The place was too beastly. Mother and I both discovered it the moment you were gone. If you must go down in a day or two, as you say, you can go alone. I won't trust it again. . . . I couldn't even wait for the car to come back and fetch us. Hallo, darling" (this to Nathalie), "how cozy you both look; I'll be down for some tea in a moment. Bigges shall bring it here."

She smiled at them both, a dazzling, beautiful smile. She was gone, and silence swept in, but now over how different a shore!

He turned to her, staring past her to the dark world on the other side of the window-frame.

"Now I'm going to catch it!" Nathalie cried, and turned almost running to leave the room. But he caught her by the shoulder. He could feel her whole body tremble.

"What do you mean?" he asked.

"Oh, Aunt Ruth! Can't you see? Didn't you watch her face? And why has she come back, do you think? How she hates me! Oh, I wish—I wish I'd never come!"

And this time she did break free of him, leaving him to a room that seemed to echo with thunder.

He sat down again. He'd got to think this out. He'd got to think out a thousand things! What a whirl of violence women could stir up when they pleased. Women! He suddenly, in a flash of lightning revelation, discovered that he knew nothing whatever about them, he who had been writing of them and for them all his days.

Martha, to whom this had always been apparent, settled down once more at his feet, her head on his shoe.

But Nathalie should not suffer. Whatever else the outcome, Nathalie, the darling, shall be safe.

Meanwhile—let him admit it—he was frightened, frightened of the next event, frightened of the noises and skirmishes, frightened, above all, of Ruth.

CHAPTER VIII

Nathalie-at-Arms

THEY had a horrible dinner that evening, the three of them, with Bigges in solemn attendance.

The silver shone, the flowers gleamed, thunder rumbled through the vegetables. Nathalie, helping herself to cauliflower (which, from her childhood, she had detested), realized that Uncle Hans was frightened. He was being terribly friendly to Aunt Ruth—"Yes," he was saying, "I quite agree with you. Egypt is too far, and nowhere nearer is really warm that month."

Nathalie trembled. What had she done? Here these two had been with their beautiful life so secure and well arranged, carpets nailed tightly to the floor, curtains hung strongly on their rings, doors closing without a murmur; and she, coming from nowhere, completely unimportant, had upset everything.

Worst of all had she upset this darling old man, who deserved, if anyone did, his quiet years of glory, she had turned all his coziness into dismay, his order into chaos. And she saw him, looking across the candied fruit and soft lights, rising like Tenniel's picture of Alice, his hands raised in dismay, the furniture falling on every side about his head.

Aunt Ruth hated her. She had turned Uncle Hans upside

down. All in a week or two. Without meaning any harm.
"No, thank you," she said to the ice cream. She had never
before in all her life felt quite so miserable.

Nor was she either old enough or social enough to conceal
her misery. She knew that Aunt Ruth and Uncle Hans were
talking with an easy fondness that covered a whole world
of uneasy displeasure. They tried at times to draw her
into this, but she was, as it were, stuck to her chair with
spiritual wax. She could not say more than "Yes" or "No."

Her face seemed to her, as she sat there, to be freezing
into a terrible mask, something without life, with fixed and
staring eyes.

She could not become used to this new fact that Uncle
Hans was frightened of Aunt Ruth. That seemed so oddly
unnatural—that Uncle Hans, the greatest of men, should be
frightened of anybody! But he was. She could see how his
eyes, timidly at times, sought hers as though for support and
encouragement. And all she could do was to sit there, a
gawky schoolgirl, with a mask for a face, a hot, dry spot
where her appetite ought to be.

Her fault, all of it her fault—and she herself must mend
it. She made the excuse, familiar to the wives of the Cave-
men, of a headache, and slipped up to her room. Lying
on her bed for hours sleepless, she knew that, as soon as
possible, she must see Vladimir. Then what? Marry him? A
strange, warning terror swept over her. In spite of everything
she was a child, lonely, inexperienced, unaware of life. She
loved him, she thought, with eternal passion. But eternal?
Passion? What do the words mean when eternity has no

boundaries and passion no quiescence? And marry him? A
Russian who did not believe in marriage, who had already
loved many women? She knew enough of life to foresee many
of the dangers, humiliation, desertion, loneliness—could
she face them? They said that such things made a woman
of a girl, and she wanted, above everything else in life, to be
a woman, ripe in experience, self-subsisting, self-supporting,
proud and strong—but if, through his treatment of her, she
should come to know him to be unworthy, mean, false,
cowardly; if her love should turn to contempt!

Her body, hot against the cool sheets, shivered. She loved
him with all her body and soul, but she knew herself well
enough to realize that she could not love when there was
nothing left to admire. She could guard, protect, assist, but
love, no. Was he then so weak? must he of such necessity
desert her?

No, it was not that he was weak, but that he was strange,
of another world in nationality, in sex, in something rough
and independent in his spirit, in his young self-confidence
and eager egotism and pride of adventure.

She had read, she had been told that men never needed
women as women needed men. That was an old platitude
but true enough, perhaps. But without him where was she?
She would never return to the Proudies, she must leave this
place—where could she go if not to him? She had spoken
bravely to Uncle Hans, but she knew well enough how little
she could do. And she wanted him, physically now, so that
she hid her face in the pillow and thus fell asleep, his arms
around her, his cheek against hers.

In the morning she telephoned to him, standing at the telephone in the corner of the sitting room, trembling every moment lest Bigges or someone should overhear her. Aunt Ruth, she knew, was safe in her room. Yes—she could hear how his voice shook with eagerness and delight as he realized that it was she. Yes, of course, he would meet her for lunch. Would he not? Oh, would he not? The little place that he had told her of, near Holborn. They would meet nobody there. It would be quiet. They could talk uninterruptedly. At one-thirty. Oh, darling—darling!

The sound of his voice had swept her into a whirl of feeling. If these few words could so excite her now, when she was with him could she resist his impulse? What could she do? What could she say? How could she remain wise?

As she passed the library door Uncle Hans crossed the passage. He drew her, without a word, into the room, closing the door quietly behind them.

He took her into his arms, kissed her, then very gravely (seeming now an old, exceedingly wise man from whom nothing in life was hid) said: "Nathalie, dear, I want you to promise me one thing."

"Yes?" she answered him, looking up at him.

"Not to take any step—any step of any kind—until you have told me about it."

"Oh, I don't know." She looked past him, almost desperately straight, into the face of the Manet, restored now to its position of grandeur. "I oughtn't to promise, Uncle Hans. It's all wrong that I've brought you into this. That

has made me more unhappy than anything else. Please ...
I can't promise——"

"You *must* promise. I won't let you go unless you do."

"But promise what?"

"That you won't take any definite step without telling
me."

"No, I can't promise that. It would make you responsible."

He shook his head like an angry, impatient child.

"Nonsense. That's absurd nonsense. I *am* responsible
already, because I love you. Promise me at least that you'll
give him, your young Russian, no definite answer until
I've seen him."

"When are you going to see him?"

"As soon as possible. Now promise me that."

She hesitated, then she said slowly: "Very well, I promise that."

He kissed her.

"That's right. Now I've something at least to go on."

She kissed him almost passionately, the emotion of the
sound of Vladimir's voice still trembling in her body.

She could think of nothing now, save that before the sun
set she would see him.

At a quarter to one she was out of the house. She walked
along to Clarence Gate, then, feeling, she scarcely knew
why, extremely defiant, she summoned a taxi. The taxi
driver, of the colour of beetroot and smelling of mice,
thought to himself cheerfully, "There's a pretty young

piece." She was wearing a dress of plum colour with silver lace at her wrists and throat. She had a little hat, pulled down tight over her head. Aunt Ruth had given her the hat, and she felt that it was wicked of her now, as things were, to be flaunting it.

She had a shop to visit in the Strand, and the taxi took her into a part of London that she did not know at all—dust on the buildings, dust on the coats of the hurrying figures, and because it was a sunny day gold-dust. And that was as it should be, because this was the entrance to the City where they all make money.

She thought, as they ran and stopped, ran and stopped, down Fleet Street, oddly enough of Peter Westcott. Millie had told her of Peter's early days in London and how he had walked down Fleet Street when he was starving and had gazed in despair at St. Paul's. Why should she think of him? A kind, solid, dependable man. He would be a friend if she wanted one, and, indeed, it seemed that she would want one very soon.

The buildings closed in and widened again. Noise and figures, figures and noise, and a whiff in an odd unexpected way, of the river.

The taxi stopped. There it was in bold letters, FARLING'S RESTAURANT. It was off the main road and the first building on the right of an empty, desolate side street that seemed to be lamenting its inability to be up and doing. She would remember all her life that the walls of Farling's were cream colour, the boarding of the door and windows dark blue, and that there was a fat black cat asleep inside the window. She paid the taxi man and timidly walked in. The room was hot and dim, and instantly she perceived that Vladimir was sitting at a table in the far corner.

She walked straight over to him like a somnambulist. Yes, she loved him more than before. She could talk nonsense about this and that, but she belonged to him for ever.

It was odd, then, that the first thing that she said to him, after she had sat down, arranged herself, given her hat a little push, smiled at him timidly, allowed him to take her hand, was:

"I've come to say that we must never see one another again."

His eyes lingered over her, absorbing the little childlike but determined eyes and mouth, the soft, gentle colour of the skin, the dark blue hat, the silver over the purple at the throat, then he answered gently, with the rather proud foreign accent that, for her, gave such distinction to everything that he said:

"All right, then—First, what will you like to eat? Then we will talk about that." Then, as she said nothing but only looked at him as though she had never seen him before: "The *sole meunière* is good here. Also the veal."

"I'll eat anything you say," she answered, speaking as though in a dream. He gave his order to the lean and untidy waiter, who obviously thought them the prettiest pair that had ever sat in that restaurant, then, holding her hand very tightly, he said to her gently:

"Why must we never meet again? You know that that is absurd."

She pulled her eyes away from him. How could she for a single moment be wise and cool and sensible if she looked at him? His eyes were enough of themselves to drown all her determination.

"It isn't absurd." She began to speak in a great hurry as though she were repeating a lesson. "It isn't absurd, because you don't really want to marry me, and I won't come to you in any other way, and if we did marry it wouldn't do. You think differently about everything. You are Russian and I am English. You are ambitious, but have very little money, and I have none at all. You don't know me in the least, and when the excitement is over you will be dreadfully disappointed in me."

She thought this a very wise speech.

"Very well," he answered her quietly. "Ve-ry well."

He rolled his r's adorably. "*C'est ça.* Now we know *where* we are. I'll be honest, shall I? Quite honest. It is true that I am Russian and that I had never intended to marry any-one. It is true, also, that I have loved other women; ever since I was fifteen I have been in love. It is true what you say, also, that I am ambitious. I am only a clerk in the City here now, but I know that I shall do great things. I am confident of that. First, I shall make money in the City, then, when I have some money, I will make them listen to my ideas— world ideas——"

He paused and very gravely, as though he were already a millionaire of middle age, ordered the wine. Then he went on, drawing a little closer to her and never taking his eyes from her face: "But you must not think that I am a con-

ceited man. I have many faults. I am not proud of myself,
but I am not ashamed either. Have we not all faults, all
men, and are not the faults the things that make us interesting? So you see me, a man with many faults and great
ambitions. Before now I have loved women. Now I love
only one woman. From the first instant I see you I love
only one woman. For ever? Who can say? That is sentimental
nonsense. Every love history has its own fortune. No one
is like another one. No one can say what our history shall
be. But we are both young and strong. We are sensible, modern people. We shall learn. We shall make mistakes
and be happy, and be angry and be happy again. We shall
have difficult times, but these difficult times make life for
us. Every adventure is dangerous, thank God. Try the sole,
darling. It is extremely good."

He smiled at her with perfect confidence, then, without
looking to see whether there was anyone watching in the
room, he put his hand against her cheek and kissed her on
the mouth. Then he turned and began with grave attention
to dissect his sole.

She stared in front of her. How was she to make him understand?

"Yes, but I can't take it like that. If, after we were married, you loved some other woman if would be terrible. And
I think that soon you would find me stupid and dull. I *am*
stupid. I've never been anywhere. I've never done anything.
How can I be sure that in a month you wouldn't hate me
and leave me?"

"Then, darling," he said, smiling into her eyes, "let us

go away for a little together, and then if we find that it won't go, we separate, and there's no harm at all."

"No—no. Uncle Hans says that, in spite of being modern, that doesn't work. And he's right. I know he's right. It might work for lots of people. I know that it wouldn't work for us. I expect it's right for heaps of people. I know it's wrong for me."

"Then let us wait a little. Let us see one another *every* day. You will find that there is something in me this time that doesn't change. I have always said before, when I was in love, 'Now in a moment this will change,' and, true enough, changed it has. I am not very fine. I am not very good. The Russian nature is always in a mess, but right in the middle of it there is something fixed. Perhaps there is not a soul. I doubt it very greatly, but there is something in a Russian's heart that is faithful in the middle of all his infidelity. Don't trust me as a man, but trust *that*, better and finer than a man. Do you understand, dearest? And eat your sole. It will be all cold."

She caught into the first part of his speech.

"I can't wait. That's just why I had to see you. I've been making a terrible lot of trouble in the house where I'm staying. Uncle Hans was settled and happy, but my coming has unsettled him, and now Aunt Ruth is angry, and I must go away. I must indeed, as soon as possible, and I'm not going back to Glebeshire. I must find some work. That's what I want mostly to talk to you about."

She knew that she was incoherent, but her urgency, she

felt, was awful. He only knew that she was adorable with that English freshness, that English naïveté, following so the well-worn simile of the rose with the dew upon it, and stirring in him, just because of its deep, positive difference, all the romance and tenderness and longing to protect that his ironic, pessimistic, doubting Russian soul allowed. Yes, the love in his heart was this time different from any that his life had known.

It had in it a sense of responsibility that was quite new to him.

Before this it had been: "Come this way and *prenez garde!* Your risk, not mine."—And well enough able to protect themselves they had generally been! But now, here, in this restaurant, at this very hour, something new was growing in him, something that, with all his skepticism, he felt that he would never lose again.

He had not heard a word that she said, but from a vast distance he caught the words "Uncle Hans."

"Ah, your uncle. He seemed a nice old boy. Does he know about us?"

"He's the finest man that ever lived. Not inhuman and grand like most famous people, but as natural as possible. You would never know he was famous. Yes, he knows about us. He noticed it the very first evening at the Westcotts'."

"And what does he say?"

"He wants to talk to you."

Vladimir made a grimace. "*Merci*—very kind. No old gentleman's going to talk to me."

"Oh, but not to preach or tell you what to do. Only to see what you're like. He's very fond of me. He only wants me to be happy."

"Well," admitted Vladimir, his eyes searching hers as though he could never exhaust for himself the beauty in them, "they say he's a fine old boy. Uncle Mihail's fallen straight—completely in love with him."

"Uncle who?'

"Mihail Klimov. The fat, bald old boy who was at the Westcotts' party. He says he'd follow your Uncle Hans to Jerusalem. So he would too. He's always getting these enthusiasms. They don't hurt anybody."

"Would you see Uncle Hans if he asked you?"

"Of course I would. I'll see anybody. I'm not ashamed of loving you."

He said this fiercely, and then glared round the room, into the eyes of the lean waiter, the stout, moon-faced proprietor, the family party, the mother busy wiping the mouths of the children, and a melancholy clergyman seated alone, reading sadly in a book. He looked at all these innocent people as though he challenged them to defy his love. No one noticed him. Smiling, he turned to her and, quite simply, kissed her again.

She drew away, looking at him, both adoring him and fearing him. "You mustn't. I'm sure you didn't hear what I said just now. I've got to leave the Frosts' house soon—very soon. Where do you think I can get some work to do?"

"Come and stay with me and we'll see."

She got up. She pulled her little hat down about her ears.

"This is serious. You won't see that I mean what I say. I am *not* coming to you and I *am* going to get some work somewhere. If you don't realize these two things it's hopeless our going on talking."

"Sit down. Don't please look as lovely as that, or I shall pick you up and carry you home."

"That settles it," she said, tossing her head. "You treat me like a fool. I'm going."

She moved, and he sprang up and caught her arm. The children at the family table turned round with their mouths open, like birds in a nest. "Sit down. Sit down. I'm sorry. Forgive me. I love you so much that I don't know what I'm saying. Listen—darling, please, please listen."

She sat down again, but as one prepared to fly out of the window at any moment.

"You shall do all you wish. I will be good. Let your uncle come, and we will have a talk. Truly, I will be wise. What I cannot understand is, why you won't marry me. You are afraid of my wickedness. Ah, try it and see—my wickedness. Perhaps it will not be so bad."

"No," she said, looking down at the tablecloth. "I'm afraid that you don't know me, that when you do you'll find me so stupid, so uninteresting—just nothing—and then I won't be able to stand it, because I love you so—so terribly —and I won't risk losing you."

And at that, without looking at him, with one of those light, swift movements, like a bird's movements, so especially hers, she slipped from him, crossed the restaurant floor, and had vanished.

He ran to the door, into the street. She was gone.

Raging, he turned to the restaurant again to find that even the clergyman was interested enough by this dramatic circumstance to put down his book and stare with sad and speculative eyes.

"Damn!" said Vladimir to the family party. "Oh, damn, damn, damn!"

CHAPTER IX

Hans Steps Out

FOR Hans, too, Nathalie presented this image of the bird in flight. She had come in early this afternoon, hastening up the stairs; he had met her halfway up—had stayed her with a hand on her arm——

"Well?" he asked her.

She was in great agitation, and had for him precisely that trembling, beating, fearing quiver of a bird caught in the hand.

"It's nothing," she answered, trying to smile. Then, looking down the stairs into the hall as though to make sure that there was no one there, lowering her voice: "Uncle Hans, would you please go to see him? He would like to talk to you."

"Of course I will——"

Quickly, as though she had not a moment to lose, she gave him Vladimir's business telephone number. He would be there all to-morrow morning. He lived in a little street not far from the British Museum—if Uncle Hans would go to see him there——

Hans looked a little bewildered. "Yes, dear, of course I'll go. But is there anything you especially want me to say?"

"No—no. Only to see for yourself. . . ."

219

They had both dropped their voices. They were talking
like conspirators. They were both aware at the same instant
that Ruth had come into the hall.

"Is that you, Hans? Are you ready? The car's there."

Nathalie vanished.

"Yes, I'm ready," Hans said, coming slowly downstairs.

He felt guilty. How absurd! He did not want to drive in
the car with Ruth, he did not want to go to the concert at
the Æolian Hall, of a Russian tenor—he did not want to do
anything, but to follow Nathalie up to her room, to close
the door behind them both, and then to discover from her
everything that had happened. Most of all, he hated to feel
guilty in his own house, and just as the other day, coming
into the house alone, he had thought it all beautiful and
radiant, so now, feeling, against his will, a secret conspira-
tor, he hated the house and everything in it.

Someone was responsible for this. Who but Ruth? He
disliked, as he felt, according to constant habit, the last rung
of the staircase with his foot, to make sure that he didn't
slip, her furs, her grey hat with the small blue feather, all
her rich appearance, her grandeur, the house's grandeur, the
car's grandeur. It stifled him. As he crossed the hall to
greet her, he was nothing at all but a peevish, discontented
old man.

But his discontent was nothing at all compared with
Ruth's. She, too, almost hated him, as she saw him slowly
descend the stairs. So the two of them had been conspiring
together again? It was happening now at every turn. Ever
since that girl had come into the house. . . .

The fool, the fool that she had been to invite her! Everything had been wrong since that moment.

Her heart was the oddest mixture of wild jealousy, physical distress (because her heart was beating in her ears, as though she had just heard that there was a fire or that someone had tumbled from a third-floor window or that there was a snake in the pantry), bewilderment and self-pity. Of these emotions, the last was the strongest. She seemed, as she stood there in the hall, to be a little girl whose mother had been called names, whose father had been caught cheating at cards, whose grandparents were moving to-morrow into the workhouse. And why? What had she done? Nothing at all, save invite to stay a conceited idiot of a girl, who had shown nothing but ingratitude and insult. She had, for years, done her duty to everyone, nobly sacrificed herself on every possible occasion, and this was what she got!

As she sat down in the car her nobility, her suffering, her loneliness, her cruel isolation, these things hurt her so terribly that she had to bite her lip to prevent the tears. And there he sat, self-satisfied, hard, selfish. Her longing for him and her disgust of him were present in equal quantities. But stronger than either was the determination to end this odious situation (which had developed, as it were, out of nothing at all, a ring of the door bell, an order to a servant, a picture crooked on the wall) at the very first possible moment.

For the first time in all their married lives together they sat in complete and absolute silence.

At the Æolian Hall, Stanislas Lermontov seemed to both

of them a shrieking maniac. Celebrated though he afterwards became, Ruth, whenever he was mentioned, said:
"But, my dear, he's dreadful! I heard him once . . ."

On such straws in the temperamental mind do the reputa-
tions of artists depend!

On the following morning Hans telephoned, and out of
that odd medley of hooting cars, omnibus conductors, the
pigeons outside St. Paul's, and a million men making and
losing a million a minute, came young Vladimir's voice saying that he would be in his rooms at Five Becket Street
that afternoon at four-thirty o'clock. "You go past Mudie's
and turn sharp to the left. . . ."

The voice faded, and all the little stir of the house resumed
its power.

He went off to the appointment as though he were a
young fellow of twenty out to capture his first job. For how
many years now had his expeditions been surrounded with
pomp and circumstance, not because he had wanted it to
be so, but simply because that was the way it had been.
Why, even were it only to drop into Mr. Bain's bookshop
in King William Street to have a chat and look at that Blake
Songs of Innocence or a Pine's *Vergil*, the car must take him,
and everyone in the shop must be aware of his presence
and there must be a sort of tum-ti-tum, tum-ti-tum accompaniment to all his words and acts. But now, as Nathalie had done only yesterday, he slipped quite furtively out
of the house, walked to Clarence Gate, and there seized
upon a very handsome taxi, with paper flowers in a silver

vase, seats of crimson leather, and a young driver with his cap at an angle.

Then, just as the house had seemed suddenly to belong to him for the first time, so now to-day did London. It was a dim autumn afternoon of smoky skies and hidden fires. He didn't doubt but that snow would shortly fall. Everything delighted him, the flaming branches of red and amber chrysanthemums in the flower stalls, the pale pearl outlines of the roofs as they cut the blue and grey of the changing sky, the hurrying cheeks and noses, hats and furs, the rising and fall of cries, the ringing of bells, the sudden flash of a window, throwing at him, as he passed, jewels and wax models, carpets and tables, fruit and china, the flaring of cinema posters, a policeman on a horse, the whirling smoke from the crowded chimneys that huddled like witches plotting their spells—all these were his now, and he was proud as Lucifer at the greatness of his possessions.

He was smiling with pleasure as he pushed the little bell that had "Vladimir Shapkin" written on a dirty card above it, climbed slowly the dingy staircase, and knocked at last on young Mr. Shapkin's door.

"Mr. Shapkin?"

"How do you do, sir? Won't you sit down?"

Hans sat down—on a faded green sofa with a hole in it. On this he carefully placed his square black hat, his gloves, and his gold-topped cane. Then, with a smile which he could not prevent (he had earlier determined that he would be stern and wise), he looked up at young Mr. Shapkin.

He smiled, because Vladimir was so very good-looking, such a young swell in this very bare and shabby room. Yes, a gentleman, and he thought once again of the room in Paris and M. Turgenev drinking tea through a piece of lemon. He had also been a gentleman. Young Mr. Shapkin rather resembled a modern version of a Turgenev novel. But no. He was not of sufficient melancholy. He suggested, however, the private pleasures and aristocratic courtesies of many generations. If he was as nice as he looked, then Nathalie would be all right. Or, perhaps not. You could never go by a foreigner's looks.

And Vladimir was thinking. "A jolly old boy. Well-preserved for seventy. He has a twinkle in his eye. He's a sportsman. I shouldn't wonder——"

"Nathalie asked me to come," Hans began confidentially. "I'm, in a sort of way, her guardian. At least she has no one else. I love her very much and I want her to be happy."

Vladimir nodded as though to a contemporary. "Yes, sir, I quite understand. By the way, will you not allow me to offer you some tea?".

"No, thank you. But I'll smoke, if I may."

Hans took out a cigar case, offered Vladimir a thin, fierce cigar which Vladimir, bowing, accepted.

"You see, sir, it's like this. Nathalie and I love one another. That is quite sure. I have asked her to marry me and she has refused me."

"She has refused you?" repeated Hans, nodding his head and then smiling at Vladimir reassuringly.

A jolly old boy with his black hair, the kindly wrinkles at

the corner of the eye, the clever, strong mouth, the thickset form sitting there, his legs spread, his back up—a fine old boy. Yes, he was somebody. You'd notice him in a crowd.

"Yes, sir, she has the idea that soon after we were married I would become tired of her. I have been honest, as I would wish to be with any woman I have asked to be my wife, and I have told her that I have loved other women. I wouldn't prophesy with certainty our future. How could I do so? Who knows about the future? But I love her, sir, with much more than physical love. I have never felt about any woman before as now. Perhaps in meeting her I have grown up."

"How old are you?" asked Hans.

"I am three-and-twenty years of age."

"And what are your means?" Vladimir, smiling, shook his head.

"They are not so great. I have a good position in the City in a shipping firm, but I have debts."

"Well, well," said Hans rather hurriedly, "the money might not be a great difficulty. But the other—that is something different. Forgive me—you have at present—no other lady towards whom you have—well, obligations?"

"Not a one, sir—not a one! There is no one in the world, save Nathalie, and I hope there will never be another. But women are beautiful. There are so many women in the world—I would never promise Nathalie that I would never look at a woman again. It would be false to say such a thing. But I have a feeling in my heart that I have never had before. I would protect her from all harm. I would not deceive her. We are sensible people, sir, and all the events of our life we would discuss together, and then we would become such great friends, that if such a time arrived I would say to Nathalie, 'Now, see, my dear—here is a beautiful lady. She has lovely legs or a fine neck, or maybe only a smile. What do you think about it?'"

"Yes, and what would Nathalie say to that?" asked Hans, greatly interested in this modern frankness.

"Oh, we would discuss it together. Nathalie is full of courage and honesty. She will grow. She is very young and I'm sure"—he went on earnestly—"I'm quite sure, sir, that I couldn't hurt her. Rather than hurt her I would take one last look at the lady's smile and then run away."

"I see," said Hans. "And what would happen if Nathalie happened to see a gentleman with beautiful legs?"

"Ah, women," said Vladimir confidently, "women are different. Women like Nathalie, once they love a man, are too terribly faithful. They don't permit themselves a moment's pleasure in any direction that isn't their husband's. But if it were so, we would discuss it sensibly, I'm sure. You see, sir, by that time we should be such firm friends and have been through so many things together that no new person coming along could be as charming. We would have done so many things, the one for the other. I would die for her!" he ended simply.

"Well, now," said Hans, "I wonder whether you would. Those are easy words. Many a lover has used them and kissed some other woman half an hour later. Dying, when you are young and strong as you are, is no fun, you know."

"I wouldn't mind dying," said Vladimir, waving his cigar

with a grand gesture in the air. "It would be harder now, of course, that I have met Nathalie, but death is no great affair, I should imagine. I would like to offer you something," he exclaimed, suddenly springing from his chair, "some tea, or if you really will not, some whisky—I have some very good whisky."

"No, indeed—thank you, no," said Hans. "Then you think that I should persuade Nathalie to trust you and take you once and for all?"

"No, sir. I wouldn't wish you to persuade her. She must decide for herself. I am sure that she will. But we must meet. We have met such a little time. And then," he went on more slowly, "I don't know whether I should speak to you of this—but yesterday she said that she was not at all happy, that she had done you harm, that she must go somewhere, get some work—— She is very young. She doesn't know what life can be. That is why I was glad that we should have a talk—because she might of a sudden do something——"

Hans, his voice sharp, interrupted, "She said that she was unhappy?"

"Yes—only that she had upset you all and that she mustn't return to Glebeshire and didn't know where to go— and she's so young——" He broke off, looking very young himself.

Hans stood up, holding out his hand. Vladimir took it, liking the strong firm grip of it—not an old man's hand at all.

"I like you," Hans said. "I trust you. We'll pull it off together, shall we?"

"Yes, sir," said Vladimir (thinking to himself, "It's a handsome style when you're an old English gentleman, that buff waistcoat with brass buttons," and thinking at the same time (so odd is life) of how terribly he loved Nathalie and how he must marry her as soon, as soon——)"We will pull it off together."

They liked one another. They were friends from that moment.

"I'll speak to Nathalie," said Hans, moving towards the door, "and then I think it would be nice if the three of us had a talk together. What do you say?"

"That would be very nice," said Vladimir, bowing.

"He's certainly a little too polite," thought Hans, "but, then, that's foreign ways. He's a decent fellow, I fancy."

"There's one thing," said Vladimir, as they reached the door. "I wonder whether you would mind doing me a favour?"

"No, indeed," said Hans. "Of course I will be delighted."

"Would you, for only two minutes, glance into the room of my friend, Mihail Klimov? It is only one flight of stairs. It will give him such extreme pleasure. He has been, for many years, very good to me, and he has so great an admiration for you. He is there, I know, making a box."

"Making a box?" asked Hans.

"Yes; he is a very excellent carpenter. You wouldn't think it, would you, when you talk to him? But so it is. One of his several excitements."

"Of course I will," said Hans.

"Thank you. It is very good of you. One flight up. His name is on the door."

They shook hands again. A grandee of Spain, a schoolboy, a nice handsome young man, a Russian philosopher, a scamp, the son of a parson, a showman, a student, an ardent but unfaithful lover, an ascetic idealist, a play-actor—all these personalities might, thought Hans, be living together in the soul of this remarkable young man. And Nathalie, a swallow in flight, was it wise to trust her to his keeping?

Stubbing his toes on the stairs, feeling that at that very moment she might have flown from the house and be beating her wings in loneliness and terror against the walls of that vast darkening London, almost forced him to turn and run straight back to Regent's Park. But no. He would see this old boy for five minutes. It might be that he, too, could help.

On opening Mihail Klimov's door and entering he beheld a strange room. High up the windows looked out to sky, roofs, and chimney pots. Near the window was a large carpenter's table, over which hung an electric light with a green shade. In the centre of the room was a large deal table without a cloth, and on this some wooden children's toys—a large, spotted horse with a red saddle, a house with a green tufted tree, an animal that looked like a tiger, and a Noah's Ark with a bright yellow roof. In the corner a bed, two wooden chairs, a bright painted chest of drawers. On one wall a white bookcase, on the other wall a series of very gay pictures, the subjects obviously Russian fairy tales. In one a

witch bent over a cauldron, in another, against a snowy
background, a crimson Russian giant with a club talked
to three dwarfs. There were also in the room two dogs and a
cat. The dogs were mongrels, one a strange cross between a
rough-haired terrier and—who can tell? This animal was
lying in a basket. One paw hanging on the edge of the basket
was bandaged. He had very soft and appealing eyes, and
a snub nose. The other was little more than a puppy with a
shaggy black head, a round body, and a long tail. He was
playing very amiably with the cat and a piece of newspaper.

Mihail Klimov himself, in his shirt and trousers, was
seated at the carpenter's table, busily engaged with a hammer. As he hammered he sang in an odd, cracked voice. His
bald head shone under the electric light. One of the windows
was open, and the room was very cold. A hideous, green-
striped linoleum covered the floor.

"Good afternoon," said Hans. The hammering and the
singing stopped abruptly. Klimov swung round.

"Dear me, dear me." He jumped up. The dog in the
basket barked. The puppy dropped the newspaper and
skipped like a ballet dancer in Hans' direction. The cat flew
to the corner of the room and stood there, eyes gleaming,
back raised, fur bristling.

"Dear, dear!" cried Klimov, coming forward, his face
smiling from one end to the other. "This is a great honour."

"How do you do?" said Hans. They shook hands. "I
have looked in only for a moment. I have been visiting your
young friend, Shapkin, below, and I thought as I was here
I would pay you a little call."

"I'm delighted, delighted," cried Klimov, pulling one of the wooden chairs forward. "And what a surprise! The pleasant surprise—I was working a little as I like to do on an afternoon. Let me take your hat and coat."

Hans kept on his coat. Here one might be living on the top of a mountain. He walked over to the table.

"What are you making here?" he asked.

"Oh, nothing. Please don't trouble. Indeed, nothing at all. A box for a child friend of mine. I make toys and boxes. You must excuse me. It must seem a fearful waste of time to a man like yourself."

"Not at all. All my life I've longed to make something with my hands. Now you write a book—who knows whether it's good or bad? Up and down it goes. Every fit of indigestion destroys it. But a box, well made, there can never be any doubt about it. There it is for all the world to agree upon."

"Indeed," said Klimov, immensely pleased. "That's very interesting. I never thought of it that way. Pushkin in *Boris* says somewhere that—— Oh, but you don't want to be troubled with Pushkin. Will you allow me to offer you some tea?"

"No, thank you. I must stay only a moment. And did you really make these toys on the table?"

"Yes. I must confess that I did. I give them to children, friends of mine. They have more personality than toys from a shop. Home-made. I find that when I'm carpentering I think more clearly. If you put a nail in straight an idea frequently goes in straight with it. Oh, but indeed I'm greatly ashamed. There isn't a comfortable chair in the room————"

It is true that there wasn't, but Hans didn't just then want a comfortable chair. He had plenty at home. He sat down on one of the hard little chairs. The puppy stretched itself on its round belly in front of him and watched him with friendly, inquisitive eyes.

"Mr. Klimov, you probably know that your young friend, Vladimir, down there is in love with a niece of mine. It happens that I'm extremely fond of that niece. She is very young, and I don't want to make a mistake. Shall I be making one if I help those two to marry?"

Mihail Klimov, who had until this moment been a little gay and disconnected (so happy was he at Hans' unexpected visit), and had been wandering, one vast smile, about the room, at one moment looking at the shavings on the table, at another patting the dog in the basket, and, in spite of himself, humming a little tune, now very abruptly pulled himself together, sat down on the remaining chair and looked very wise, with a distinct resemblance to Mr. Dick engaged in advising Betsy Trotwood.

"Oh, yes, indeed. Very delightful. I *have* heard of it. You care for your niece, Mr. Frost—I am exceedingly attached to Vladimir. He is more to me than I like to realize, because I believe that in life one must be entirely independent of human beings. One must be courageous enough not to depend on the human affections. That's my theory, but in practice I am, as indeed in everything else, very weak. But, of course, I am fond of the boy, because he has been very good to me. There, again, I hold that gratitude doesn't belong to a man who is superior to life. It is undoubtedly one of the weaker emotions. I find myself, however, quite unable not to be grateful to Vladimir."

"You see," said Hans, "Vladimir, if I may call him so, has been very honest with my niece and has told her that he has had relations with women before, and refuses to promise that he won't have relations with them again. She is naturally afraid of marrying him and being very unhappy. She has had no experience of life at all. This is certainly the first time she has ever been in love. Now, I want her to be happy. If anyone can be happy I want her to be. How much chance has she, do you think, of happiness if she marries this young man? You know him—what he is, I mean—and can judge."

Klimov brought his chair very close to Hans' and, bending forward, laid his broad hand on his knee.

"Vladimir is good. Yes, he is truly good. I have watched him in every situation, and he has nobility of spirits. Certainly he is handsome and young. I, who was never handsome, have loved many women, but I have been faithful only to one. And I am faithful still. But I am not as noble as Vladimir. I am not, in fact, noble at all. But it seems to me, my friend, in life that it takes two fine people to make a fine relationship—one is not enough. And when two fine people meet and love one another, let them take their risk. The result must be fine, whichever way it goes. The trouble in life comes because a fine person meets one who is not so fine. I know I'm a fool, and can never keep an idea in my head for more than a minute at a time, but what I am telling you is true."

"And from what he's said to you," asked Hans, "you think that he truly loves my niece?"

"Vladimir is a strange man. Sometimes I think that he will one day be a great man. But I don't know. There are many ways that it can go. And, as with all men, love will not ever be the only thing in his life. He has great ambitions and fine ideas. He sees beyond life and beyond persons, and there are times when no one is of much account to him, but he has a good and tender heart. He will care for her and guard her against unhappiness and make her life richer, that I swear."

"Thank you," said Hans, rising. "That's what I wanted to know."

Klimov also rose. He looked at Hans with a rather pathetic, anxious gaze, as though he were a little bewildered and afraid now of being left alone.

"It has been a great honour, your coming to visit me. Will you come again?"

"Of course I will."

"And may I say this—possibly an impertinence to a man like yourself—but if you are troubled and disturbed about this matter will you allow me to know of it?"

"I promise that."

"Thank you. I admire you very greatly, and that makes it difficult for me to speak."

"Not at all." Hans was embarrassed, as all Englishmen

are at spoken emotion. But he liked him. He seemed this afternoon to be liking the whole Russian nation.

"We'll meet again soon," he said cheerfully, to cover his embarrassment. "Good-afternoon, Mr. Klimov."

His last glimpse of the room was of Klimov returning slowly to his carpenter's table, the puppy tumbling after him, the evening breeze blowing the curtains as the wind outside rushed the clouds along their course.

CHAPTER X

Ruth Is Honest

FOR three days Nathalie had been like a captured animal, bewildered by her confinement.

She kept to herself as much as was possible. She sat in her room, looking out over Regent's Park, watching the stripped branches writhe in the wind and rain (the weather now was terrible) and hearing the cries of the animals in the Zoo. Their cries were hers. She did not know how to get out. She had lost her trust in herself, and she did not know how to regain it.

All her life it was this upon which she had especially prided herself. As a tiny child she had said to herself, that she was alone, belonged to nobody, nobody belonged to her. Tying up her boots one morning in her little room in Polchester (she saw it so often with its faded wall paper of robins, its view of the Cathedral—if like Charles Lamb you perked up in bed on your haunches to catch it—and its battered copies in the little brown bookcase of *What Katy Did*, *Queechy*, and *The Dove in the Eagle's Nest*—the hole in the carpet, and the wind that whistled in the wall), stinging red in the face, hearing someone call from far down in the house her name, standing up, her boots yet unlaced, she said out aloud, "I don't care—I can manage it myself."

And always afterwards, when things were difficult, she saw the unlaced, gaping boots, the robins, the little brown book-case—"I can manage it myself."

Now it seemed that she could not—and she could not, because she was so dreadfully in love.

She was dreadfully in love, but didn't trust him, or rather didn't trust her own power to hold him.

He wrote to her every day. He wrote a long letter after his talk with Hans, telling her what the old boy had said, and what a sporting old boy he was, and demanding of her that she should herself speak to the old boy and find out from him his opinion.

She did speak to him, but very briefly. She had a queer conviction that by dragging Uncle Hans into her small affairs she had ruined his life. He was changed—anyone could see it. The whole house was changed, and Aunt Ruth was furious. So she stood away from him, didn't kiss him (although she was longing to do so), spoke to him in a tight, reserved voice and altogether behaved quite unlike the modern girl that she fancied she was.

He told her to wait for a little while, that he liked her young man, but that he must see a little more of him. Yes, wait. But how? Where?

Aunt Ruth hated her. That was now the central fact of her situation, the one fact that must be altered. She had never been hated by anyone before, never even, so far as she was aware, disliked. The sense of it was new to her, horrible, frightening, sinister, like a witch's story. She could not help herself. She wanted always to be liked. She had her pride, but she had also her sensitiveness that came, perhaps, from her lonely start in life; and now that she knew that Aunt Ruth hated her, the only thing was to get away at once, and far, far away, where she could not feel Ruth's iron, implacable dislike.

At what moment had she been aware of this hatred? Only one week ago they had, it seemed, loved one another. She was to be Ruth's companion, to cherish her old age. Ruth had been so kind, so generous.

The change had come, perhaps, one afternoon at tea when, the three of them alone, Uncle Hans had said something enchantingly funny and kind, and Nathalie impulsively had gone to him, put her arms around him, and kissed him.

Something that Aunt Ruth had said a moment later had told Nathalie she must never kiss Uncle Hans in front of Aunt Ruth again. It was like the things that in her childhood she had learned that she must not do, must not make a noise when Mr. Proudie was writing his sermon, must not speak of "stomach," must not say of a pudding that she loved it, must not stare at strangers—but there were reasons for these laws, and they were friendly laws. Now it was as though with that one embrace of Uncle Hans she had been pushed out of one room into another, out of a room full of light and bright colours into one gloomy, close, hot, and stale.

She had not the knowledge yet of life to enable her to track that action of Aunt Ruth's to its true conclusion. She was rather inclined to believe that the evil emanated from her grandmother's room. That first visit had been also her last; she had never been invited again, and she had concluded from that that her grandmother did not like her. She most certainly did not like her grandmother, and these things were always mutual. She thought of that bedroom as of a witch's cave, where spells were brewed and enchantments muttered. Ugh! A nasty old woman to have for a grandmother!

But come whence it might, Aunt Ruth wanted her out of the house, and her pride told her that she must go before she was sent. Her pride also told her that she must show Vladimir how independent she truly was, that she could stand on her own feet, that she was somebody, a modern girl who could manage her own life without *anybody's* help. And then, having shown him these things, she would marry him.

So, sitting on her bed staring out of the window, loving him, longing, aching for him, she resolved.

Well enough. But where to go? What to do? She had a little money, ten pounds or so; she had a gold locket that had belonged to her mother, a gold wrist-watch that only last week Uncle Hans had given her, and that she most foolishly in her naïve delight had exhibited at once to Aunt Ruth—she could live for a week or two on these. But in what direction could she find work?

She searched the columns of the *Times* and the *Morning Post*. It seemed that ladies wanted companions; gentlemen, secretaries; and one old woman in Kensington a girl to look after her dogs. Well, then, there you were!

On this same rainy afternoon, alone in her room at exactly four of the clock, she came to her resolve: she would tell Aunt Ruth that on the following Monday her charming visit must terminate, she was to stay with a friend, it had been most kind of Aunt Ruth. . . .

And so, happier than she had been for three days, she sprang off her bed, washed her face, tidied her hair, and went down to tea—stepping at that same instant, although she did not know it, from girlhood into maturity.

Aunt Ruth was alone. Nathalie stood hesitating at the door. She wanted to come forward boldly, but the furniture itself seemed to stop her. "We don't like you," the chairs shouted at her, and the silver on the tea table shivered at the sight of her. Meanwhile Ruth said, in her kindest voice (she had some five or six voices very carefully graduated), "Ah, it's you, dear. . . . Come in, I'm sure you're dying for some tea." As she saw the child standing there, she thought: "This will be a good opportunity to explain to her that she can't stay here for ever."

And so it would, and she behaved to her very nicely indeed. She was always unhappy unless she was quite sure that she was behaving with tenderness and generosity. Swiftly, minute by minute, the pictures passed, giving money to a blind man with a dog, approaching at a party some poor woman whom everyone else had neglected, protesting against the ill-treatment of a horse, patting a child seated in a cottage door, and there were so many of these pictures that she had very little time to examine her real actions.

So now she had for several weeks been dreadfully unhappy; all her life, she told herself, lying on the little dark gold sofa in her bedroom, pretending to read a novel, had been sent tumbling about her ears; her husband, for whom she had done everything, suddenly selfish, indifferent, and (who could ever tell?) unfaithful.

This chit of a child—and here her eyes sought the different things in her bedroom, her silver crucifix, her toilet articles, her crimson-furred bedroom slippers, who having known her so long could testify to her character—was the cause of this ruin. But was the child to blame? No, no. Only a really selfish and egotistic woman would make such a child responsible. Little did she know what she had done— only she must return to the place whence Ruth had so generously brought her, as soon, yes, as soon as possible.

So she beckoned very graciously indeed to the place on the sofa beside her.

"Come, dear, sit here beside me, the water is just boiling. Well—and what have you been busy about to-day?"

Nathalie's heart felt a rush of eager gratitude. This was the Aunt Ruth of a week ago, before this horrible change. This was the Aunt Ruth whom she had been eager to adore. Perhaps, after all, they would find one another again, and all would be well. How much had not Nathalie imagined? Or it might be that Aunt Ruth had been very unwell during this last week with neuralgia or headache. And how beautiful Aunt Ruth was this afternoon in her dove-grey dress, with the single row of pearls and the silver shoes.

"Oh, I haven't done much to-day—written to the Proudies—and this afternoon I went for a walk in the Park— quite a little one—it was raining—and what have you been doing, Aunt Ruth?"

"Well, dear, it's been a busy day—and yet it's hard quite to remember. Let me see—try one of those little rolls. They're very good and quite fresh."

Nathalie tried one. Looking around her a little, she knew that even now with all Aunt Ruth's kindness, the room wasn't very friendly—perhaps it never had been. Vladimir wouldn't be comfortable here, and Aunt Ruth wouldn't like him.

"Well, now, let me see—what have I been doing? This afternoon some necessary shopping. One has to do things oneself, as you'll discover one day, when you have a house of your own, or everything goes wrong. And it's not been a nice day. I can't say it has. Wind and rain—terrible. And so many poor people out in it. Really our climate is too awful! If I had my way I'd never spend another November to March in England again. But of course London is the only possible place for your uncle, and now that he is older one must study his comfort. Why, only the other day, when we went down to the country, I saw at once that he was miserable, and ordered him straight back to town. He misses his books and his regular life. If I didn't force him out, he would become a perfect recluse."

"Are you and Uncle going out to-night?" Nathalie asked.

"Yes, dear, the Beaminsters. Frank Beaminster is the Duke of Wrexe's first cousin. A very artistic man. He collects French pictures. He has a lot in common with your uncle. The old Duchess of Wrexe, years before you were born, was a great figure. Before the Boer War. Doesn't that seem centuries ago, and hasn't the last terrible war made it

seem a tiny affair! I don't suppose that a great figure like
that would be possible now. Society has changed so utterly.
There's very little ceremony left, I'm afraid." (And she
saw herself a splendid figure moving magnificently across
the old Duchess's drawing-room. "Ah! That's a noble face!
And what a lovely poise." And behind the picture she was
thinking: "Now in a minute or two I will be able to tell
her that another week is just as long as I can possibly have
her——") "Have you had all the tea you want, dear? I'll ring
to have it taken away. You're nearer the bell. Thank you
so much, dear." (She was still only a raw little country girl,
in spite of the dresses that had so generously been given
her. Nothing would ever make her smart. Nothing. A
country town was her proper *milieu*.) And behind this—
restless, ceaseless—were thoughts about Hans. What was
he doing up there in his library? Soon, when she had rid
herself of this tiresome child she would go up and see; one
word, one glance, and all the old certainty, the old security,
the old safety of their mutual relation would return; this
odd strangeness that had lately seized him would fly away,
and she would be happy once more!

The tea was removed. They sat side by side on the little
sofa, staring into the fire.

Nathalie, at least, was happy again, happy as she had not
been for many days, touched, grateful, longing to show her
gratitude.

"Aunt Ruth, I have been wanting for a long time to thank
you for all that you have done for me, you and Uncle Hans.
I think it's simply wonderful of you. One day I hope to be

able to show you what I feel. That you have let me come and stay here so generously, and that you and Uncle Hans have been so good to me. . . . At one time I was a little afraid that I had been in the way, and I want you always to tell me if there's anything I do wrong, and if I'm stupid about something, because of course I've got so much to learn . . ." she broke off, smiling into her aunt's face.

"I've got so much to learn!" The words were alarming. "So she intends to stay. She's here for ever!"

Ruth's voice was sharper than she had intended.

"There's no reason for gratitude, dear, your uncle and I have loved your being with us. I wish we could have you always. But we mustn't be selfish. They must be missing you badly in Polchester."

"I'm never going back to Polchester," Nathalie said. So her aunt had run in before her? She had not been quick enough. Her pride, the quivering sense that already, after all, she *had* outstayed her welcome shivered through her body. The room *was* hostile and unfriendly, and her aunt——

"Never going back to Polchester! But my dear, *what* do you mean? That's your home."

"No, it isn't. When I left it the other day, I left it for good. I can't possibly be dependent on them any more. Later on, when I've made my way, I'll go back for a visit."

"Made your way? But how?"

"Oh, I have friends in London, and I shall make my living."

"Make your living! But do you realize——"

Ruth was aware of something very near to terror. So the girl would remain in London, would be at Hans' elbow, would be meeting him, disturbing him, plotting——

Tired, nervously excited by the events of the last fortnight, she saw everything at once melodramatically, the chairs and tables swelling to twice their natural size, the clock ticking with frantic insistence. She dragged her excitement down, laid her hand upon it; there, under her palm, it stayed quivering.

"Now, Nathalie dear, listen to me. You're only a child. You know nothing about life at all. Take the advice of your aunt and don't try any experiments with London—yet awhile at least. Go back to Polchester and live there quietly for a year or two. Perhaps I did wrong to give you a peep at London so soon. But I only wanted to be kind. I was a little impetuous maybe. It's gone possibly to your head— ever so slightly. And oh! I understand it so well. I should have been just the same at your age—all the fun of London after the quiet of a little town like Polchester. But Polchester's the place—for a year or two at least. Believe me, it is. Your grandmother feels as I do, and although she's an old lady now she knows life. Believe me, she does."

"Grandmother," said Nathalie slowly, "doesn't know anything about me at all. She's only seen me once, and then we never talked about anything."

"Now, that isn't very grateful, Nathalie. Your grandmother's an invalid and a brave one too. But because she has to stay in her room so much doesn't mean that she knows nothing of what's going on outside it. Indeed it doesn't."

Nathalie saw her grandmother, the dark, stuffy room, the creaking black silk dress. So that old woman thought she would be safer packed away in Polchester?

She seemed suddenly to confront that old dried dark figure here in this room, a shadow thickening the air, fading the light colours of the chairs, the stuffs, the pictures. Her hands were trembling a little on her lap, but her voice was steady enough as she answered.

"I know, Aunt Ruth, that you think me very young and ignorant. Perhaps I am. But I've been alone all my life. Everyone has been very kind to me, but I've always longed for the time when I should be able to be independent. I've taken people's charity so long, and that's over—I'll never be dependent on anyone again. I'd rather starve. I will indeed!"

And as she spoke she thought of Vladimir, whom she loved with all her heart, but to whom she would not go before she was earning her own living. No, not if he said he would never see her again!

But Ruth knew nothing about Vladimir. All she knew was that in spite of her kindness and generosity this pig-headed girl, to whom Hans had most unfortunately taken a most dangerous fancy, now that she realized that she had found an important association, was determined to cling like a limpet.

Well, she should not, and in another minute or two Ruth, even though she hurt the girl's feelings, would make this plain.

"Nathalie, I'd better put things honestly. You're talking nonsense, my dear child. Make your way in London? How can you possibly? Do you realize what London is? Do you realize how many people at this very moment are 'making their way' as you call it? If you had to help people continually as I have to; if you were for ever meeting the terrible tragedies, often enough just the result of trying to 'make their way,' you'd realize the hopelessness of it. I wish I could take you into some of the homes where my work often lies, hear what some of these women say, how they repent that first step, which you are so lightly proposing. No, Nathalie, go back to Polchester. That's your home. Put these grand ideas out of your little head."

Ruth saw herself moving from door to door, dispensing food here, money there, advice everywhere, and grateful faces looked up to her, faces that had been sullen and scowling, lighted now with a new hope, a new faith in human nature.

But "little head"! That was an unfortunate word. Patronage is the hardest thing in the world for the poor to endure. Nathalie had no intention of enduring it. "I'm sorry, Aunt Ruth"—and her voice was very firm now indeed, even a little arrogant—"but I don't think you quite understand me. How could you, when I've only been here so short a time? But, indeed, I'm neither so young as you think nor so ignorant. I had made up my mind when I came down this afternoon to tell you that I would be going away next week. I'd made my plans. You've been ever so kind, you and Uncle

Hans, and I'll never forget your kindness, but—but—I'm
not a little schoolgirl, you know. I realize perfectly what I'm
about. I shall manage very well indeed. I shall really."

The impertinence! Here was the girl's true nature coming
out at last! This matter must be dealt with, once and for all.

To have the girl running loose about London, Hans making secret appointments with her, leading him into all kinds
of company, encouraging him to oppose her wishes in
everything.

Her voice shook a little in spite of herself as she answered:

"Well, Nathalie, you force me to be frank. I didn't intend
to hurt your feelings—I hope I shan't now—I hate to hurt
anyone's feelings—but I think that as you've said what
you have, it's my duty. This visit, as I tried to hint just now,
has gone to your head, my dear. I made a great mistake in
bringing you up here. It was one of my foolish, impetuous
impulses. You *are* a little schoolgirl, so far as knowledge of
the world goes. Like so many girls these days, you think
you know everything, and you know nothing at all. It has
been only too obvious, I am afraid, these weeks here, how
ignorant you are. I don't want to be unkind, but I must
speak the truth. You've given both your uncle and myself
a lot of trouble and anxiety during your stay with us. We've
been glad to have you, but there's no doubt both your uncle
and I are agreed that you will be better and safer in Polchester."

"Uncle Hans said that? That's a lie!"

Nathalie had sprung to her feet; her voice was a cry.

"A lie! Nathalie, you're forgetting yourself!"

"It *is* a lie. Uncle Hans never said that. Uncle Hans loves me. He wants me to be with him always. It's you that hate me and have always hated me since first I came here!" She turned and challenged the room, the house, the nasty old woman in her nasty chair, the town, the world. Ruth also had risen.

"Oh! so that's what you think, is it?" (Shame, shame that she, who had been so good, so generous and patient, should have to face this savage ingratitude.) "Do you know what you have done since you've been here? You've managed in a few days to disturb everything that your uncle values. With your crude selfishness, never thinking of anyone but yourself, you have interrupted your uncle's work, his privacy, his comfort, everything that I for years have been protecting. It is because he is a great man, and a great gentleman, that he hasn't pointed one or two things out to you. If you had been less selfish and less conceited you'd have realized what your visit has meant to him. Only last night he said to me: 'Is that girl never going? Am I never to be left in peace?' That's why to-day I was trying to tell you as gently as I could——"

"It isn't true! It isn't true! He never said that!"

(But indeed Ruth was sure now that he had said it. She saw him standing in the door of her bedroom, she caught again the very accents of his voice: "Ruth, is that girl never going?")

"Now, Nathalie, that's enough. You've forced me to tell you the truth. And take my advice. See yourself as you really are. Don't flatter your attraction to men; you are an ordinary little uneducated girl from a country town. I've been greatly to blame in——"

"It isn't true! It isn't true!" pantingly she interrupted again. "He never said that!"

But perhaps he had! Oh! perhaps he had! Like a blow in the heart she saw herself as Ruth saw her, an ignorant, uneducated girl, flattering herself that he loved her. That had been possibly his kindness, his generosity. How could she tell? This woman must know him better than she.

She looked at Ruth. "If he really said that—I'm sorry. He is so kind, he wouldn't want to hurt me. You needn't worry. I'll go."

With her head up she left the room.

CHAPTER XI

Farewell to Tapestries!

HANS had, during these three days, been in a strange mood.

All his life he had been subject to overwhelming times of lethargy—not laziness, not idleness, but conditions that were dreamlike, submerged beneath long shadows, as it seemed to him, of green and purple colour, when everything was dim to him. When he wrote, but scarcely knew what it was that he was writing, when figures moved before him like ghosts, and the hours flew before his eyes like scraps of paper.

Now that he was old these moods were more frequent. He would sit in his chair in the library like a man under a spell, happy, indifferent, and when he had energy enough, scornful.

In his youth he had thought that these moods were the creative ones and had been proud of them. Now he didn't care whether they were creative or no. He had done, it might be, with creation for ever, and a good thing too. What, after all, had he even created? Witch talk and a passing cloud, the ripple of a stream and a flare in the night. Only he was not so picturesque about his creations. "Crétins" he was in this and that sort of a mood inclined to name them. He had had his moments, had snatched a

251

perch or two out of the flaming lake with his worm on the
end of a string. There had been salmon for cleverer fisher-
men.

These moods, however, were for the most part happy
ones. This time they had been acutely unhappy. He sat in
his chair, not moving, his velvet cap on his head, his deep-
set piercing eyes staring into nothing at all.

And in this nothing shadows shifted—Nathalie, Ruth, his
cursed mother-in-law, the Russians. Who were they? What
were they about? And in a dimmer distance the One-eyed
Commander sulkily overhung his gaze. What was the fellow
doing there? He didn't want him. He was done with creation. He wouldn't stir a finger to help him out of his obscurity. No, he would not look his way or catch the purport of
his whisper. He was done with creation.

And later he thought, as his eye scornfully moved about
the room, they had all been done with it. Dante, Milton
and his dummy heaven, William of the playhouse and the
second-best bed, Euripides and his melodrama, Balzac and
his dressing gown, Keats and his young woman, Byron and
his game leg, Wordsworth and his daffodils, Dostoevsky and
his lunacies, Tolstoi and his arrogant peasantry, Pope and
his malice, Cervantes and his windmills, Browning and
his dinner parties, Chaucer and his daisies, Homer and his
blindness, Lord—what a cackle about a fire in the gorse!
Stuff your guts and tickle your phallic sensibilities—only
he was too old even for that these days.

Yes, the fire died to ashes, the clouds, above the house,
spreading, thinning, the streamers in great battalions ad-

vancing across the sky, shutting out the light, throwing darkness upon the earth, prophesying the end of all these vanities. Out of nothing into nothing. After the whistle of the wind and the stir of the hissing flame, the long blessed silence.

He moved about the house, lay on his bed staring into darkness, listening to the clocks, hearing his body fall into decay.

Then on the third morning he burnt his finger lighting a cigar. He cursed like hell, danced about the room, kicked Martha, came to a stop, still cursing, in front of the Manet.

Well, that was a darling, certainly it was a darling. There was justified creation with those women and the delicate colour in the air. He would have liked to know those women, to have kissed their ears and lost his hands in their dark-lit hair.

He yawned and scratched his head, picked up Martha and stroked her forehead over her eyes (which she adored), stretched his body. Where was he? What about Nathalie? He hadn't done a thing about her. He had talked to her these days—or had he not? And he loved her. He tingled suddenly with love of her. He was awake again.

Those Russians—could you trust 'em? That young man, he had talked long enough about wanting to die for her, but everyone knew that you couldn't trust them a yard. And the old boy, and the people in the street, the shops and houses, the rain gurgling down the water pipes, the girls ogling the men at the street corner. . . . Dante wasn't so bad; Goethe knew a thing or two.

And if, as toward the silent tomb we go,
Through love, through hope, and faith's transcendent dower,
We feel that we are greater than we know.

Do we, by God? That's just the question. But Nathalie,
at least, should be happy. That's one thing he'd see to before the earth choked his nostrils, and standing in the middle of the room he felt life run fiercely once again through
the old veins, tingle at the heart, flame in his eyes, fire his
brain.

It happened on that afternoon (the afternoon of Nathalie's
little tea party with Ruth) that he had to be present at a
meeting of authors and publishers. Seldom indeed, now, that
he went to these gatherings. This occasion, suggested to him
weeks ago, had stirred some interest—he had forgotten now
what it was.

But he went through the rain, dressed in his best, sat there
sardonically at the long table, looking to them all (as they
remarked to one another in confidence) "exceedingly ancient"; then back in the car through the rain again, up to
his library where he slept for two hours. Woke to the touch
of Bigges' hand on his shoulder. "Time to dress, sir. Going
out to dinner to-night."

He woke in a panic of apprehension. What was the matter?

"Bigges, what's up?" Half awake he stared at that
solemn countenance.

"Nothing at all, sir. Only you're dining out and it's gone
seven."

As he dressed the apprehension remained with him. He
had half a mind to look into Nathalie's room. He moved

indeed to the door, then paused. No, he would settle it all in the morning. Scandalous the way he had allowed these days to pass. But he would settle it all in the morning. He would go along with her to young Shapkin. . . . Everything should be arranged.

Nevertheless, when he had finished dressing, he tapped on her door. No answer. He tapped again. She was downstairs maybe. A damned incumbrance, these dinner-parties. He would make an excuse and stay at home. The two of them should enjoy a perfect dinner alone. He smiled, standing there in the passage, at the thought of the pleasure of it. But, no, he must go carefully with Ruth until the business was arranged. No risking Nathalie's happiness. But he would see her for a moment at least before he went.

His first word to Ruth, standing waiting in the hall, was:
"Where's Nathalie?"

"Up in her room, I think."

"No, I knocked on her door."

"It's late, Hans. They live right over in Cadogan Square." So he suffered himself to be led into the car, arrayed for the sacrifice, this vague apprehension still clutching him.

In the queer, muffled silence of the car the apprehension grew. Ruth was strange; something had happened to her. Whatever else had been true of her, she had always been protected by her self-confidence.

Now she was not protected. He knew it by her nervous movements, her slight, hesitating sentences, her oddly restless gestures.

He was himself uncomfortably restless. He did not want

to go to this damned party. He wanted to have an hour with Nathalie. The newly awakened consciousness of the lethargy of the last three days was irritating him now the more with every passing moment.

They exchanged few words, but once held up at a street corner, lights illuminating the interior of the car, he turned to her and said:

"Ruth, what's the matter?"

"Nothing," she answered sharply.

"Yes, there is," he said. "I know."

"Oh, why don't we go on? We shall be terribly late."

"This damned party," he growled. "This is the last dinner you ever get me to."

She sighed, but didn't reply; and he was suddenly touched by her; she seemed to him, for perhaps the first time in all their married life, lonely and desolate—Ruth, who had always been so self-sufficient. Had he been unkind during these weeks? The trouble was that he didn't care if he had been. For years and years, because he was fond of her, and because she had done so much for him, and because he was lazy, he had been anxious to save her every distress, even the tiniest. Now when he knew that he was desperately bored with her, and would for the rest of his days be so, he was sorry and felt a great tenderness towards her—the tenderness and kindness that one feels for people who have been very good to one, but whom, thank goodness, one will, after to-morrow, never see again.

He put out his hand and took hers.

"Tired?" he asked.

To his amazement her hand was trembling. He thought for a moment that she was going to cry.

"No," she said. "It's all right."

He held her hand, but they spoke no more until they reached their destination.

The Beaminsters were very kind and hospitable people. They were not very clever. Everyone went to their parties because the food was good; moreover, you never knew whom you might meet. The great and interesting were as greedy as the others, and probably at the Beaminsters you might watch them feeding.

Marjorie Beaminster was born a Medenham. She belonged to the Beaminster clan. The Beaminsters and the Medenhams lived in these days on the past. They were great no longer—but the younger members of these families did not wish to be great—a colossal Victorian bore, that idea of greatness! . . .

A figure like the old Duchess of Wrexe seemed to Marjorie Beaminster a fantastic waxwork. There were few left alive any longer who, by personal reminiscence, could give her reality. And a good thing too, thought Marjorie, who lived for her friends, bridge, dancing, and hunting in its due season. She and Frank were not, thank God, intellectual.

They invited, however, the best intellectuals to their parties, just as they invited the best politicians, actors, painters jugglers, saints, and missionaries. Ruth always accepted, and Hans was in general quite glad to go. He tolerated Frank, who, with his round red face, long limbs, and wide-staring eyes, looked like an ox being led dumbly to the slaughter. And Marjorie was young and pretty. And they were kindly. And he seldom met there his confrères.

To-night, however, he was miserable. He was only longing for the thing to be over that he might hurry home and reassure himself about Nathalie.

He was seated on the right of his hostess and, as usual, she treated him with a mixture of chaff and reverence. She thought him an old pet and also, as everyone knew, he was a great man. And although she did not believe in great men she liked to entertain celebrities. She had not read a line that he had ever written. He never seemed to her in any way extraordinary, just a charming, rather handsome old man who could, when he wished, have charming manners, who liked pretty women and good food, who possessed a bore of a wife (she thought Ruth, with her social manner, her chatter, and her assumption that she was important, too terrible for words).

Hans seemed to her an exception to the general rule that writers were not gentlemen—and by the word "gentlemen" she meant nothing to do with birth, but rather social ease and companionship.

She saw that to-night Hans' mind was elsewhere. He seemed old and tired: probably that wife of his had been bothering him, and she glanced (without seeming to) across at Ruth, who seemed to be made all of a piece, shining with colour—rose—gold. She was talking eagerly and gaily. It was one of the unhappiest evenings of her life.

All the several people at dinner watched Hans, sooner or

later, and made their comments. This, the last dinner-party of his life, had, although they didn't know it, its importance.

Two of the commentators were Clare Ronder and a young man, a barrister. Clare Ronder was a large, stout woman, who had, for thirty years or more, written clever, witty stories, more autobiography than story, depending for their success on a rather sharp and cruel wit mixed with a light and sophisticated sentimentality. She had reached the age when literary egotism, unless watched and guarded, becomes devastating. Every thought, every breath passing through the world seemed to her to have reference to herself and her work. Clever though she was, she could not conceal her sensitiveness, her eagerness for praise, her hurt at another's success. She was naturally kindly, generous, and warm-hearted, but she was lonely and ageing, and clutched her literary reputation to herself passionately, the only love left to her.

The sight of Hans irritated her. There was a convention that he was a great writer, and she guessed that he did not care whether he were so or no. That indifference hurt, because it was not hers.

Over her fish she murmured to her companion:

"Well, what do you think of the great man?"

"Frost? He's astonishingly young-looking for his years. He had his seventieth birthday the other day, hadn't he?"

"Yes, his wife coddles him like an infant. He might have been a great man once, if he hadn't married as he did."

"Don't you think much of him then?"

"Oh, I know it's the fashion to praise him. England's

always got to have her great man of letters. All you've got
to do is to live long enough."

"I don't know. Some of his things are fine—*Goliath* and
The Scornful Sun. Wonderful how he's kept it up."

"Oh, you think he has? Can't say I do. Derivative stuff.
Galleon and water, most of it."

"What's he like personally? Do you know him?"

"He can be charming when he likes. Pretends he's indifferent to praise, but he's as proud as Lucifer underneath.
His wife's built up a kind of Chinese pagoda over him. That's
her over there in the rose-coloured dress. Frightful snob.
It's a pity he's succumbed to all that. Just lets himself be
coddled."

"Well, hang it, he's over seventy. He deserves some pet-
ting. He looks a grand old boy to me. Finest eyes I've ever
seen. It doesn't matter what his job might be—he'd go to
the top in anything."

("Stupid ass," thought Miss Ronder. "Too naïve for
words. I wonder what the man's like on the other side of
me.")

Meanwhile, on the other side of Hans, there was a young
girl whose first year in London this was. Marjorie Beaminster had put her next to Hans, partly because she knew that
he liked pretty girls, and partly because of the thrilling
excitement it was to the girl. Marjorie liked people to be
happy.

The girl was so terribly moved by the event that she had
not as yet dared to speak. They had reached the middle of
dinner before Hans discovered her. He was pleased at once

when he saw her, because she resembled, a little, Nathalie.

"Are you enjoying yourself?" he asked her, smiling for the first time this evening.

"Yes."

"I don't mean this dinner. I mean life generally."

"Yes. Some of it—when I can do the things I want to."

"What are they?"

"I don't like parties much—not all the time I mean. I want to paint, but my mother wants me to marry as soon as possible. I've got six younger sisters, you see. But I don't want to marry."

"Well—what are you going to do about it?"

"Everyone says I'm selfish if I don't marry. I'm stopping my sisters' chances. I want to go away and lead my own life. Then my sisters can go ahead."

"Do you think you'll be a good artist?"

"I don't know. I don't care. That's all I want to do." Then greatly daring, looking at him rather timidly:

"Did anyone try to stop you writing when you were young?"

"No, nobody. Perhaps it would have been better if they had. I began too soon—before I knew anything about life."

"But some people think"—she was growing, encouraged by his kindness, very courageous now—"that some of your early books are as good as the later ones."

"Better perhaps. But that doesn't alter the fact that they'd have been better if I'd waited. Don't worry. If you're meant to paint you will, nothing will stop you."

"Oh, do you think so?" Her face lightened up. She was

at the moment beautiful. "You've made me so happy by telling me that. I'll never forget it."

"You're like a young friend of mine—a niece I'm very fond of. She's starting out into life too. And I'm starting out as well, the two of us together."

"You starting out?" She stared at him, not knowing at all what he meant.

"Yes. . . . We'll drink one another's healths, wish one another luck."

They drank to one another.

Ruth saw them do it. "Any pretty girl's enough," she thought bitterly.

An hour later he gave Ruth a sign. They were the first to leave. In the car she longed to reassure herself against the old age and desolation that had approached her from the eyes of the young girl at dinner. Also she could not escape from Nathalie. She saw her, had seen her through the evening, standing and crying, "That's a lie."

So almost timidly she put out her hand and touched his knee. He started as though he had been sleeping.

"Hans," she said, "Nathalie told me at tea time that next week she must leave us. She is going to some other friends in London."

His whole body quivered.

"Leave us? What other friends? She has none."

"I don't know. She didn't tell me their names."

"Nonsense!" He flung himself up and away from her. His gleaming top hat slipped to the back of his head.

"Of course she mustn't leave us. I hope you told her so."

"No. . . . She is determined. There is some job she wants to do."

"She can do her job at our home. Our house is her proper home."

He had never spoken directly about Nathalie to her before, and a fierce fiery jealousy gripped her and shook her.

"Oh! she can't live with us always. It would never do. She wouldn't like it herself."

"Have you been telling her so?"

"Of course not. . . . She knows it without my telling her so."

"She does not." Then he felt a sudden consciousness of selfishness and ingratitude.

"I beg your pardon, Ruth; I'm rude. It's a thing we must discuss. I don't think it's a bad thing for us to have a young thing like that in the house. It keeps us lively."

"Yes—and separates us." Her voice was shaking—this day seemed the worst and hardest of all her life.

"Separates us?"

"You know it does. From the moment she entered the house you have been different. We have never been so far apart in our married lives before as we are now. Whose fault is it but hers?"

He answered her quietly.

"That may be. We will come together again—but differently. I was dying and you were dying. You were too good to me, Ruth, and I was stifling."

She said nothing. He went on: "Why shouldn't we tell one another the truth? We've been married long enough.

You don't really love me. You have probably never loved me. You love the life you've built out of me. You shan't lose that. I'll see to that, but now I'm going to build a life for myself."

She answered him rapidly.

"I don't perhaps see love as you do. I have never been romantic. It is hard after all these years to be reproached . . . Because a girl . . ." She was on the verge of tears. She lifted her hands with a pathetic gesture and let them fall on her cloak. "You can't begin again now. You can't get on without me. . . . No, no. . . . Try it and see."

He turned to her, his eyes full of affection and kindness. "You are the best friend I have in the world. You have been wonderful to me for many years—but we must not make one another prisoners."

They had arrived. He got out, helped her out, put his hand through her arm, felt for his latch-key. The storm was over, there were stars in the sky; all the trees in the Park trembled after the rain.

Hans swung his hat and coat to Bigges, turned to her, and said:

"I'll be down in a moment—it's early yet," then slowly went up to the library.

She stood there without stirring. She was thinking with that sharp intensity that was hers sometimes at a crisis. This was a crisis now.

What must be her next move? Should she prepare him to-night for the things that Nathalie would tell him to-morrow? How she hated that girl! How she *hated* that girl! She crushed in her hand one of her gloves. . . . But hatred was no use as a policy. She must be cleverer than that. Things, however they might seem to change, must not alter in reality. She would give him all the freedom that he thought he wanted, and in a fortnight's time have him as he had been before. He was old, he was tired, he was lazy. . . . Above all, the world must know nothing. That cat, Clare Ronder, had been watching to-night—and Marjorie Medenham had said something. . . . Silly idiotic old man to want to break loose *now* when she had made him so comfortable. Then she saw him coming down the stairs. She knew at once what had happened. She saw the note in his hand.

"She has gone," he said, giving her the note. His eyes were terrible. Through all their lives together she had been afraid of his eyes. Of all the properties of his body, she had possessed them the least. She had kissed him, flattered him, petted him; they had never been hers.

She read the note.

DEAREST UNCLE HANS:

I can't stay any longer. I haven't meant to be tiresome. She says that I have disturbed you and that you want me to go. I don't know whether that's true. You've been so kind. But one day I shall ask you. Good-bye.

Your loving
NATHALIE.

"Did you tell her that?" he asked her.

"I told her that she disturbed you—yes. And it was true."

"I'll never forgive you that lie." He turned towards the staircase—"I'm going after her."

His head was clear. He walked firmly and quickly to his

bedroom. After the first anger he did not think of Ruth
again. His only thought was that Nathalie might do something desperate. He must stop her. And he would never
enter this hateful house again.

He changed his clothes rapidly. He found a bag in the
cupboard in the bathroom. He found shirts, collars, ties.
Anything would do. He could send for other things that he
needed. . . . There were some books on the table beside the
bed. *Pride and Prejudice*, Carlyle's *Life of Sterling*, a volume
of Proust, *John Buncle*, and a volume of Lamb's *Letters*.
He laid them carefully in the bag.

He closed it. Passing the library he remembered Martha.
When he went out to a dinner-party Martha always remained in the library until his return. He went in. Martha,
who had been sleeping in front of the fire, yawned, and
came gently towards him.

"Come on," he said. "We're leaving."

Then he saw the Manet.

He picked it up, wrapped it in the leaves of the *Times
Literary Supplement*, and laid it in the top of the bag.

He went downstairs, Martha at his side.

He went to the cupboard at the end of the hall and found
his coat and hat.

Ruth was standing just where he had left her.

"Hans," she said, "wait—wait until to-morrow. I was
wrong to speak to Nathalie. She shall come back to-morrow."

"Oh, no, she won't," he said, cocking his hat a little
sideways on his head. "She knows better than that. So do
I."

His cocking his hat infuriated her.

"Very well, then," she answered. "If you go now like this, it's the end."

(And underneath her fury something said to her, "You silly fool—temper's no good.")

"I expect so," he answered, going to the door praying that Bigges would not appear and that there would be a taxi passing.

There was a taxi. He hailed it. As he closed the door behind him he heard Bigges' voice.

He climbed in slowly. Martha jumped in delicately after him.

He gave the man the address of Vladimir Shapkin.

END OF PART II

Part III

TO ST. SERVIAN!

CHAPTER I

A Lodging for the Night

HE SAT in the taxi, leaning forward, his hat still cocked, like a pirate who has escaped, against his expectations, with all his booty intact.

His soul was, indeed, divided—one half of it cried, "To Nathalie! To Nathalie!" The other half of it called, "To Freedom! To Freedom!" —and it is this divided domination which has bewildered artists since the first trembling of this star.

Martha knew also that the chief event of her life had just occurred. She too sat forward, her tongue out, her eyes gleaming; once and again she turned and licked Hans' hand to show him that she was with him in this adventure.

He had no doubt that he would find Nathalie, and that very soon. She would have gone either to Vladimir or the Westcotts. If Vladimir knew nothing, he would go to the Westcotts.

But, beyond all else he was free—he had only this bag and Martha in all the world—no wife, no mother-in-law, no house, no fame, no stupid friends, no stupider acquaintances, no one to fuss over or trouble him. He might die in a ditch and no one prevent him. Oh, perfect liberty!

At least for a day and a night he might do so! How to

keep his freedom, that was the question. As the taxi lum-
bered along he felt that he would like to ride in it for ever
(although it was an ancient taxi).

He was so deeply excited that when he put his hand on
Martha's neck it trembled, but it was the excitement of
happiness. When he found Nathalie they would live together
somewhere, in some extremely remote place, until she was
ready to marry her young man, and after that——— Why, he
would live all by himself! (Why was it that that thought
gave him the deepest throb of happiness of all?)

He adored Nathalie—she was his child, his darling, his
beloved for ever—but to be quite alone—he and the One-
eyed Commander! . . .

"We three!" he said to Martha, who, her eyes shining
desperately, barked sharply once, then yawned.

The taxi stopped.

He got out, took his bag, and looked up at the dark and
sinister building. Not a light in any window. It was then,
standing in the quite empty street, the taxi waiting for
a moment behind him then buzzing into activity and vanishing—after, not a sound save the distant rumble of traffic—
that he realized that he was indeed at the beginning of
an adventure. He had been for so long enclosed and
guarded and watched that he had now in spite of himself
a moment of apprehension. This was what it was to be
alone, to stand in a dark street under the stars before a
dark house that did not know of your approach, and, moreover, did not care.

But the One-eyed Commander was at his side. He felt

him—tall, the silver buckles glittering on his shoes, the silver at his wrists, that hawk-like nose, the stern relentless gaze. "Well, go *on* with it. This is your adventure. Not mine. I have my own affairs, as you'll soon discover."

So he went on with it. He walked forward and pushed Vladimir's bell. He waited. There was no answer. He looked up the street and down the street, then, shouldering the bag (he was aware at that how his excitement had tired him), he turned the handle of the street door. The door would not open. He waited. He rang Vladimir's bell again. Still no response. It was chill, and a breeze had sprung up, around his feet as it seemed—a cold breeze with the shiver of snow on it. He looked up at the sky and saw that the stars were slowly vanishing; wisps of grey cloud, thicker and darker than the night sky, were spreading above the chimney pots.

He rang the bell above Vladimir's—Klimov's bell. A window at the top of the house was flung up. A figure leaned out.

"Who is there?"

He called back, feeling intensely ludicrous and ironically helpless, his name. The window closed. The street door with a creaking noise slowly opened. He climbed the dark stairs, stumbling at every step, dragging the bag. Now he was very tired and felt foolish. The One-eyed Commander had departed into the stars.

On Vladimir's landing there was a light, and Klimov standing in a faded red dressing gown, his mouth open.

"But what——?" he cried.

Hans, panting, put down the bag. "Wait a moment. I'm out of breath. This damned bag . . ." Then he gasped: "Where's young Shapkin?"

It did him good then to see Klimov's delighted pleasure.

"Here, give me the bag. Come up to my room *at* once. Shapkin is away—since yesterday. He returns to-morrow. But why? . . . what? . . . no, but come. Rest in my room."

He almost ran up the further flight of stairs, bumping the bag after him. Hans and Martha followed. Mihail's room was in a splendid confusion. The dog and puppy ran to meet them, barking excitedly. Klimov had been carpentering, the floor was littered with shavings, newspapers, clothes. On the table beside the wooden toys were piles of books, the remains of a meal, and a large blue china bowl full of chrysanthemums. The bed was neat in the corner, on it laid very modestly a white nightshirt with a red border. Klimov was in his shirt and trousers and a pair of shabby clapping slippers.

Hans had put down his bag and stood looking about him. The dog and the puppy were investigating Martha, who herself was inquisitive, aloof, and coquettish.

"I must explain," Hans said. "If Shapkin is away, can you tell me where I can find him?"

"He has gone—yesterday, he has gone to Bristol on business. He was very reluctant to go, but he had no choice. He gave me orders that if there was a message from the young lady I was to send him a telegram. There has been no message."

"She hasn't been here then this evening?"

"No, no. Certainly not."

"And when does he return—young Shapkin?"

"To-morrow afternoon."

"Oh, I see. Then I must enquire at the other place."

His fatigue subconsciously getting the better of him, he sat down, almost without knowing it, on Klimov's bed.

"What time is it?" he asked.

"Nearly midnight."

"It's too late to go to them—but I might ring them up. Have you a telephone, Klimov?"

"Yes, next floor. I'll go with you."

They went down together. Near Vladimir's room, in a dark corner, there was a telephone.

"You put in pennies," explained Klimov.

Hans found his pennies, gave the number which he had found in the old tattered book, waited eagerly. Suppose they were all in bed! How could he ever rest?

"Ah, is that Mrs. Westcott?"

"Yes—who is it?"

"It's Hans Frost speaking."

"Oh, yes."

"I apologize for ringing you up at this hour, but—have you heard anything of Nathalie this evening?"

"Yes, Mr. Frost. She's upstairs asleep at this moment."

"Oh, thank God!" He sighed with relief. Klimov, standing beside him in the darkness, smiled with delight. He could tell from the sigh that the news was good.

"Was she very upset? What time did she come to you?"

"Yes, she was—very upset. She was quite hysterical. She got here about half-past five. She arrived with a small bag, said she'd only come for a minute, and must go out instantly and make her living! She's refused to tell us anything more. The only thing she said over and over again was that no one must know where she was. She said she'd been a burden on you, and when you'd been so good to her that was wicked— that she wouldn't see anyone again until she was on her own. . . ."

"Poor child, poor child!" Hans murmured. Klimov sighed sympathetically in the darkness.

"I told her she was a fool. I scolded her. I thought that was the best way to treat her. She was on the edge of hysterics. I told her she was imagining everything. At last I persuaded her to lie down for an hour or two—to wait until my husband came in. She did, and then I gave her—although she didn't know it—a sleeping draught. She's slept soundly ever since."

"Poor child, poor child—yes, you did absolutely right, Mrs. Westcott. I'm most grateful to you. May I come round in the morning?"

"Yes—please do. If you could show her that she hasn't bothered you——"

"Bothered me! Good God! . . . All right. I'll be with you first thing in the morning. Thank you so much."

He turned round to Klimov.

"It's all right. She's gone to friends. I'm so relieved."

They went back to Klimov's room, where they found that Martha had already established her power, having ejected the dog from the cushion in front of the fire and ordered the puppy to keep its distance, which it most obediently was doing.

And now what was Hans to say? How much was he to explain? He looked at Klimov and decided to tell him everything.

"Look here, Klimov. We're friends—I felt that we were from the first. Here's a secret—not a soul's to know. I've had a quarrel with my wife about this girl. I'm not going back home to-night. Can you put me up somewhere, just for to-night?"

"Everything I have, it is yours," said Mihail, his bald head crimson with pleasure.

"Thank you, that's a noble answer. But I only want to lie down somewhere for an hour or two. I don't suppose I shall sleep very much anyway."

"There's Vladimir's room."

"So there is. The very thing."

They moved down together, Klimov insisting on carrying Hans' bag, Martha following.

Vladimir's room was clean and empty. A bed in one corner, a shelf of books—everything neat and in order.

"Yes, I can make this do nicely," said Hans.

He shook hands with Klimov, who bowed, then said:

"I'm proud that you let me assist you. Very proud."

Then he went.

How strange, then, the silence of this empty room! He undressed, washed, put on pyjamas, switched off the light, lay down on the bed.

He could hear Martha moving round in this strange new place. She moved round and round the room, scratched at the carpet, lay down, sighed, got up again, scratched again, sighed, lay down, padded here and there. Then there was silence. He knew what she was doing. She was standing beside the bed, looking up, wondering whether for once she might do what had always been forbidden. After all, this was a strange uncouth place—unlike everything she had ever known in smell and substance. Should she dare? He must be feeling strange himself to-night. She hesitated. Then she jumped. She was on the bed. She waited, expecting the protest. None came. Encouraged, she scratched among the bedclothes. Wrapped in his dressing gown he was lying under the counterpane. She advanced, sniffed at his face, then finding that he did not scold her, with a sigh of great content, lay down, fitting into the hollow of his thigh. This was what all her life with him she had desired. She had, long ago, abandoned all hope of its realization. But you never could tell. Everything came if you waited for it. Then when he put out his hand and laid it on her head her happiness was complete.

He lay there, his body aching with weariness, but unable to sleep. Figures, pictures of the past crowded about him. The old days when creation had come upon him so fast that he had scarcely time to breathe, the old days of Henley and Stevenson, the old days of *The Duchess of Paradis* and *The Blissful Place*, and *Queen Rosalind*.

It seemed that all the intervening years had been rolled away. All the hours since his illness were like a scroll rolled up. His body might be old, but the spirit was once again young.

Yes, his heart was young—but as he lay there he realized with a splendid sense of ease and lightness that it mattered but little what his heart might be. He had never before in all his creative life been so completely conscious of his passivity, of the way in which in the past his body and soul and mind had been used, whether he wished it or no, by something that had regarded himself, his happiness, misery, content, ambitions, with a sweeping indifference. One glance, and he was used, and the spirit passed on. So it had been that day at Portofino, when, finding with great luck the chapel open, he had walked in, stared at the altar and the candles, and thus staring, had been seized, held, had *The Silver Tree* thrust upon him; or walking back on a blind, foggy night, after saying good-bye to Carlotta Hegel (ugly, angry, selfish thing of a German) heart-broken, it had seemed, and then suddenly—free! No more running round to the rooms in Parchment Street with the spotted wall paper and the rustling everlastings, no more meeting her at the restaurant in Soho—what was it called? He had forgotten now even the name—and imploring her over the *fritto misto* which she adored and was so greedy about, to divorce the hideous Hegel and marry himself; no more of that high shrill laugh and the canary-coloured dress with the silver buttons—and realizing then, in the middle of the fog, his freedom, how Laura Merrilees had come to him, Laura the woman of fifty, with her grasping maternity, her selfish self-sacrifice, her greed for love, her clutch on her weak, feckless sons—and how, grasping the railings that he might not fall, he had shouted for joy, fetched Laura a "clout" and carried her helpless home, then for months and months battened on her body!

Or the misery once in the English Lakes, staying in the farm near Ravenglass, fighting with *The Philistines*. How the book, a quarter created, died and withered under his hand, how he waited day after day, day after day, for something to come of it, how the people—that beastly family, the Crocketts, who had started so well—simply vanished from before his eyes, lay down, died, and passed away. That miserable country, how it rained and rained! That wretched day at Wastdale Head, staring up at the gloomy Gable, listening to the climbers in the dark, smelly room of the inn, with their eager, selfish (as it seemed to him) absorption in their trumpery climbs—and then, even then, wandering wretchedly into the little church, suddenly the Crocketts had come crowding about him again. Milly with her sarcastic smile, and Henry with his ambitious selfishness, and Old Mother Crockett with her thieving good nature. Directly after that the weather had changed. He had moved on, he remembered, to the little inn at Dungeon Ghyll, and the sky had been a glory of coloured clouds, and the earth musical with running water!

But himself—he had had nothing whatever to do with it. He had not even learnt the rules of his craft. And there were no rules. The great men came along, broke all the rules; then came the critics, and made the very breaking of the rules new laws for the next comer to go by.

No, he had not even written the kind of books that he wanted to write. He admired supremely, in literature, the *simple* style. In English, Defoe of prose writers and Wordsworth of poets (yes, even the Wordsworth of the Ecclesiastical Sonnets) had seemed to him the great exemplars. And yet, in the end, in *The Duchess of Paradis* and *Green Parrots* and *The Silver Tree* he had written some of the most fantastic and bejewelled prose in the English language.

Everything had been as he would not have it. No book that he had ever written had been the book that he had wanted to write, no praise that he had ever received (save a word or two from Galleon) had been the praise that he had desired, no criticism (and he had had plenty) had seemed to him to hit the mark (he knew how feeble in many ways all his works had been). He had not even lived the life that in his youth he had longed for. "Oh!" he had cried at twenty-five, "when I have money enough, and fame enough, the freedom, the energy, the breadth that my life is going to have!" And, behold, his life had not had either freedom or breadth. . . .

He sighed, drifting now towards sleep—and even as he sighed the One-eyed Commander came to him. Not, as he had come to him hitherto, unattended, driving up in the rain to the dark and sheltered house, but moving now in thick and fast company. Near to him was a woman with flaming red hair, a young man halting a little in his walk, an old woman with a bent back. The long room was lit with candles: the red-haired woman was playing at the piano. The One-eyed Commander, pacing the room, stopped at her side, laid a hand on her shoulder. She looked up, smiling. The young man came with halting step towards them, then stayed.

All the candles blew out. The Commander was alone. He turned and, raising his hands in the dark, felt his way blindly. The woman, also blindly, waited, steady against the wall, for his coming. . . .

But this woman, although he would possess her, was not the prize that the Commander needed. At every turn he missed his desire. . . . The funeral was creeping up the hill. The bearers stumbling under the heavy black coffin; the two women darkly veiled; the Commander grimly impatient at this idiotic ceremony that he must attend; the little graveyard on the hillside; the priest's robes blowing in the chilly wind; below, on the right, the house sunk in the trees, his destination on that rainy night months before; the words of the priest; the sinking of the coffin into the thick, damp soil; the smell of dung and rotting leaves; the cawing of the rooks in the little wood near by. . . .

So it goes . . . So it goes . . . Coming, coming, coming. . . .

The last trees, the last cloud fading into dusk. . . .

Hans, his hand on Martha's warm, smooth neck, fell asleep.

He awoke, instantly aware that he was deeply refreshed, and happily excited to a consciousness of Klimov standing over him. Martha was still asleep, and did not move when he sat up.

"What time is it?" he asked, rubbing his eyes.

"Nine o'clock," said Klimov, smiling.

"Oh, Lord!" He tumbled out of bed. "Nathalie!"

"I have some breakfast ready in my room," Klimov said; "and there is a bathroom down the passage."

Klimov had made coffee and boiled eggs. He sat rather silently while Hans ate and drank. He seemed to be lost in a sort of dreamy ecstasy that Hans should be there. He asked no questions, and Hans, was too deeply preoccupied with Nathalie's affairs to notice Klimov.

He was quickly dressed and bustling away. By ten o'clock he was at the Westcotts' door.

Millie let him in.

"She's gone," she said.

"Gone!" Hans cried. Then impatiently he went on: "Oh, you shouldn't have let her go! . . . Oh, why am I so late? . . ."

"We couldn't stop her," Millie said. "She woke me very early, knocked on my door. I went, and there she was fully dressed. She told me that she was going. I said where? She she'd decided to go back to Polchester, not to live with the Proudies again, but because she couldn't at present stay in London. There were circumstances that made it impossible. She might, she said, stop with the Proudies for a night or two, but only while she was looking for something. I asked her what kind of thing. She said that there were lots of old ladies down there who wanted companions. I told her then that you'd rung up last night. That seemed to excite her very much. She had been very calm and collected until then. She begged me to tell her what you'd said, so I told her exactly. Tears were in her eyes. She was tremendously moved. She said that if you came this morning I wasn't to tell you where she'd gone to, but to let you know that as soon as she had a real position she would write to you. She repeated the words a 'real position' as though they were very important. She also said that she loved you, and always would. . . . She is a darling, Mr. Frost, she is indeed. My children are more to me than anything on earth, but, honestly, I'd leave them, and my husband too, just now for Nathalie. But she wouldn't hear of my going with her, or giving her money or anything at all but breakfast. Then Peter, my husband, woke up and came out and joined us in his pyjamas. And he seemed to understand in a moment what she was feeling. He really did. And he'll go down at once to Polchester if she wants any help."

"He needn't," said Hans. "I'm going down myself."

"Oh, are you?" said Millie, a little doubtfully. "That's splendid."

"I'm going down to-day by the very next express train."

"Oh, yes," said Millie, still more doubtfully. "Only—I oughtn't, I suppose, to have told you where she's gone. I promised not to."

"That makes no kind of difference," said Hans. "You were quite right to tell me. I promise not to give you away. I suppose there's another express train to-day?"

"Yes," Millie said. "I know there's one in the afternoon—about three."

She found an ABC. Yes, there was a train from Paddington at three.

"She had enough money?"

"She said so. She was very proud, and very independent. . . . Mr. Frost, can you tell me at all what happened?"

"Yes. She had a quarrel with my wife, who unfortunately
said something that made her feel she was in the way. This
happened while I was out. I didn't know until I got back
from a dinner-party last night that she'd gone. She left me a
note."

"Yes," said Millie. "Also, she's in love with young
Vladimir Shapkin, but is afraid to marry him."

"Now, Mrs. Westcott, you introduced them in the first
place. Tell me, what do you think of that young man? Is he
a good sort or no?"

"Yes," said Millie, nodding her head, "I think he is. I
don't know him very well; but Peter likes him and trusts
him, and Peter's a splendid judge of people. Of course he's
a Russian, but that only means that he sees some things at
a different angle from ourselves. He's got a good brain and a
good heart. He's very kind."

Hans agreed. "I've only had one talk with him, but I
liked him."

He was aware of a pleasurable, excited interest in everything. He liked the room into which the sunlight was glancing, he liked Millie in her soft, crocus-coloured dress, he
liked the dark chrysanthemums on the table, the voices of
the children from upstairs—all of the world was here in
this room, flowing about him.

"Well," he said briskly, "I must be going along."

("Dear old man," thought Millie. "How smart and spruce
he looks! I hope Peter's like that at seventy.") She wanted,

though, to return to the children now. Nathalie was safe if the old boy was going to make her his charge. She wanted to get back to the children. No knowing what they were up to. . . .

Hans, returning, found Klimov on his knees near the window playing with the puppy. He was drawing a piece of string across the floor. The puppy, lying flat, pretended not to notice, then suddenly made a frantic dash. Martha was watching the door, wondering where in this strange new world could her master be. The other dog was watching Martha.

Klimov, not at all embarrassed at being caught over so childish an employment, got up.

"Well," he said, "there you are. Have you seen her?"

"No," said Hans. "She left at eight this morning for a town in the south where she'd been living before she came up to London."

"Yes," said Klimov, beginning to hum a tune, then checking himself.

"I'm going down there. There's a train this afternoon at three."

"Yes," said Klimov. He appeared of a sudden extremely doleful. The corners of his mouth drooped. He looked out of the window.

"You'll be able to tell young Shapkin," went on Hans, "something of what has happened. Not everything. I don't want you to tell him where she's gone. I'll write to him when I've seen how things are down there. You can tell him that. Tell him also——"

"Oh, Mr. Frost——" broke in Klimov, but timidly, nervously, twisting his hands together.

"Yes?" said Hans, smiling.

"I suppose it wouldn't appear to you possible. . . . You'd dislike it extremely—if—well—I want to come with you. Just for the journey. I've never been to the south of England. I haven't indeed. I know that this suggestion is most audacious, but I'd leave you immediately you wished—I would indeed. I might be of some assistance——"

He broke off. He looked like a child entreating from its elder some incredible joy.

Hans looked at him. Why not? He wasn't sure whether in spite of this splendid new-found liberty he wanted to be quite alone. He liked the man. Why not?

"Come, then," he cried. "We'll go on the adventure together."

He had a horrible fear for a moment that Klimov was going to embrace him. But all that Klimov did in reality was to sit down at the carpentering table and begin frantically to work.

"The box," he said, "must be made before I leave. I promised it to Nancy by to-night. Now come, you devil! See what a fine box we can make together."

CHAPTER II

The Train

HANS was aware against his will, as they started for the station, that Mihail Klimov was an odd-looking travelling companion; against his will he realized it because he was now in the open world, free of all prejudices, caring nothing for appearances.

Nevertheless, Klimov's appearance was too individual—a faded green jacket of the hunting sort, gay knickerbockers and gay worsted stockings, a large black hat of the kind worn by unsuccessful artists.

He carried also a kind of alpenstock, and conducted on a lead his dog Tray. ("Why Tray?" Hans had asked him. "The name," Klimov had answered, "of every dog in English poetry.")

Hans was the more aware of Klimov's costume because his own was so official. He had at the moment only the clothes in which he had escaped last night from what he now called "the Zoo"—his dark London clothes with the buff waistcoat and the black hat. Martha was in attendance, exceedingly scornful of Tray's bondage, and of this Tray was most unhappily aware.

It was a chill day, with wisps of fog clinging to windows and doorways, unsuspecting lampposts, and indignant street

288

corners. Everyone looked as though marriage were a failure and dyspepsia the common lot. In the half-light, faces were pale and backs bowed. All the wrong horses were winning the wrong races; the Balkans were feeling very uncomfortable about Italy; there had been earthquakes in Japan, and two millionaires had committed suicide. Russell Square dribbled at the mouth, this street had a cold in the nose, that a sore throat. The afternoon was closing quickly into a thick yellow twilight and the pavements were slippery under a paste of thin filmy mud. No sparrows twittered—human voices were hushed, and all the mechanism of the new triumphant world creaked, yelled, thundered its progress.

"I'm escaping! I'm escaping!" Hans thought joyfully, sitting beside Klimov in the taxi. "It's fitting that it should be on such a day." But his joy was nothing at all to Mihail Klimov's. Klimov was busily engaged in "keeping himself down." He had told himself that beyond and above everything he must not bore Hans Frost. He must show himself worthy of this, the greatest, most unexpected glory of all his life. Because, ever since he had been a little round boy in the Moscow Government spelling out for himself the easier poems of Pushkin, ever since his father had taken him one never-to-be-forgotten day into the nearest town to witness a performance of an Ostrovsky comedy, he had thought men of letters the greatest creations of the Almighty God. It had been his lot, however, only to know the lesser ones— the so-much-lesser ones that, try as he might, he could never reverence them as he should.

Once, spending a holiday in the Crimea, he had had pointed out to him the attenuated figure of Tchekhov. That had been indeed a tremendous moment for one who had worshipped, as he had done, Stanislavsky and Knipper and Kochalov in *The Three Sisters* and *The Cherry Orchard;* a great moment that he carried like a picture always in his heart—the brilliant sky, the shining front of the hotel, the figure, standing on the hotel steps, looking out, lonely and whimsical, into the infinite distance. That had been his nearest approach until now.

This present event was nothing less than a miracle. He had a true sense of what was fine in the Arts. He had long ago savoured the uniqueness, the odd alliance of irony and sentiment, of fantastic beauty and rigid formalism, of almost wild poetry and realistic prose in *The Duchess of Paradis* and *The Silver Tree* and *Goliath* and the others.

And here the man himself was presented to him, so to speak, straight out of heaven's pocket. The man himself, so attractive, so human, so kindly, so unpretentious.

Mihail Klimov was a very humble man, although he would stand up at any moment with hot indignation for the ideas in which he believed. He was always very unconscious of himself, for ever losing himself in enthusiasms, devotions, ideas, protests, labours, projects. He lost himself now completely in Hans Frost, and it made him exceedingly happy to do so.

They reached the station and found a porter. He looked with great suspicion at the two dogs.

"They won't bite, will they?" he asked.

"Dear me, no," said Hans indignantly.

"Because if they bite anybody there'll be a bit of trouble. Anyway, you can't take them in the carriage with you. They'll have to go in the van."

"Not take them with us!" cried Klimov. "But we must. I insist. I'll pay extra. My dog will be terribly unhappy by himself."

"Can't help it, sir," said the porter, who was a little shrivelled man with a hoarse voice. "Ain't allowed. Must go in the van."

"I'll see about it," said Klimov confidently. "I'll speak to the guard."

"Speak to 'oo you like," said the porter, digging down into his trousers for his voice, then, failing to find it, ending in a whisper: "It's the law."

Tray meanwhile, greatly depressed in the taxi by Martha's (as he felt, deserved) contempt, had just discovered a lady Pomeranian tied to a stout lady in furs, and, in order to establish in Martha's eyes his adequate masculinity, started in pursuit. This involved Klimov and his alpenstock in many confusions—porters' barrows, piles of luggage, and the legs of passengers.

Certain lookers-on were smiling. Hans had a moment (of which he was greatly ashamed) of wishing that he had never met Klimov. It was difficult to rid himself completely, all in an instant, of twenty years' traditions. So he went off and bought the tickets. He bought third-class ones. He suspected that that would suit Klimov's pocket more appropriately.

When he reached the train he found Klimov, hot, his hat on one side of his head and Tray wound about his legs, discussing the situation with the guard.

However, it could scarcely be called a discussion. The guard had but little time to spare.

"Sorry, sir. Rules; no dogs allowed in with passengers. Quite all right in the van, you'll find. Always settle down."

With anxious absorption Klimov followed the guard, dragged forward indeed by the now exceedingly excited Tray, who supposed, it seemed, that he was heading straight for a paradise of bones and lady Pomeranians. Martha, always wise before the event, followed demurely.

Tray was tied to a pillar in the middle of a sea of boxes, Martha to a staple in the wall. Klimov knelt beside him, whispered in his ear, patted him, pulled his ears. Tray, straining at his cord, panting, smiling, wagging his tail, considered this excellent fun. But the moment arrived.

"Now, sir—only three minutes. You must go to your carriage."

"But I wish to remain here."

"Sorry, sir, no room to-day. Very heavy luggage."

It was true enough—no room to squeeze a cat. Klimov tumbled onto the platform, dust on his knees, his cheeks, straw in his hair. Hans, in a state of nervous exasperation, was waving to him to hasten. He was dragged into a compartment completely filled, so that at once he was pressed down between a stout ginger-faced woman, a man with knees widely spread, a little boy and a little girl. Hans, on his side, had a young man in a bowler hat, a little man with pince-nez and a newspaper, and an old goatish man with a white beard.

But this audience was exactly what Klimov needed. He seized upon them, compelled them to force the highways and hedges of their British surly shyness, made them partners and co-sharers of his wrongs, injustices, outrages and intolerable treatments, forced from them compassion, sympathy, argument, and general emotional chorus.

A new Klimov was revealed to Hans, a challenging, ferocious, melodramatic, abusive Klimov. What was the British Government to him? Had he not paid a ticket for his dog, and if he had paid his ticket, was not the dog entitled to some special convenience? Was it right or just that he should be tied up like a criminal to a post without bread or water, without a friend in the world, that he should be allowed to howl his heart out from loneliness and terror, and nobody care? He, moreover, a dog who lately had been sick, his leg sprained, and having for weeks to be most especially tended. And it was not as though he were a dog of evil or malicious tongue—the mildest dog ever seen, only, of course, a dog with natural feelings, a human, tender-hearted dog, who would feel this injustice as possibly no other dog in the whole country would feel it. . . .

And suddenly, because he was short of breath, Klimov ceased, and with a most unexpected (because he had been crying out in a very ferocious tone) beaming smile looked round upon the company.

He had them all in his power. They might not indeed agree with his opinions or accept all his views. The little man with the newspaper enquired rather fiercely whether he considered that the comfort of other passengers ought not to be considered, and the stout man at his side said that he hoped that he realized that when the Labour Party came into power everything would be very different.

But in general they were all with him, sympathizing, understanding, his little sisters and his little brothers.

Then what intimacies poured forth! Who is it who has complained that the English are a reserved and reticent people? Reticent! Give them an inch of encouragement and they will return you ell upon ell of personal experience. The ginger-faced woman had a dog; the man with the wide-spread knees had two dogs; the prophet with the white beard had had kennels of dogs; the little man with the news-paper had an Alsatian; even the small children hoped to have dogs.

All these dogs were led forward and presented to Klimov; he was urged to consider their coats, their noses, their appe-tites, their tricks, their injustices, their triumphs, their humanities, their passions. And behind this world of dogs hovered an atmosphere, pleasantly stimulated, of a general disgust with the idle, selfish, exorbitant, malicious, unedu-cated British Government "going to the dogs," as the little newspaper man, who had plainly a pretty wit, humorously suggested, but so far, so far, inferior to their destination!

And what of Hans during this eager excitement? He sat there, taking indeed no part, but revelling in this close con-tact with his common humanity. How could it be that he who had hated Bigges so bitterly that it had been all he could do not to kick his posterior, who disliked increasingly any sort of dinner-party, who had been creeping more and more into a reserved and isolated shell, should feel now this warm sympathy, humorous participation? He did not mind in the least that the compartment was already close and stuffy, that the young shiny-nosed man on one side, the goatish prophet on the other, were pressing in upon him and leaning, because of their interest in the general argument, right across his chest. Strange to say, forgotten impulses and agitations were rising in his breast. He was savouring life once again, real life, at first hand, as for years he had not savoured it. Not that he would wish to spend immortal years in this compartment, to be condemned for ever to the company of the ginger-faced woman and the goatish old man—but he was in contact once more with his own people. These were those from whom he had sprung, the real children of the world, to whom birth and death, labour of the soil, contest with earth and sky, and at the last an eternal God-given truce, were the unescapable facts. No escape, no flinching, no specious argument—acceptance of life.

After these grand thoughts he felt for his pipe, with apologies for troubling his neighbours pulled down his bag and extracted Charles Lamb, looked out at the dim and misty landscape, and began comfortably to read.

The hubbub fell as quickly as it had risen. Everyone slipped back into his or her proper individuality, but they were all friends together now, and would support one another if occasion arose against all the world.

Klimov looked smilingly about him, and then, a little anxiously, at Hans Frost. How had he taken all this noise and excitement? Ah, there! Once again he had forgotten, in the stir of the moment, to control himself, and as always when ashamed of his behaviour he saw, standing before him, his huge fat nurse, her bosom creaking behind the crimson bodice with the gold buttons that she used to wear. She had had a dark moustache and a hairy mole in the middle of her right cheek, and she would scream at him and raise her great flat hand. But she never struck him. In the middle of her temper she would smile and catch him to her and give him something to eat. He could feel still the soft warmth of her cheek and neck and the smell of milk and cabbage soup that seemed always to hang about her. He looked at Hans just as all those years ago, there in the huge empty wooden rooms of the house in the Moscow Government, he had looked at his nurse.

But Hans was all right. He was reading in a thick squat crimson book, *The Letters of Charles Lamb*. Klimov felt in his coat pocket and produced from it, very shabby and dog-eared, *Tristram Shandy*. It was his favourite book in the English language, and in between the pages he listened for the howls of Tray.

After a while the train stopped at a station, and the young man, the goatish old man with the beard, and the little man with the newspaper got out. They all seemed to part from Klimov with great regret. They smiled and nodded and said good-day. Klimov smiled and got out and stood on the platform wondering whether he had time to visit Tray. He looked about him with wide-open childish attention, but just as he was prepared to make a valiant dash he was ordered back into the train.

Hans had moved now to the window and Klimov sat opposite him. The fat man had disappeared. There remained now only the woman and the two children. Yes, they also were going to Polchester, to a sister. Not a good time of the year, but the sister's husband had gone to Canada and the sister needed company. The little boy had new boots which he showed to Klimov. Klimov patted his head. Then, seeing that Hans was not reading but was gazing out of the window, he began to talk to him. He talked about art. Did Hans remember how Dostoevsky in his *Journal of a Writer* defended the artist against the utilitarian critics, how he said that the only thing the artist had to bother about was to write well and to give his fellow men as much beauty as there was time for, and never to bother as to whether he were useful or no? Did Hans agree with that?

"Certainly I agree with that," Hans answered. Gazing out of the window he saw how a faint pale dusk, dimly gold, had invaded the world, and against this dim world the streams, the fields, the trees were like vaporous shadows.

A dim, dim world—beautiful in its silence, its loneliness, its remoteness.

"I don't know anything about art," he went on hurriedly. "I never have known anything. I can't talk about those things; I never could. I've always been quite passive as a

writer. I've never had many ideas. Something comes to me
and forces itself out of me. I'm not a true artist at all. If I
were I'd hammer and hammer away to make something
more beautiful. I'm not a poet. I've never known—what
shall I call it?—a frenzy of inspiration. I'm not a novelist
either, or only a very little one. People do compel me to
let them out sometimes. I do it reluctantly. I resist them as
long as I can. I suppose I'm best at fairy tales. And those
are what I admire most in literature. But not the sort of
decorated, elaborated fairy stories that I've written. I'd
rather have written like Hans Andersen than anyone. Or
La Fontaine. Or your Kryllov whom I've read in French. Or
Robinson Crusoe. There's a book! Wonderful! But I can't
do it. I can't be simple and natural. Only once in these
popular poems before the war. Not that they were good;
but they were simple, natural."

"So you've never tried to be useful?" asked Klimov,
drawing the little boy close to his side.

"Useful! Lord, no!"

"You've never planned any Utopias?"

"Utopias! You can see how useful my Utopia would be
when I tell you that my favourite book of that kind is old
Morris's *News from Nowhere*. No one reads it now, I suppose.
I should like just such a world, beautiful men and women
moving happily along flowery meads, singing as they row
up the river, carving boxes and painting missals. . . . No, I
suppose I should hate it really. But politics are unmean-
ing to me. I just do what I'm told by the man in power,
and curse at having to do it, like every other man. There

have to be men in power, I suppose. One of them is very like another."

Klimov sighed. "At least you've given happiness to thousands of your fellow men; that is enviable."

"Perhaps. But have I ever made a single human being happy? An artist is a godless egoist. Everything must be sacrificed to his trumpery little creation. So soon as an artist allows another human being or a cause or a religion to dominate him he becomes a bad artist. He must be selfish and vain and petty and tyrannical. I've been an artist long enough, and not a good enough one to justify my tyrannies. I should like before I die to see life at first hand a little, to know one or two human beings as they are, not as the creatures my art makes of them. . . ." He tapped his book. "Here was a man. He loved his sister and his friends like a man, and he wrote divinely. Although he knew great tragedy and was often unhappy, he was one of the most fortunate men who ever lived, and one of the greatest . . . Saint Charles—Thackeray's damnable sentimentality, but for once truth, was justified."

"When I was a young man," said Klimov, "I thought that I was going to be a great artist. I could write a little and paint a little and play the piano a little. I thought I had great ideas. I would walk for hours beside the canals in Petrograd and think how great my ideas were. But nothing came of it. I had no application. I never could think anything out. And yet I've had a very happy life. I used to have visions. I often talked with God. He wasn't a weary old man with a white beard, but young and lusty, rather arrogant, and very

wrong-headed about many things. I used to argue with him
and point out where he'd made mistakes. He would come
and walk with me and curse the stupidity of human beings.
He was always showing them the right way to do things,
but would they go the right way? Never. Obstinate as
mules he would say they were. But he would grow wiser
himself in time—or he hoped so. That's the one hope of
the world in my opinion, that God himself should grow wiser
as time goes on. . . . There is not at present much sign of it.
Ah, here we are at another station! Let's go and see the
dogs."

They hurried down the platform, found the van, and
there were the dogs lying like the lion and the lamb, or
more pertinently, perhaps, like Cophetua and the Beggar
Maid, almost in one another's arms.

They were in fact only languidly interested at the sight
of their masters. Martha had scarcely ever been out of her
master's sight before, and she found this new world uncertain, puzzling, but filled with interest. This strange dog was
after all to be sniffed at, and there were many humans who
appeared, paid their due by open admiration, and passed on.
She had been fed, too, with biscuits, pieces of sandwiches, and
the jammy fingers of two young children. Her strict home
diet gave her deep appreciation of the many pleasant ad-
ventures possible in a world without discipline.

Tray, a vain and inexperienced dog, was overcome with
pride at his apparent conquest of Martha. It was true (as
is, alas! so frequently true) that now that she had given
him her companionship, she was not after all so very inter-

esting, but his tail was "up." He had vindicated his incipient manhood.

He rose to greet his master, but yawned several times, and then at once lay down again, his head resting very pleasantly on a mail bag.

"They seem to be all right," said Klimov, in his heart disappointed that his dog didn't need him more. All his life it had been the same. No one had ever needed him very much. A woman who had loved him once for three days in Petrograd told him that it was because he was too eager about people, showed them too plainly that he liked them.

"You should be more indifferent," she had said, yawning, and powdering her cheeks. "Never send women telegrams." And she had been so fond of him the first evening!

Returning to the carriage, looking out of the window rather sadly, he admitted that this was probably true.

It would be the same shortly with Hans Frost. Then cheering up—no matter, this had been a great adventure, a wonderful piece of luck that he would cherish all his days. With him "cheerfulness was always breaking in." He had a puppy's excitement in the moment and trust of the future.

Hans, meanwhile, opposite him, was feeling exceedingly weary. He was not seventy now, but seven hundred. All the weariness of the world sat upon his eyelids. He wondered why the devil he wasn't sitting in his marvellous chair in his library, a crackling fire at his side, Martha at his feet, the Manet before his eyes. What fly had bitten him? He loved Nathalie—she was the apple of his eye, his heart rejoiced when he thought of her—but wasn't an old man a

fool to give up his beautiful home for a young girl who considered him, when she considered him at all, an ancient
Methuselah?

It was true that Ruth was a bore, and her mother a horror,
but Ruth ran the house extremely well, and he needn't see
the mother. What was he doing sitting on a seat so hard
that his ham bones throbbed with ear-ache, a seat also so
filthy that every germ in the world must have its country
home in the creases, sitting staring into the fat, cow-fed
cheeks of a country woman, and the oily, shining counte-
nances of her offspring? What was he doing, too, in the company of this amiable, but too utterly childish, Russian, who
now had seized him and would never let him go again? What,
what had possessed him at his age to break his settled, comfortable life into pieces, all for a whim, for a moment's anger,
because of a scrap of paper, Bigges' posterior, Ruth's irritation, his mother-in-law's insults?

A profound melancholy seized him, a horror as of approaching death. He saw himself seated there, an ugly,
lonely failure of an old man, not needed, ludicrous, despised
by the young, rotting to the grave. . . .

They were summoned to dinner in the restaurant car.
Sulkily, silently, he bumped along the corridor, gloomily
he sat down to the congealing soup, the fragment of turbot
with the glistening blue eye, the stolid mutton and water-
soaked cauliflower, the tasteless apple tart, the cheese and
poisonous watercress.

Not a word did the two of them exchange during the
meal. The train went bumping along, lights flashed, rivers

whisked by, hills and roads flashed out under a pale, dim moon that had risen gently into a misty heaven.

The sea rolled up to the train, flashed a breaker or two and was gone. They bumped back again to their carriage.

Hans picked up the Lamb again, and, warmed now by food and drink, was a little happier. Saint Charles, knowing his case, came along and sat beside him.

"You are feeling a little low," he said. "You shouldn't. Take a pig, for instance. To confess an honest truth, a pig is one of those things which I could never think of sending away. Teals, widgeons, snipes, barn-door fowl, ducks, geese— your tame villatic things—Welsh mutton, collars of brawn, sturgeon, fresh or pickled, your potted char, Swiss cheeses, French pies, early grapes, muscadines, I impart as freely unto my friends as to myself. They are but self-extended; but pardon me if I stop somewhere. Where the fine feeling of benevolence giveth a higher smack than the sensual rarity, there my friends (or any good man) may command me; but pigs are pigs, and I myself therein am nearest to myself."

Seeing then that Hans was already more cheerful, was smiling indeed, and pricking up his ears, he proceeded to tell him and Samuel Taylor Coleridge the adventure of the Cake and the Beggar Man:

"One of the bitterest pangs of remorse I ever felt was when a child—when my kind old aunt had strained her pocket-strings to bestow a sixpenny whole plum cake upon me. In my way home through the Borough I met a venerable old man, not a mendicant, but thereabouts; a look-beggar, not a verbal petitionist; and in the coxcombry of taught charity, I gave away the cake to him. I walked on a little in all the pride of an Evangelical peacock, when of a sudden my old aunt's kindness crossed me; the sum it was to her; the pleasure she had a right to expect that I—not the old imposter—should take in eating her cake; the ingratitude by which, under the colour of a Christian virtue, I had frustrated her cherished purpose. I sobbed, wept, and took it to heart so grievously, that I think I never suffered the like—and I was right. It was a piece of unfeeling hypocrisy, and proved a lesson to me ever after. The cake has long been masticated, consigned to dunghill with the ashes of that unseasonable pauper."

"Good!" cried Hans aloud. "Damn good! Good indeed!"

Then aware that he had cried out aloud in a public conveyance, looking about him to see whom he might have disturbed, he realized that no one was paying him the slightest attention.

Klimov had gathered the two children close to himself, and was telling them a story. They were sitting like little coloured statues, without motion, mouths open.

"And when the little boy," Klimov proceeded, "came near to this part of the town his heart bounded within him. He had come across the shining, glittering snow to the doors of the great church. The doors were of beaten gold, and on all the walls the saints of the church were painted in every colour. The towers of the church were like a cluster of tulips, crimson and purple and orange and green. And above the towers all the silver stars were shining in a sea of glory. And even as he looked, holding onto his father's hand very tightly, his eyes starting from his head, all the bells began to ring, jangling together across the snow. And from every part of the town came flocks of people, all hastening into the church to return thanks to God. Little Ivan, with his father, passed in too, and then indeed he had to draw a great breath. Because there in front of him were thousands and thousands of candles, all shaking in the breeze, and glittering, like the stars above outside. Then all the people knelt down and offered thanks to God——"

"Polchester! Polchester!" cried the guard, passing down the corridor.

"Polchester! Polchester! Here we are!" cried Hans. "Well, upon my soul. I've never enjoyed a journey so much in my life before!"

CHAPTER III

Progress through Polchester

HE awoke next morning in his bedroom in "The Three Feathers" to awareness that it was nearly nine o'clock, that it was a day of sunshine, and that he was bewildered as to his surroundings. The wall paper was of a mottled yellow, with birds that looked like green canaries. There was a large print of "Carrying Home the Yule-log" that reminded him instantly of his mother-in-law. His mother-in-law! Ah! she was, thank God, abandoned and deserted. He remembered, instantly, everything, and especially the train journey of yesterday, the dogs, the talk with Klimov, the company of Charles Lamb, Klimov's story, the country people. . . . A glorious and vigorous satisfaction with life attacked him. He sat up, stretching his arms. Of course he was free, free— free! Here he was in Polchester, where not a soul (save Nathalie) knew him, he had had a divine sleep, better than any that he had known for years, and to-day he would see Nathalie!

He rang for his hot water, and twenty minutes later he was down in the breakfast room, drinking bad coffee, and marvelling at the sensational stories in the *Daily Post*.

It was an old-fashioned, thoroughly English hotel. The rooms seemed to echo with the click of billiard balls;

in the lounge there was an ancient wall paper with yellow chrysanthemums, Frith's "Railway Station," a little spotted with time and weather, and large red vases with everlastings.

He stood in the doorway of the hotel and looked out on the shining, cobbled street. People were moving about in a lazy, happy fashion. Only now, although it was nearly ten o'clock, some of the shops were losing their shutters; as he walked, from some high distance the cathedral bells rang the hour. Here Klimov found him. He arranged with him to meet him at the hotel at one o'clock, and with Martha (who had against all rules been smuggled last night into his bedroom) started up the High Street to find the house of the Proudies.

Now, as he moved up the street (and many people turned to glance at this very distinguished-looking old gentleman with the peculiar-shaped hat), all his excited love for Nathalie had returned. The events of yesterday had for a moment dimmed his vision of her, but now, in a minute or two, he would see her again, the darling—the darling, and he would have her in his arms again, and pet her, and reassure her, and show her that he was her friend, and would look after her to the end of his days, and maybe after that.

He passed under the Arden Gate and stood for a moment looking at the splendid breadth and size of the cathedral basking now like a splendid great animal under the warm autumnal November sun. Just to think that he had allowed all these years to pass and had scarcely visited England at all, had never seen many of the English cathedrals, and indeed none of them since his early youth. There was great peace and quiet here. Two clergymen moved slowly across the grass, and an old man passed him pushing a wheelbarrow pressed down with dead leaves and faded flowers. Martha walked in dignity beside him, as though this were the very place and atmosphere for which she had been always intended.

He had found the address of Canon Proudie in the directory and soon discovered that it was one of the little houses, its garden bursting with chrysanthemums, that looked out across the grass to the cathedral.

He rang the bell and, when the maid came, presented his card. He would like to see Mrs. Proudie, if he might, on a matter of considerable importance. The maid took his card, said that Mrs. Proudie would see him if he did not mind waiting for a moment, led him up the stairs into a drawing-room full of sunshine and photographs of Proudie relations. He sat rather stiffly in a very old and not very comfortable chair, leaning forward on his stick. In another second Nathalie would be in his arms!

But Mrs. Proudie came in alone. She was a big, stout woman with a beaming smile and the air of one who has spent her life in taking pots of conserve out of an aromatic storeroom to bestow upon large and greedy families.

She greeted him like an old friend.

"Mr. Frost, how good of you to come! This is an honour— and most unexpected!"

"Yes," he said, feeling rather like a schoolboy, "I hope I'm not here at an inconvenient hour. I arrived late last night in Polchester. I hope you'll forgive me not giving you any warning, but I was so impatient to see my niece Nathalie——"

"Oh, dear!" Mrs. Proudie broke in, "Nathalie's gone!"

"Nathalie gone!"

"Yes. She went an hour ago. She arrived here, as I suppose you know, only yesterday afternoon—about tea time. Most unexpected. We had no idea, of course, that she was coming. She just walked in. We were all having tea, my husband and three children. Having tea in here. She simply sat down without a word of explanation and had tea with us, just as she used to do."

He was bitterly disappointed. He wanted now to see her, there standing right in front of him, as (so he felt under the unexpected blow) he had never wanted to see any human being before.

"Oh, dear! Oh, dear!" was all that he could say.

She saw how grievously disappointed he was and was very sorry for him.

She and Canon Proudie had, last night in their bedchamber discussion, been angry with him. Nathalie had refused to tell them a thing, but they could see, of course, that there had been grievous trouble somewhere, and they had thought it very wrong of Mr. Frost to allow so young a child to go off, then, without a word to anybody.

But now when she saw him, she could not be angry with him. A dear-looking old man and not at all alarming for such a celebrity. It was pleasant that she would be able, for many weeks to come, to describe the event to her friends— to Mrs. Nash and the Chancellors and the Burrows and those supercilious busybodies the Swintons. "No, he was charming—not a bit conceited. He just sat there, and we talked. He'd never been in Polchester before. Wonderful for his age—oh, well, he must be over seventy——"

All this passed through her mind as she went on.

"Yes, we thought it, of course, most peculiar. She had never sent us a word of warning. She just arrived. And she would tell us nothing. She was most reserved—not at all as she used to be, the dear child. She was quite friendly, but grave, and a lot older, we all thought. All she would tell us was that she wasn't going back to London again and that, at once, she must find work of some kind. That was the only thing she could think about. She began right away, looking in the advertisement columns of the *Glebeshire News*, and before she'd finished her tea she'd found several that she said she was going to try."

"What kind of advertisements?" asked Hans.

"Oh, people who wanted companions, being read to, having their dogs looked after, that sort of thing. She found one that she thought looked especially promising. A lady who is staying in St. Servian and wanted a secretary."

"St. Servian?" asked Hans. "Where's that?"

"It's a little fishing place on the coast about twenty miles from here. That's where she's gone off to this morning."

"That's where I'm going off to too," said Hans, rising.

"Of course," said Mrs. Proudie, "Nathalie may not like the look of the lady or the lady might not like the look of her. My husband begged her not to be so precipitate, and to write a letter and stay quietly here for a day or two. I'm sure we're all simply delighted to have her. But Nathalie was absolutely determined, she wouldn't hear of anything but that she must go off at once. Certainly a week or two in London has strangely changed her. I do hope"—Mrs. Proudie hesitated, then went on—"that Nathalie hasn't done anything disgraceful in London. You see, she's almost like our own child. She's been with us so much."

"No, indeed," said Hans warmly. "Nothing disgraceful. How could she? Why, she's wonderful. She's brought something into my life——"

He broke off. Why should he disturb Mrs. Proudie with the story of his life? "Why," asked the eyes, noses, and chins of the photographed cousins, brothers, sisters, grandfathers, and aunts, "should you disturb our Mrs. Proudie? This is not *your* home. You don't belong to us at all."

"It's only," said Hans, gently rubbing his black hat round and round, "that there's been something of a love-affair. A very innocent and harmless one, but Nathalie was determined to show her independence. And—well, this is the way that she's showing it."

"I see," said Mrs. Proudie (although she didn't see in the least). "I'm greatly relieved, I'm sure, and so will my husband be. We're so very fond of Nathalie. And now, Mr. Frost, I do hope you'll stay to luncheon. My husband will be so very disappointed if he doesn't meet you. We have it at one-thirty. Just ourselves——"

"No, thank you," said Hans, moving towards the door. "That's extremely kind of you, but I—I would like to get to this place—what's its name?"

"St. Servian."

"St. Servian, as quickly as possible—you say that it is twenty miles. One could motor, I suppose?"

"You could motor, of course"—Mrs. Proudie was very doubtful—"but I don't think I'd recommend it. It is one of the most out-of-the-way places in Glebeshire, or Cornwall either, for the matter of that. And we've had a lot of rain lately. The roads will be terrible. I would recommend that you take a train to Treliss and then drive from there. I know that there's a good train to Treliss at 3:30 in the afternoon. You should be in St. Servian by dinner time."

"I see," said Hans. "It certainly *does* seem very remote. Is there a hotel or anything of that kind?"

"Well, there's an inn, but it's very primitive, I'm afraid. You see, it's really a tiny place—very few visitors find their way there, even in the summer. And it will be quite empty at this time of the year. You're sure to find a room; it doesn't matter just for one night what it's like, does it, if it's clean?"

"Not at all," said Hans. He felt oddly excited about St. Servian. He felt that he would want to go there now, even though Nathalie were not there. The curious happiness that had been slowly pouring in, like a welling stream, upon his heart during the last two days, seemed here, at this moment, in this quiet sunlit room with peace in the air, colour everywhere, and the sunlit cathedral still and beneficent beyond the window, to reach a height that swung with a lovely rhythm around, beyond, and about him.

It was within him and outside him. St. Servian! St. Servian! St. Servian!

"Thank you very much. My friend and I will take the afternoon train."

"Then won't you come to luncheon?"

"I think not, Mrs. Proudie. You are very kind. I have a number of things that I must see to."

He had, when he liked, a beautiful old-fashioned courtesy. He liked now. Mrs. Proudie, after he had gone, stood there without moving, thinking that she had never met so beautiful an old gentleman. She determined to go that very afternoon and find several of his books at the Library.

He crossed the green and went into the cathedral. The great place was empty, save for an ancient verger. He saw several beautiful things. He saw the splendid tomb of the Black Bishop. He saw the six windows known as "The Virgin and the Children." As he looked at these with their deep rich colour, the one in which the Virgin bends down to watch the Baby Christ at play, the one in which St. John and the Christ paddle in the stream, the one in which Jesus is playing at his Mother's feet, while the ox and the ass and the three dogs with the large heads gravely look on, as the colours, purple and green and blue, falling now in great splashes onto the floor, moved his heart, he felt the tide of happiness in him move yet higher.

And he saw the Brytte monument, one of the loveliest things in all England, with its Mino da Fiesole babies. He wondered, indeed, what he had been doing for so long in the house in Regent's Park.

He walked about the town. He walked down the High Street into the market place, and then up Orange Street to get the view, and then through the market place again to the street that led down to the river. Here, hanging over the Lower Town, he found under a tree a brass tablet which read:

HJALMAR JOHANSON.
FRIEND OF THIS TOWN,
DIED OCTOBER VII. MCMVII.

"Hjalmar Johanson!" An odd name to find in a little English town! He wondered who he might be. There was beside the tablet a lovely little fountain of eighteenth-century work, so rare and beautiful that for a long time he bent over it, examining its details. Who had this Johanson been, and what had he had to do with the fountain? He did not know. He did not want to know. There was beauty here, and that was enough. He drank some water out of the little metallic cup chained to the fountain. He drank; during these days he seemed always to be obeying some inner commanding instinct. Then, jauntily, Martha at his side, he found his way back to "The Three Feathers."

Here was Klimov waiting for him.

During luncheon Hans told him the news. "So we will catch the 3:30 train," he ended.

"I too?" asked Klimov.

"Of course you too."

"Well, for a day or two perhaps———"

Klimov looked a little unhappy.

"I have been doing this morning considerable thinking. I sat inside the cathedral, I went up onto the hill and looked down to the river. I became very uneasy about mankind."

"Oh, dear," said Hans, looking with some doubt at a shining purple slice of cold meat that, attended by some congealed beetroot and a little forest of ancient lettuce, testified to the splendid and courageous impertinence of English hostelries. "Oh, dear! Don't get upset by such general questions. I believe that's always been your way in Russia, and look what it's led to! Think of individuals if you like— and especially of yourself—but this general commiseration— it leads to nothing but stomach-ache and bad temper."

Klimov looked at Hans with admiration.

"What a clear mind you have! You always know just what you think!—and I never do. I'm in a hundred moods in one morning. But it's such a beautiful day, and this town is so charming. And when I realized how happy I was, and how fortunate for me to be with a man like yourself, and what miserable lives many people had to lead——"

"Oh, damn! damn! damn!" Hans broke in, pushing his plate away from him. "This beef is bloody. What I mean is, that I really do dislike raw meat. And I dislike all this misery, I do, indeed. If only everyone would be cheerful on their own little dunghill and leave other people's dunghills alone. Now, here I am. I've been a selfish man all my life. I regard myself as someone I've got to look after, because if I don't, certainly no one else is going to. And here I am, too, at a very advanced age, suddenly discovering that I've been living all the wrong kind of life—submitting to other people out of laziness, just passing into corruption in an armchair. And I've been jerked out of that like a Jack-in-the-box. I'm going to lead my own life from now on. I shan't care a damn for anybody, and I'll die in a ditch with a bottle of whisky in my hand and nettles in my hair, and the worms will eat me, and no one will know I've even gone—only a star or two or a sleepy duck in a green pond, or a water hen, or possibly the village constable. Do you know what would have happened otherwise? I'd have died in my bed, and there'd have been three doctors, oxygen in a bag, and rows of medicine bottles. My wife would have closed my eyes, my mother-in-law would have danced the saraband, there would have been articles in the newspapers, and the Authors' Society would have sent a wreath to the funeral. A memorial service in a church, and no one caring a damn. A word or two at some dinner-parties and then—silence. And my poor ghost tearing its windy hair, because for all those years I was in prison and didn't know it. I might have been free and wasn't. I might have kicked my heels and eaten my eggs and bacon in a tuppenny inn, and bought liquorice at the village shop, and ridden on a char-à-banc to Margate, lived in a world with decent noises and long silences. Thought one or two things through to the beginning, slept till midday or got up at five and nobody caring—and I sacrificed it all, for what? For a ceremony that has always bored me to death, for people who are less than shadows to me, for a convention that is a gilded sham. I don't want to make the world better. I never did. God knows, I don't want to have any truck with the world at all. What's the world to me or I to the world? I'm but an old man with two eyes and a nose. *My* eyes and *my* nose. I've been letting them out on hire. I'm never going to give anyone the use of them again. I've been playing Blind-man's buff for seventy years. . . . Do you know," he said, looking up at the waiter, "what your cheese is like? It's like soap. And then soap. And then more soap. Do you know what your apple tart's like? It's like plaster and a cold in the nose. Do you know what your coffee's like? It's like ink and sawdust."

"I'm very sorry, sir," said the waiter. "Most gentlemen speak very well of the food here."

"Most gentlemen," said Hans, getting up from the table, "are liars."

Klimov followed Hans into the hall.

Hans turned round and put his hand on Klimov's shoulder.

"I've been talking like a book. I apologize. But I'm excited to-day. I haven't been so happy since I was a boy. I like you, Klimov, you're a good fellow. Now the train's at 3:30. Let's go down to the market. It's market day. Lots of sheep and pigs. The nice sort, not the human variety. We'll have an hour there—and then for St. Servian!"

The market place was in a fine bustle. It was crowded with stalls, human beings, and animals. There were sheep and cows and dogs, old women and young women, stout farmers and thin farmers, flowers and fruit, and shirts and handkerchiefs, noise and sun, and the wind blowing from the sea.

Hans and Klimov had a tremendous time. They bought ridiculous things—apples and coloured cotton handkerchiefs, a tin train, two trumpets, a dog collar for Tray, two shilling volumes of Milton's poetry (this was Klimov's purchase), a looking-glass, a bag of sweets, a book of Glebeshire ballads, and an old eighteenth-century map of Polchester, and the *True and Entertaining History of Anthony Keech, Pirate.*

They talked to everyone, were trodden on, pushed, and hustled. They went back to "The Three Feathers" loaded with parcels and dust and disorder.

"Now for St. Servian!" said Hans.

CHAPTER IV

The Tawny Sand

HANS, sitting by Klimov in the bumpy old car, thought, as the light left the last lingering fields: "How like a dream this is! And all the best moments of life have been dreams."

That was it then—never to force anything into too positive a shape, to avoid at all costs, if one wanted to remain happy, this modern passion for seizing something and looking at it in and out, up and down, as a small boy seizes his railway train or his birthday watch and investigates the works.

The car was an open one, and it was cold. There was a strong wind from the sea, a wind that bore on its wings salt and savour, seeds and clods of earth, wet leaves and the tang of fishy scales. The two men sat close to one another, and the dogs clung to them for safety. They were taking with them all the things that they had bought in the market—the toys, the coloured handkerchiefs, the book about the pirate, and the eighteenth-century map.

The earth, crouching expectantly beneath the oncoming sweep of darkness, was filled with sweet scents. Sea gulls and rabbits, sea pinks and dandelions, the dung of the animals and the thick secrets of the high hedges all sur-rendered to the night. Only the lights were beginning to

319

shine in the windows, and the stars in a cloudless heaven. They didn't talk to one another. They were becoming real friends now, and speech wasn't needed.

"All my best moments," thought Hans, "have been dreams, and now I'm an old man. This is my last adventure and perhaps my best."

He was knowing again, for the first time for many years, some of that sharp and acrid flavour of expectant excitement that he had felt as a young lover going to meet the lady of the moment. Why? Was it Nathalie? Not entirely. He could not tell what it was, but he thought of himself as most men, when they are honest men, do: "Well, here I am—not so bad and not so good. But I'm ashamed of nothing, and I wonder what the next thing's going to be like."

They had found an open Ford with an ancient, decrepit driver outside Trellis Station. They had stood for a moment looking down on the shield of the bay as the last sun slashed the thin glasslike waters with purple. They had sniffed the sea, then filed into the car. For a while they had kept to the main road, but now they were leaving it and were bumping horribly over country lanes. They all bumped together—themselves, the dogs, the parcels, the bags. The car creaked, wheezed, groaned. No houses now were visible. The stars were rushing into the sky, and at every bump the scent of the sea became stronger. Now they seemed to be on the very edge, then down they plunged, almost, as it seemed, on their very heads.

"I suppose it's all right?" Hans shouted; but nobody answered him, only Martha frantically scraped at his knees,

pulled herself onto his lap, and lay there, her body trembling.

They turned sharply a corner, and the car appeared for an instant to stand on end, three wheels in air. Then it bumped down again, giving the earth a resounding smack and, like a horse that scents his stable, plunged eagerly forward. Little houses, clustered tightly together, came out to meet them; and a moment later, with a jerk as though all the paper wrappings had with one rough gesture been torn off the parcels, they were flung onto a little cobbled square with nothing but sea in front of them. Another step, and into the sea they would surely all have gone.

Unless they had been destined for America, they, had arrived.

The Ancient inquired their address.

"Do you know good lodgings?" Hans asked him.

He considered them as a fisherman may consider fish so small that they are best, perhaps, returned to the sea. He looked at them with contempt and indifference. Then he pointed to lighted windows, apparently high in air.

Accepting ungraciously their invitation, abandoning doubtfully his car, he led them over the cobbles up a flight of wooden steps, through bushes that smelt of thyme and blackberries, to a cottage door. He knocked.

A tall, thin woman, with hair tied in a knot on the top of her head, appeared in the doorway, carrying a lamp.

"I'm sorry to disturb you," Hans said, "but my friend and I have come over in a car from Treliss. I wondered whether you could give us lodging for the night."

She raised her lamp that she might see them both.

"Dogs?" she said.

"I beg your pardon?"

"You've got dogs with you."

"Yes," said Hans. "We have."

"Never take dogs."

"I'm sorry," he said, turning away. "We'll find some-where else."

But Tray, excited by the smell of food, had pushed past her into the lighted room beyond. Thus, unwitting, he in-fluenced Frost's remaining days.

Very indignant she hurried in. Tray, trailing his lead, was sniffing the legs of the table.

"Shoo!" she said, as she might to chickens. "Shoo!" But now the others had followed her; they were in a kitchen, spotless, gleaming, a great fire blazing. Three small children, seated on high chairs, were eating their suppers. At the sight of Tray they broke into a chorus, jumped from their chairs, rushed to him and began to pull his tail, his ears, shrieking with pleasure.

It was evident that discipline here was not very stern.

"My daughter's children," she said grimly. "My daughter and her husband are in China—Shanghai," she added un-expectedly.

"I have never been in China," said Hans politely; "a very picturesque country."

"I really can't allow dogs," she said again, but now with less decision.

"It's probably for a night only," said Hans; "but I'm sure there are other places."

"Now Lottie—Harold, Emma. What are you about? Where's your manners? The dog will bite you."

"Indeed it will not," said Klimov indignantly. "It's never bitten anyone in its life. It's very fond of children."

She regarded Klimov with considerable astonishment.

"You're not a German gentleman?" she asked sternly.

"I am not," said Klimov with dignity. "My native country is Russia, and I was compelled to leave it owing to the monstrous tyranny——"

His eyes would soon be flaming, his hair on end, as he considered Lenin standing on a tub in the Nevski Prospect, Trotsky ordering innocent people to execution, the ice of the Neva floating, a crystal green, down past the palaces. . . .

But the Ancient wanted his money. "I've got to be getting home——"

She seemed to come to a decision.

"I happen to have two rooms. They're small, of course, but they're clean, and considering the time of year if it's only for one night——"

They all moved up a tight and winding staircase. First little room. Second little room. First little room full of whitewash and, in the daytime, you must believe, the sea. Second little room also full of whitewash—in the daytime a view of Mrs. Agerson's house.

How clean the rooms were, how they smelt of whitewash, moth ball, sand, and seaweed! On the white walls there were texts. In each room three. In the sea room—"Thou God seest me," "A little child shall lead them," and "Thou

shalt love thy Father and Mother"; in the other room—
"Behold the Lilies," "The Lord is My Shepherd," and
"Feed My Sheep." No other ornament, save in each room
two large, inquisitive seashells. Hans, seeing them, knew at
once that it was here that he was going to live. When Klimov
had departed, he would have both rooms, one to sleep in,
one to work in. He didn't know it, but in the bed at which
he was now looking he would one day die.

Turning from the bed, he looked at the lady and smiled.
Surprisingly she smiled back at him.

"Whether you like it or no I am going to stay here."

And she oddly answered: "Yes. It is always very quiet
here."

Once more in the kitchen, she told them that her name
was Mrs. Iglesias. This astonished him greatly. She explained laconically that her husband had been half a
Spaniard. And then, addressing only Hans, who seemed now
to have a strange attraction for her, she added: "He was a
good husband to me, although he had strange ideas. I have
never been farther than Treliss in all my life—never needed
to, somehow. This was a cramping place to him. He was a
sailor, though, and had plenty of travelling. He was content
to die in this quiet place at the last."

She herself was quiet. She seemed to spread quiet like a
colour over all the scene.

So it was settled with no more questions asked, only
would they be having something to eat? Yes, in an hour's
time. Hans went off to find Nathalie.

He had got the address from the advertisement in the

Glebeshire News. The lady to whom Nathalie had gone was Miss Thorne, and the address was Barham Villa. Mrs. Iglesias' home was called Saltgrass Cottage.

Barham Villa was easy to find, even in the dim light that was threaded with half-seen cobbles, twinkling stars, and the sudden flashing of white-topped waves. The villa stood so close to the sea that the spray stung Hans' face. He rapped the knocker. A little maid came to the door. He asked whether Miss Thorne was staying here. Yes, sir, she was. Then with thumping heart he asked whether Miss Nathalie was also staying here. (Was he once again to be disappointed?) Yes, sir, she was. And was she just now at home? The little maid would see. She left him there with the sea thundering into his back, and the little hall, dimly lit, watching him with a gentle and apprehensive eye. A moment later Nathalie was there.

He dropped his stick. His arms were round her, her lips against his, her hand stroking his cheek. For a long, beating, triumphant pause, they stayed thus on the edge of a thundering sea. Then she drew him inside, stood him beneath the little hall lamp that she might see him better.

"Oh, you're just the same! just the same! And you aren't angry. Look out for the aspidistras. Quick! Come in here. Miss Thorne is praying upstairs. She'll be another half hour at least."

"Praying?"

"Yes, for the peace of the world—so we've got twenty minutes anyway. Come along in here. Look out for the photographs. Don't bang yourself against the table. There's a candle here somewhere. We haven't got electric light. Matches. Matches. . . . Oh! I'm so glad you've come. I've watched all the time. I knew you'd find me, but I didn't think you would so soon. . . . Here by the window. . . ."

They sat down, close together, hand in hand, on a red plush sofa, and the candle, rickety and dribbling, watched them with drunken solemnity.

"Well, now," he said, "answer to me for all your sins. You're up for judgment."

"You've really taken all this trouble, you've followed me here—just to look after me?"

"Just to look after you."

"Who told you I was here?"

"Your friends the Proudies."

"Oh, yes, of course But you've been so quick——"

"You've been quicker. I've always been just an hour behind you. For all I knew you might have been back in Polchester by now."

"I would have been if Miss Thorne hadn't taken a fancy to me. I've only been here since lunch time. I got the early train to Treliss, then came on by bus. I walked into this house just as she was sitting down to her egg and boiled water. I said, 'I hear you want a secretary.' She looked at me and said, 'Have you any references?' I said, 'No.' 'Can you type?' I said, 'No.' 'Do you know shorthand?' I said, 'No.' 'Have you ever been secretary to anyone before?' I said, 'No.' 'I'll try you then. Sit down and have a boiled egg with me.' She never asked me another question, but all the afternoon she's been dictating her pamphlet to me, and as she speaks quite slowly it's been easy. I'm to try for a month and see how we get on."

"What an extraordinary woman!" said Hans. "What's she paying you?"

"A pound a week and all found."

"And what's her work? What's her pamphlet about?"

"The Peace of the World. It's the only thing she ever thinks about. She has a plan."

"A good plan?"

"I don't know. We were dealing with poison gases all the afternoon, and we didn't get beyond the fact that they exist. We shall squash them to-morrow."

"Do you like her?"

"Yes," said Nathalie. "I like her because she doesn't know any of the world that I know. It's so peaceful. She'd never heard your name, for instance, and when I said you were a novelist she said 'Tchut!' and when I said you were a poet she said 'Tchut!' again. But I'm sure that no one in this village has ever heard of you."

"This is the place for me." He drew a deep breath, then tightened his hand on hers.

"Now tell me. We must have this out before we go any further. Why did you treat me so damnably? Why did you trust me so little?"

She looked in front of her, staring into a little mirror that hung crookedly on the wall opposite her.

"I didn't know. I believed what she said. Because she hated me so, I disbelieved everybody. I'd never been hated by anybody before."

"Wouldn't it have been fairer to me just to have waited and asked me?"

"I couldn't wait. I wanted to get out of that house—at once, at once I wanted to go where no one I knew could see me. I felt shabby, mean. I was ashamed."

"Yes, you thought of yourself. You were selfish. You didn't care about the pain you were giving——"

"No, why should I? I didn't matter enough to anybody to pain them."

"You thought that?"

"Yes—I—I——"

She burst out crying, turned to him, clinging to him. He held her, stroking her hair, kissing her. He let her cry. Then he began to talk, to give her time to come quietly back to herself again.

"You did me an injustice. But we won't say any more about that. After all, it might have been the other way. I'd reached the state when I was as peevish as an old woman if anyone interrupted any of my arrangements. And I didn't know I was peevish. I had caught my wife's idea of myself as something very grand, Olympian, that had to have its own laws and rules. But no—that isn't fair either. I never thought I was grand. I'll do myself that justice. But I was lazy, and getting lazier and lazier—and your aunt, my dear, liked me to be so. It made her own plans easier. It's terrible the seriousness with which women set about a jol. It's devastating. Talk about making a mountain out of a molehill. It's their perpetual business. And the worst of it is that the molehill is compelled to feel a sort of gratitude for being made into a mountain although he may have greatly preferred the molehill state. But after all the work and the labour, all on his behalf, what can he do but say Thank you? It was your aunt's life work to transform my cottage into a palace. She was very clever about it, she set all the right people to work, saw that the proper lights were turned on, arranged the criers and banged the drums. It usedn't to be difficult in England. It's been much harder since the war, I fancy, but by that time, because no one ever read me any longer, it was easy enough for them to say in a lazy way that I was a great man. And then there were a few fanatics, of course. . . . That was all your aunt wanted. And I slumbered in the middle of it all like the Sleeping Beauty until you came and woke me——"

"I didn't mean to," Nathalie said; "and you're quite wrong about nobody reading you. Aunt Ruth may have done something, but it would have been none of it any use if your work hadn't been splendid."

"Splendid? Splendid? My dear child, what words! I've failed in everything I've tried."

"Doesn't every real artist think that when he looks back on what he meant to do?"

"Yes, that's the general consolation for Mr. Tuppenny. Ah, well, this isn't the fine thing I meant it to be, but every great man in the past has been disillusioned in the same way. It isn't true, that's all. Milton was arrogant with pride over *Paradise Lost*, Balzac burst buttons off his dressing gown over *Illusions perdues*, Wagner couldn't contain himself after *Tristan*. Every truly great artist is arrogant and selfish, and greedy and mean, and a maniac. I've written some pretty little things. I've had some great times writing them. Now I'm going to have some great times living them. A little late. But no matter. . . . That's enough about me—and now—Vladimir?"

Nathalie said: "I've had a telegram from him——"

"Already?"

"Yes." She hesitated. "It was weak and cowardly of me, but just before I left London I sent him a telegram giving him the Proudies' address in Polchester. I couldn't bear somehow for him not to know where I was. A telegram came to the Proudies early this morning."

She took it out of the bosom of her dress.

This was the telegram:

Just returned London found your telegram Please return London otherwise will come Polchester Love you terribly always Vladimir.

"I don't know what the post-office people must have thought."

"Oh, post-office people get wires like that every minute. What are you going to do?"

"Well, Miss Thorne is going up to London in three days' time, to attend a meeting at the Albert Hall about the next war and how to prevent it. She said at tea time that she wants me to go with her. It's only for a week. I'll see Vladimir then."

"And tell him you'll marry him?"

"No, of course not. I won't marry him until I'm quite independent. Then, if things go wrong, I've got my own life to turn back to. And he'll respect me more—and perhaps he'll love me longer when he doesn't own me. I'll seem more valuable."

How she had developed, he thought, since that first evening when, going into her room, he had found her in tears. And in so short a while! From a child to a woman. He loved her the more for that. She seemed to him now to have in her all the great womanly elements—she was lover and mother and child, courageous, tender, touchingly inexperienced, wise, and humorous. Yes, men weren't in it with women for the grand big things in life.

Sitting there beside Nathalie he saw his sex as a huddled, labouring, mannequin crowd of Nibelungen with bent backs bowed to the heavenly whip. A poor, blind lot. He chucked them out of the window into the tramping, insolent, regardless sea. They vanished as though they had never been, himself among them.

"Uncle Hans," said Nathalie, rolling the telegram tightly in her hand, "does love never last? Why is it that Vladimir is so sure that he isn't going to care for me later on? Why must marriage be so unsuccessful?"

Hans put his arm round her.

"Love can last if you get two people who are fine enough. But they must both be fine, and the trouble is that the right people so seldom meet. You see it sometimes. A man has had the luck to encounter a woman who compels all the grand things in him—unselfishness, honour, gaiety, gladness. Yes, he has the luck. But for the most part people aren't patient enough, and they blame others for their own failings

—and the body's a strange thing. If you take a permanent step on some temporary bodily impulse, of course you get nowhere. You must play a waiting game. Women are good at that—men no good at all. That's why women always think they're unfairly treated. But don't you worry, my darling. You've got character and pluck, so you'll take Vladimir as though he were a long, long story—not over in one chapter or two. And you won't turn the pages over to see what the end's going to be. You'll write the end one day yourself. And you won't throw a fit at every cat-and-monkey trick he shows you. You'll be patient, and then patient, and then patient once more. And gradually his soul will be delivered into your hands, bit by bit you'll have had the making of it. He won't know it. He'll think he's made it all himself. You won't try to possess him. Ownership of one human being by another is the sin against the Holy Ghost, to my thinking—but in the end he'll be yours. He's worth having. He's got fine lines on his map. And when you're unhappy there is your old uncle, covered with seaweed, barnacles on his nose and jellyfish clinging to his boots, but just alive enough to give you a fish dinner if you care to take the train to Treliss."

"But Uncle Hans—you're going to live here?"

"Yes. I'm going to live here."

"Here—with nothing—nobody——"

"Here with Mrs. Iglesias, Martha, Lottie and Company —what more do you want?"

He rose slowly. There were aches in his joints. He was very weary.

"Your employer's prayers must be just about over. I'll be seeing you in the morning."

"I'll walk with you to your house."

So through the dark, arm-in-arm and without another word, they went along to Saltgrass Cottage.

They kissed and said good-night, then he went in. He was so grossly tired—felt such a very old man that he sat down on the first kitchen chair that he came to, one near the door. Klimov, sitting near the table, deeply intent, was carving with his pocketknife something out of a piece of wood. The three children watched him with absorbed eagerness. The smallest one, a fat round child, stood, resting her hand on his thigh. The three children and Tray, who, his mouth wide open, was sitting on his haunches, as though he expected at any moment the coming of the Kingdom, made no noise. They seemed scarcely to breathe. A grandfather clock loudly ticked and chattered. Martha was asleep in front of the fire. Mrs. Iglesias, moving about very softly, was preparing supper. Hans as he sat there, his stick between his knees, knew that he had never before been in contact with such peace. And it was timeless. He might have been here already for a thousand years.

No one seemed to notice him. Then suddenly Mrs. Iglesias asked him whether he wouldn't prefer to be in the sitting room. No, he thought not. Well, wouldn't he like to look at it? He went with her and found the customary chilled, stiff, and deceased room crowded with shells, photographs, woollen mats, and horsehair sofa.

"I shouldn't be happy in here."

"No, likely not," she said. "When the other gentleman's gone away you can have his room for your sitting room."

Then she knew that he was going to stay? How did she know?

But he only said "Yes."

They had supper, and very shortly afterwards Hans went up to bed, Martha following him.

He never remembered to have known such weariness as he felt now. He could scarcely pull off his clothes. He blinked at the Manet which was propped up against the little swinging looking-glass. He arranged the two or three books, the Lamb, *John Buncle*, and the others, on the table by his bed. As soon as he had, with the same movement that he had used as a little boy, turned on his right side, curled into a ball, his head cupped in his hand, he was asleep. He slept like the dead.

He woke up abruptly, as though someone had called his name. He lit his candle and looked at his watch. It was a quarter-past six. Through his open window came the swish and sigh of the sea; the whole world was still intensely dark. He blew out his candle and lay flat on his back thinking. He was tired no longer, but beautifully refreshed, intensely happy, at peace. Thoughts swam, lazily, easily, across his consciousness. He thought of Nathalie. Once or twice in a man's life, if he is lucky, he loves someone, man or woman, with complete trust, with a great sentiment of honourable dealing, understanding, noble generosity, and is loved in return in truest fashion.

After their talk last evening he knew that they felt, and

now would always feel, such a love for one another. Nothing could touch or harm it. He had not in all probability now many years to live, he was no certain believer in the survival of personality after death, but it seemed, as he lay there in that quiet little room listening to the rhythm of the sea, that it was very unlikely that his love for Nathalie would cease with physical death—it was so unphysical, although he delighted in her youth and prettiness and charm. There can be a grandeur and nobility in human relations that is beyond chemistry, something with a light and fire so strong and penetrating that the great loose word immortality does not seem a foolish word to use.

Then he thought of Ruth. With that he passed out once again another world of experience. There was no immortality in his contact with Ruth. Nor had there ever been. But he must achieve some relationship with her that would be clean and honourable. All irritation with her had passed away—only he would never return to that other life again. Maybe there would be a letter from her this very day. Before he left London he had written her a brief note, and she knew the Proudies' address.

She seemed to him now, in this rhythmic darkness, infinitely far away.

But behind Ruth, and even behind Nathalie, he knew that there was now something more important than either of them, a great sense of eager expectancy. Soon, soon he would be at work again. At the mere thought of it his heart began to beat fiercely, he felt energy pulse through his body. He saw no figures. The Commander was not there in the room with him. But he was almost ready; it was like the moment before the rise of the curtain, before the ringing of the little bell, when the orchestra stops its preliminary playing, the lights go down and with a soft whisper the curtain quivers. . . .

For months now these people had been assembling the scene, preparing the idea that would form all the scattered forces into one shape and pattern, gathering power. . . .

Soon, in a day or two, the voice would be heard: "Now— BEGIN!"

And he lay there, seeing with all the clarity born of the silence how all the little circumstances had arisen, one after another, to bring him to this point—the seventieth birth-day, the Manet, the dinner-party, his discovery of Nathalie, his dissatisfaction with the party, the evening at the West-cotts', the Russians, the visit to the country, his talks with Klimov, Nathalie's flight, his hatred of his mother-in-law, his own flight, the journey in the train, Lamb's *Letters*, Klimov's fairy story, Polchester, the cathedral, the market place, Nathalie's journey to this place, the Ancient's direct-ing them to this house—omit one of these elements and he would have lost his prize! He held his breath lest even now, after all, he should have lost it!

His room was flooded now with the early morning sun. It was half-past seven. He got up and went over to his win-dow. He gave a cry of pleasure. All the little cove was shin-ing in the sun. Directly in front of him was a roughly cobbled square. On this, boats were drawn up and, beyond it, bright yellow sand ran out to a misty, glittering sea. Cluster-

ing around it were the heaped cottages, white and grey, two
of them with green shutters, one with blue; little flights of
steps ran irregularly to the higher tier of little houses. In
front of some of them, as they climbed up the hill, were small
gardens with chrysanthemums and fat deep green bushes.
It was all like a painted scene. Thin purple smoke rose from
some chimneys into the thin papery blue sky; some gulls,
crying in the distance, hovered over the sea. These were the
only movements. Not a human being was to be seen. The
light—the brilliant, smoky, frosty light of an English Indian
summer—burnt with fire upon the cobbles, the yellow sand,
the sea, the glittering Chinese white of the cottages, the red
and amber colour of the autumn trees hanging to the hill.

Hans felt the sun on his head and his bare chest. He raised
his hand that it might shine too upon his palms.

> The Sounds and Seas with all their finny drove
> Now to the Moon in wav'ring Morrice move,
> And on the Tawny Sands and Shelves
> Trip the pert Fairies and the dapper Elves.

He turned back into the room and climbed into bed
again.

"Thou God seest me," said the text on the wall.

Hans scratched his chest, saw that Martha also was
lazily scratching. In another moment he would be asleep
again, floating off on the sunlight.

But sleepily be murmured: "The Sounds and Seas. . . .
The Sounds and Seas. . . ."

And, scenting the crisp odour of frying bacon, he swung
off into a cloudless space of light and misty sun.

CHAPTER V

The Silver Feather

Two wonderful, miraculous days, and then a telegram from Ruth:

Arrive to-morrow morning about midday Motoring from Polchester.

On the morning that Nathalie was going, Ruth was arriving. Nathalie would be away for a week, Klimov was going also because he had fallen in love—not with Miss Thorne but with Miss Thorne's idea, with the Peace of the World.

The idea was made for Klimov, and Klimov for the idea. Miss Thorne, introduced to him outside her house by Nathalie, knew at once that he was the man for whom she had been waiting. She said: "M. Klimov, there is the great work in the world waiting for you," and Klimov, his eyes shining as though paradise had been opened before him, answered: "This is what, for years, I have been looking for."

Nathalie's eyes also shone, not because of the Peace of the World, but because in twenty-four hours' time she would see Vladimir, and now proudly independent she would be able to hold up her head when she saw him. So the Peace of the World had already done one good deed.

Miss Thorne, who was short, round, and stout, with flaxen hair and rosy cheeks (not at all what you would have supposed), was distressed when she heard from Nathalie that one day she intended to marry.

"How you can," Miss Thorne wondered, "when there are so many really important things to be done!"

"Someone must marry," said Nathalie, "for the next generation."

"Not at all," said Miss Thorne, "that must be a State-arranged affair."

"Poor babies, with only the State for their mother."

"Better than nine mothers out of ten."

However, Miss Thorne had taken a fancy to Nathalie and was ready to forgive her a good deal. She ended:

"When you've seen what this work really is, you'll think better of marriage."

Nathalie smiled.

She had a little walk with Hans after breakfast, just before the Treliss bus started.

The Indian summer was still smiling on the land.

Already Hans belonged to the place, to the country within a radius, perhaps, of three miles.

Hans walked with Nathalie past the cove, over the irregular little steps to a narrow beach closed in with trees. A wooded valley ran straight from the beach into the heart of the inland, a stream tumbling over white shining stones, raced out over the valley through the sand into the sea. As they walked, they, this stream, the sea, two sea-gulls were the only live spirits in this little world.

Nathalie had only ten minutes before she must go, but she would be back in a week.

As they walked he realized that this was the last time that they would ever be truly alone together. To-morrow she would see her young man, and after that, whether she liked it or no, however she might wish to assert her independence, she would be always part of him.

He had an instant—which he was to remember afterwards as part of the thin faint colours of the day, the singing stream, the brown bare trees—of acute, almost agonizing loneliness.

An old man by himself, that was what by his own impulse he had chosen to be.

"When are you coming back to London?" she asked him.

"Never."

"Never? . . . Oh, but you must. . . . If I have to work up there. . . ."

"Maybe I'll come to see you one fine morning, just for an hour, and then vanish again."

"You won't want to see me."

He could tell that for the first time she was realizing now that some change had come, that something had happened to him.

"My dear, you won't want me. You'll have some work or other—and you'll be married——"

"No, never if it's going to keep me from you——"

"Never! Stop a moment. Think, just now, here on this beach, isn't it really Vladimir of whom all the time you are thinking? You know that it is. I'm a very pleasant old gentleman; you're fond of me, you'll be always glad to see

me. But your life—your life—that isn't with an old man
of seventy. It can't be. It shouldn't be."

He spoke almost passionately. He was at that instant
as far from her youth as once only a month ago he had
fancied himself in contact with it. An odd air seemed to
be creeping upon him, a whisper, a foreboding as though
all the doors were closing about him. He hadn't thought
it would be like this, he hadn't expected it, but he realized
that he was waiting with an eager curiosity for the next
step—would it perhaps be death?

"Oh, you're wrong," she cried, seizing his arm, pressing
her body close to his. "I don't feel your age, I haven't from
the first moment that we met. I love Vladimir. I'm terribly
glad that I'm going to see him again so soon—but you are
different, you are more important to me than anybody.
Yes, really, than anybody. And you always will be, I know
it."

"You dear child." He bent down and gently kissed her.
"I'm glad you think that—if it's even for a moment. We
love one another—of course we do. But I'm passing into
a place where you can't come. It's all right. That won't
prevent our being together. We may find that our contact
is eternal. Who knows? There is a kind of sniff of immortality about our love for one another. But here, now, on this
earth my adventure is almost over and yours is just beginning. I shall write one book perhaps—I don't know. I feel
as though I shall. But from now onwards I shall be alone.
I want to be. It's what for years I've wanted, although I
didn't know it. And you have finer and finer contacts,

events, fusions, more and more exciting and thrilling. I'll watch you for a little, but I'm not going to cling on and cry, as tiresome old men do, because no one comes to see them, and beg to force a situation that isn't really there. Ever since I first saw you on that afternoon of my seventieth birthday, I've been travelling to this place. I didn't at first know the direction I was going in. Now I do."

She nodded her head. "Ah well, you talk like this, but soon you'll see. I'll be back here in a week. I'm not going to marry Vladimir for ages. Perhaps I never shall. I'm in a sort of excited dream about Vladimir. I don't feel that he's real. I don't want him to be real. But you're real. I don't know whether I shall love Vladimir six months from now. I know I shall always love you."

"Of course you'll always love me. I'm a very charming old gentleman. But beware of the old however charming they are. They're preoccupied people—the old are—and they'll eat up the young if they get half a chance. I'm very charming just now, but you accustom me to your society, make yourself necessary, and see how greedy I get and the demand I make. Besides I want to be quiet, I tell you. I don't want your life to drive in upon mine. I'm selfish, as selfish as a pig, and I grow more selfish every moment. I've seized on this place, and I'm going to make it mine—yes, every stock and stone of it. That won't hurt the place. It's stronger than I am. But what would you say if I came in and demanded your life and Vladimir? Don't encourage me. Keep me in my own little box. You can come and feed me sometimes—but beware of me. An old man let loose with his sentimentalities, reminiscences, complaints, greedy ailments, is the devil."

Then a miraculous moment that he afterwards caught again and again the echo of for his exquisite pleasure—standing there on the little beach, she pressed her body against his, kissing his eyes, his mouth, her hand against his heart—"Yes, yes, but isn't that selfish? What of me? Don't you know that I'm frightened without you, that I must always be close to you and have you love me? I need you terribly. I'll never need anyone so much. I'm going to have my own life, yes, and I'm going to make it as fine as I can, but it's only if you're with me that I'm able. . . .

"You can't lose me. You can't get rid of me. You never will. Whether you're with me or not with me, I'll love you, love you, love you for ever and ever and ever."

"Well, Nathalie," at last he answered her, "we'll make an immortal pair."

Exultingly he thought: "Now I shall never die. It will pass on and on. . . . There'll be something always to remember. In Hades I shan't be lonely."

Ten minutes later he was saying good-bye to them all, to Miss Thorne and Klimov and Tray and Nathalie. The old bus was crammed to bursting with human beings, baskets, hens, dogs, and rabbits. The noise was tremendous.

Hans had a fear that Klimov would embrace him, but Klimov's eyes were fixed upon the Peace of the World. With Tray between his knees and his arms absent-mindedly round the hutch that contained the rabbits, he sailed off into eternity, busy with his divine mission.

At quarter-past twelve exactly Ruth arrived in her motor from Polchester.

Hans saw her from behind his window. She got out of the car and stood looking about her.

Her car was very handsome, she herself was very handsome; Hans, stroking the pane of the window softly with his fingers, knew, when he saw how handsome she was, that he had escaped from her for ever. Round her little hat was curled a silver feather. St. Servian had never seen a hat with a fine silver feather in it before. Hans as he stepped out on to the cobbles, smelt the fish and the tar and the salty air, was happily aware that it would never see such a feather again.

She greeted him very easily.

"Dear Hans, how well you look!" He kissed her, then led her away.

"Where would you like to go? A walk? Or I have a fire in my room."

She shivered. "Let's sit in your room. I've been dying of cold in the car. What a funny little place. It is out of the world, isn't it?"

"It is," he assured her.

He led her in, through the kitchen, up the dark crooked little stairs into the bedroom. The other little room, just vacated by Klimov, would be ready for him to-morrow morning. Oh! how beautifully it would be ready, with the whitewashed walls, the deal table, and the Manet!

She looked round her, at the little brass bedstead, the

texts on the wall, and the old armchair with the hole in the seat. But there was a bright fire burning.

She went to the window and looked out at the sky, now grey like a bird's wing, the sea of silver streaked with purple, the ghostly mist, the floating sand.

She shivered again.

"How can you!" she said. He pointed to the armchair.

"But where will you sit?"

"In this one." He drew forward a little wooden chair.

"Oh, but you will be so uncomfortable!"

"Not at all, I assure you."

She took off the hat with the silver feather and laid it very carefully on the bed. She looked in the cracked glass, patted and stroked her hair. Her lovely silver fur lay stretched on the bed like the ghost of superior fashion, overcome by this rustic crudity. She sat down in front of the little fire, sticking out her feet. She began at once.

"First I want to apologize to you for my wretched behaviour the other night. I have been perfectly miserable ever since. Nathalie exasperated me, and I'm ashamed of myself for that—but I'm more ashamed of my unkindness. I haven't, as a matter of fact, been myself for weeks—nor, dear Hans, if I may say so, have you, quite."

"Don't you think so?" he asked, smiling at her.

"No, I don't. I've been thinking it all out, and what we both want is to get away from the house, from Mother, from everything. Now—what about Egypt?"

"Egypt?"

"Yes, Egypt. We've never been. Oh! it will be heavenly, the warmth, the light, the colour! And so interesting! I'll leave you alone. You shall go and excavate as much as you like by yourself. All I shall want is to sit and feel the sun in my bones."

"No, I don't want to go to Egypt."

She paused a moment, then rather more sharply said:

"Well, where *do* you want to go then?"

"I want to stay here."

She rattled her shoe against the little fender.

"Hans, don't be absurd. How can we stay here? What, in the winter! Here! Why, I should perish of cold and misery."

"I'm not suggesting that you should stay here."

She sighed.

"Now, Hans—you're still angry with me, aren't you? That isn't like you. You're always so generous. I've confessed my fault. I've said I'm sorry. You must forgive me."

"I'm not angry. I've never had anything to forgive. It was quite natural of you to be exasperated with Nathalie."

She turned sharply round to him.

"Nathalie has been here?"

"Nathalie was here first. It was because she was here that I came here."

"Nathalie is here now?"

"No. She left for London this morning."

Ruth moved impatiently.

"Can't we keep Nathalie out of this? After all we've had all our married lives together without her. This is between us. What I want to know is, why you are still angry with me, how long you're going to continue to be, and when you're coming back to live with me again?"

"I'm never coming back to live with you again."

There was a long pause. At last Ruth said in a low voice: "That's absurd and rather insulting to me."

"It's not absurd" Hans answered gently, "and it's not insulting."

"You're in love with that girl," she burst out.

"No," he replied. "She's my niece, you know. I'm not as modern as all that. . . . Besides I'm too old."

She turned to him. He thought for a moment, so angry she was, that she was going to strike him.

"You're lying to me. There's someone in the background. No man's ever too old. But don't imagine that I'm going to let you make a fool of yourself. I warn you that I can protect myself and you too—I warn you——"

She suddenly turned away from him and burst into tears, hiding her face in her hands.

He was filled with pity for her, filled with boredom too.

"Ruth—listen. Let's be honest with one another for once in our lives. We never have been. Never. There is no one in my life, no one at all. I'm tired of people, tired of human beings. Nathalie is a darling, but I'd be tired of her too if I saw very much of her. It isn't my fault, and it certainly isn't yours; you've been a splendid wife to me for many years. Now your job is over. You're not really fond of me, you haven't been for ages. Perhaps you never were. If all the truth were known I shouldn't wonder if I'm not more fond of you than you are of me. But I'm not very fond of anyone any more. I'm not fond of myself either. I'm tired of all personal relations. I want quiet and silence. For a long time I've wanted those things, but I didn't know it. There are, I'm sure, millions of people to-day who want those things, but there is such a row going on that they can't hear themselves think. Someone soon will found a new contemplative order. It will have nothing to do with any kind of religion. It will simply be for people who want a quiet hour or two. A great success it will be, I'm sure. Well, I'm founding my own contemplative order—membership of one. A little late in the day, I'm afraid. But still there it is."

"You're mad," she said, through her sobs. "You'll be sick of it in a week. It is a crazy impulse, because we had a pretty girl in the house and I lost my temper."

"No, I'm not mad," he answered quietly. "I'm not mad— but I'm very determined. Nothing that anyone can say will make the slightest difference."

He waited. She pulled herself together.

"Then listen to me. If you're not mad, you're selfish. After all I've done for you, for years and years, you throw me over. You think only of yourself. You don't care what the world says, what my position is——"

"Ah," he said, "that's the truth. Why didn't you come out with that before? You've never cared for me, but you've cared for the position that you could make through me. And you were perfectly right. That was our bargain. You were to give me a comfortable life, and I was to give you a position of importance. You've certainly done more for me than

I have for you. I've got to make it up to you for that. And I will. Let's discuss that and see what we can do."

But she broke in passionately: "You're wrong. You're wrong. I do care for you. I've always cared. I would have loved you more, much more, if you had let me. But you've always been so cold. You forget that I'm younger, that I want some life of my own. But I've always put yours before mine. I have indeed."

"Yes, I think you have, and that's what's been wrong. I acquiesced lazily and let you do what you wished. As to love—I don't want to be ungallant, but at the beginning I loved you passionately. And—we're being honest, you know—you were bored with my passion. Do you remember one night—at Caux? A night in July. We were high above the lake; there was a great red moon. We had been dancing and came up to our room; I knelt at your feet, imploring——"

"Ah, that . . ." She shivered, moving forward to the fire again. "I don't mean that, by love. Not such violence——"

"Not such violence—and afterwards not such indifference. You are exacting, my dear. We were both to blame, and out of our fault came a kind of compromise, as in many marriages, and buried deep in the compromise love died. Died years ago. You know it. You have been bored with me for centuries, wondering what people saw in me, but glad that they saw something because that helped our grand position. Bored by my books, too, for which indeed I don't blame you. I wasn't even the kind of artist you could understand. I wasn't on the one hand eccentric enough, I didn't wear old clothes, drink like a pig, leading mistresses into your bedroom. I was never very modern. Always years behind the latest thing. On the other hand, you could never quite rely on me. I would have my moods. I would escape you sometimes and you didn't know when I'd give in. You could never be quite sure that I wouldn't shock your friends. The only thing that you could be sure of was that I wouldn't shock them in the really interesting way. You wanted people to talk about me, you wanted them to think me a genius, but because you were so sure in your heart that I wasn't one, you were for ever afraid that they would wake up one day and discover the truth. You have always had a fear that one day I'd be discovered for a sham and vanish. . . . Well, now—I've vanished."

While he had been speaking her mood had changed. Her face had hardened, as indeed it could harden! Now she had a curious resemblance to her mother. In another twenty years, he thought, looking at her, she would be her mother's spitting image.

"Yes," she said. "There is something in all that you say. As we're going on now, yes, honestly I'll admit it, I haven't understood the fuss that people have made over you. You've put your side of the case, but have you ever for a moment realized how patient I've had to be? You say I built up the situation for my own advantage, but it hasn't been so simple as all that. I suppose I've felt maternal to you. You have seemed to me so silly, so childish, so ignorant of how to manage for yourself, so upset by tiny unimportant things, so selfish. I know that all men are childish and selfish—otherwise women would never bother about them—but it touched me to see you thinking yourself a great man, and other people thinking you important when I knew that you were neither great nor important."

"Now, come," he interrupted, smiling at her. "You know that I have never thought myself a great man."

"Oh, I know that's your pose about yourself—to tell yourself that you don't think yourself a great man, but you wouldn't have to tell yourself that so often if you didn't really think yourself so."

"That's clever of you," he agreed, nodding his head. "You've been reading modern novels. But never mind whether I think myself great or no, the point is, that at last we've been honest with one another. You can't really want any longer to look after anyone you despise so thoroughly."

"I've no one else," she broke out unexpectedly.

"You have your mother."

"I hate my mother. . . . Yes, you didn't know that, did you? With all your cleverness you've never seen that. I've often wondered that you could be so blind. We've been in a kind of league, my mother and I—that's what you supposed. My mother and I have detested one another for years. It has been her pose to say that I'm wonderful, so that she may get a kind of glory out of it. And she does think me wonderful in comparison with you. She does think I've made something out of nothing—but her conceit is such that she can't bear to see me carrying anything off, even while she praises

me for it. So, you see, you're all I've got. I've grown accustomed to looking after you, and I've always sworn that
nobody should take me from you. And nobody shall. You're
coming back to Polchester with me in half an hour's time."

"No. We say good-bye here. Here, in this room," he
answered quietly. "You shall have all the glory of the
separation. It will be easy enough for you to put all the
blame upon me. I shan't say a word, you can keep everything
up in style. You can call me every name under the sun."

"Yes, and have everyone despise me and laugh behind
my back at the mess I've made of it. No, thank you."

"No one will despise you. You'll have plenty of money,
and a good cook. No one to-day despises anyone with a
good cook. And think how fine you'll be! No stupid old man
to arrange for! Your own complete mistress. All the glory of
being my wife, with none of the bother. 'Poor Hans,' you'll
say, 'I thought it best that he should stay quietly in the
country for a bit. I go down to see him whenever I can.'
You can come down here sometimes, you know—just to
keep up appearances."

"Down here! You don't mean that you are really meaning
to live here?"

"Yes. Really."

She looked at him with an odd expression of regard and
interest, such as he had never seen in her eyes before. Their
talk had altered their relations. They saw one another with a
new respect, perhaps, and, at the same time, realized how
far they had travelled the one from the other.

She got up, walked about the little room, then went to

the window and looked out. A thin sea mist had come down and obscured all the landscape. Little trickles of water tumbled on the panes.

"Here!" She turned round to him. "In this awful, awful place! Alone! You're mad. You must be. Or no. It's a momentary reaction from London. You'll come back in a week or two. You will have had enough of this. I'll go back and wait for you."

"Yes, do that." He, too, got up. "Wait for me—but don't expect me ever to return."

He felt that she was a little afraid of him—that now she wanted to be gone. He knew that already her brain was busied with her London plans, with the new arrangements in the house, the new combinations of friends and acquaintances, the fresh ground that she could now occupy entirely on her own account; the tiresome and irritating people whom she must no longer invite, because they had come only for his sake, never for hers; the pictures that she would paint of his oddness, eccentricity, impossibility; the parties that now she would have, gayer, more modern, younger admirers, possibly even (with all discretion and control) lovers. . . . He knew that in those swift minutes, these views, these fresh glittering landscapes were almost against her will unrolling before her. Against her will!

"Well"—she picked up her lovely cloak and the little hat with the silver feather—"I leave you then. But only for— how long shall I give you?—one week, two—before you are back again. The library will be waiting for you."

She went up to him and kissed him. "Look after yourself:

don't catch cold in this chilly place. Come up the moment that you are bored."

He looked at her. Odd. Once he had loved her passionately. He had knelt before her pleading. . . . He helped her down the crooked little stairs. He handed her into the motor. She smiled and nodded. Turning back to the cottage, he felt the thin friendly rain caress his cheek.

CHAPTER VI

The Wave—Silence

EARLY in the afternoon the misty rain slipped away, and a world was revealed of faint pale colour and a saffron light shed by a dim sun.

Hans had his meal all to himself in his new little sitting room. He had cold beef, salad, potatoes in their jackets, and blackberry and apple tart and thick yellow cream.

Mrs. Iglesias served it and never exchanged a syllable with him while he ate. He had discovered *Robinson Crusoe* in the kitchen; he read it, the volume propped up against the jug of water.

After the meal he went out. He walked over the steps to the little beach where he had been with Nathalie.

Everyone was gone—Ruth, Nathalie, the Russians. And every place was gone—London, Paris, Vienna, Shanghai.... And every memory was gone—Germany, Italy, early London struggles, triumphs, mistresses, toothaches, ambitions.

There was not a soul in sight.

After the rain the wood, the beach, the bare trees were thin and unsubstantial. The colours were faint ivory, dim amber, the grey surface of steel. The sea heaved without breaking, then threw a line of foam in white froth upon the sand. Then a little wave broke far out, another nearer. Several raced together to the shore.

Hans watched, waiting. He was eagerly expectant; then, as though to answer his expectancy, from the long expanse of trembling silver a wave rose, shook its shoulders, tossed its head, leaped up. It hung before his eyes in an arc of crystal green, clear glass green, shelving in a half-circle of lovely, purest colour. Thus it hung, waiting, before his eyes. Then with a final grand shudder of ecstasy it came crashing, tumbling down, and leaped with white edges of triumph spilling to the shore.

At that moment, in Hans' ears, a voice cried:

"NOW—BEGIN!"

He turned, crossed again the stone steps, mounted the steps to the cottage, climbed the dark stairs.

He entered the little white room, closed the door behind him, sat down at the deal table, drew the pad of paper before him, wrote:

THE ONE-EYED COMMANDER
I

Then his pen moved swiftly.

THE END

BRACKENBURN,
 Sept. 10, 1927.

HUGH WALPOLE

AN ENGLISHMAN who loves his England and understands his countrymen the better because he has spent so much of his time away from home, Hugh Walpole has become the chief exponent of the beauty of the traditional in English fiction. Born in New Zealand, brought to New York in the glorified nineties, when the horse-car still rumbled up and down Broadway, he has been travelling ever since. Russia, the continent, all have given something of richness to his work. London knows Walpole periodically. Since he resigned as master of an English provincial school at twenty-three, and came to London with £30 in his pocket, determined to be a novelist, he has been busy at his task of seeing life. During one month, says Arnold Bennett, "it is impossible to 'go out' to London without meeting Mr. Walpole, and then for a long period he is a mere legend of the dinner tables." He is probably in a hidden spot in Cornwall which only the postman knows. Here he wrote many of those novels which have made him outstanding among his contemporaries, *The Dark Forest, The Captive, The Cathedral, Jeremy, Wintersmoon,* and now *Hans Frost* which returns to the fascinating background of *The Duchess of Wrexe.*

' The arrangements for her funeral which she had set down in her will were carried out, and in accordance with them, nothing more was spent on her funeral than on that of any of her Daughters, for she declared that if they proceeded otherwise it would be a declaration of her unworthiness when dead of resembling a true Daughter of Charity and servant of the members of Jesus Christ although she regarded no other title as so glorious.' On the day after Louise de Marillac's death, S. Vincent de Paul himself sent word of it to all the houses of the Sisters of Charity and of the Priests of the Mission. In one of these letters, he said, when announcing the sad news : ' Mademoiselle Le Gras died on the 15th of this month. I recommend her soul to your prayers, although she may not, perhaps, be in any need of this help, for we have every reason to believe that she now enjoys the glory promised to those who serve God and the poor in the manner in which she has done.' On July 24, 1660, S. Vincent de Paul, more and more infirm and no longer able to walk, summoned the Sisters of Charity in Paris to Saint-Lazare for a final conference on the virtues of Mademoiselle Le Gras. It was a specially touching reunion at which ' the most honoured Father invited each of the Sisters to tell all she knew of their holy foundress whom she should always keep before her eyes as a model.' They were all so deeply moved that they burst into tears and they had to pause from time to time for a new outburst of weeping. Saint Vincent, too, like his hearers, wept. These were the last words of his conference and they form the best panegyric of Louise de Marillac.

' He added,' says the Sister who drew up the account of the conference, ' that for the thirty-eight years he had known the lady, he had never thought her anything but the purest of souls : pure in her youth, in her marriage, in her widowhood, and that, at confession, she wept so bitterly over the slightest faults that it was very difficult to console her. From these different remarks, our most honoured Father drew the conclusion that each of those to whom he was speaking should do her utmost to be really and truly interior, that is to say, should occupy herself only with God, look to Him alone in all her actions, and in this way, said he, when you feel tempted to yield to some unruly impulse, you should say to yourselves : " I am a Daughter of Charity and therefore a Daughter of Mademoiselle Le Gras who, despite the inclinations of nature, was so well able to conquer self and be occupied only with God. Ah ! I wish to overcome myself and follow her example." '

The remains of Louise de Marillac, after having been transferred to different houses of the Sisters of Charity and miraculously preserved from profanation during the French Revolution, repose to-day in the Chapel in the Rue du Bac, where they are piously venerated by her faithful children.

It was only in recent times, on June 10, 1895, that the cause of Louise de Marillac's Beatification was introduced in the Court of Rome. After the preliminary process of enquiry in 1886, by an ecclesiastical commission appointed by the Archbishop of Paris, His Holiness Pope Leo XIII, signed the findings of the commission. The cause of her Beatification was thus introduced and is pending before a commission of whose decision there need be little doubt. Two hundred and ninety Cardinals, Archbishops, Bishops and Superiors of Religious Orders signed the petition for the introduction of her cause. If the traditional and prudent delay of the Court of Rome in such matters, should retard a decision, the definitive result seems to be assured and everything leads us to hope that we may soon be able to invoke the help of S. Vincent de Paul's faithful collaborator, together with that of her spiritual father and guide. By the mere fact of the cause of her Beatification having been introduced, the holy foundress of the Sisters of Charity has the title of ' Venerable ' and her life may thus be included amongst the lives of the Saints.

At the end of this life so admirable in its simplicity, so truly, so completely Christian, so astonishing in its marvellous fruitfulness, we shall say very little, for words are powerless to express one's feelings at the sight of such manifestations of Divine Grace, which rather incite us to silent admiration and adoration of the works of God. We shall merely say that when Louise de Marillac died in 1660, the Company of the Daughters of Charity numbered about two hundred and fifty Sisters in sixty different houses. At the present day, after nearly three hundred years, the number of Sisters of Charity has reached twenty-four thousand, scattered over the whole world in three thousand houses. At the sight of such a prodigious development and of such vitality in the midst of all the social changes and revolutions the world has since experienced, one cannot but think again of the little grain of seed of which our Lord speaks in the Gospel which, planted in a good soil, bears fruit a hundred-fold.

The few poor ' country girls ' gathered around Mademoiselle Le Gras, who formed at first that modest, humble ' little Company,' have now grown into a great tree which cannot be uprooted by any tempest because it was planted in the good soil of the love of God and of Christ living in our neighbour. The tempest may shake and injure, but cannot destroy it, and the Sister of Charity in her grey-blue dress and white coif, known and revered by all, may still be seen moving modestly and cheerfully, like a true Daughter of Louise de Marillac as she visits the poor, nurses the sick, teaches the young, and comforts the afflicted as their Mother exhorted them to do three hundred years ago.

NOTES ON CHAPTER VII

[1] *Letters of Barbara Bailly*, p. 271.
[2] *Letters of Louise de Marillac*, No. 254, p. 424.
[3] *Op. cit.*, No. 277, p. 465.
[4] Baunard, *op. cit.*, p. 499.
[5] *Op. cit.*, p. 500.
[6] *Letters of Louise de Marillac*, No. 333, p. 539.
[7] *Op. cit.*, No. 489, p. 795.
[8] Baunard, *op. cit.*, p. 544.
[9] *Conferences of S. Vincent de Paul*, No. LIV, p. 289 (1902 edition).
[10] *Letters of Louise de Marillac*, No. 451, p. 733.
[11] *Conferences of S. Vincent de Paul*, No. XCIII, p. 515.
[12] *Op. cit.*, No. LXI, p. 391.

[13] *Op. cit.*, No. LXXXIX, p. 467.
[14] *Letters of Louise de Marillac*, No. 334, p. 557.
[15] *Op. cit.*, No. 561, p. 895.
[16] Louise de Marillac, *Thoughts and Writings*, p. 90.
[17] *Letters of Louise de Marillac*, No. 644, p. 1025.
[18] *Op. cit.*, No. 649, p. 1033.
[19] Gobillon, *Life of Louise de Marillac*, edit. 1886, p. 151.
[20] *Letters of S. Vincent de Paul*, p. 434.
[21] Baunard, *op. cit.*, p. 606.
[22] Baunard, *op. cit.*, p. 606.
[23] Gobillon, *op. cit.*, p. 153.
[24] Gobillon, *op. cit.*, p. 154, etc.
[25] Baunard, *op. cit.*, p. 610, etc.

BIBLIOGRAPHY AND SOURCES

1. *The life of Mademoiselle Le Gras*, foundress and first Superioress of the Daughters of Charity, by M. Gobillon, Doctor of the House and of the Society of Sorbonne, parish priest of S. Lawrence, Paris, 1676. Has been frequently reprinted. The last edition was published in 1886, Bruges, Société Saint-Augustin.

2. *History of Mademoiselle Le Gras, Louise de Marillac*, by the Countess of Richemont, Paris. Poussielgue, 1882. 4th ed., 1894.

3. *Life of Louise de Marillac*, by Mgr Baunard, Rector of the Catholic Faculty of Lille. Paris, Poussielgue, 1898.

4. *Conferences of Saint Vincent de Paul to the Daughters of Charity*, followed by extracts from letters of S. Vincent de Paul to the Venerable Louise de Marillac, Paris, at the Mother House of the Daughters of Charity, 140, Rue du Bac, Paris, 1902.

5. *Thoughts and Letters of Louise de Marillac*, Mademoiselle Le Gras, foundress and first Superioress of the Daughters of Charity, servants of the sick poor. Selections. Bruges, Société Saint-Augustin, 1886.

6. *Letters of Louise de Marillac*, widow of M. Le Gras, foundress of the Daughters of Charity (1197 pages, MS.).

7. *Letters of S. Vincent de Paul*, addressed to Mademoi-